Clayton

Clayton

A Story of a Small Town Living and Loving God's Way

Densel Raines

Xulon Press

Xulon Press
555 Winderley Pl, Suite 225
Maitland, FL 32751
407.339.4217
www.xulonpress.com

© 2024 by Densel Raines

All rights reserved solely by the author. The author guarantees all contents are original and do not infringe upon the legal rights of any other person or work. No part of this book may be reproduced in any form without the permission of the author.

Due to the changing nature of the Internet, if there are any web addresses, links, or URLs included in this manuscript, these may have been altered and may no longer be accessible. The views and opinions shared in this book belong solely to the author and do not necessarily reflect those of the publisher. The publisher therefore disclaims responsibility for the views or opinions expressed within the work.

Unless otherwise indicated, Scripture quotations taken from the English Standard Version (ESV). Copyright © 2001 by Crossway, a publishing ministry of Good News Publishers. Used by permission. All rights reserved.

Paperback ISBN-13: 978-1-66289-539-5
Ebook ISBN-13: 978-1-66289-540-1

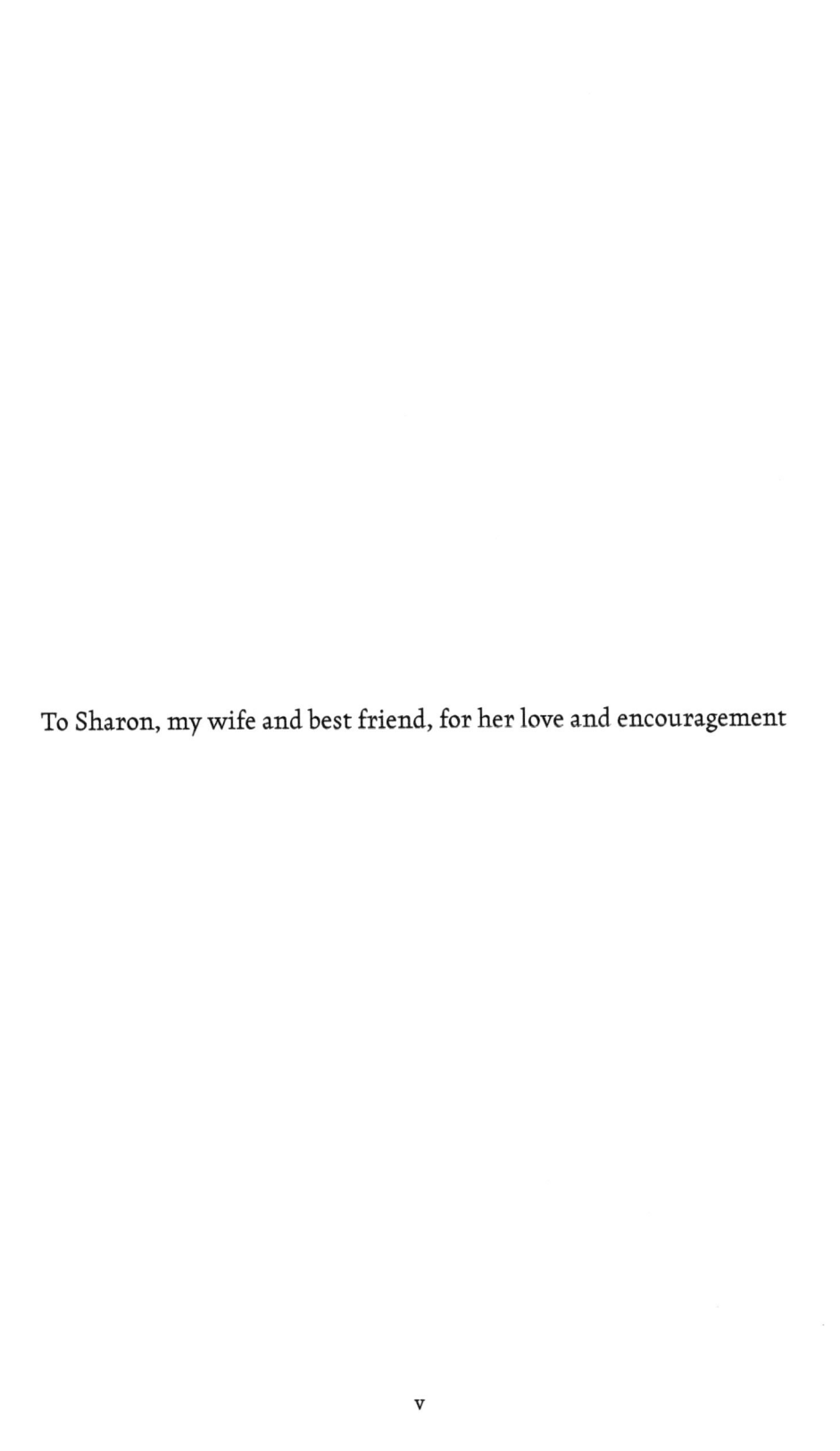

To Sharon, my wife and best friend, for her love and encouragement

Table of Contents

CHAPTER 1 1
CHAPTER 2 11
CHAPTER 3 17
CHAPTER 4 20
CHAPTER 5 23
CHAPTER 6 28
CHAPTER 7 34
CHAPTER 8 42
CHAPTER 9 46
CHAPTER 10 55
CHAPTER 11 62
CHAPTER 12 70
CHAPTER 13 79
CHAPTER 14 87
CHAPTER 15 97
CHAPTER 16 104
CHAPTER 17 113
CHAPTER 18 123
CHAPTER 19 135
CHAPTER 20 144
CHAPTER 21 151
CHAPTER 22 165
CHAPTER 23 172
CHAPTER 24 180
CHAPTER 25 187
CHAPTER 26 195
CHAPTER 27 204

CHAPTER 28	212
CHAPTER 29	223
CHAPTER 30	233
CHAPTER 31	241
CHAPTER 32	251
CHAPTER 33	262
CHAPTER 34	272
CHAPTER 35	280
CHAPTER 36	289
CHAPTER 37	300
CHAPTER 38	307
CHAPTER 39	315
CHAPTER 40	324
CHAPTER 41	334
CHAPTER 42	344
CHAPTER 43	356
CHAPTER 44	364
CHAPTER 45	371
CHAPTER 46	380
CHAPTER 47	389
CHAPTER 48	398
CHAPTER 49	406
Author Notes	411

CHAPTER 1

IT WAS A clear early fall afternoon deep in the Appalachian hills of West Virginia in 1892. Archibald Raines, "Archie," was harvesting vegetables from his small garden when he heard shots fired deep in the woods behind him. Quickly, he ran to his little shack to get his gun just in case he needed to protect himself. He suspected it was Hank, who lived down the hollow and over the hill about a mile away. Hank hunted whenever he didn't have customers who needed lumber from his sawmill. Archie continued his work in the garden but kept an eye out for trouble just in case it wasn't Hank. He needed to finish his work in the next few days so that he could go into town on Wednesday to work for Widow Henry.

Just as Archie was putting the last squash into his wheelbarrow, he saw two men running across the tree line with dogs chasing them. More than likely, the Harless boys were being tracked down by the sheriff.

Jim and Paul Harless were known to be moonshiners and thieves. Lately, they had been suspected of stealing from the general store and other businesses downriver in Elkview. Sheriff Fred Griffith had been looking for their still for months, but the intensity of this chase made it seem like there was more to it than just "shining."

Even though the sheriff had his dogs, the Harless brothers knew these woods better than anybody. When it looked like the sheriff was closing in, Paul yelled to his brother, "Let's go toward the creek!"

Paul knew the dogs would lose their scent if they could get in the water, but even more importantly, he had left their horses tied up to a tree near the water. Ducking branches and running as fast as their legs would carry them, they jumped about ten feet off a cliff and ran down to the creek and over the small knoll to the safety of their horses. This time, they got away but knew they would have to move out of Sheriff Griffith's territory to a safer county further down the Elk River.

As Archie was putting the last of his vegetables in the underground cellar he had dug under his shack, he heard the sheriff's dogs. "Hi, son," said Sheriff Griffith, "Did you see where those Harless boys were running? I've chased them all day, but they keep getting away."

Archie looked at the sheriff and answered, "Sir, I saw them running over the ridge with your dogs after them, but that's it. I haven't seen them around here before. I'll watch for them and let you know if I see anything."

"I doubt they'll be back here since they know I'm looking for them, but thanks anyway."

As Sheriff Griffith walked away, Archie yelled," Sheriff, you want some water to drink and an apple? I've got plenty!"

Sheriff Griffith turned around to see the twenty-three-year-old young man reaching into a basket for apples. It was clear that he barely had enough for himself, and though his willingness to share was touching, he couldn't accept his generosity.

"No thanks, son; I've got to get going if I'm going to get back into town by sundown."

When Archie settled down for the evening to a pot of stew he had made, the warm glow of the fire made the cool evening comfortable. He knew that cold weather wasn't many weeks away and there was much work to be done. He planned on cutting down an oak tree in the morning, and after cutting the branches into usable lengths for firewood, he would split the trunk and stack it to dry over the winter. He wanted to expand his shack and build a cabin where he hoped to settle down and raise a family someday.

Things were usually quiet in the hills, the only excitement being an occasional bear or coyote. Although he loved the freedom living in the mountains alone provided, he longed for a family.

Wednesday morning, just before dawn, Archie began his walk to Widow Henry's. He wanted to get an early start on the work that she needed done. He was exhausted from cutting down the giant oak tree the day before but knew that this might be his last paying job before winter, and he needed the money to buy supplies.

The two-mile walk to the small town of Clayton would take a while, with the fog as thick as it was. Archie knew he had to be careful in the fog not only to keep from falling but also for bears. At this time of year, bears tried to fatten up before their hibernation, so they hunted constantly. Black bears didn't usually attack people unless they got too close to their young or were startled, so Archie knew that the more noise he made, the less likely he was to surprise a bear looking for berries. But this morning, as Archie hiked over the little dirt road into town, he was thinking about his future and not worrying about bears. Building the cabin and enlarging his garden were the most important things he had to do before he could even think of looking for a wife, or at least that's what he thought.

As the fog lifted, he looked down from the hill he was on to see the little town. When West Virginia became a state during the Civil War, the counties split their territories into districts. Clayton was in the Henry District of Clay County along the Elk River. The area was mainly populated by farmers who brought extra crops to the local general store and traded them for needed goods. The church was in the middle of town, with the schoolhouse down the only street fifty yards. The children had to meet twice a week at the church with some ladies from town to get their lessons since the school fire in late August had destroyed most of the school building.

A group had raised some money to help rebuild it, but volunteers would be needed to do the work. A committee had been formed to coordinate the building project and to search for a second teacher. The small town had grown in the last few years to the point where the children needed to be separated so the older ones had a better opportunity to learn.

Martha Henry, known by everyone as Widow Henry, lived at the end of the street in a house left to her by her late husband, Colonel James Henry. He had fought for the Union Army during the Civil War and was killed at Gettysburg. Before the war, he owned a lumber company in the Charleston area and land along Cabin Creek. After his death, the lumber company did very well.

All of the South needed lumber to rebuild after the destruction brought on by the war. Bridges, railroad tracks, buildings, and houses were being constructed in all the cities. It was a time of prosperity for many but of destruction for the pristine forests of Appalachia. The need for timber had never been greater, but no thought was given to reforestation.

Widow Henry was a sweet lady in her early fifties who had lived in Clayton most of her life. She was active in the church and community groups, including the committee raising money for the reconstruction of the schoolhouse.

As Archie approached her house, she greeted him with a warm, welcoming cup of coffee. She liked to start her days sitting on her front porch, sipping coffee and reading her Bible. Today, Archie provided her with a much-desired guest. Archie was a little anxious, knowing how much work needed to be done, but the widow seemed in no hurry for him to get started. She asked him how his cabin was coming and if he had heard from his father lately.

Archie had left home several years earlier and seldom received letters from his father, Stephen. Archie's mother, Sarah, had died six years earlier when Archie was seventeen. His mother's great-grandfather had immigrated from Scotland to Ohio and farmed like many others from Ireland and Scotland. Archie's father worked in a factory in addition to farming to help provide for his family, and though he was close to his son, he seldom found time to write to him. There was a great need for workers since an estimated seven hundred thousand men lost their lives during the war, and many who survived were injured so severely that they could not provide for their families.

Widow Henry showed Archie the fallen trees in the pasture behind her house and asked him to cut them up for firewood. The winters were long and cold, and she needed all the wood she could get. Last year, Archie had cut down another tree for her, so he knew the routine. Move the aged wood to the woodshed next to the house and stack the new wood to dry near the old oak tree where he had built a lean-to using an old door to keep most of the rain and snow from getting the wood wet.

Widow Henry left Archie to do his work and walked down to the general store to buy some flour and coffee. She was going to make apple pies for the church fall picnic this coming Sunday afternoon and needed more flour. While at the store, she met a young lady named Maggie Garrett, who had just arrived from Canton, Ohio, to help her injured aunt, Carol McCombs. Her favorite aunt had been injured trying to help extinguish the schoolhouse fire in August and needed her.

Carol McCombs was the teacher at Clayton's one-room school. She lived alone in the boardinghouse across the street from the school. One early evening in mid-June, she heard a commotion outside her window and ran to see what was happening, only to discover her beloved school was on fire. Like everyone else in town, Carol ran to help put out the fire. Desperate to save the books she had brought from Ohio, she ran into the building to retrieve them, only to find the fire had grown out of control and barely escaped before the front part of the building collapsed. She had been burned on her arms and left leg and had also broken her ankle when she fell running out of the building.

Doc, as everyone called him, wasn't a doctor but had served as a medical assistant during the Civil War. Now in his sixties and suffering from arthritis, he moved slowly but helped care for the local town folks. When Doc arrived at the school, he found Miss McCombs lying on the ground with a cold wrap on her head, crying from the pain. Doc set the ankle and put salve on the burns. Though the pain was severe, Carol refused the moonshine offered to her by Doc to help relieve the pain. A few days later, she was able to write to her sister in Canton, Ohio, and ask if her daughter Maggie could come for a while to help her during her recovery.

During their conversation at the general store, Widow Henry asked Maggie if she would like to come to her house the next day for some fresh apple pie. Maggie gladly accepted the invitation and agreed to go around three o'clock in the afternoon.

Thursday afternoon, the aroma of fresh apple pie floated through the air as Maggie walked up the street to Widow Henry's house. She had looked forward to getting to know the town matriarch better and learning more about Clayton. When Maggie entered the parlor, she noticed a young man working on firewood in the back of the house. Her glancing eye was caught by Widow Henry as they sat down. While enjoying their pie and coffee, Maggie asked many questions about the town and its history. Widow Henry explained that it was a settlement surrounded by farmers and craftsmen. Until lately, it had been quiet, but with the population growing across the country, more people were coming to the area. She said that when they rebuilt the school, they planned to add a second room and hire an additional teacher. As they talked, Maggie could not help glancing at the young man working in the yard.

"What's his name?" she asked. "Does he work here often?" Suddenly, she realized her face was blushing and felt embarrassed at her direct questions.

Widow Henry, wanting to relieve Maggie of her awkwardly asked questions, smiling, said, "Oh, Archie, yes, he does come by often this time of year."

Quickly, Maggie changed the subject to answer an earlier question about how her aunt was doing. She explained that she had to change the burn bandages several times a day. She then went on to explain that since Aunt Carol couldn't get out until her burns healed, she was becoming depressed, missing her students and teaching. Realizing she needed to return to the boardinghouse to check on her, Maggie thanked Widow Henry for the wonderful dessert and conversation and left. Walking home, she could not stop thinking about the handsome young man.

Archie went to the front porch where Widow Henry was sitting. She went inside to get him a glass of water to help him cool down. As they sat on the porch, Widow Henry asked Archie if he was planning to attend the church fall picnic on Sunday. She knew Maggie was planning on being there and looked forward to introducing them.

There was more than a little matchmaker in the Widow. She enjoyed seeing young people meet and hopefully fall in love. Her only prayer was that they would love each other as much as she and her beloved James loved one another.

Archie hadn't been to church for a while because he spent every minute clearing his homestead and preparing logs to build his future home. Though Widow Henry encouraged him, he declined, knowing he didn't have much more time left before it would be too cold to work on his farm.

Friday morning came quickly for Archie. He slept in the old barn behind the house rather than going back and forth from town to his place. He had been eating apples he had brought along with some jerky he had purchased from the general store. Archie hoped to finish his work by midafternoon to return to his shack before dark. He only had another two yards of firewood to split and stack, so he started as soon as the sun came up.

It was a beautiful fall day with the leaves a glorious orange, red, and yellow and the sky as blue as he had ever seen. When afternoon arrived, Archie noticed he was thinking more and more about Widow Henry's invitation. He knew he wanted to get his place ready for winter. Still, the thought of a relaxing Sunday, enjoying good home-cooked food, was enticing, and so was the possibility of seeing the young girl who had visited Widow Henry the other day. When he was about to leave, Widow Henry came out to her front porch to give him the ten dollars he had earned that week and to try one more time to encourage him to come on Sunday.

"Archie, why don't you work at your place on Saturday and come stay in the barn Saturday evening? Besides, I would like you to work on the barn doors on Monday before it gets too cold if you can."

Much to her surprise, Archie said he would come. The next thing he said, though, was even more surprising.

"Who was the young woman you had pie with the other day?"

With a smile, Widow Henry told him that it was Maggie Garrett, the schoolteacher's niece from Ohio.

"You know, she'll be at the picnic as well. Maybe I can introduce you."

Archie blushed and said," Oh, I was just wondering."

Sunday could not come quickly enough for Archie. He worked on his farm Saturday from sunrise until around three o'clock, then went to the creek to clean up. He wanted to look his best, so he packed his only other pair of pants and a shirt he owned and started his journey back to town.

It seemed to take forever to get there, but Widow Henry saw him from her parlor window as he arrived. She had been baking apple pies all afternoon and came out to greet him, smiling with flour on her cheek and a glass of water in her hand.

When evening came, Archie sat on a log in the backyard, thinking about his decision.

> Yes, the farm needed work to be done before winter, but what was the purpose of that work? After all, he hoped

to build a cabin to raise a family, but what good would it be if he didn't meet the right woman? He would have a nice place to live but end up alone.

Sunday morning's sermon was on trusting the Lord with all your life and not living as if you had a better plan. Most people live only asking God for advice when their plans don't go as they wanted. God wants us to trust Him with every detail.

The message was unsettling for Archie. He had been raised in the church and knew what the elder said was true, but he had spent the last two years working on the little farm he had purchased, designing his future, and hoping the right woman would come along. What if God's plan was different?

The fall picnic was the biggest celebration in town since the Fourth of July. The townspeople gathered every fall to share their harvest and enjoy time together. People came from miles around, bringing food to share. Games for the children were set up. A bucket was filled with water so the young people could bob for apples. Some tables were set up for the pie-tasting contest. There was food everywhere as laughter filled the air. As hungry as Archie was, he was more interested in meeting the young woman he had seen a few days earlier.

Suddenly, the children stopped the three-legged races and began shouting.

"Miss McCombs! Miss McCombs!"

Walking on crutches, being helped by her niece, was their beloved teacher. They had not seen her since the fire, and as they all rushed up to her, joy returned to her face. She loved them so much and had missed them beyond measure. Maggie looked up as the children rushed to hug her aunt and saw Archie, and though she hadn't met him, she, too, began smiling.

Not missing a beat, Widow Henry noticed the look on both of their faces and came out to meet Maggie.

"There's someone I would like for you to meet Maggie." As she locked her arm around Maggie's, they walked toward Archie, smiling.

Archie had fought a pack of coyotes, killed an angry bear, and chased wild hogs out of his vegetables, but never had he felt so nervous. What would he say? Did he forget to comb his hair, or worst of all, was his fly closed? As they drew closer, for some reason, he calmed down completely. Something or Someone gave him all the confidence he needed. She was perfect!

Widow Henry introduced them and told each of them a little about the other one and then conveniently had to help set up the pie-tasting contest. Neither could remember what they talked about that afternoon, but they knew they couldn't wait to see each other again. His humble honesty was most attractive to Maggie, and her heart for others was even more important to him than her beauty, for Maggie was very beautiful. Her reddish blonde hair, blue eyes, and dimples on her cheeks every time she smiled were striking.

As the picnic ended, Maggie said goodbye and helped her aunt back to the boardinghouse, and Archie went back to Widow Henry's barn. As he laid back, looking out of the loft opening at millions of stars, he wondered how this would work. Maggie was from Ohio, and with her aunt getting better, she probably wouldn't stay around much longer. He had no reason to be in town after his work was done, so how could this work out? The excitement of meeting Maggie transitioned to worrying about ever seeing her again. However, as he began calming down to sleep, the elder's message drifted into his mind like the sweet smell of Widow Henry's apple pie. Trust God?

CHAPTER 2

Reverend Seamus McConnell had been a minister, traveling throughout the mountains teaching at different churches and sometimes in people's homes for the last seven years since graduating from Seminary, feeling called to bring the Word to the unchurched backwoods people of that part of the country. When he arrived in Clayton, he was ill. He had been traveling during a chilly rain all week and had gotten sick. Seeing someone coming from the general store, he asked if a doctor was in town. Rather than pointing out where Doc's office was, the young lady took him to his house.

Immediately, Doc saw he was very sick with a high fever. After doing what he could to help him, Doc told Seamus that he needed to go to the boardinghouse in town to get the rest he required while recovering. Doc promised to check in on him regularly for the next few days until his fever broke. Reverend McConnell told Doc that he did not have enough money to afford to stay at the boardinghouse, but Doc insisted, saying, "Don't worry about the money; it will be taken care of; just rest."

The itinerant minister had been invited to preach Sunday at the little church in town when he had passed through on his way to the backcountry a few weeks earlier. Usually, he stayed in a tent he carried with him so that he wouldn't inconvenience anyone, but he couldn't turn down the offer of a warm bed. Seamus did not leave his room for the next several days but slept and read, praying that his sickness would pass. His fever had been high the day he went to see Doc, so every afternoon, Doc stopped by to check on him.

During his stay, Sarah Adkins, owner of the boardinghouse, had been giving him some of her chicken soup and biscuits. Three days of a warm bed and chicken soup did the trick, and Reverend McConnell began feeling much better.

On Friday, he was feeling stronger and asked Sarah if she had some paper he could use to write. He wanted to prepare his sermon for Sunday. The following day, he was strong enough to go downstairs to the restaurant on the first floor of the boardinghouse to have a cup of coffee and more of Sarah's chicken soup. He brought his Bible and the paper to continue preparing the message for Sunday. Sarah noticed he could use more coffee and brought him a fresh cup. To be polite, she asked him what he was reading.

"I'm reading Luke 10:30-37 today; it's the parable about the Good Samaritan. It's one of my favorites." He talked about the parable for the next half hour and shared the scriptures with her in a way she had never heard. "Will you be coming to worship this Sunday, Mrs. Adkins?" asked the Reverend.

"I don't think so. I used to attend church but haven't been there in two years. I don't believe like I used to," responded Sarah.

"Perhaps someday we can talk about it when you are ready. I am here to help." He could tell something was bothering her, but he knew it was better to wait for her to feel comfortable enough with him to talk about it.

Suddenly, a beautiful little girl ran into the restaurant. "Mama, can we go to the general store today? I want to get new pencils and paper for school."

"Excuse her, Reverend McConnell; she is excited about school and forgot her manners."

"And what is your name? "asked the Reverend. "My name is Elizabeth, but everybody calls me Lizzy. What's yours?" asked Lizzy.

"My name is Seamus McConnell. What grade are you in this year?"

Lizzy explained how she couldn't wait for school to start again with Miss McCombs' teaching. She explained that they would meet in the church until the schoolhouse could be rebuilt. Her excitement caused her to talk faster as she continued, "I'm going to be in the second grade, and Miss McCombs is going to be back. She was sick for a long time after the fire, but she's fine now."

Mrs. Adkins put her hand on Lizzy's shoulder, signaling that it was time for her to return to her room and get ready to go to the store.

"Sorry, Reverend, she gets overly excited at times. It's good to see her happy. We've had a hard two years," explained Sarah. With that, she excused herself and returned to her room to get money for their shopping.

People came from all around Sunday morning, as word had spread that there was a preacher in town and that he would be preaching Sunday morning. The church hadn't had a full-time minister since the passing of Reverend Hutchins a year earlier.

Seamus was overwhelmed by how many people came, as he was used to smaller groups of ten or fifteen people. His sermon was about the Good Samaritan, but today, the parable meant more to him than anything he had learned in Seminary.

"All week, the people of this community have been the Samaritan Christ spoke of in the parable." With deep emotion and a quivering lip, he explained how people had loved him, a stranger, all week. They had sheltered him, cared for him when he was sick, and fed him. He concluded by simply saying, "Thank you for being the hands and feet of our Savior; thank you."

After church, people kept asking him if he would stay as Clayton's full-time preacher. Many folks invited him to their homes for dinner and fellowship. It was clear to Reverend McConnell that the Lord had brought him to Clayton, and he would stay if he believed he was called to.

After everyone left, he returned to the boardinghouse to change into more comfortable clothes; he didn't want to get his Sunday clothes dirty;

he only had one suit. Sarah Adkins came out as he walked through the restaurant, upstairs to his room.

"How was church service today? It sure looked like there were a lot of people."

Reverend McConnell looked at the single mother and said, "I was so happy to see how the community turned out. I was honestly surprised at how friendly everyone was. I had only met a few people since I came here earlier in the week, being how sick I was, yet everyone was so welcoming."

"Did you talk about the Good Samaritan?"

"Yes, I did talk about the Good Samaritan and how you had been so kind to me while I was recovering. God used you and Doc to be the hands and feet of Christ. I was sick and hungry, and you and Doc fed and nursed me back to health. Neither of you knew me; neither of you had any reason to help other than to care for a stranger who needed it."

As he shared with Sarah, she felt tears welling up. She remembered how the town folks had comforted her when her husband was sick.

Charles Adkins opened the boardinghouse with Sarah several years ago when they first moved to Clayton. Three years after their arrival, Elizabeth was born. Their lives together could not have been better. Sarah loved to cook, so she prepared the food for the restaurant, and Charles ran the business and did handyman work in the neighborhood.

One day, Charles began feeling tired, and later that evening, he became nauseous. The following day, he had a fever. Doc stopped by to see him and recognized the symptoms. "I'm afraid you have malaria, Charles; you must stay in bed and rest. Sarah, keep a cold compress on his forehead and make sure he stays in bed. He needs all the rest he can get."

Word of Charles' sickness made its way around town, and people began bringing food for the family and enough for any boardinghouse guests they had. Tom Campbell, owner of the general store, and his wife, Nancy, offered to take Charles to Charleston to be cared for in the hospital. Everyone did what they could, but it wasn't enough. Charles died two weeks later.

The entire community came to his funeral. Reverend Hutchins spoke about Charles's strong commitment to the Lord and how his example had encouraged many in the community. Elizabeth and Sarah cried uncontrollably as his coffin was lowered into his gravesite behind the church.

Widow Henry gathered them into her arms and stood with them as they mourned the loss of a husband and father. After most of the town folks left, Widow Henry said she and the Campbells would be by shortly to bring them dinner. The town matriarch walked slowly with them back to their boardinghouse, telling them she would return soon, "just rest for now."

As those memories returned, Sarah began crying. Reverend McConnell said softly, "Losing someone close to you is the hardest experience we must deal with on this side of eternity. Imagine God's grief watching His Son die on the cross for our sins. It had to be for us to be reconciled to our heavenly Father, but the grief was genuine, too. Sarah, God has felt every pain you have and is always here to comfort you and help you bear the burden. His arms are open to hold you in your sorrow; trust Him."

"How could He let Charles die?" asked the sobbing widow.

"God's ways are not our ways. Many things he does are hard to understand. You must know that He is faithful to do all He has promised, so while you miss Charles, know that you will someday see him in heaven. We must live this life trusting the Father to lead us in everything, including moving on from our losses."

Later that evening, Reverend McConnell had dinner with the Campbells beside the general store at their house. As they discussed the desire of the church elders to extend a position to Reverend McConnell as their preacher, Tom could tell something was bothering him. "Reverend, what's on your mind? You seem troubled?"

Seamus told Tom and Nancy about his discussion with Sarah Adkins.

Tom knew that she had struggled since Charles' passing but didn't know that her grieving was still so deeply felt.

Reverend McConnell looked at Tom and said, "You know, Tom, maybe she is one of the reasons God has called me to Clayton. Christ talked about how a shepherd would leave the flock to find the one lost sheep; maybe He wants me to lead her back."

"Tomorrow morning, I will show you the facilities and the parsonage in the back of the church, and if you still want to be our full-time preacher, you can let me know then," said Tom. He knew this was a crucial decision for the Reverend, and he wanted him to be sure it was God's calling, not just the people of Clayton.

Seamus thanked the Campbells for their hospitality and went back to the boardinghouse. As he lay in bed that night, he saw that the people in Clay County wanted and needed a pastor. Closing his eyes, he prayed that God's will would be done.

The following day, Tom stopped by the restaurant and had a cup of coffee with Reverend McConnel before going to the church.

When they had finished their coffee, Tom looked at Sarah and said, "Sarah, I have an idea. Why don't you bring some of your incredible cookies to the store, and I'll sell them for you? People are always looking for sweets!"

"Thank you, Tom, that is a wonderful idea."

Walking down the street, Seamus knew that he was going to stay. Tom's offer was the beginning of ministering to his hurting friend, for he saw how a caring neighbor was already reaching out to a grieving single mother.

CHAPTER 3

PAUL HARLESS HAD been in trouble with the law before, but this time it was different. Sheriff Griffith was a local lawman from Clayton, not a Federal Marshal, which meant the law was closing in on him and his brother. For years, they had made "shine" in the deep woods of Appalachia undetected. They would fill their wagon with jugs and slowly move around the area on ridge roads, staying out of sight of the locals. When the moon lit their way at night, they would meet at designated sites to sell their goods. Usually, Jim would hide, with his gun ready, in case of trouble, and Paul would take the cash from a few local "distributors," who would then sell the moonshine to their customers. The meeting spot was never the same. Often, they would bury the cash in case they were ambushed on their way back to the still, then return for it a few days later.

Jim went to a local sawmill to have a false bottom constructed for his wagon while Paul disassembled the still equipment, preparing to leave the Clayton area. The sawmill operator, Hank, knew more about what Jim was up to than Jim imagined. Jim told Hank what he wanted done to his wagon.

Hank was a formidable man in his mid-fifties who lived alone in the woods about a mile from Clayton. He didn't like being around people, so the solitude pleased him. He told Jim he would build the wagon for two jugs of moonshine. Hank hadn't had any "shine" for years, but the temptation was more than he could handle. Jim was surprised Hank knew what he and his brother were doing and said he did not know what Hank was talking about.

Hank looked at Jim confidently and explained that one night, he was hunting and heard a voice he did not recognize talking to another man about the shine he had just bought from the Harless brothers. After they passed, Hank backtracked to see where they had been. After about twenty minutes, he saw Jim and his brother leaving in their wagon.

Jim knew they would be in trouble if they didn't do as Hank asked, but even more importantly, like his brother, he realized that too many people knew what they were doing, so they had to leave the area. After agreeing to Hank's payment, Jim rode away on his horse, leaving the wagon, to get the jugs Hank demanded.

The next day, Jim slowly returned to the little sawmill where Hank was finishing the project. Hank built the wagon bottom just as promised, adding a compartment under the wagon seat to hide their cash. He showed Jim his work, nervously looking all around to assure himself that no one was looking; he did not want to be accused of being an accomplice to their crimes. Jim was pleased with the work and gave Hank the two jugs, then quickly hitched the horse onto the wagon. They had to get moving soon before Sheriff Griffith came around. As Jim rode off, Hank opened a jug and began drinking. He hadn't had any good shine in over ten years.

When Jim returned to the still, Paul had gotten most of it apart so they could move. The plan was to go further downstream, away from the Clayton area, and settle along the Elk River in the Elkview area.

Paul and Jim Harless left the Clayton area that night and headed south. The creeks feeding into the 172-mile-long Elk River were perfect water sources, but they didn't have any farmers they knew to get the corn they needed. Paul felt that since it was so late in the year, they should lay low until spring, hide their equipment, and begin meeting farmers they could do business with next year. As it turned out, that would be the wisest decision the boys ever made. U.S. Marshals and their deputies conducted raids all over Clay County and the Elkview area, arresting sixty-three moonshiners only two weeks later.

With their competition in jail and the Marshal believing the area had been cleaned up, Paul and Jim could easily find the corn they needed the following summer. Paul decided, however, that they should purchase land to grow their corn, eliminating the worry of a farmer finding out what they were doing, and it would reduce their costs. During the winter, they would look for land to buy and plant corn the following spring. What could go wrong?

CHAPTER 4

The week after the church fall picnic, Widow Henry stopped by to see Sheriff Griffith to see if he could go by Archie's place and tell him she wanted to discuss something with him. Sheriff Griffith said he intended to head out that way to see if anyone had seen the Harless brothers. He believed they had left the area after his latest confrontation with them but wanted to make sure. The Sheriff took the safety of the people of Clayton very seriously and wanted to make sure the boys were nowhere near there.

The following day, Sheriff Griffith left for Archie's to see if he had seen the Harless boys. After talking with some farmers, he stopped by the sawmill to see Hank. As he arrived at Hank's cabin, he couldn't help noticing an empty jug near the door. Based on a comment Doc had made a few days earlier, he knew Hank had a source to get moonshine.

Sheriff Griffith ran into Doc on his way from the general store earlier that week. Doc complained about how hard it was to get alcohol to use in his "practice."

"Only thing I've got to help folks is some moonshine I got from Hank."

Doc had gone out to Hank's sawmill to have some boards cut to repair his front porch and happened to notice Hank had some moonshine. When Doc asked where he had gotten it, Hank didn't want to tell him but offered to sell him the remaining jug. Doc had not drunk since the end of the war, but the thought of some good shine for "medical" purposes sounded good to him.

"Morning, Hank. How have you been?" Sheriff Griffith greeted Hank as he rode up to his cabin. Sheriff Griffith had known Hank since he moved to the area and thought that deep down, he was a good man, a little rough at times and a bit of a recluse, but still a good person. Something bothered the sheriff, though; Hank was secretive about his past and sometimes seemed almost afraid. To make Hank a little uncomfortable, Sheriff Griffith looked at an empty jug outside his cabin for a few seconds.

"Where'd the jug come from, Hank? Looks like the kind the Harless boys use."

The day Sheriff Griffith had chased the Harless boys through Archie's place, he had found one of their jugs that they had dropped, so he knew what theirs looked like.

"Found it in the woods one day while I was hunting," said Hank. "Is there a problem?"

Sheriff Griffith looked at Hank and said, "I know where you got it, Hank. Don't lie to me! I'm looking for the Harless boys, and I think you might know where they are."

"Let's look around your property, Hank. I don't think you're telling me everything you know."

As he said this, Sheriff Griffith began walking toward the mill. As he looked around, he noticed some old boards about the size of a wagon with a familiar aroma.

"Should I get my hounds out here to check out your mill, or do you want to tell me why you would have old boards with spilled mash on them?"

Hank was terrified; he did not want to go to jail. Earlier, Hank realized that he had allowed the temptation to drink to cause him to make a bad decision. After just a couple of swallows, he poured the rest out on the ground, not wanting to return to the person he had once been. With his head down, Hank humbly told Sherriff Griffith that he had gotten into a bar fight long ago and accidentally killed a man. He spent ten years in jail before being released when a new judge ruled it had been self-defense. Hank spent every penny to his name, hiring an attorney to help him get the re-trial. When he left jail, he wanted to live away from everybody else, especially any place with a bar. Alcohol had caused him to lose ten years of his life, and he did not want to have anything to do with it again.

"Please, Sheriff, I didn't do anything wrong. I wanted some moonshine, and the only way I could pay for it was to build a wagon bottom for Jim Harless. It has a false bottom and a small case attached to the bottom of the seat. I didn't do anything wrong!"

Sheriff Griffith asked Hank why he would do something illegal like that; after all, didn't he know that would make him an accomplice to their moonshining crime? Selling moonshine itself wasn't an official crime, but not collecting and paying for licenses and the sales taxes was an offense.

Hank broke down and began to tear up, something he never did. "I can't go back to jail, Sheriff, I can't. I'd sooner die!"

Sheriff Griffith had been surprised to learn of Hank's previous jail time, yet there had always been something he knew Hank was keeping to himself. He could tell Hank was a broken man and that alcohol had been at the core of everything.

"Hank, I'm sorry for what happened to you. It wasn't right, but I think you know the real problem. You have got to promise me never to touch alcohol again! Agreed?"

"No sir, never again!"

"Now, can you tell me if those boys are still around?"

Shaking from fear, Hank looked directly at Sheriff Griffith and thanked him. "I don't know where they were headed, but I got the impression they were in a hurry to get out of here."

Sheriff Griffith thanked Hank for the information and rode to Archie's place to tell him that Widow Henry needed to speak with him. He was upset that he had not been able to catch the Harless', but he was glad they were out of his area and wouldn't bother the fine people of Clayton again.

CHAPTER 5

WATCHING SHERIFF GRIFFITH ride away on his horse, Archie was excited to learn that Widow Henry wanted to see him; it could give him a chance to see Maggie. He hadn't stopped thinking about her since he left town early Tuesday morning after the fall picnic. Although the creek water was beginning to cool down quite a bit, he didn't mind the discomfort of washing up after a long day stacking timber to dry; he wanted to be his very best, just in case.

He decided to leave early, just after sunrise, to get there as soon as possible. After seeing what Widow Henry needed, he thought he should bring the ten dollars he had earned to buy a few winter supplies at the general store. After building a fire to cook his dinner and help keep him warm during the night, Archie leaned back against the shack door frame and dreamed of seeing Maggie again.

He had never felt like this and wasn't sure what to do next. His cabin wasn't built, nor was the field ready for planting next May, but he was sure he would never have an opportunity like this again. After eating the rabbit he had killed earlier that day, he lay in his cot, his gun by his side, and drifted off to sleep. Rest came easy; he was exhausted from the day's work, yet he kept waking up hoping it was daylight and he could go.

The trip to Clayton was uneventful but seemed slower than usual. As he walked into town, he looked down the street, hoping to get a glimpse of Maggie. Widow Henry saw him from her parlor window and walked to her porch to greet him.

"Let's go inside, Archie; it's a little cool for me this morning."

As he settled down in a chair facing the window, hoping to see Maggie, Widow Henry went to get coffee. When she returned to the room, Archie's heart was pounding with anticipation. What did she want to tell him? Was it something to do with Maggie? Thoughts rushed through his mind so rapidly that he could barely think.

Widow Henry handed Archie his coffee and slowly sat down on the old rocking chair she often used to read her Bible during her morning meditation. "Archie, with winter coming shortly, the school committee met last week to discuss how we could get the new school rebuilt and how soon. There isn't much money for the project, but we had an idea I wanted to run past you."

Archie anxiously waited to hear what Widow Henry was going to say. He didn't see what this had to do with him since he was a farmer living in a shack two miles out of town, but he was curious and hopeful.

"We would like you to gather all the lumber you can for the construction before it gets too cold. We have enough money to pay Hank to cut logs to make the floors and walls. You can begin building the school once you have brought the lumber to the work site. The Campbells have donated enough dried lumber from their inventory behind the store to build the framework. Some of the town's folk have agreed to help with the initial framework on Saturdays, but it will be up to you to build the rest of the structure. Reverend McConnell said he would help when he didn't need to visit the sick, and Sheriff Griffith will help you get the framing done when he has time."

"How will I get the lumber to town from Hank's place? He's a mile out of town. Where will I stay once I get the lumber into town?" Archie had many other questions, but inside, he desperately wanted to do the work because it would mean he would hopefully be able to see Maggie.

Widow Henry had anticipated most of Archie's concerns and was well prepared to assure him everything would be fine.

"Reverend McConnell said you could stay at the church in a classroom to save money. You can stay here in the barn until the room is ready.

The town folks have volunteered to bring food, and the Campbells will let you use their horse and wagon to move the lumber."

Archie knew this was an opportunity he could not pass up and agreed to do the work. Widow Henry said they could pay him ten dollars weekly for his work, which sounded like a fortune to Archie. He would have enough money to buy his own horse by spring to help build his cabin and till his land for planting.

"Mrs. Henry, do you know if Maggie plans to stay in town? Her aunt seems to be doing much better?"

Widow Henry smiled as he asked the question and said," I think so, but perhaps you need to ask her yourself."

Archie's heart was pounding so fast he couldn't breathe. As he finished his coffee and got up to leave, he thanked Widow Henry for offering him the job and the morning coffee. He had grown to have a deep respect for the elderly lady. She seemed to always be at peace and cared for everyone, regardless of who it might be.

Archie closed the front door to Widow Henry's house and briskly walked down the street to the general store. He had to see Maggie and tell her the good news.

Maggie was attending to a customer when Archie walked into the store and didn't notice him at first. When she turned around to take the goods to the cash register, she saw Archie, and her face lit up. It was all she could do to finish the purchase and count change as her hands shook excitedly. She, like Archie, didn't know if they would see each other again after the fall picnic or how they could have a meaningful courtship with him living out of town.

"Archie, I'm so glad to see you. I was hoping you would come to town before too long." Her smile was even more beautiful than he remembered.

"Maggie, when can we talk? I want to tell you something, but now, while you're working, isn't the right time." The excitement on his face made it clear to Maggie that he had good news to share with her. Little did Archie know that she also had news for him.

Tom Campbell was stocking shelves and overheard the two of them talking. He was on the committee and knew what Archie wanted to tell Maggie, so he said to Maggie," I can handle things in the store; why don't you take the rest of the day off."

Archie remembered that there was a bench in front of the church that they could sit on while they talked. He did not want to do anything inappropriate; being alone with her in public was the proper thing to do. As they walked down the street, Maggie could not wait to hear what Archie wanted to tell her, but she respected that he wanted to do it calmly and respectfully. As they neared the church, Archie remembered that this was where he had first seen Maggie as she escorted her aunt to the picnic, so he asked her how Miss McCombs was doing.

"Aunt Carol is almost completely healed and excited to return to teaching. Until a new school is built, she will use the church for classes. I believe she said they were going to start next week."

"Does that mean you are going back to Ohio?" Archie asked with a sunken heart.

"Aunt Carol has asked me to stay with her and teach the younger children while the school committee finds another qualified teacher to teach them. There are so many more children than when Aunt Carol first started; they want to split the classes," said Maggie. "We will be able to see each other when you are in town!"

"Praise God!" Archie blurted out without thinking.

"Archie, what did you want to tell me?" Maggie asked somewhat impatiently.

To her, staying in town for a few months longer didn't change their situation much; it just offered them more time to get to know each other whenever Archie came to town.

Archie told Maggie everything Widow Henry had said about building the new schoolhouse, staying at the church, everything. Archie would be in town while Maggie was still there teaching, and nothing could have made either of them happier.

The two walked across the street to find Aunt Carol. Maggie went into her room and told her that Archie wanted to ask her something. Maggie's smile made what Archie wanted to ask her evident.

"Miss McCombs, may I have the privilege of courting Maggie? I will be in town for the next few months, and I desperately want to get to know her and spend as much time with her as you will permit," asked Archie.

Looking into Archie's eyes, Carol McCombs could see that he was very sincere, and the look on Maggie's face told her how happy she was at the prospect of spending time with Archie.

"Thank you for being a gentleman, Archie, and asking for my permission. Yes, you and Maggie may court with my fullest blessing."

CHAPTER 6

After Archie left, Maggie rushed back to Aunt Carol's room, where she found her aunt on her knees beside her bed praying. She did this every day, but today, Maggie was close enough to hear what she was praying.

"Dear Father, thank you for healing my ankle and the burn wounds and bringing Maggie back into my life. She has been such a tremendous help. I pray, Father, that you will be with her as she begins her courtship with Archie, and if it is your will, they may be happy together for the rest of their lives. I have never seen her this happy; thank you, Lord. Father, I pray for the children, Lord, that I will be able to teach each one of them to love reading and learning. If it is your will, Father, please help me find books to replace the ones lost in the fire. I ask only that you lead me in the months ahead to guide each child to grow in learning and to grow to know You more by what I say and, more importantly, by what I do. In Jesus' name, I pray."

Maggie stepped back out of sight for a few seconds and reentered the room with a different attitude. She knew that she would marry Archie if it were God's will.

"Aunt Carol, thank you for allowing Archie to court me. He is the most humble, caring man I have ever met. I want to spend as much time with him as I can. I will be with you during the day teaching the little children, and Archie will be rebuilding the schoolhouse, but after work, we can see each other, even if just for a little while."

Maggie explained where Archie would be staying and how so many of the townspeople had given money and supplies, would provide food for Archie, and help with the construction. She was so excited that she didn't notice the tears welling up in Carol's eyes.

Carol was so happy for Maggie and profoundly touched by how these poor folks gave what they could to help rebuild the schoolhouse. As she hugged Maggie, tears rolling down her face, she whispered, "Thank you, Lord."

Archie had stopped by to see Tom Campbell to ask if he could use the horse and wagon to get all the dried wood from Hank that he had in stock and to see when Hank could get started cutting additional boards. Tom assured him he would not need the wagon or horse for a couple of days but needed them back on Friday morning to go to Charleston to get supplies for the store. It would take him all morning to go downriver to Charleston. He had planned to stay with a friend before loading the wagon and heading back on Saturday, assuming the weather was good. Sometimes, the river flooded the river road, making getting back to Clayton exceedingly tricky.

Archie went back to Widow Henry's to have dinner and to discuss in more detail what needed to be done. As they ate fried fish Widow Henry had prepared, they talked about the new design for the schoolhouse. Archie was excited to start but knew he should go over drawings with Reverend McConnell and Tom Campbell when he returned to town Saturday evening to ensure he understood exactly what was expected. Tom had asked an architect friend in Charleston to do the drawings needed to build the new schoolhouse.

Tom's grandfather had immigrated from Scotland like so many others. Still, unlike most Scots, the Campbells had owned land and houses they rented to people and, therefore, came to this country with significant wealth, ready to prosper from their business knowledge and the expanding population. Little did they or any of the others understand how the Scots and Irish would be discriminated against. There was no work for them in the cities as signs were posted: "Scot/Irish need not apply." Moving west to the mountains was not only necessary but exciting. The hills of Appalachia reminded them of their homeland. Many farmed, while others had enough children to tend to the crops so the fathers could work clearing timber for lumber companies. If they could save enough money from the extra work, they would be able to buy land. Most had never owned land. The thought of owning their homestead was a dream. In addition to the lumber companies, new coal mines were beginning to open, and there was talk of oil being discovered further south of the Pennsylvania oil fields.

Archie went to the general store to hitch the horse to the Campbell's wagon the following day. While there, he looked for Maggie to tell her where he was going. When he was coming around to the front of the store, Maggie was running around the corner to see him, and they accidentally ran into each other's arms. Both quickly jumped back, blushing but completely overjoyed by the brief encounter.

They talked briefly about what each would do the next couple of days when Archie blurted out, "Can we have dinner Saturday evening? Widow Henry told me it would be fine with her if you joined me. It's my last night staying there before I move into the room at the church."

Maggie was so thrilled to have been asked to have dinner with Archie that she could not contain herself. Running to the boardinghouse, she rushed up the stairs to tell her aunt the fantastic news.

"Archie has asked me to have dinner with him at Widow Henry's. Widow Henry will be there, of course, but I get to have dinner and have time to talk and be with him."

The look on her face warmed Carol's heart. She had never known love like that, though she had courted a young man back in Canton before deciding he was not the one she intended to spend her life with. They embraced and briefly talked about what she would wear. Aunt Carol had some dresses that might fit her, and if not, they had a couple of evenings to alter them, but for now, they were off to school.

Archie drove the wagon, unaccustomed to riding, for he had never owned a horse, let alone a wagon. The chestnut brown horse was experienced pulling the wagon and seemed to understand Archie was uncomfortable. Archie began to get the hang of it as they continued over the road to Hank's, or at least that's what he thought. The small dirt road was narrow, with holes everywhere, so the going was slow. The late fall air was crisp, with a mild frost covering the valleys. The trees were beautiful, with their leaves at their peak colors. Everything was picture-perfect as the day began warming up and the frost melted. Archie usually didn't pay attention to such things as he was working hard cutting trees, clearing farmland, or hunting for game, but today, everything seemed perfect. His heart was full of joy thinking about Maggie and how different everything was from just ten days earlier.

Pulling up to Hank's sawmill, he noticed Hank seemed more upbeat than usual and was the most talkative Archie could ever remember him being. Archie did not know about Hank's meeting with Sheriff Griffith. Hank felt free of his past secret now that the sheriff knew, a feeling that was new to him. He took the reins from Archie and tied the horse to a tree.

"I'll get him some water and be right back, Archie. The horse looks thirsty." Hank grabbed his bucket and ran down to the creek to get water, and on his way back up the knoll, he asked Archie what he was doing with the Campbell's wagon.

Archie and Hank sat on a couple of logs Hank had placed next to his fire pit to talk. Archie explained why he was there and what the town folk were doing to rebuild the schoolhouse. Archie explained that they had raised money to buy any useable dry wood he currently had and that they wanted to hire him to cut as many boards as he could before it got too cold so that they could dry out during the winter. His skill was appreciated by the people of Clayton so much that he would be the only sawmill they planned on using.

Hank did not know what to say. Just two weeks ago, he felt isolated and lonely, hiding his past from everyone. He lived from the few crops he could grow and what game he could kill. He saw no future, only existence. His reaction to the confidence of the townspeople, knowing that they had very little to give and yet they trusted him to provide, was all the encouragement he needed. In two short weeks, his life had changed entirely.

"Archie, why wouldn't they use wood from Widow Henry's lumber yard in Charleston?" asked Hank.

"I don't know Hank, but Widow Henry is on the committee and insisted they use you," Archie said.

"Archie, tell everyone how grateful I am for this opportunity; I won't disappoint them."

He led Archie around to his sawmill to collect all the dry boards he had in inventory. After they loaded the wagon, Hank told Archie he would cut some trees along the road so that it would be easier to navigate and use them up for lumber.

"I'll store them inside the mill for winter to dry, so you'll have what you need next spring."

As Archie was pulling away, he turned around and asked Hank," Why don't you come into town to get paid for the wood and the work you will be doing? You could use the money for winter supplies and thank some of the folks yourself."

Hank shook his head no; he was uncomfortable around folks other than Archie.

The trip back was even slower, with the wagon filled with wood. The afternoon heat was beating down on Archie and the horse. When he was about halfway back to town, Archie stopped to let the horse rest and drink from a nearby creek when suddenly he saw a black bear off in the distance eating berries. The bear wasn't interested in them, but Archie did not know how the horse would react, so he decided to stay where he was and let it pass. After almost an hour, the bear was still in the area eating berries, and Archie needed to get the horse back to town so

Mr. Campbell could take it to Charleston Friday morning. He took his shirt off, wrapped it around the horse's head, covered his eyes, and began singing as loud as he could. The noise startled the bear, who, begrudgingly, wandered off from the berry patch as Archie slowly walked the horse down the road. Archie would stop singing every few minutes to calmly speak to the horse and rub his neck to assure him everything was fine. When they were out of danger, he took the shirt from the horse's head, climbed back on the wagon, and road into town.

It was later than he had expected to get back, but the rough road and the bear had slowed him quite a bit. He took the wagon to the back of the schoolhouse property to unload the boards and cover them with a tarp Tom Campbell had loaned him. After securing the tarp, he walked the horse to its stable behind the general store to wash and rub him down. He would be as good as new in the morning with fresh hay and cold water. As Archie pushed the wagon to where Tom usually kept it, he heard a now familiar sound. It was Maggie asking him how the day had gone. As they walked back to the front of the store to let the Campbells know he had returned their horse, he told Maggie about the meeting with Hank and the bear. Maggie wasn't too happy hearing about an incident with a bear; he could have been hurt.

Archie explained that black bears were usually relatively easy to avoid, but being from the city, Maggie didn't know if he was telling her the truth or just trying to keep her from worrying. Maggie asked if he had eaten yet because if he had not, she had saved some of her dinner to share with him. As they left the store, having told Tom he was back, they went to the boardinghouse to meet Aunt Carol, who was also anxious to hear about Archie's adventures.

That night, when Archie returned to Widow Henry's place, there was a spring in his step. "What a great day," he whispered, "what a great day."

CHAPTER 7

The following day, Tom hitched his horse onto the wagon and began his trip to Charleston. He knew the ride would take about three hours if there weren't any rain. A few times, the Elk River overflowed its banks, making the road impassable. There was another way, but it required going over the hill on the river's west bank and down a steep, narrow road that most people avoided.

As Tom rode along, he thought about the little town he and Nancy had settled in twenty years ago and its wonderful community. The people were friendly, caring folks, but he did worry about the lack of a doctor. Doc was good at what he did, but the town needed an actual doctor. He also thought about his land holdings and how now would be the time to purchase additional acreage. Tom and Nancy had formed a corporation shortly after settling in Clayton that bought land in the area and rented it to the local farmers. Each farmer paid rent and had the first right of refusal to purchase it when it was placed on the market. Most intended to buy their land, so they built homes, barns, and other buildings, taking the chance that their labor and expense would not be for naught.

Tom formed the company so that the townspeople would not know who owned the property, which could potentially make people uncomfortable.

Mostly, however, Tom thought about all the changes taking place. People were moving further west every year to settle down on land they could claim or go to California to look for gold or to the open spaces of the west, to towns that didn't exist twenty years ago. Locally, Tom saw a change in how people lived. In the past, most had been farmers, but now more men were working in coal mines or salt packing factories, sending money home to care for their families, coming home a couple weekends a month. The country was becoming much more industrial than the agrarian culture he had immigrated to years earlier.

Making his way along the river road, he noticed two men heading up a hill with guns, no doubt deer hunting. This time of year, the woods were peaceful, with the fall breeze gently blowing the bright leaves from the trees and the sky a clear blue. Autumn was in the air, and part of him wanted to join them to walk in the forest and enjoy the bright, sunny day. Today wasn't the day for that; there was much to be done before the cold weather set in.

The road went downstream toward the Kanawha River, part of the Mississippi River watershed leading eventually to the Gulf of Mexico and New Orleans. Tom knew times were changing when he got to the river and saw six steamships lined up being loaded with logs and other goods. Three barges were carrying coal from a nearby coal mine. He had heard of mines being dug upriver near Cabin Creek but, until then, had not given it much thought. It was apparent that industry was moving into the area, and the Kanawha River would provide a way to transport products inexpensively.

Tom rode into town to the distributor he dealt with to get supplies for the general store before meeting his friend. Harry Clark had owned the warehouse for thirty years, having moved to Charleston from Cincinnati. His father had been in the same business, so Harry learned to operate a successful warehouse early on. As Harry's employee loaded the supplies into the wagon, Tom could not help noticing that his inventory was lower than usual, so he asked Harry what was happening.

Harry looked at Tom and said, "I'm selling the warehouse, Tom, and moving back to Ohio. My father is ill and asked me to take over his store."

This was quite a blow to Tom since this was his leading supplier, but he respected Harry's decision. "Where will I be able to get supplies, Harry?" Tom asked with concern in his voice.

Harry understood Tom's dilemma and told him about a few places not far from his place. "If you've got the time, I'll go with you to introduce you to Jim Hoffman; he's a good guy, you'll enjoy working with him."

Tom asked Harry if he could stop by after meeting with a friend of his downtown for a while, and Harry agreed. Tom left his wagon in the warehouse and walked about a mile to Howard McDougal's office to review the drawings he had made for the new schoolhouse.

Howard had known Tom since he first moved to Charleston. He had designed the general store and became one of Tom's best friends. They discussed the new schoolhouse, and Howard showed Tom how, with little effort, the building could be added to as needed.

"All the administration offices and storage rooms will be in the back part of the building so that a mirror image could easily be constructed to the back end of the property when needed."

Howard went over the drawings in detail with Tom so that he could explain them to his builder. As they concluded their meeting, Tom asked Howard who was buying Harry's warehouse.

"Some outfit from Columbus, Ohio, is moving to the area to look for oil and wants to use the space to store their equipment," Howard explained. "No one's ever found oil in these parts, but for some reason, they believe there could be oil around here. They're not telling anyone where they are looking, but word has it, they are leasing hundreds of acres."

Tom thanked Howard for his help and, noticing how late it was getting, rushed down the street to see his attorney to instruct him to buy more land in the Clayton area.

Tom had been regularly depositing money from the store's profits, along with capital he had brought from Scotland when he and Nancy came to America. With that money and what Tom had inherited from his father, they could add to their holdings when the price was right.

Thomas Franklin had worked with Tom before in helping him purchase property in Clay County, so when Tom asked to meet with him, he suspected there was a piece of property he was interested in.

"Thomas, I'm sorry to be so rushed, but I need to meet the new warehouse owner in a few minutes. I just wanted to ask you to be on the lookout for some property for Nancy and me to buy. I think it is a good time, with the growth occurring all over the state," said Tom.

"I think the ten acres in the south end of Clayton is about to be put on the market," said Thomas.

"Let me know more when you have the details. Sorry, I need to rush. I will see you the next time I'm in town."

Quickly, Tom returned to the warehouse where Harry was waiting.

"Sorry it took so long, Harry; I forget how much bigger Charleston is than Clayton."

Harry was unconcerned as they got into Tom's wagon to go to Jim Hoffman's place. When they pulled into Jim's warehouse, Tom couldn't help noticing that "Hoffman's" was a more diverse establishment. They had supplies for the general store and carried building supplies, dishes, and canned food. Back in the corner, Tom caught a glance of what looked to be a library and walked over to see what kind of books they were.

On the way, Harry explained to Jim that Tom was from Clayton and was probably interested in the books to see if they could replace the ones destroyed by the fire last summer.

As Jim approached Tom, he asked what he might be interested in.

"The books are from my wife. She used to teach school before we were married. She brought them to the warehouse just in case anyone was interested."

Tom wrote down the titles to show Carol McCombs. He couldn't believe he found schoolbooks in good condition in a warehouse. He told Jim he would let him know if these were books Miss McCombs needed.

As they walked around the warehouse, Tom looked at what Jim carried and discussed pricing and availability. When Harry and Tom were leaving, Tom thanked Jim for showing him around and that he would be in town to see him next month before the cold winter snow prevented safe travel.

After dropping Harry off at his warehouse, Tom went to Howard's house to spend the evening with him and his wife.

Howard's wife, Vivian, was glad to see Tom. It had been two months since Tom had been in town to purchase fall supplies for the store.

Vivian had met Howard when he was in college in Morgantown. They courted for two years while he finished school and were married shortly after graduation. Moving to Charleston had worked out beautifully for them. The city was growing faster than any city for hundreds of miles, and new buildings were being built everywhere. An old cattle farm had become the east end of town. Churches, office buildings, and houses were being built at an alarming pace.

Vivian had prepared dinner for the three of them that afternoon. Howard asked how Clayton was doing as they enjoyed their chicken, mashed potatoes, and beans. Tom was proud of his little town and thoroughly enjoyed the smaller setting, but it did not compare with the big city. He explained that, besides a new schoolhouse going up, only a little had changed since Howard's last time there.

"Nothing like Charleston. Wow, this place is growing fast!"

Howard looked at Tom and said, "Maybe too fast."

Howard explained that the lumber business had been good for the local economy over the last few years, but it seemed to be slowing down. New people were moving to the area and leasing vast amounts of land. These people didn't seem interested in the local community; they were only interested in business.

They didn't use local professionals for their legal work, banking, or, for that matter, architectural work. Charleston had a few larger firms, but these companies were different. Their employees did not come from this area, and while they said they planned on hiring local people once operations were underway, the core group was rough.

The following day, there was a slight drizzle, and the sky was gray. It looked like the trip back to Clayton wouldn't be as enjoyable as the ride the day before. Tom covered everything the night before to protect it from the weather in case it rained. Tom said goodbye to Vivian and thanked her for a wonderful dinner. Howard walked to the back of the house to see Tom off and help him hitch the wagon when Tom remembered something he had meant to ask Howard the night before.

"Howard, would you keep an ear out for a doctor for Clayton? We don't have a real doctor, and with the town growing, it is becoming an issue."

Howard told him he would see what he could do and said goodbye to his friend. In some ways, he envied Tom's life in a small town where things were more straightforward and people could be trusted.

The trip back proved to be more complicated than Tom had hoped. The rain the night before and the steady cold mist made the road muddy and difficult to move through. The only good news was that there hadn't been enough rain to cause the river to flood. Accepting the situation, Tom slowly drove his wagon back to Clayton. It had been an eventful day with a few surprises. A new supplier, drawings for the schoolhouse, and the sad news about the change in the Charleston economy. While growth was exciting and provided opportunities for people, he, like Howard, wondered at what cost.

Tom arrived in Clayton after dark, quickly unhitched the wagon, and moved it into his shed. After feeding and giving his horse water, he went into the house, exhausted and cold. After changing clothes, he entered the kitchen, where Nancy had made him a warm cup of coffee as she finished dinner. She could tell something was on his mind but waited for him to explain after warming himself at the potbelly stove. Tom did not say much during dinner and wanted to go to bed afterward. It had been a long day, and he wanted to rest.

The following day, Tom was back to his usual self and, over breakfast, told Nancy all about the trip and everything that had happened. He went into their bedroom, changed into his Sunday church clothes, and happily escorted his wife to worship, thankful for the life he was given.

After church, Tom asked Carol McCombs if she could stop by sometime that afternoon. "I've got something that I think will interest you."

Later that afternoon, there was a knock at the door. Tom went to the door expecting Miss McCombs, but Reverend McConnell was there instead. He had forgotten that before going to Charleston, he had asked the preacher to stop by Sunday after church to review the new schoolhouse's drawings. So much had happened over the last two days that it had completely slipped his mind.

"How was your trip, Tom? Glad to be back? I hear Charleston is growing like gangbusters!"

Tom acknowledged that he was glad to be back and even more grateful for the small town he lived in after spending the day in Charleston. They discussed how things were changing in Charleston and how Clayton was growing.

"The difference, Reverend, is the people that move here want to be part of our community. Thank God we haven't experienced what Charleston is going through."

Tom pulled out the drawings to show Reverend McConnell just as there was a knock on the door. Miss McCombs had stopped by to see what Tom wanted to show her. Tom realized that they should all discuss the building and the books; after all, Miss McCombs should have input on the new schoolhouse, and the Reverend might be interested in the books Tom had discovered.

Carol walked into the room as Nancy was bringing water for everyone. Setting the pitcher down, she went into the kitchen to get glasses for their guests.

"I'll be in the kitchen if anyone needs anything else."

Tom was excited to tell Reverend McConnell and Miss McCombs about the drawings and all the effort Howard had put into them to accommodate further expansion when needed. As they reviewed the renderings, Carol glanced at the Reverend and noticed how genuinely excited he was about helping the town's children. As both looked closely at the drawings, Carol said that she felt her office was too large and suggested that it be smaller so that a second office could be added to accommodate an additional teacher. Reverend McConnel liked what saw he only suggesting that hooks be put in the front of the school so the children could hang their coats up to dry as they entered class. Tom could not help noticing how Reverend McConnell and Miss McCombs worked so well together and seemingly enjoyed one another.

When they finished reviewing the drawings, Tom shared the list of books he had found in Charleston the day before. To his surprise, tears began flowing down Miss McComb's face. These books were exactly what she had wanted for the children.

Reverend McConnell looked at Miss McCombs and was moved by how much she loved her students and what these books meant to her. He reflected on how fortunate Clayton was to have a schoolteacher who so deeply cared for each of her students. As he got up to leave, excusing himself, he realized he had a clearer understanding of the real Carol McCombs.

He had known her over the last few weeks but only from afar. He felt it was inappropriate for him to spend too much one-on-one time with any female from town, so he had maintained a casual acquaintance with her, only talking after services.

When Carol left, she thanked Tom for getting the schoolhouse drawings and especially for finding the books. She was overwhelmed and told Tom she hoped to get the books to read to her students as soon as possible.

Tom promised her that there was enough money in the new schoolhouse fund to pay for the books and that he would soon have them shipped from Charleston.

After their guests were gone, Tom and Nancy sat in their parlor and discussed what they would like to do for Carol.

"You know, a school isn't often blessed with a teacher that cares as much for their students as she does. We have enough money in the treasury for the books, but we also don't know how much rebuilding will cost. You and I could donate the money to buy the books," said Tom.

Nancy approvingly smiled at her husband; he was such a wonderful man. She looked into his eyes and said, "I think that is a great idea, Tom; thank you; that means a great deal to me."

CHAPTER 8

ARCHIE AWOKE EARLIER than usual. The sun wasn't up yet, but he could not wait to get started on the schoolhouse. He decided to carefully inspect what structure was left after the fire, to salvage as much as possible, and to determine the extent of the work that had to be done.

As he headed out of the front gate, Widow Henry yelled, "Are you going without having breakfast?"

She had been up, preparing the coffee and waiting for Archie to make breakfast.

She had grown fond of the young man and knew he would be restless to start his day and, perhaps even more so, about his dinner with Maggie that evening. Archie hadn't wanted to bother Widow Henry, but the smell of fresh coffee, bacon, eggs, and biscuits was more than he could resist.

"I didn't want to wake you, Mrs. Henry, it being so early."

Widow Henry laughed and said, "Young man, I always get up early to enjoy the sunrise and to have quiet time with the Lord. You didn't bother me at all. Now sit down and have some breakfast."

As they sat and talked about what Archie planned to do that day, enjoying their coffee, Archie thanked her for all she had done for him.

"You've done so much for me: food, shelter, and work; I just don't know what to say but thank you."

Widow Henry looked at him like a mother would to a child and said quietly, "I'm thankful for the young man you are, Archie; it's been a joy to share my blessings with you."

Archie wanted to ask her a question that had been on his mind for a few weeks, but he didn't know how to ask it without being too personal.

"Widow Henry, I have noticed that you read your Bible every morning and spend time quietly thinking, why? I know it has to do with your faith, but I have never seen anyone spend so much time reading the same book repeatedly. I like to go to church on Sunday, and sometimes I remember to pray, but when I see you, I wonder if that's enough."

"Well, Archie, to me, it's simple: I want to have a deep personal relationship with the Lord, and to do that, I need to get to know Him, not just know of Him, so I spend time every day reading what He says to me through His Word. I learned a long ago that to know someone, you must spend time with them, and the Lord's no different."

"Oh, I see. Thanks for sharing with me. It makes sense, "said Archie as he carried their dirty dishes to the kitchen. "I'll see you later this afternoon. I want to get cleaned up before dinner and take my things to the church on my way to pick up Maggie."

Archie walked down to the school and considered Widow Henry's statement, "a relationship with the Lord."

When Archie got to the general store, he picked up some tools Tom had left for him and went to the schoolhouse to begin his day. The fire had destroyed most of the building, but some sections could be used. As he stacked the burned boards and debris, he noticed something shiny on the ground. When he dug it up from the ashes, he could see it was a heart-shaped necklace that might have a picture inside. Archie put it in his pocket to show Tom later when he returned the tools.

As the day wore on, Archie began to get excited about his dinner with Maggie. At first, he was anxious about what to talk about. He had been a loner most of his life, living alone on his farm with no one to speak with or care about, so conversation did not come easy. He moved there about a year after his mother died to start his own life and had not spent much time getting to know people in Clayton.

Maggie was visiting the area, which might make conversation easier for them, but he still worried all afternoon. At about five o'clock, the work he had planned to do that day was complete, so he packed up the tools and set out for the general store to see Tom. After he left the tools in Tom's shed, he looked to see if Tom was inside the store and, seeing him behind the counter, went in to show him what he had found. Tom opened the necklace, saw a picture of a mother and daughter, and thought he recognized the girl.

"Archie, I'll clean this up for you so you can give it to Miss McCombs; I think this is a picture of her as a young girl with her mother."

"That would be great. Thanks, Tom, see you in the morning."

After Archie had gotten ready for dinner, he packed his things and walked down the street to the church to move into the room Reverend McConnell had shown him the day before. On his way back, he kept thinking about Maggie and how quickly life had changed. When Archie entered the general store, Maggie looked up to see him and smiled. She was beautiful!

Archie nodded to Tom and put his arm out for Maggie to hold on to as they walked. Tom looked over at Nancy, and both smiled knowingly as if to say, "These two are falling in love."

Archie wasn't the most graceful; after all, this was the first time he had ever courted, but he did remember enough about proper manners to open the door for Maggie as they got to Widow Henry's house and to pull out her chair when they had been asked to join Mrs. Henry for dinner. Archie's mother had taught him everything she knew about acting correctly. She was the daughter of a minister in Canton, Ohio, and had helped her parents with small dinner parties from time to time.

Widow Henry had gone all out. She had been cooking all afternoon and was happy to present the two of them with fried chicken, baked squash, fresh green beans, and biscuits. As they were about to serve the food, Widow Henry surprised Archie and asked him to give thanks.

Awkwardly, Archie bowed his head and, without any forethought, thanked God for the food that had been so lovingly prepared and for the overwhelming care Widow Henry had shown him these last few weeks.

After completing his prayer, he noticed Widow Henry was wiping her eyes and smiling.

Widow Henry helped the conversation as dinner progressed, asking how the schoolhouse looked and what Archie would do first to get the project going. She asked Maggie how her aunt enjoyed her first day back teaching the children since last summer's fire.

Archie asked Maggie about her life in Canton. What did she like about the big city, what were her friends like, and how was the search for a new teacher coming along? All his questions affected their future and helped him better understand the kind of things Maggie liked to do.

As she was talking, Archie listened intently, wanting to know all about her. He mentioned he had grown up in Canton but left when he was eighteen after his mother had passed away. They had not lived near one another since Maggie's father worked in town and Archie's family lived outside of town on a farm, but they did know some of the same places.

Maggie told Archie she liked Canton but had grown to love the small town of Clayton. She enjoyed working with the younger children and secretly hoped the committee would take their time finding her replacement.

Widow Henry brought in the coffee and her famous apple pie while they continued talking. The three of them ate their dessert and laughed at stories Widow Henry shared from days gone by in Clayton.

As the evening ended, Maggie and Archie thanked Widow Henry for the beautiful meal and for hosting them. When the door closed and the two young people walked down her stairs, Widow Henry had the same knowing smile that Tom and Nancy had earlier that day.

Archie escorted Maggie to the front of the boardinghouse, told her how much he had enjoyed the time with her, and asked if he could see her again. Maggie suggested she pack a picnic dinner and bring it by the schoolhouse after the children left school. With a huge smile, Archie said he could not wait.

CHAPTER 9

THE WEATHER WAS getting colder as winter was fast approaching, and Archie knew he had to get the structure to a point where he could close it in to work indoors during the cold months ahead. After meeting with Tom that morning to confirm the dimensions of the building, he went about gathering framing boards to be used for the walls, making sure each was cut to the same length so that the work would be easier on Saturday. Several town folks said they would help raise the walls and frame in the basic structure. Archie stacked wood for the four sides and those for the truss work. The back section of the school had not been destroyed by the fire but needed to be cleaned to remove the smell of the smoke. Archie decided it would be best to take it apart and use the boards for the exterior so they could be painted. He didn't want the odor from the singed boards to remind the children of the horror of the fire.

The work was slow since the boards would be reused, but Archie knew it was the right thing to do. By the end of the day, Archie was covered with black soot and looked like a chimney sweep. Maggie arrived around five o'clock, just before dark, with the picnic dinner she had prepared. Archie was embarrassed by his appearance, but Maggie quickly assured him she did not expect him to look any other way, "After all," she said, "you have been working all day."

They talked until it started getting cold. Archie walked Maggie back to the boardinghouse and then returned to ensure the work site was cleaned up for the next day. He took the tools Tom had loaned him to the church so that he could start working that much sooner the following day.

As he washed in the basin pastor McConnell had brought into the room that day, he noticed a note on his bed. "Come by my place when you are finished for the day, Seamus McConnell."

After laying out his belongings and making his bed, Archie walked to the back of the church where the parsonage was located and knocked on the door.

"Good evening, Archie," said pastor McConnell, "I'm glad to see you. I thought you could use some company in the evenings. Frankly, I could use the company too. As a pastor, unless someone is in need, my evenings are lonely, too."

Archie felt a sense of relief for some unexplained reason and was glad for the company. The two men sat in Seamus' small living room and talked about the schoolhouse project, Archie's farm, and Seamus' travels through the mountains before settling in Clayton and the coming winter. As the evening progressed, Archie began to see Seamus differently. He wasn't just a pastor but a regular man like Archie with many of the same desires and goals for his life. When it started getting late, Archie thanked Seamus for inviting him over and got up to leave. Seamus told Archie to come by whenever he wasn't busy, "I enjoyed getting to know you."

That night, as Archie was falling asleep, he again looked back at the last few weeks' events and how none of them were anything he had planned. "How can life change so quickly? "

Archie saw Maggie every day and Seamus McConnell most evenings after dinner for the remainder of the week. Archie had asked Maggie if she would have dinner with him at the boardinghouse in the evenings after he had finished working; he would bring food people had prepared for him to share with her. He desperately wanted to see her, and this was the proper way, in public, so there wouldn't be any questions of impropriety.

On Friday evening, Seamus asked Archie if he and Maggie would join him for dinner on Sunday evening. "I don't know what we will have to eat since some of the people from the town are providing the food, but

I am sure it will be delicious, whatever it is." Archie gladly accepted the invitation, excited to have more time with Maggie.

Saturday morning arrived, and it seemed like everyone had come to town. The women brought food to the church for a potluck dinner after the schoolhouse raising while the men joined Archie and began working on the framing of the school. Archie had worked hard doing as much as he could alone, putting together the framing and trusses so there would not be any wasted time. The men attached ropes to Archie's frames and pulled them into position while others secured them temporarily with supports. The roof truss work was the most time-consuming. Sheriff Griffith and Tom built a pulley system so the men could raise the support beams to be attached to the wall structures. Hank had come into town Friday to help prepare the truss joints, making them more substantial, and stayed at the church with Archie that evening. By the end of the day Saturday, the schoolhouse was completely framed and ready for the exterior walls and the roof to be built.

All the men went to the church, where the ladies had been busy moving the pews and setting up tables. Everyone filled their plates and sat down to eat, but before eating, they all waited for Archie and Maggie to take their place with them. Reverend McConnell asked the blessing, and afterward, Tom stood up and thanked everyone for all their hard work.

While the town folks were enjoying their dinner, Reverend McConnell, Tom, and Widow Henry stood up and spoke, praising Archie for his challenging work that week, allowing the raising to go so smoothly. Seamus McConnell looked at Archie and said with deep emotion how he was moved by everyone showing up to work on the schoolhouse and what a great community this was to live in. He said he and Archie had spent several evenings getting to know one another during the past week.

"This young man cares about doing what is right, and regardless of how tired he is by evening, he is always happy, looking forward to what he can get done the next day. Archie, you're a good man; I'm glad to call you my friend." The audience applauded, showing their appreciation for Archie.

Maggie beamed with pride, for she knew from conversations with Archie that he had never looked at himself as belonging. He had been a loner, working the little piece of land he owned, staying to himself. He knew he wanted a family someday but was timid and thought he had little to offer. Tonight, Maggie could see from Archie's face that he knew he belonged and that this community was home.

The remainder of November continued to get colder as Archie spent every minute of daylight working on the schoolhouse. Hank went to town one day to help Archie with the pulley system, lifting the shingles to the school's roof. It was backbreaking work for both of them, but by the end of the day, all the shingles were either nailed to the roofing slates or in place, ready to be fixed the next day.

Thanksgiving was Thursday, winter was fast approaching, and Archie wondered if he could finish the exterior before the season's first snow. The previous year, the first snow of the season surprised everyone. The Friday after Thanksgiving, it started snowing and didn't stop until Sunday morning.

To Archie's surprise, on the Wednesday before Thanksgiving, men from all around came into town to help him finish his work. They worked all day and completed the exterior of the building. As they were leaving, Carol McCombs came by to see how everything was going. When she saw the outside was finished, except for the windows and door, her eyes filled with tears, thanking each of the men for all their hard work.

When they were gone, Carol looked at Archie and asked him if he would like to come to the boardinghouse for Thanksgiving dinner with her and Maggie.

As Archie was thanking her, he remembered that Seamus would probably be alone and asked, "Would it be all right if I asked Reverend McConnell to come as well? I will eat less, so there will be plenty for him. I feel bad that he spends so much time alone."

Carol was surprised by the request but, at the same time, comforted in knowing how compassionate Archie was. Carol noticed how Archie was different from just a couple of months ago. Somehow, he was confident and still gentle. Maggie had also seen the change and told her aunt that he felt he belonged for the first time in his life.

That evening, when Archie stopped by Reverend McConnell's home, he told him about Thanksgiving dinner with Carol McCombs. Although surprisingly excited, Seamus told Archie he had been invited to Widow Henry's for dinner and could not go. Archie was glad he had dinner plans; being alone on a holiday would have been terrible.

Archie worked Thanksgiving morning building a door so the schoolhouse could be closed in the evenings. Tom was going to Charleston on business the following Monday and would pick up the windows while he was there. With the door finished, Archie returned to his room to prepare for dinner. After cleaning up, he changed into his Sunday clothes and headed for the boardinghouse. When Carol opened the door and did not see Reverend McConnell, she surprisingly felt disappointed but tried not to show it to her guest. Archie explained that Pastor McConnell had been invited to Widow Henry's for Thanksgiving.

The restaurant was filled with the aroma of turkey, stuffing, and fresh biscuits. Archie settled into a comfortable chair and tried to take it all in. It had only been two months, and yet everything was different. There he was in a warm, comfortable restaurant, preparing for a beautiful Thanksgiving dinner instead of cooking something over his open fire in his little shack. He had new friends, and most importantly, he knew he had met the woman he wanted to spend the rest of his life. He did not allow himself to get emotional, but today, in this setting, he was filled with joyful thanksgiving.

Before dinner began, Archie reached into his pocket and pulled out the necklace he had found. Tom had cleaned it up for him and brought it by the schoolhouse the day before.

" Miss McCombs, I found this the other day, and I believe it is yours."

When he showed Carol the necklace, she quickly opened it and looked at the picture inside. "Look, Maggie, that's me when I was a little girl with my mother! Oh, thank you, Archie; I wondered where it was. It is my favorite necklace. Thank you."

Dinner was even better than it smelled, and to his surprise, there was pumpkin pie! He hadn't had pumpkin pie since his mother had died seven years ago.

Archie looked at Maggie as they enjoyed dessert and asked if she was happy. Did she like Clayton enough to live here instead of Canton? Maggie smiled and told Archie she loved the town and couldn't think of a better place to settle down. When Sarah took the dishes into the kitchen, Maggie jumped up to help her. Sarah and Lizzy had worked so hard to make this a wonderful evening that she wanted to do something to help. With Maggie out of the room, Archie asked Carol if she could write down Maggie's address in Canton; he knew he wanted to ask her father for her hand in marriage.

When Archie left the restaurant, Carol brought him his coat and slipped a piece of paper into his front pocket so Archie would see it. Archie was on top of the world as he walked down the street to the church. As soon as he got to his room, he looked for some paper and began to write a letter to Mr. Garrett asking for his daughter's hand in marriage. He felt it was also important to tell him how he planned to take care of her and what his prospects looked like. Not feeling completely comfortable with the letter, he went to the parsonage to see if his friend was home yet. When Reverend McConnell opened the door, he saw something was on Archie's mind and asked him, "What can I do for you, Archie?"

"I need your help. I'm writing a letter to Maggie's father, and I want to make sure it is written so that he can feel comfortable giving me his permission," said Archie in a rush.

"Permission for what, Archie?" asked Seamus, knowing what Archie was probably doing. The two of them sat down, and Seamus read the letter and, when he had finished, looked directly into Archie's eyes and asked him if he was prepared to love Maggie, regardless of their circumstances, for the rest of his life.

The look on Archie's face gave away his answer as he told his new friend, "Seamus, I've never been this sure about anything." After finding an envelope and addressing the letter, Archie left. He planned on going to the general store as soon as it opened to ensure it was in the mail as quickly as possible.

The following day, at ten o'clock, Archie went to the general store and asked Tom if he could mail a letter for him. Archie gave it to Tom for the mail carrier to pick up later that day. As Tom put the letter in the mailbox, he noticed who it was addressed to and smiled.

The next three weeks went by very slowly for Archie. His work at the schoolhouse was going as planned. He had installed the floor and the new windows. Every day, he would go by the general store to see if there was any mail for him, and every day for three weeks, there was nothing. He continued seeing Maggie daily and spent time in the evenings with Seamus. Still, nothing seemed to matter, despite everything going so well for him, until he received Mr. Garrett's approval.

One Thursday in mid-December, a letter arrived at the general store for Archie. Tom noticed it and asked Nancy if she would look after the store while he made a special delivery to Archie. Archie was working on the ceiling when Tom walked into the schoolhouse. He almost fell off the ladder when he saw Tom had a letter in his hand. Grabbing the letter from Tom's hand, thanking him for bringing it to him, Archie's hands began shaking as he read it.

"Dear Archie, I have heard about you from letters Maggie has sent me these last two months. I have never known her to be so happy. She told me about your work ethic, compassion for others, and gentleness. I can think of no one else I would consider for my daughter's hand than someone of your character. Promise me you will always take care of my little girl. With all my blessing, I give you permission to marry Maggie."

Archie began jumping around the schoolhouse like a little boy on Christmas morning. "He said yes, Tom, he said yes!"

Tom was happy for Archie and excused himself to return to help Nancy at the store after congratulating him. When Nancy heard the good news, she screamed, "Praise God!"

Archie could not continue working; he was too excited. Rushing back to his room, he cleaned up and began thinking of what he wanted to say to Maggie and where.

As he left his room to go to the boardinghouse, Seamus came home and saw him. "Where are you going, Archie? Did you hear back from Mr. Garrett?"

Archie told Seamus the excellent news with a smile that went from ear to ear. Archie asked Seamus, "Do you have a minute? I want to run what I want to do by you." Seamus was honored that Archie felt close enough to him to seek his advice. Archie told him what he planned to say, and the only advice Seamus had was, "Just relax and be yourself."

School was out, and Maggie was in her aunt's room in the boardinghouse. Archie knocked on the door, and Carol opened it and knew immediately what Archie wanted. The look on his face was unmistakable.

"Maggie, Archie is here to see you," announced Carol.

"Maggie, I know it's a little cold, but could you come with me to the bench in front of the church?" asked Archie. This was the place they had spent their first time together in October. Maggie agreed, and as they walked down to the church, she asked Archie what this was all about.

"I've got something I want to ask you, "said Archie. When they got to the bench, they sat down, and Archie described how his entire life had changed these last few months and how he wanted to be with her every day.

"I cannot imagine ever spending a day without you, Maggie Garrett; I love you. Will you marry me? I have gotten permission from your father. I have nothing to provide you but my complete love and devotion."

Maggie began to cry and said, "Yes, Archie, that's all I need. I love you too." Archie reached into his coat pocket and pulled out his mother's engagement ring that his father had given him before he left home. As he placed it on her finger, they kissed for the first time.

Overjoyed, they ran to the boardinghouse to tell Aunt Carol. "Aunt Carol, Aunt Carol, Archie asked me to marry him!" said Maggie as they burst into Carol's room. Maggie showed Carol the engagement ring Archie had given her and told her it had been his mother's.

"It's beautiful!" exclaimed Carol as she hugged them both and asked if they would join her for dinner downstairs at the restaurant. When they sat down, Carol asked what their plans were. Archie hadn't thought that far ahead and said he wanted to get married as soon as possible. Maggie said that she wanted to see if her parents could make the trip from Canton, Ohio, before a date was set, and Archie completely agreed.

December went by slowly for the young couple. Archie kept working at the schoolhouse, and Maggie taught school at the church, waiting to hear from Maggie's parents, wanting desperately to be married. The week before Christmas, Maggie received a letter from her father telling her they could not come to Clayton before spring but agreed that if she wanted to get married before then, it would be with their blessing. In her letter, Maggie mentioned they wanted to marry in January if possible. After learning that her parents would not be able to be there, Maggie and Archie decided to set the date for Saturday, January 21, 1893.

Since neither had money to spend on a wedding, they planned a simple ceremony with their closest friends. Seamus McConnel would preside. Guests would be limited to Aunt Carol, Widow Henry, Tom and Nancy Campbell, and Sarah Adkins. Lizzy would be the flower girl and ring bearer.

As the day approached, Maggie received a box in the mail from her mother, and in it found her mother's wedding dress along with a note that said, I love you. That same day, Tom asked Archie to stop by the store to look at something. After working, Archie stopped by only to find a suit Tom had ordered from Charleston. Embarrassed, Archie said he did not have the money to pay for it when, to his surprise, Tom said, "It's my wedding present to you, my friend!"

CHAPTER 10

Christmas 1892 in Clay County was not like most places. There was very little gift-giving since most people were poor, but there was an abundance of thanksgiving for what blessings they did have. For many years, Widow Henry had secretly taken food and toys to many of her neighbors who didn't have money to spare on such things. She enjoyed sharing her blessings with friends and neighbors. The first thing she did was make candy and cookies for the little ones.

The week of Christmas, when school was out, she asked Carol and Maggie to help her prepare food and deliver the baskets to her neighbors. They were not supposed to tell anyone who had given them the food and toys, but most people suspected it was Widow Henry. Her genuine love for people was evident throughout the year, especially during Christmas.

The joy of the holiday was heartfelt and brought the community closer together as they celebrated the birth of Christ. Everyone gathered outside the church on the Monday before Christmas to decorate the Christmas tree and sing Christmas carols. The Campbells provided hot chocolate, and candy canes were given to the children. It was a Clayton tradition that everyone looked forward to throughout the year.

January arrived with a harsh wind and colder-than-normal temperatures, but Maggie and Archie hardly noticed. Their wedding was only three weeks away, and much was to be done. Widow Henry helped alter Maggie's wedding dress and Archie's new suit. When Tom was in Charleston, he purchased more candles than usual to decorate the church with candlelight for the wedding.

As a surprise, Nancy had gone with Tom to shop for some special things for Maggie. But what Archie and Maggie did not know was that the word of their upcoming wedding had caused quite a stir around town. Everyone understood the importance of keeping the wedding small and inexpensive, but they all wanted to celebrate with the young couple they had grown to care for so much.

Saturday finally arrived. The day began as most of the month had gone, cold and dreary. Around three o'clock, the clouds cleared, the sun shone, and temperatures warmed slightly. It was a beautiful winter's day. At four o'clock, Archie was at Seamus' house nervously waiting for the ceremony to start while Maggie was with Aunt Carol in one of the classrooms in the church finishing her preparations. Surprisingly, there was a knock on the classroom door; Widow Henry brought flowers she had shipped from Charleston for the young bride.

As the nervous couple made their way to their places in the church to begin the wedding ceremony, they both noticed a stirring in the sanctuary they had not expected, given how small the wedding party was to have been. When Maggie walked around the church to the entrance with Aunt Carol and Archie to the front of the church, both were overwhelmed.

Before Archie could see Maggie, he saw the church was full of friends from all around; even Hank was there. Maggie saw all the town folks and the children from school. Both were moved deeply by the outpouring of friendship. These people didn't have an extra penny to their name, yet they each took the time and effort to make their way into town to celebrate the wedding of their new friends.

The church pianist played the piano as Lizzy strolled down the aisle with a small pillow and the wedding rings. She beamed with excitement. Maggie had put one of Widow Henry's flowers in her hair to help her feel special. Maggie made her way down the aisle arm in arm with Aunt Carol. Archie could not believe how beautiful she looked and how incredibly blessed he was to marry such a loving young lady.

Reverend McConnell spoke to everyone about the importance of marriage and how a couple grows closer through the years as they keep their hearts focused on God.

"As two people are focused on the same thing, they are drawn together in love and spirit. One God, one faith, one love."

Lizzy gave Reverend McConnell the two wedding rings, and after exchanging their vows to one another and God, they placed them on each other's fingers. "Archie, you may kiss your bride."

When they kissed, the audience broke into a thunderous cheer. With their faces glowing with happiness, Archie and Maggie walked to the back of the church, arm in arm, while everyone came to congratulate them. There were tears of joy that afternoon, for this young couple had become like family to many.

While the young couple talked with neighbors, the men began bringing food into the church, and some moved pews to make more room. As things started to quiet down, Reverend McConnell announced to Archie and Maggie," Your friends want to celebrate with you to show how happy they are for you. We are all very blessed."

Widow Henry had invited the newlyweds to live in her guest room until Archie finished the schoolhouse construction. After that, they would move to Archie's cabin to live.

The young couple grew close to Widow Henry as winter wore on. Her joyful spirit, caring attitude for others, and, most of all, her deep faith made a lasting impression. Archie and Maggie began reading their Bibles daily and would discuss what they had read with Widow Henry in the evenings while they sat in her parlor around her fireplace.

Maggie helped in the kitchen and learned many of Widow Henry's secret recipes. Archie did some repair work around the house while keeping the firewood in sufficient supply. It was a good time of growth for both of them, but sadness began creeping into their thoughts as spring approached. Although they were excited to start their life together on their property, they would miss Widow Henry and the friends they had made in Clayton.

The school committee had yet to find a replacement for Maggie, so it was agreed that she would finish the school year before relinquishing her position.

Archie had completed the building itself and was now in the process of building desks for the children. A potbelly stove was purchased, and Archie installed it in the middle of the room so the children would be as warm as possible during the frigid winter months.

Hank had also been busy making boards for the inside of the schoolhouse. He had carefully made each panel the same length and width. He wanted to impress the school committee and especially Widow Henry with his workmanship. He knew he had only gotten the work because Widow Henry wanted him to get a fresh start in town and hopefully be used to provide lumber for the new people moving into the area when they decided to build. After all, she owned a large lumber mill south of Clayton in Charleston and could have quickly filled the order.

Hank began to feel more like a part of the community like he belonged. For so long, he had kept to himself, never sharing anything about his past until the day Sheriff Griffith visited. Now that the sheriff knew, rather than condemn him, he seemed to like him. Being the only black person in the area didn't seem to matter; everyone treated him just like everyone else. He knew of a black community east of Charleston near the mouth of Cabin Creek, but he didn't feel drawn to live there. The people of Clayton were becoming his friends now, and Hank was happy for the first time in his life.

In late March, Hank filled his wagon with lumber and came to Clayton. It was still cool, but spring was in the air, and Hank looked forward to seeing Archie. When he arrived, he and Archie began unloading the lumber when Hank said," I think I'll stay in town for a couple of days and help you put the siding on the walls, Archie; I know you want to get everything done here so that you can get out to your place."

Archie gladly accepted Hank's help, and they worked hard for three days until the entire school was finished. When Hank was leaving town to return to his cabin, he asked Archie to stop by his place on the way to his cabin.

The following Monday, Archie started painting the exterior of the school. He thought it would take a week to do the job correctly, and then he would head out to his place. One day, while Archie was working at the schoolhouse, Maggie began feeling bad and asked Carol if she could escort her to Widow Henry's house since the children had all left for their homes.

That evening, she couldn't explain it, but she didn't feel right. She went to bed early, skipping Bible study with Archie and Widow Henry. By morning, she was sick to her stomach and couldn't eat. Maggie felt terrible for several days, so Widow Henry brought Nancy to visit her.

Nancy had helped deliver babies for several years and knew what was probably going on. Maggie told Nancy about her various symptoms, and Nancy assured her that she was not sick but pregnant. "You'll know for sure in a few more weeks, Maggie, but I'm positive that is causing you to feel this way."

As Nancy left, she winked at Widow Henry with a knowing look and a bounce in her step.

Widow Henry prepared dinner for the three of them but told Maggie, as Archie was cleaning from work, that she needed to visit a friend and would not be there for a few hours. She wanted Maggie and Archie to have time alone so that Maggie could share her news privately.

When Archie entered the dining room, he wondered where Widow Henry was and asked Maggie. Maggie replied that she had to visit a friend and would not be home for dinner. When the two of them sat down, Maggie was not interested in eating much; she was too excited to eat. After giving thanks, Archie began eating dinner when Maggie said she had something to tell him. Archie looked at Maggie, wondering what was on her mind, but the look on her face gave it away.

"We're going to have a baby!"

"What?" Archie cried, "Are you sure? Are you all right? When?" He couldn't control his excitement and just kept firing question after question. They laughed and cried and hugged each other for a very long time. Then, after calming down a little, Archie told Maggie he wanted to lead them in prayer for their unborn child.

"Father, you know how happy we are with this blessing you have given us, and all that we ask is that you would guide us to be the parents you want us to be. We trust you with everything."

As the days warmed and the flowers bloomed, Maggie started showing that Nancy had been correct. Maggie committed to finish teaching through the school year but looked forward to being able to rest more during the summer months. Archie had completed the schoolhouse and was planning on going out to his farm to till the soil so that he could plant crops in May.

With the money he made constructing the schoolhouse, Archie went to Charleston with Tom and bought a horse. They found a two-year-old that looked to be precisely what Archie needed. On the way back to Clayton, Archie shared with Tom how excited he and Maggie were to move to their place, but sadly, that also meant leaving Clayton. He also mentioned to Tom his concern that no doctors were in the area if something went wrong with Maggie's delivery.

Tom told Archie that he had a friend looking for a doctor who might want to move to Clayton but that, in the meantime, Nancy had helped deliver many babies over the last few years. He suggested that Archie might want to buy a wagon to use on his farm and make the trip to town more comfortable for his new family.

"Archie, if you have a wagon, you can bring your family into town much more easily and often."

"Where can I get a wagon that I can afford, Tom? I don't have that much money left over from what I made building the schoolhouse," asked Archie.

Tom thought for a while as they rode back to Clayton. As they continued along River Road, Tom asked what names he and Maggie had picked out and if Archie had been able to get his cabin ready for their move. Archie replied that he was planning on building a crib the next time he went to their place, and he knew Maggie was planning on shopping at the general store for some things they would need for the baby. He also told Tom they had not decided on a name but had been talking about it the last few evenings.

Suddenly, Tom stopped the wagon, looked at Archie, and said, "Archie, I will sell you this wagon; I've been thinking of getting one of the new ones I saw in Charleston the other day."

"How much do you want for it, Tom?" asked Archie.

"I'll take sixty dollars for it, thirty now and the remainder when you can afford it. You could bring any extra vegetables you grow this summer to the store for me to sell, and I'll buy them from you."

Archie understood the importance of having a wagon but knew he only had ninety dollars left after buying the horse. A few minutes later, he thanked Tom for the offer and gave him the thirty dollars he had in his pocket. "It will make things a little tight, but I need a wagon. Thanks, Tom."

Archie would keep his new horse with Tom's behind the general store in his stable for now. Widow Henry's old barn needed a few repairs before he could use it. If he had time after planting his crops, he would see what could be done to repair it.

CHAPTER 11

SHERIFF GRIFFITH WAS planning on going to Elkview to ensure the Harless brothers did not intend to return to his county when he ran into Tom coming home from church.

"Tom, I am going to go to Elkview next week; if you plan on going to Charleston, I could join you part of the way."

Tom wanted to go to Charleston to pick up his new wagon and meet with his attorney about land opportunities. "Sure, Fred, I'm going Monday morning at sunrise."

"I'll see you then, Tom," said Sheriff Griffith.

The following day, the two friends headed down River Road together. "I've got some business to investigate in Elkview. I will stay in town until around three o'clock before I head back to Clayton in case you finish your business early. I want to ensure the Harless boys never return to our county again. They're trouble, and they are not welcome around Clayton. I'm sure they are making moonshine again somewhere. I knew their father, and he was always in trouble. Guess folks don't change much."

Tom was surprised the sheriff would go so far out of his way to protect Clayton and was comforted to see how seriously he took his position.

"I'll probably be late, Fred; I have to meet with some people about a project I am considering doing. I hope you're wrong about the Harless brothers. It's such a waste to live life like that."

When they got to Elkview, Tom said goodbye to Sheriff Griffith and kept going down River Road toward Charleston. Sheriff Griffith went to the local sheriff's office to ask him questions and warn him about the Harless.'

"Hello Matt, how are you doing? "asked Sheriff Griffith, entering the office.

"Been fine, Fred, how about you?" responded Sheriff Lincoln. "What brings you to Elkview Fred? It's been a long time since I've seen you."

"Well, Matt, I wanted to check around for a couple of moonshiners that I think have settled in this area. They were a big problem in Clayton before I chased them out of town last fall, and I am fairly sure they are around here. I know about the raids you and the Federal Marshal had last year, so it makes sense that these brothers would have figured out that they could do well here with their competition in jail."

"What's their names? I may have heard about them recently?"

"Jim and Paul Harless," responded Sheriff Griffith.

"That's what I thought. I was talking to the County Real Estate Commissioner the other day, and he mentioned that a couple of strangers had bought some land last month. Let's go to the County Courthouse and see what we can find out."

As the two of them walked to the courthouse, Sheriff Griffith told Matt what he had found about the wagon with its false bottom and hidden drawer in case he ever ran into them. When they reached the courthouse, Sheriff Lincoln introduced Fred to the County Real Estate Commissioner and told him what information they needed.

Sure enough, the brothers had purchased some farmland along the Elk River, and then just downstream, they also bought an island in the middle of the river.

Sheriff Lincoln rubbed his beard as he thought about the purchases and then figured out what they were doing.

"The farm is to grow their corn, but the island, now that's smart. They can see any trouble before it gets to them, so they can quickly escape downstream on the other side of the island. Let's pay them a visit, Fred; I think I know a way to the farm that they will never see us coming."

Paul was tiling the field when his brother came running, shouting, "Sheriff Griffith's coming! I saw him at the river getting water for the horses."

Jim was scared and didn't know what to do, so Paul calmly said, "There is nothing to worry about. All we are doing is planting corn; we haven't broken any laws. Why don't you circle around and keep out of sight, and I'll take care of this?"

"Since when did you become a farmer, Paul? The last time I saw you, you were running from my dogs down a hill to get away from me."

Paul looked up at Sheriff Griffith as he kept working and said, "You made an honest man out of me, sheriff; I'm a corn farmer now."

Suddenly, Sheriff Lincoln came up from the river with Jim. "Is this one of the brothers you told me about, sheriff? I found him hiding by the river near a little cave."

"Paul and Jim, meet Sheriff Lincoln from Elkview. I've told him all about you boys and the trouble you have been in Clayton.

"We're just farmers now, sheriff, honest," said Paul. "We don't want any trouble."

Both knew Paul and his brother were lying, but at this point, they hadn't done anything against the law in Elk County. As they turned to leave, Sheriff Lincoln said to Paul, "I'm glad to know you aren't going to be any trouble, but just in case, I will be keeping an eye on you two."

As they continued to walk away, Matt turned to Paul and asked, "Why would a farmer need a false bottom in his wagon, Paul?"

After the two sheriffs walked away, the boys were rattled. "How'd he know about the wagon, Jim?" asked Paul angrily.

"Only person that knew about it was that stupid old slave that made it for me," replied Jim. "I'll get that darky; he's ruined everything!"

When Sheriff Griffith returned to town, he said goodbye to his friend, looked at his watch, and noticed it was almost three o'clock, so he headed for River Road to see if Tom was coming.

The day had been a busy one for Tom. He had stopped by Jim Hoffman's to pick up his new wagon and store supplies. This time of year, he usually purchased seed for the farmers to buy, plow parts, nails, small tools, and the usual foods, but today, he had something else he needed. Nancy wanted Tom to look for things to help make Maggie feel more at home than living in a small shack would offer. Jim had some fabric that could be made into curtains for the one window and a mattress to replace the old, worn-out one Archie had made many years ago from corn husks. Tom also found a set of dishes and utensils. When he had finished buying the things he needed, he went downtown, leaving the wagon in Jim's safekeeping, to meet his attorney, Thomas Franklin, to review some property he had found for sale in the Clayton area.

When Tom arrived, he found Thomas waiting for him along with his assistant, Elizabeth Coffee. Liz had worked with Thomas her entire career and was highly efficient in handling the detailed paperwork needed to complete real estate transactions in Kanawha County. With Charleston growing as quickly as it was, many real estate transactions took place, so it was essential to have a professional reputation for doing everything correctly and promptly.

As they sat down to look at some of the properties Thomas had discovered, Tom noticed a plot of land on the east side of Clayton for sale not far from the schoolhouse. He recognized that it was the little house where Doc lived. In the back of the property were three acres of land that Doc had never done anything with the entire time he had been in Clayton.

Tom wondered why Doc was selling his house but told Thomas to purchase it for the asking price, even though it was higher than the property was worth. Tom suspected that Doc was considering leaving Clayton and perhaps moving to Ohio to be near his daughter. Maybe Doc felt he could no longer serve the folks in Clay County the way they needed to be taken care of; after all, he was getting on in years. When he completed signing the offer papers, Thomas told Tom of an area beginning to show promise upriver from Charleston called Cabin Creek.

"Tom, an oil company from Columbus, Ohio, has been leasing thousands of acres in the area, and coal mines are beginning to be dug. I was considering buying in the area and wondered if you would like to go in with me to buy a thousand acres."

The two men talked for over an hour about the expanding industrial growth in the area and the overall changes in the economy from agriculture to industrial. Tom knew this was different from the type of venture he was comfortable with, but he also saw more opportunity in the Charleston area than in Clayton.

Eventually, they agreed to buy the acreage together. Thomas would handle the paperwork and any negotiations needed.

Thomas also got more information about the ten acres Tom mentioned during his last visit. It was on the southern side of Clayton, and the asking price was reasonable. The owner had bought it several years ago but never did anything with it, so it was uncleared timber land that could be used for many different purposes.

The trees could be harvested and sold to a lumber yard, and the land developed. Tom gave Thomas directions to purchase the land in his corporation's name. He would sign the papers to close the transaction when he received them in the mail. The seller wasn't in a hurry for the money, so that would work fine. Tom wasn't sure when he would return to Charleston again and wanted to finalize everything quickly. With his business complete, Tom said goodbye to Thomas and returned to Hoffman's.

Returning to Jim's to pick up his wagon, Tom stopped by to see Howard McDougal for a minute. Howard was finishing with a client as Tom walked into his office, and when Howard saw him, he motioned for Tom to please wait a few minutes; he needed to talk with him. After Howard's client left, he motioned for Tom to come into his office.

"Tom, that was David Smith, a recent graduate from the university's medical program. He told me he only has six more weeks left in training at the Charleston hospital until he can begin practicing. He also told me his vision was to help the poor in areas like Clayton. I have been meeting with him for the last two months on some other matters and mentioned Clayton's need. I think he might be interested."

Tom could not believe what he was hearing; he had just heard that Doc was planning on leaving, and two hours later, a doctor was interested in a little town like Clayton.

"I'd like to meet him, Howard; I want to know more about what he wants to do. Why don't you see if he would like to come to town so I could show him around and spend time with him? "

Howard agreed to talk further with David and would let Tom know if it would be possible for him to get away from the hospital long enough for a visit to Clayton.

When Tom left Howard's office, he noticed it was after four o'clock and knew he had missed going back to Clayton with Sheriff Griffith. Tom stopped by Jim's and thanked him for watching after his wagon and supplies. After hitching his horse to the wagon, Tom headed for Clayton; he hadn't noticed a box Jim had put into his wagon.

On the trip back to Clayton, it began to rain, so Tom stopped in Elkview to secure the wagon's covering to protect his supplies and to get a quick cup of coffee to warm himself. Paul Harless saw him on his way out of the restaurant and growled," Tom, tell Hank I know what he said to Sheriff Griffith. He'll pay for his mistake!"

Tom was shaken as he climbed into the wagon. He had never seen Paul that upset, even though he could tell by the smell of his breath that he was drunk. He knew he needed to tell Sheriff Griffith when he got into town. The further he went, the harder it rained, and the river began to rise. Tom knew he needed to take the road up the mountain to avoid problems with high water. The road was narrow and, in a few places, steep, but at least there wasn't high water to worry about. As Tom reached the crest of the last hill before going down to Clayton, he looked down on Clayton and thought to himself, Clayton is also changing.

It was dark and cool when Tom got to town, but he knew he needed to see Sheriff Griffith before unloading his new wagon. When he knocked on the sheriff's door, he saw Doc inside talking with Fred, who motioned for him to enter.

"Hi Doc, I haven't seen you in a while," said Tom.

Doc had a saddened look on his face. "Tom, you might as well know what I just told Fred. I am moving from Clayton. This town needs a real doctor. I think I will go to Ohio and spend time with my daughter and grandchildren." The look on his face did not convince Tom or Sheriff Griffith that spending time with his grandchildren was his real motive.

"Doc, we've known each other for twenty years, and you have always taken care of the folks here in Clayton, so why the sudden change of heart?" asked Tom.

"With more and more people moving to the area, I just can't keep up with their needs, and most of all, they deserve someone better trained than I am. I'm having trouble doing what I used to be able to do, much less more. "

Tom realized he needed to tell them about the possibility of a new doctor moving to Clayton. "Doc, I have arranged for a new doctor to come to Clayton to see if this would be a place for him to practice. I haven't spoken with him directly, but I have been told he is a fine young man. He's finishing his training in Charleston and hopefully will come to Clayton for a visit. Doc, as well-educated as he is, he's new and needs help from someone who has been taking care of all of us for years. Please stay and work with him if he decides to come to Clayton. I would like it if you would help me interview him. You can see what you think; after all, it will be your friends that you have taken care of for all these years that he will be taking care of in the future."

"I'll think about it, Tom. This is a hard decision for me, but working with a new doctor may be useful," said Doc. "I have another problem, though; if I decide to stay for a while, I will need a place to stay because I have put my place up for sale."

"Don't worry about that, Doc; there is always a place for you in Clayton."

Doc left and seemed a little more cheerful than he had appeared earlier. Tom thought about what he said and began to understand that maybe Doc was not only seeing the town needed a better-qualified doctor but also that he no longer felt he had a purpose.

Tom turned and looked at Fred and told him about his run-in with Paul Harless in Elkview. Sheriff Griffith was worried for Hank and told Tom he would go out to his place in the morning.

"Those boys are trouble, Tom; I need to help Hank."

That evening, as Tom unloaded the supplies for the store and the merchandise Nancy had asked him to get, he noticed the box. Nancy was pleased with the fabric and dishes and thought the mattress was a great idea. Tom showed Nancy the box and told her he did not know what was in it. Both of them sat down and carefully opened it, and on the top, they found a note from Jim Hoffman, "My wife and I wanted to give these to Miss McCombs. Enclosed is her complete collection of Louisa May Alcott. These books have inspired her, and she hopes they will be as meaningful to Miss McCombs."

That night, as Tom and Nancy settled into bed, they talked about everything that had happened in Charleston earlier. Nancy was a little uncomfortable with an investment in land that wasn't local but understood Tom's reasoning. Times were changing, and divesting their assets in different areas was important. Tom assured her that Thomas was a good attorney whom he had known for years and that he trusted. Tom also told Nancy that there was a good chance a new doctor would be visiting Clayton to determine if it was where he wanted to practice.

Nancy was relieved to know a trained doctor might move to Clayton; she was always a little frightened at the responsibility she had undertaken in helping with deliveries. The two of them settled in for a night's rest, comforted by the possibility of a new doctor but unsettled by the threatened violence.

The day had been full, reflecting changes coming to Clayton and the entire area. Some were good, but others were concerning.

CHAPTER 12

EARLY IN THE morning, Archie went to the general store to get his horse and wagon to make the journey to his property. He had never been away so long and wasn't sure what to expect after the long winter. The horse ate hay Tom had left that morning, so Archie hitched the wagon while it ate and prepared to leave. Before leaving, Archie thought he should run into the general store to thank Tom for caring for his horse. Tom was stocking the store with the new merchandise he had bought in Charleston.

"Hey Tom, I just wanted to thank you for caring for my horse while it was here. In the future, I will stop by and do whatever is needed until I can get a barn built or repair Widow Henry's."

Tom looked up and saw Archie looking around at the new merchandise with an eye on the household items in particular.

"Let me know if there is anything you want, Archie; I'll put it in the back until you can afford it. How's Maggie feeling?"

Archie looked up and responded," She is a little better but getting uncomfortable. I'm headed out to my property for the day. Is there anything I can do for you?"

Tom looked at Archie and remembered that Sheriff Griffith said he was going to Hank's, so he told Archie in case he wanted company part of the way. Archie rode over to Sheriff Griffith's just as he was about to leave and asked him if he would like for him to ride out with him. As the two of them left town, Archie asked Sheriff Griffith why he needed to see Hank.

"The Harless boys have threatened to hurt him, and I need to tell him to be on the lookout, "said Sheriff Griffith.

"Those brothers have been trouble ever since I can remember," said Archie. "What can I do to help?"

Sheriff Griffith didn't want to get everybody involved but knew it would take many eyes to discover if the Harless were in the area, so he said, "Please let me know if you see them or hear of them being in the area."

When they arrived at Hank's place, Archie said hello to his friend and then headed out to his farm.

Archie arrived at the farm and quickly determined what needed to be done and in what order. First, he would pick up fallen branches and load them into his wagon for later use as firewood. After that, he would tie a rope to a hitch on his horse's collar and remove as many tree stumps as possible. Since the horse had never pulled anything, it took Archie a while to train him. After about an hour, the two of them began working well together; however, Archie decided it would be better to rest his horse while he dug around the stumps to make their removal easier.

After several hours of digging, Archie hitched his horse to the ropes again and removed the stumps. This time, it worked much better, and they were able to drag six stumps to the side of the open field to be burned after they had a chance to dry out. Archie and his horse were very tired by this time, so Archie took the horse to the creek for water and food while he rested. He planned to go back to Clayton to be with Maggie but decided that in the future, he would stay at the cabin for three days at a time to get more work done. Widow Henry would be close if Maggie needed anything.

After resting, Archie climbed on his horse and headed back to Clayton. He had decided to leave the wagon since he was returning the next day, and it would be easier on his horse. Archie gently patted his horse's neck and began talking to him as they rode along.

"You know, boy, you need a name. Buddy or Blue? Oh, I know, Buck. Yea, what about Buck?"

Immediately, Buck whinnied, giving his approval, or at least that's how Archie interpreted it. When Archie and Buck arrived back in Clayton, Archie took him behind the general store, washed him down, and brushed him. After giving him water and hay, he left for Widow Henry's to see his bride. He felt good about what he had gotten done but, perhaps for the first time, understood how much needed to be done to make his shack a home for his new family.

When Archie walked into Widow Henry's, Maggie sat in the parlor with the Widow. The two of them had been discussing a letter she had received that day.

"Archie, we got a letter from my father today. He and Mama are coming to see us in early June!" Maggie was excited to see her parents for the first time in over a year. Archie didn't have the heart to share with her how he felt. This only gave him a few weeks to get the farm looking like a home they would be glad to know their daughter was living in. Widow Henry, however, noticed the hesitation in his voice.

After a late dinner, Archie explained his plan to prepare the farm for the growing season. Widow Henry agreed to be there for Maggie. Neither Archie nor Maggie wanted to be apart, but it would be too risky for Maggie to travel out to the farm.

That night, as they lay in bed, each had different thoughts going through their minds. Maggie was looking forward to seeing her parents. She knew they would love Archie and be excited for them becoming new parents. However, Archie was afraid that Maggie's parents would be disappointed in the remote, rustic little place they would live in. Both prayed before going to sleep, but their silent prayers were quite different.

Archie climbed on Buck the following day and headed out to the farm. Widow Henry had prepared food for him that Archie put into a large bag and laid over Buck's neck.

When Archie approached Hank's place, he saw Hank working in his sawmill cutting boards and rode over to say hello. As Archie got closer, he could tell Hank was upset.

"What's wrong, Hank? You look upset," asked Archie.

"Sheriff told me the Harless brothers are furious with me. They told Tom Campbell they would be after me."

Archie had never seen Hank act this way, so instead of rushing to work on his farm, he got off Buck, tied him up, and walked over to Hank. "I'll be here for you, Hank, and I know Sheriff Griffith will be looking for them, so I'm sure everything will be all right."

Hank looked at Archie and stopped cutting lumber. "Archie, I know you believe what you said, but you have never been a black man in this country. It's not the same," as his voice quivered. "Archie, you've never had to live as a slave. You've never seen your daddy whipped and your brother sold. When I was a little boy, I learned to be quiet, keep my head down, and work as hard as I could, and maybe I wouldn't be beaten. My daddy lost his temper with the foreman on the plantation we worked for when he started hitting my mama. He was beaten and then whipped until I thought he would die. So, when I heard that the Harless brothers were coming to get me, all I could think about was how it was before the war. You and Sheriff Griffith are the only white folks I've ever told about this, but I thought you should know." With that, the big, strong sawmill operator broke down. He was scared!

Archie was shaken by what Hank had said. He couldn't imagine living that way: always afraid, not trusting others around him, never knowing how people felt about him. Archie put his hand on Hank's shoulder and quietly said," I will be here for you, my friend. You can trust me."

For the next hour or so, Archie listened as Hank told him stories about his past. After Hank had sat quietly for a little while, Archie looked him in the eye and said, "I'm sorry you have had to endure this on your own. I'm here for you. You don't have to ever feel alone again."

Hank was thankful for Archie's sentiment, but he knew deep down that some things would never change. There would always be people who would treat him differently. Archie made his way over to Buck, and as he was about to leave, Hank said he would be out later that day with a load of lumber.

The ride to his farm was much different than it ever had been. Archie couldn't stop thinking about what Hank had told him. How terrible it must have been for him all these years. With a saddened heart, Archie arrived at his farm with a resolve to make a difference in Hank's life somehow. Archie hitched Buck to the plow and began trying to get the field ready for planting; unfortunately, Buck had never plowed either. Once again, Archie patiently worked with his horse until he understood what to do. Plowing took several hours, but when he was done, the field was ready for planting. Archie took Buck down to the creek for water and rest while he walked up to his shack to get the seed he had purchased from the general store. He planted corn, tomatoes, squash, melons, potatoes, and green beans for the rest of the afternoon. When Archie was about to put stakes in the ground for the beans, Hank rode up with the lumber. Archie showed Hank where to store the wood, and the two began unloading the boards.

When they were finished, Hank asked Archie what he planned to do with his little cabin. Archie pointed out how he wanted to expand it to make it a home for his new family.

Hank walked around the cabin, looked closely at the property, and asked Archie if he could have permission to make a suggestion.

"Of course, Hank. You don't need permission. What are you thinking?"

"The ground up the hill is much flatter than around your shack and would be easier to build on; plus, it would be drier during storms," said Hank." You could build a nice place up there and use your shack to store your farm equipment and tools."

"I agree, but I can't afford to build a new house."

"I'll tell you what, Archie, I'll sell you the lumber you need at my cost and help you build it when I have time."

"Wow, Hank, that's nice of you. Thanks, my friend, thank you!"

"You have a pencil? Grab a piece of wood and draw what you want your house to look like."

As Archie began to draw, Hank said he would return with the rest of the lumber in the morning and rode off.

That night, as Archie finished the dinner Widow Henry had made for him, he began thinking about the house and what they needed. Suddenly, a thought struck him; there he was, thinking about a new home, and just down the road, his friend was probably having a hard time even considering going to sleep, afraid he might be attached.

The following day, Archie made coffee and began drawing the basic dimensions of his house. When he finished roughing out his home, he hitched Buck up to the wagon and went down to the creek to see how many large rocks he could find for a foundation. He heard a noise behind him as he struggled to pull a stone from the bottom of the stream. It was Hank with the lumber he had promised.

"Let me help you with that, Archie; it's almost as big as you are," laughed Hank.

The two of them struggled to get the rock into the wagon, getting wet and muddy but eventually succeeding. Buck jumped a little at the weight of the new stone but settled down after Archie ran up and began rubbing his neck.

Archie and Hank rode up the hill to the farm, each with their respective cargo. After they unloaded the lumber, Archie took his wagon further up the hill to the location Hank had pointed out the day before to begin unloading the rocks. It took both of them longer than they thought, but eventually, the stones were placed close to where they could be used.

Archie asked Hank if he wanted to rest awhile as he walked Buck down the hill to unhitch the wagon.

"Sure do; that was a lot of work," said Hank.

The two sat on a log Archie had placed around his fire pit and shared the lunch Widow Henry had prepared for Archie. "Hank, why don't you stay with me tonight? You'll rest better knowing there's someone with you to help protect you if the Harless boys show up."

Hank looked at Archie and realized that, for the first time in his life, he had a real friend.

"Thanks, Archie, but if we both drove our wagons to my place, we could fill them with the rest of the lumber I have ready and bring it up first thing in the morning," said Hank.

"Good idea," said Archie, "I'll meet you after I finish working this afternoon."

With the seed planted, rocks moved, tree stumps out of the way, and lumber ready, Archie sat down to make a cradle. He took boards and cut them but only put them together once he had sanded them to make them as smooth as possible. He wanted it to be perfect for his little baby. When the wood was ready, he assembled a rectangle and then added rounded boards to either end so it would rock. He had needed to plane the bottom rockers and sand them, so they rocked quietly. When it was finished, Archie went down to the creek to get Buck, hitched him up to the wagon, and headed down to Hank's.

When Archie arrived at Hank's place, he noticed Hank had already loaded his wagon and cut enough lumber to fill Archie's.

"You've been busy," said Archie.

The two of them enjoyed the rest of the evening, telling stories and trying to relax.

Around four in the morning, Archie awoke to the sound of both horses stirring. Quickly, Archie woke Hank to tell him something was bothering the horses as he ran out of the door to check on them. Hank jumped up to go to the sawmill to check it out, but just as Hank was leaving his cabin, he was jumped by Paul Harless and hit on the head with the butt of his gun.

"I'm going to kill you!" slurred Paul. Hank could smell moonshine on Paul's breath and knew he was in serious trouble. Paul staggered as he raised his gun, and just as he put his finger on the trigger, Archie came running into the cabin and tackled him, knocking the weapon to the ground. The gun discharged, hitting Hank in the leg.

The shot had gone into his right calf, ripping flesh as it exited the other side. Paul was startled, not expecting anyone to be there except Hank. As Paul reached for his gun, Archie dove ahead and grabbed it. Paul tried to wrestle it away from Archie but was not able to. Seeing Hank crawling over to his gun, Paul let go and stumbled out the door, slamming Archie against the wall.

Jim Harless had set fire to the sawmill and was coming to do the same to Hank's cabin when he heard Paul yelling, "Run, Jim, Archie's got my gun." Both men ran down to where their horses were hidden and rode off into the night.

Archie fired the gun in the air to scare them off and ran back into the cabin to see about Hank. Archie saw Hank looking at his leg when he entered the cabin door. "It's not too bad. It looks like it only got my muscle and didn't hit the bone," said Hank as blood poured from the wound.

Archie found a rag and soaked it in water Hank had beside the fireplace. "Here, see if you can get it to stop bleeding while I see if I can get the fire out."

Archie ran out to see if the sawmill could be saved. Rushing down to the creek, he gathered buckets of water and poured water on the fire until sunrise. Hank limped out as Archie poured water on the burning mill to see the damage. The little mill was destroyed, along with all of his equipment. The only thing left was the wagon and his horse. Dejected, Hank rested beside an old oak tree while Archie continued pouring water on the smoldering embers.

With the fire out, Archie helped Hank get in the back of his wagon. After tying Hank's horse to the wagon, they headed to Clayton to see Doc. Nothing much was said on their way into town. Archie couldn't imagine how Hank must feel. He could see the dejection and sadness in his friend's face but felt helpless to do anything about it.

When they arrived in Clayton, they went directly to Doc's.

Noticing the wagon headed down the street with Hank in the back, Sheriff Griffith ran over to help Archie get Hank out of the wagon. "What happened, Archie," asked Sheriff Griffith.

"Harless brothers tried to kill him and burned down his sawmill. Paul's gun went off as I was wrestling it away from him. Jim burned the mill and was headed to the house to set it on fire when Paul ran out, yelling for his brother to run. The two of them got away. It was horrible, Sheriff! Horrible!"

Doc looked at Hank's leg and saw that the bullet had left a hole in the front and back of his calf. "You'll be all right, Hank; I've taken care of worse in my day. I am sorry this happened to you, Hank," said Doc solemnly." We'll get those hoodlums!"

Sitting on the examination table in one of Doc's patient rooms, Hank could tell that Doc was upset. "You all right, Doc?" asked Hank.

Doc looked at Hank, clearly bothered, and responded, "Oh, I'll be okay; I have never understood why people do such terrible things to one another. I spent four years in the U.S. Army treating the wounded and saw things I wish I had never seen. Anytime I see someone shot, it brings back those memories. I'm glad you are all right, Hank, I really am. "

CHAPTER 13

ARCHIE STAYED IN town the next day to be with Maggie and to do some repairs around Widow Henry's house. He repaired the stairs going out of the back door and painted them to match the front of the house. After finishing his work, Archie went to the general store to speak with Tom. While he was looking around the store, Carol came in to purchase some things and, seeing Archie, asked how Maggie was doing and if he thought she would mind if she stopped by to visit later that day. Archie assured her that she would enjoy the company, "You don't ever have to ask to see her; she loves you." Getting out was becoming more complex as time passed due to the heat and Maggie's discomfort, so a visit from Aunt Carol would be just what she needed.

Tom could tell Archie was waiting to ask him something, but he seemed anxious.

"Archie, how did your place look the other day? It's the first time you haven't been there through the winter. Was there much damage from the wind and snow?" asked Tom, trying to help Archie to open up.

"It wasn't too bad, Tom; it took me a few hours to straighten things up before I could clear the tree stumps from the field to prepare it for planting."

Then Archie looked at Tom and asked, "Can I be honest? Yesterday was the first time I realized how much needs to be done for my shack to become a home for my family. I can do everything that needs to be done, but the lumber I need is only part of the problem. To make it a home for Maggie, I have decided to build a new house up the hill from my shack with more room. Hank has agreed to help me when he can, but now, with his leg healing, I doubt he will be able to do that much for a while."

Archie was no different from any other man. He wanted to be able to take care of his family, but farming wasn't going to provide enough money to buy the things he needed for the new house. The transition from single farmer to husband and father would change how Archie lived and worked.

As Archie left the store, Tom remembered how others in the community had struggled when they first started a family. He and Nancy had always had enough money from their inheritance, but most people had to start from nothing. Suddenly, Tom had an idea and rushed out the door to catch Archie before he had gone too far.

"Hey Archie, I have an idea," said Tom." Come back to the store, and we'll talk about it."

When Archie entered the store, Tom asked him to come around to the back where they could speak privately.

"Archie, I think I can help you. You own your farm outright, correct? Almost everybody who has property has a mortgage on it. I could loan you money based on the property's value and take back a mortgage. You could make payments from the money you make working around Clayton or whatever work you can find in Charleston."

Tom knew that, like most men, Archie didn't want debt, but what Archie didn't understand was that most men didn't own property that they could leverage to improve it.

"You know, Archie, building a house on the property and doing the work yourself will increase the property's value, so if you decide to sell it someday, you can pay off the mortgage and have money to put in your bank account."

Archie was taken aback. Why would Tom do this for him? He did not want a mortgage, but he understood how it could be helpful. He told Tom he would think about it and left the store. "See you in the morning, Tom, and thanks for the offer. I will talk about it with Maggie."

The following day, as Archie loaded his wagon, Tom came to help him.

"Well, what did you decide, Archie?"

Archie thought for a minute about how he would answer and then said, "I will do it, Tom, but after I am finished building the house, I will find work so that I can make regular payments. But Tom, I have to ask you, why are you doing this for us?"

Tom stopped loading the wagon and, looking directly at Archie, said, "Archie, Nancy, and I have never had children, and as we have watched you and Maggie this last year, we have grown in our admiration for both of you. You are a humble man who works hard at everything you do, and Maggie has become the daughter Nancy never had. We have noticed how you have changed from a shy, tough farm boy to a caring, giving man of faith. Your time at Widow Henry's has affected both of you; everyone can see it. Your faith shows clearly, and your character has become more Christ-like. I'm sorry, I didn't mean to go on, but I guess what I am trying to say is, if Nancy and I had been given children to raise, we would be happy if they turned out to be like you and Maggie."

Archie was moved, as was Tom. Both men fought back the urge to tear up and hugged.

Archie climbed in his wagon and headed out for a long day's work. Along the way, he again thought about how his life had changed entirely in less than a year and began weeping, thanking God for the many blessings he had been given.

Archie worked all day, putting in the poles he had started earlier and adding string between them for the beans to climb. He moved most of the rocks for the house's foundation and placed the split logs to form the house's base. He wasn't as skilled as Hank in cutting the joints on the logs but finally got them to fit the way Hank had shown him when they worked on the schoolhouse. As the evening was approaching, Archie gathered his tools and headed back to town. On his way, he stopped by to see how Hank was doing. Doc had told him to keep his leg above his head and stay in bed for the first week. He was supposed to see Doc the next day to see how it was healing.

"I'll take you into town, Hank; I'm headed that way. You can stay with us. I'm sure Widow Henry will love your company. I'll bring you back after you visit with Doc. I'm starting to set the house's base and have lots to do."

"That would be great, Archie. I sure could use a ride. Coming out here on my horse was more painful than I had expected. Are you sure Widow Henry won't mind me staying there?" asked Hank.

Archie took his wagon straight to Widow Henry's house before going to the general store. Widow Henry was sitting on her front porch and saw Archie coming with Hank in the back. As they approached, Widow Henry walked down the front steps to great Hank and Archie.

"How are you doing, Hank?" asked Widow Henry. "I heard what happened to you. I am sorry, Hank, that people like those Harless brothers are around. I don't understand what causes people to be that way."

Looking into Hank's eyes, she saw pain she had never noticed." Will you stay with us tonight? I don't have another bedroom, but you can sleep in the parlor."

"That's nice of you, Widow Henry, but are you sure? People might talk, me being a black man and all," said Hank humbly.

"Of course, I am sure Hank! You are my neighbor, and need a place to stay for the night. You lost everything you own in the fire and are injured; of course, I want to help you. People in Clayton would all do the same if they had the opportunity.

"Archie, help him get down out of the wagon. I'm going in to put another plate on the table." With that, Widow Henry turned and quickly walked back into her house, glad she had the opportunity to help her friend.

During dinner, there was talk about the pregnancy and a little prying into what names had been chosen. Maggie said she didn't want to tell anyone until after the child's birth. Maggie discussed her excitement about her parents' upcoming visit, but what consumed most of the talk was what Hank would do to replace the sawmill.

While all of this was happening, Widow Henry was putting together an idea that would benefit the entire area.

After dinner, Archie invited Hank to join them in the parlor. "Every evening after dinner, Hank, we sit in the parlor and discuss what we read earlier that day in the Bible. Would you please join us?"

Hank had started attending church occasionally but wasn't sure about "studying" the Bible.

Archie could see the hesitancy in Hank's face and said, "Come on, we promise not to bite."

The three had been reading Paul's letter to the believers in Ephesus. Archie said that he never knew that Paul had been in prison when he wrote this letter but that despite that, he was still encouraging fellow believers.

"In chapter two, Paul explains how being saved is a gift from God, not something we have done to earn it. So, am I right, Widow Henry? Are we supposed to do good to others because God loved us first, even though we were sinful and deserved to be condemned? It's not to gain anything but to love others like He loved us."

"That is right, Archie, we care for others out of love for God. It is an act of worship to our Heavenly Father. I get tremendous joy in doing what little I can to help folks. I don't need anyone to thank me or any recognition; my happiness comes from Jesus. It's essential, Archie, to understand that whatever you do for someone, the ultimate purpose is to glorify the Lord. It's our responsibility to help lead them to faith in Christ.

"Here's my Bible, Hank. Why don't you read the next chapter, and we can talk about it?" asked Archie.

Hank looked embarrassed as he was handed the Bible. Widow Henry saw the look on his face and gently said, "Hank, if you're not comfortable reading, you can give it to Maggie; it's fine."

As the evening wore on, Hank began relaxing, and as he later would tell Widow Henry, he learned a lot. He saw how all believers, regardless of race, wealth, or nationality, were one in Christ.

The following day, Widow Henry had a big breakfast prepared for everyone. Hank couldn't remember ever having such a delicious breakfast. Archie helped Widow Henry take the dishes back to the kitchen when the meal was finished before taking Hank to Doc's.

"Archie, when you're finished with Doc, stop by on your way out of town today, and I'll have lunch for you two," said Widow Henry.

"Oh, thank you, but you don't have to do that; you've already done so much," answered Archie.

Widow Henry looked at Archie and said, "Weren't you paying attention last night, young man? This is my joy. Now get on down to Doc's," said the smiling hostess.

Archie helped Hank to one of the examination rooms, and after Doc finished talking with his patient, he came into the room to look at the wound. Doc removed the bandages, examined the injury, and was pleased to see it healing well.

"Just take it easy for another week, Hank and you should be fine," assured Doc as he wrapped Hank's leg in fresh gauze and bandages.

"How much do I owe you, Doc?" asked Hank.

"Don't worry about it, Hank; I hardly did anything. Just take care of your leg."

"You sure?" Hank couldn't believe the way the folks in Clayton were treating him.

Archie helped Hank back into the wagon and rode down the street to Widow Henry's house. When Archie jumped down from the wagon, Widow Henry told him to see Maggie before he left; she wanted to talk with Hank. Coming to the back of the wagon, Widow Henry asked Hank how everything had gone at Doc's and if his leg was healing. After answering, Widow Henry softly asked Hank a question.

"Hank, can you read? I don't mean to embarrass you, but was that why you didn't want to read last night?"

Hank looked down and answered, "No, ma'am, I never had anyone teach me. It was against the law when I was a little boy, and after the war, I just did what I had to do to get by."

"I'll tell you what, Hank, I will teach you. Stop by my place whenever you are in town, and we will work on it. You'll get it in no time!"

When Archie returned from seeing Maggie, they headed for his place. Hank had asked Archie if he minded if he looked at what he had done with the foundation before he did much more to his house.

During the ride, Hank asked Archie, "Why does the Widow Henry do everything she does for people? Is it her religion? Sure, seems like it to me. She is the nicest person I've ever met, next to you."

Both laughed before Archie answered. "Hank, it's not her religion that makes her the way she is; it's her relationship with Jesus."

Hank allowed what Archie said to sink in before saying anything. "I've never heard of anything like that before. Is that why she is so peaceful and happy?"

Archie thought about how he wanted to answer Hank's question before saying, "Widow Henry is full of energy and does more than most people know around these parts, but the difference is she doesn't do anything until she has prayed about it for many days so that she is confident that what she is doing is what God wants her to do, not what she has decided to do on her own. She is different; I only wish I could be more like her. Knowing that what she does is from God's direction gives her that happiness you see, and when tough times come, she's calm knowing that God will always be there for her."

The ride to Archie's place took about an hour. Archie didn't want to do anything that would cause Hank's wound to hurt or possibly open up. Archie helped Hank down from the wagon when they arrived at the shack and handed him the crutches Doc had given him until his leg was completely healed. Walking slowly over to where Archie had started laying the rocks, Hank looked at the foundation and showed Archie two stones that should be adjusted so the house would be on level, solid ground.

"You have gotten a lot done, Archie. I'm impressed, but I don't know where you will get the lumber you need to finish the job. Even if I had the money, it would take weeks for me to rebuild my sawmill; maybe you can go into Charleston and get more."

Archie took Hank back to his cabin and gave him his lunch from Widow Henry." I was too busy to eat; Hank here, take mine."

CHAPTER 14

WIDOW HENRY WENT to the general store to meet Tom, Nancy, and Revered McConnell for a school committee meeting. As the four of them began their discussions, Nancy brought out a pitcher of water and glasses. When the drinks were poured, Tom asked if anyone had heard anything regarding a replacement for Maggie. Tom understood Archie's new family's financial issues, but he also understood the local tradition. It seemed in everyone's best interest that they ask Maggie if she could teach for as long as she was physically able, allowing her to make some money while giving them more time to find another teacher. They all agreed that it would be better for the children to be separated to facilitate the older children's learning. Tom said he would continue asking around every time he visited Charleston.

After their short meeting, Widow Henry brought up some community concerns she had been praying about.

"I feel badly for Hank. I thought about offering him a job at my lumber company, but the more I prayed about it, the more the Lord made it very clear to me what I should do. Doc told me that the Harless boys yelled hurtful racial slurs and called him terrible names when they attacked him. He is a good man and as much a part of our community as any one of us, so I thought we might be able to do something special for him to show him how much he means to all of us.

"I understand that the ten acres just south of town were sold recently. I am wondering if the new owner would be willing to sell three of the acres to my company. I have been thinking about building another sawmill in this area to serve the needs of the people moving to Clay County.

I didn't want to consider such a move while Hank was operating his mill, but now the need has never been greater. If I can purchase the land and have a new mill built, I would ask Hank if he would run the operation for me, and of course, if he were working here in town, he should also live here. Reverend, do you think the congregation would help build Hank a house here in town next to the mill? I know I am getting ahead of myself, but I think this is an opportunity for all of us to help a neighbor in need."

"Widow Henry, you always amaze me with your heart for others. I am positive the men will help. Maybe he can make the lumber Archie needs for his cabin."

"I'll check next week when I'm in Charleston and see if the owner is willing to sell part of the land," said Tom.

After their meeting, Widow Henry purchased extra supplies for Maggie's parents' visit. Maggie's parents would be in town on Monday, and she wanted plenty of flour, coffee, and groceries for dinner.

Archie used the remainder of the lumber Hank had delivered to his farm along with the wagon load that was supposed to have been delivered the day of the fire. Three feet of the exterior logs had been placed on the stones laid earlier, and flooring boards were laid on top of the base supports Archie had applied with Hank's instruction. However, the project was stopped until additional lumber could be brought in from Charleston.

Archie took Hank back to his place and headed to town to prepare for his in-law's visit. He was still extremely nervous about how his in-laws would feel about him. He had told Maggie's father in his letter that he didn't have much, but he doubted her father could have imagined how little he did have. When Archie returned to town, he stopped by the general store as usual to wash down Buck and store his wagon. Reverend McConnell was leaving the store and saw Archie taking care of his horse in the back.

"Long day, Archie?" asked Seamus McConnell. "You look tired."

"Yes, it has been a long day, Seamus, and now I've got to get ready for Maggie's parents to visit," said Archie with a voice of concern.

"Archie, I sense you are a little worried about their visit. When you and I used to talk during your stay at the church, we talked about how the Lord had always been there for you, so why do you think he won't be this time? Relax, my friend; you will be exactly the son-in-law they have always wanted."

Monday arrived, and Maggie nervously walked back and forth in the parlor while Widow Henry made apple pie. The trip from Canton brought the Garretts to Charleston by train, and then they would meet Archie at the train station for the long ride to Clayton.

When Archie went to the general store to hitch Buck up to his wagon, Tom came out and said, "Archie, why don't you take my wagon? It's larger and more comfortable. Maggie's parents will be tired from the long day on the train and want as much comfort as possible; besides, you'll have more room for their baggage."

"Are you sure, Tom?" responded Archie. It sure is nicer than my old wagon, which I've been hauling lumber and rocks in the last few weeks."

"Take it, Archie, it's my pleasure."

The trip to Charleston was uneventful, which was a blessing because Archie kept thinking about Maggie's parents and what they would think about him. Archie arrived at the train station half an hour early. After tying Buck up, he entered the station to wait for his guests. Out of the corner of his eye, he saw Paul Harless. He and his brother sheepishly took tickets they had just bought and walked to the side of the station to avoid being seen. When they were out of sight, Archie went to the ticket window and asked where the tickets he had just sold to the two men were going.

"Those two wanted tickets to Cincinnati, but all I could sell them were tickets for Huntington. Once they get there, they'll need to buy a connecting ticket to Cincinnati," said the ticket salesman.

"Is there a sheriff around here?" asked Archie.

"No, but he usually stops by here around one o'clock."

"When he does, please tell him the law wants those two in Clayton for attempted murder. I've got to pick up my guests in a few minutes, so I can't stay much longer, but if he misses them, he could telegraph the Huntington sheriff. Their names are Paul and Jim Harless," said Archie.

"Thanks for your help. In case the sheriff needs to know, Sheriff Griffith in Clayton knows everything. Thanks!"

As the train pulled into the station, one going the opposite direction was pulling out with the Harless brothers on it.

The excitement had distracted Archie from his anxiety about Maggie's parents. Just then, James and his wife, Phoebe Garrett, stepped down from the train and looked around for their new son-in-law. Noticing a couple searching the crowd, Archie approached them and asked if they were the Garretts. After introducing themselves, Archie grabbed Mrs. Garrett's bags and directed them to the wagon.

Archie drove the wagon to a restaurant nearby to freshen up and get something to eat before heading to Clayton. After helping Phoebe into the back seat, James jumped to the front seat next to Archie.

"Nice looking horse, Archie," said Mr. Garrett, "what's his name?"

"His name is Buck, sir; he's a perfect horse," bragged Archie.

"I can see that, son; you did a fine job picking him," replied James.

With that exchange, Archie began to relax. During the trip to Clayton, Archie told the Garretts about the area and the fine people who lived in Clayton.

Early that evening, the wagon pulled up to the boardinghouse where Sarah Adkins was serving dinner to one of her guests.

"Welcome. You must be Maggie's parents," said Sarah. I'll be with you in just a minute."

Archie unloaded the bags from Tom's wagon and brought them into the boardinghouse.

"Archie, please take them to room number three if you don't mind," said Sarah.

After finishing with her guests, Sarah looked at the Garrett's and said, "Your daughter is such a wonderful young lady. You must be very proud of her. Let me take you to your room; I'm sure you will want to freshen up before you go to Widow Henry's to see her."

When James and Phoebe entered their room, they were pleased to see fresh flowers next to an open window. The early evening breeze had begun cooling the room. A full jar of water was next to the basin for them to clean up, and a pitcher of water with two glasses was on the chest of drawers for their refreshment. When they came downstairs, Sarah asked them if everything was all right.

"You have a lovely place, Mrs. Adkins, thank you," said Mrs. Garrett.

James asked Archie how far it was to Widow Henry's, and when Archie pointed it out just down the street, he suggested they would prefer to walk.

"We could use the exercise and some fresh air."

Archie left the horse and wagon at the boardinghouse and walked with them, showing them all the buildings that comprised Clayton. Tom and Nancy were leaving the general store, and when they saw the three of them walking, they yelled, "Welcome to Clayton. We're glad you're here."

Seeing her parents walking toward Widow Henry's, Maggie could hardly contain her excitement. She loved her parents so much and had missed them greatly. When they opened the front gate to the yard, Maggie ran out to meet them. Maggie and her mother hugged and kissed, openly sharing how much they had missed each other. Mr. Garrett was less comfortable embracing, but when Maggie reached out to him, he held her warmly and kissed her on the cheek.

"Let me look at my little girl," said Mr. Garrett.

"You look glowing," said Mrs. Garrett. "It's so great to be with you!"

Maggie and Archie escorted their guests into Widow Henry's house, where Widow Henry met them with a hearty welcome.

"Please, please come into the parlor; let's hear about your trip," said Widow Henry.

Maggie and Archie shared stories about the wedding and how everyone came to celebrate. Maggie told them how much she enjoyed teaching the children with Aunt Carol, and Archie told them about his work rebuilding the school. As Maggie and Archie went on and on, both of Maggie's parents could see how much they loved each other and the people of Clayton.

"We've enjoyed our evening, but it has been a long day. I think we need to retire for the evening," said Mr. Garrett.

"Oh, I understand. Please come back in the morning for breakfast. We enjoy starting the day off with a good meal," said Widow Henry.

"I promise you; it will be the best breakfast you have ever had," said Archie.

With that, everyone said good night. The Garretts, with Archie escorting them, returned to the boardinghouse.

"Good night, Mr. and Mrs. Garrett; I'll see you in the morning," said Archie.

Archie headed to the general store to return Tom's wagon and care for Buck. When he was finished, he ran down the street to Widow Henry's house but noticed a light on in Sheriff Griffith's office. Archie knocked on the door, and Sheriff Griffith came to let him in.

"Just the person I hoped to see," said the sheriff. "I got a telegram this afternoon that the sheriff in Huntington had captured the Harless brothers as they got off the train from Charleston. He said that the ticket salesman in Charleston said a young man from Clayton told him about the brothers. I bet that young man was you, wasn't it, Archie?" said Sheriff Griffith.

"Thank you for all your help, Archie. Who knows if they would ever have been caught if they had gotten away? Thank you."

Archie explained what had happened and how glad he was to know they were behind bars." I need to let Hank know; I don't think he has slept very well in a long time," said Archie.

The following day, the Garretts walked down to Widow Henry's house. The aroma of bacon and coffee filled the air with the promise of the wonderful breakfast Archie had told them about the night before.

"Good morning," said Widow Henry, "I hope you rested well."

"We did, we were both tired," said Mrs. Garrett.

When breakfast was ready to serve, everyone went to the dining room table when James exclaimed," This is quite the feast. Everything looks terrific!"

Widow Henry asked Archie if he would ask the blessing when everyone was settled. Without hesitation, Archie thanked God for the beautiful new day and the food they were about to enjoy. Before he finished, he thanked the Lord for the safe travel his family had enjoyed the day before and for Widow Henry's blessing to him and Maggie. As breakfast was being enjoyed, Mr. Garrett asked when they could see their farm.

Archie told them that he would be glad to take them out to the farm that morning and then somewhat hesitantly began to explain that he was in the middle of building a new house, but since the fire, there hadn't been lumber for him to continue working on it.

As he continued, Maggie said she would like to join them. "I'll be fine. I've been feeling much better lately. I haven't been out there since last fall and am excited to see everything Archie has done. He works so hard for us!"

"I'll pack you a picnic lunch," said Widow Henry.

Archie rushed over to get Buck and hitch him to his wagon, concerned that there was no seating for everyone. When he rode up to Widow Henry's house to pick up everyone, Widow Henry gave Mrs. Garrett the picnic basket she had prepared. Mr. Garrett took the basket from his wife and helped her up to the front seat. Archie assisted Maggie to the seat next to her mother while Mr. Garrett put the basket in the back of the wagon.

"I'll walk beside Buck, Mr. Garrett; you can ride in the back," said Archie.

"If you don't mind, Archie, I would rather walk with you," said Archie's father-in-law.

The foursome headed out to see the young couple's new homesite.

When they reached Hank's place, Archie asked if they would like to rest for a minute while he briefly spoke with his friend. When the women got down from the wagon, Mr. Garrett stayed with them and poured them a glass of water.

Archie approached Hank's cabin to tell him about the Harless brother's arrest. Hank was excited to hear the news and thanked Archie for stopping by.

"Why don't you come over to the wagon and meet Maggie's parents?" asked Archie.

"Are you sure they want to meet me, Archie?" asked Hank.

"Don't be silly, Hank, of course they do," with that, the two of them walked over to the wagon.

"Mr. and Mrs. Garrett, I want to introduce you to my best friend, Hank." Both of Maggie's parents reached out their hands and warmly said hello.

"Any friend of Archie's is our friend as well," said Mr. Garrett.

After their brief meeting, Hank said goodbye as the wagon made its way up the hill to the farm. James looked at Archie as they walked along and said, "I heard from Mrs. Adkins how you saved Hank's life last week. You're a good man, son; I'm glad you're in our family."

The wagon rounded the final hill, and the vista opened. Below was the spring-fed creek, and to the left, vegetables were growing in the field Archie had planted earlier in the year, and on the right, up on a knoll, was the house Archie had begun building.

Maggie began to weep. "Archie, it's beautiful! I can't believe how much you have done since last fall."

Mr. Garrett helped his wife down from the wagon while Archie did the same for Maggie. Archie locked his arm through Maggie's as they walked down the hill toward the shack, where Archie tied Buck to a post. The four of them walked around the property, first looking at the vegetables, and then, as they walked over to the house, Mrs. Garrett said to Archie, "You have made us incredibly happy, Archie. This is going to be a wonderful place to raise your family. It's a bit of a ride from town, but once you're here, it is worth the effort."

"Thank you, Mrs. Garrett; I can't begin to tell you how much your approval means to me."

James Garrett had built a house when he first moved to Canton, and he knew how much work it would be for Archie to attempt to do it himself.

"Archie, after we return to Canton, let me know when you get the lumber you need. I will leave Phoebe with a friend of hers and come out to help you for two weeks. My boss is always on me for not taking time off, so I am sure he will not have a problem with it. You've got a lot to do before winter. I know you said Hank would help you when his leg healed, but I doubt he will be strong enough to work as hard as he used to, at least for another month or so. I want to help you, Archie, and frankly, I look forward to spending more time with you."

Archie was shocked at Mr. Garrett's offer. He had spent the last two weeks worrying if he would approve of him, and all he wanted to do was spend time with him, helping build the house.

"Thank you, Mr. Garrett; you don't need to come all this way to help. I can take care of it," said Archie, unsure how to respond to such an incredible offer.

"Archie, I want to help you and Maggie get into your new house by the time the baby arrives. I don't have much to give the two of you, but I know a little about building a house," said Mr. Garrett as he extended his arms to hug his son-in-law.

On their way back into town, the Garretts invited Archie and Maggie to the boardinghouse for dinner. That evening, the four of them talked until late, sharing childhood stories about Maggie and her sisters.

Archie told them where he used to live in Canton, and Mr. Garrett told him he had a close friend who lived near that area.

"If you don't mind, Archie, I'll stop by to see your father to let him know how well you are doing and that we are family now."

Archie had written his father about meeting and marrying Maggie but hadn't received a reply. Archie's father wasn't one to write since he didn't know how to write very well. It had been something he had never shared with his son because of how embarrassed he was about it.

"That would be wonderful, Mr. Garrett; I haven't heard from my dad in years."

It was an excellent evening for them to grow as a family. When the time came for them to leave, Maggie told her parents that Widow Henry wanted to host dinner tomorrow, and with that, Archie and Maggie left to walk down the street to Widow Henry's home.

The rest of the week was spent enjoying each other's company. Mrs. Garrett and Maggie shopped at the general store for baby clothes with Aunt Carol while Archie and Mr. Garrett looked at tools and other building supplies.

"Archie, if you want, I can purchase windows for you at Hoffman's Supply while I'm in Charleston Friday," said Tom Campbell.

"I will need four windows, but I'm afraid until I get more lumber, it will be a while," said Archie.

"Oh, didn't you hear? Widow Henry is having two wagon loads of lumber brought into Clayton next Monday to help," said Tom. "You know her; she always is one step ahead of the rest of us," laughed Tom.

When the week ended, Maggie insisted on riding to Charleston with Archie and her parents to be with them for that much longer. She was feeling better every day. Once again, Tom had loaned Archie his wagon so everyone could ride comfortably.

It was a beautiful day along the river. The somewhat cooler breeze and the shade from the trees made the journey relaxing. Archie helped load the Garrett's baggage onto the train when they arrived at the Charleston train station as everyone embraced, saying their goodbyes. It had been a fantastic week for Maggie. She had gotten to see her parents and received their approval of her choice for a husband, a concern she hadn't shared with Archie. Archie had gotten to know each of Maggie's parents and felt they were happy he was in their family.

The ride home was peaceful. It was still a beautiful day, but both felt an unspoken relief. They were family, and it was wonderful.

CHAPTER 15

Friday morning, Tom hitched the wagon to his horse and began the trip to Charleston. The morning was warm, but riding along the river was relaxing. Tom had several errands he needed to handle while he was in town, in addition to getting supplies for the store at Hoffman's.

Jim Hoffman saw Tom as he arrived and walked out to greet him as he tied his horse to the hitching post.

"Jim, I'm glad to see you," said Tom." I need supplies for the summer season and some fireworks if you have any. With the Fourth of July coming up, I wanted to shoot fireworks at our town picnic."

Jim looked at Tom's list and said he had everything he needed but only had a few fireworks left for the Fourth.

"I assume you need to go downtown, so leave your wagon here, and I'll have your things loaded for you when you return," offered Jim.

"Thanks, Jim; I'll see you later this afternoon," replied Tom.

Walking down the busy street to see Thomas Franklin, Tom noticed how crowded the busy streets were and how the people were all rushing to get to wherever they were going. He didn't see anyone saying hello to one another, and no one smiled.

Is this progress?

When Tom arrived at his attorney's office, his assistant, Elizabeth, greeted him and showed him into Thomas' office.

"What can I do for you today, Tom?" asked Thomas.

"I want to sell three of the ten acres I just purchased south of town," answered Tom." Widow Henry wants to build a sawmill in town as a branch of her business here in Charleston."

"Her company is doing quite well in Charleston," said Thomas, "You should be able to make a nice profit."

"I'm not interested in making money from a friend, Thomas. She is building this to help our community, especially Hank. His mill was burned down, and she wants to build a new one in town and hire Hank to run it. I want to help make that happen. Please have Elizabeth draw up the papers from my corporation. You can sign them as our attorney. I have other business in town today and can pick them up in a few hours if possible."

"Sure," said Thomas, not understanding how such a good businessman was willing to give up making money, friend or not.

With that, Tom thanked his attorney, especially Elizabeth, as he left to meet with his friend, Howard McDougal.

"Tom, it's so good to see you," said Howard. "How's Nancy? "

"Let me take you to lunch, and we can talk about your project. I worked right through my lunch time and am starved," laughed Howard.

"Sounds great to me, Howard; I could use a bite myself," replied Tom.

After lunch had been served, Tom talked about an idea he and Nancy had to give Clayton a place for families to relax and enjoy each other's company.

"Howard, as you know, when the town folks get together, we always meet in front of the church and use the little yard for picnics or celebrations. I am selling three of the ten acres I bought a couple of months ago to Widow Henry, who is going to build a sawmill and a house. Still, the rest of the property could be used for a community park—a beautiful creek runs along the southern end of the property, and a meadow in the middle.

"I could remove trees, and the sawmill could make the lumber we need. There could be a gazebo in the middle of the park, a little bridge or two over the creek, and picnic tables everywhere. I want to give the town a place where they can go with their families and enjoy themselves. Do you think you could make drawings for the gazebo and the bridges? I know this is not the intricate drawings you develop for all the buildings you have worked on, but I want everything done correctly. I will pay you; I want this to be a special place for our friends. Clayton has been good to Nancy and me, and we want to give something back to our community."

Howard looked at his friend and shook his head, saying, "Tom, you and Nancy are two of the nicest people I have ever met. I would consider it an honor to draw the plans for the gazebo and bridges at no charge. I want to help, too."

The two friends continued talking about the park, and as they left the restaurant, Howard said, "Maybe a park is something the people of Charleston could use; perhaps coming together at events in a park would begin to bring back a feeling of community."

Tom could see the wheels turning as Howard talked about getting some of the more prominent landowners to give a portion of their land to build a park in the middle of town. Howard was genuinely excited about bringing the idea of community back to Charleston. When they parted, Howard thanked Tom for his vision and told him he would have the drawings ready in two weeks.

Tom walked back to Hoffman's with a spring in his step. It had been a wonderful day. On the way, he stopped at Thomas' office to pick up the papers from Elizabeth. As Tom was about to leave, Thomas rushed out of his office, asking Tom if he could please come into his office to discuss something.

"Tom, I just received an offer to lease five hundred acres of our land to a coal mining operator from up north. They have offered us five hundred dollars monthly plus five percent of their monthly gross sales. It's a good offer, Tom, excellent."

Tom agreed that the offer was good but did not like the idea of leasing to a coal mining operator.

"Thomas, I have read that the conditions in the mines are terrible. The miners are paid with company currency that they can only spend at a company-owned store. The housing is terrible. People glue newspaper to the walls to keep the frigid air from blowing in. I don't want to be part of anything like that."

After thinking for a while, Tom said, "I have an idea. Why don't we split the acreage? You keep the five hundred acres they want, and I'll keep the other five hundred acres."

Thomas looked at Tom, shaking his head, and said," You would walk away from this kind of money on principle? I've never met anyone like you, Tom, never. If that's what you want, I will draw up the papers to dissolve the partnership, allocating the northern five hundred acres closest to the mouth of Cabin Creek to you. No one has been mining that section of the creek, so I'm not sure what you will do with it."

"God will provide Thomas," responded Tom.

"I'll mail you the paperwork tomorrow to sign. If you change your mind, send them back unsigned, and I'll understand," said Thomas.

When they had finished discussing the issue, Tom shook Thomas' hand, thanked him for the opportunity, and then quickly headed up the street to Hoffman's.

Jim had everything Tom had ordered loaded in his wagon. After paying his bill, Tom thanked Jim and started back to Clayton, knowing how pleased Nancy would be.

On the way back to Clayton, Tom had an idea for the park's name, and he knew Nancy would love it. About halfway back, the wind began to blow, and the sky darkened.

Looks like a summer storm is headed our way, thought Tom. Stopping to cover his supplies, Tom noticed his horse was beginning to get nervous, prancing around and raising his front legs in the air.

"Let's go, boy, maybe we can outrun the storm!" yelled Tom. The horse responded, and Tom carefully guided it at a quicker pace. He did not want the horse to run from fear, so controlling his pace was necessary. Fortunately, the storm was headed east rather than north toward Clayton, enabling them to escape most of the rain. After a while, Tom slowed down and returned home, thankful for his good fortune.

Tom took the papers to Widow Henry's house the next day for her review. The two old friends sat on the porch enjoying a cool glass of water, talking about the new sawmill. Widow Henry asked Tom if he would take her to Hank's place. She had approved the asking price and signed the documents to give to the mail carrier the next time he was in town.

"You could wait until Sunday and talk with him after worship," suggested Tom.

"Yes, I could do that, but I would prefer to talk with him at his home. I think it would mean more to him if I did. He's hurt Tom and needs to know that he's our friend, regardless of how the Harless brothers treated him."

"I will pick you up in a half hour after I tell Nancy," said Tom.

Widow Henry had not been to this part of the county for several years and was surprised to see two other families living along the way.

"Place sure is growing, Tom; we need to get to know these new folks and ensure they feel welcome."

Continuing along the road, the beauty of the area was inescapable. Old tall trees shaded much of the road; two different creeks flowed along the way with deep blue water from the springs that fed them. Down in the valley was a boy fishing with his father.

"It's so peaceful here, Tom. I can see why Archie and Maggie like it so much."

Hank was tending to his vegetables when they arrived. Looking up when he heard a horse, Hank was surprised to see Widow Henry and Tom. Dusting himself off the best he could, he walked over to meet them.

"Hi, folks, good to see you," said Hank. "What can I do for you?"

When Tom helped Widow Henry down from the wagon, Widow Henry reached into the back of the wagon and brought out one of her apple pies to give to Hank.

"Hank, we've missed seeing you lately. Is everything all right? Are you feeling better," asked Tom.

"Sure, I'll be fine. It'll just take me some time to figure out what to do. The mill will be too expensive to replace until I can save money. I have been thinking of going to Charleston to look for work."

After handing Hank the pie, Widow Henry sat on the log beside him, reached out her hand, and put it on his forearm.

"Hank, I can't imagine how you must be hurt because of what happened to you. I know you understand that the people of Clayton are not like the Harless brothers."

"I wanted to visit you in person to ask if you could help me."

Hank looked at Widow Henry as if to say, "What?"

"Hank, you know I own a large lumber mill in Charleston. Well, with all the new people moving to this area and settling down, I am considering opening another mill in Clayton. However, I need someone to help build it and run it for me full-time. You were the first person I thought of. Would you be interested? It will be a lot of work, but I know you can handle it."

The big, rough-looking man looked into Widow Henry's eyes and could see her sincerity and true friendship. He started to thank her when his voice cracked, and his lip quivered. Stopping to gather himself, Hank said, "Yes, of course I will do it. Thank you, ma'am, thank you!"

Tom told Hank that the churchmen wanted to help build his house on Saturdays after the mill was open. "After all, Hank, you should live in town next to the mill." Hank was speechless. Never in his whole life had he felt he belonged or that he was cared for, and yet these people were reaching out to him in his hour of need and caring for him like he was one of their own.

Everyone was excited as they shared apple pie and discussed the new mill. Widow Henry told Hank it would take two weeks for the lumber to begin the project to arrive from Charleston. In the meantime, he was invited to come to town and walk around the property with her to discuss where to put the mill and house.

When the day ended, Widow Henry and Tom had left for Clayton; Hank did something he hadn't ever done before. Kneeling, he prayed, thanking God for this new opportunity and for keeping him safe during the attack but, most of all, for bringing people who cared for him into his life.

CHAPTER 16

The trial of Paul and Jim Harless in Elkview required Sheriff Griffith, Hank, and Archie to provide testimony about what had happened. Archie and Hank were nervous about appearing in court. As the three of them rode down River Road, Sheriff Griffith tried to assure them that all they had to do was tell the judge what had happened. Just before getting to Elkview, Archie asked if they could stop while he prayed. Stopping the wagon, Archie bowed his head and prayed, asking the Lord for clarity of thought, peace of mind, and strength to deal with all the questions he was sure would be asked. Archie felt better about his responsibility to testify when he returned to the wagon, even though he had never been in a courtroom.

During the trial, Archie was asked to share what he remembered the evening of the fire. Hank had been asked to leave the room with the bailiff, so he could not hear what Archie said. Confidently, Archie told the judge and jury what had happened that night. The defense attorney tried to create doubt about Archie's testimony, asking him why he was at the cabin with Hank. Archie told him that his friend was frightened knowing the threatening comments Paul Harless had made to Tom Campbell, and he wanted to be there for him. When he had finished, the judge asked Archie if there was anything he wanted to add to his statement. Stopping momentarily thinking about everything he had told the court, Archie looked solemnly at the judge and said, "No sir, I've told the court everything I remember."

When Archie stepped down from sharing his testimony, Paul Harless glared at him. The judge noticed Paul and reminded him that any threat to a witness was also a crime. Later, after the court took a recess, Hank was asked to tell what he remembered from that night. Hank's story agreed with Archie's, but Hank had a look of terror on his face when he talked. The judge noticed but didn't say anything at the time.

Sheriff Griffith testified that the fire destroyed the mill to confirm what had been said earlier. He wanted to tell the court about all the times he had chased the moonshiners but had been warned that he was not allowed to bring up anything not directly involved with this particular instance.

After the defense presented their case and summaries were given by both sides, the jury was dismissed to consider all that had been said. After only a half hour, the jury returned with a guilty verdict. The judge read the ruling from the jury, stating that the brothers were convicted of arson, attempted first-degree murder, and threatening a witness, and sentenced them to thirty years in jail. They would be transported to the Moundsville prison in the northern part of the state the next day to begin their sentence.

When the courtroom cleared, the judge asked Hank if he could see him for a minute. As Hank entered the judge's quarters, he became frightened and asked the judge, "Have I done something wrong, your honor?"

"No, no," said the elderly judge," please sit down." I noticed how upset you were when you gave your testimony. I can understand the fear you must have felt then, but you acted as if there was more to the story."

"Well, your honor, I grew up as a slave in Virginia. I was beaten just like my mama and daddy. My brother was sold to someone from Georgia, and I haven't seen or heard from him in over thirty years. My life has seen the harshness of slavery from a very personal level. When I was on the witness stand and looked out at the audience, all I saw were white folks, and it brought back all the fears I lived with growing up. Until recently, I was afraid of all white folks. I thought all of them hated blacks, and people like the Harless brothers were typical whites."

"You said until recently, what has changed?" asked the judge.

"Sir, I live in Clayton, and the people there are different. They treat me just like their own. I can't explain it, but I feel safe there. I know one thing: all the people I know there are born-again Christians. I'm fairly sure that has a lot to do with it. They have told me that they love me as a brother. Now, isn't that something, sir? It sure feels good," said Hank, smiling.

The judge shook his head and softly said, "I can't imagine what it was like for you, sir. Please forgive me for any part I may have had in overlooking slavery instead of trying to do something to stop it. The war didn't divide our great country; attitudes did, and attitudes are taught. We have much healing to do as a country, and it starts with love and changing our attitudes."

As the judge stood up, he reached out his hand to Hank and thanked him for sharing. Before going out the door, the judge asked Hank what his brother's name was.

"George, sir. We were slaves in Lexington, where Stonewall Jackson lived before the war. We worked at a tobacco plantation outside of town," replied Hank.

The trip home was much more relaxing than the trip to Elkview. Sheriff Griffith thanked both of them for sharing their testimonies. When Hank left them to head back to his cabin, he thought about what a difference it was to go from slave to having white friends who genuinely cared about him. "Glory, Glory, Hallelujah! "He sang at the top of his voice.

For the remainder of the month, Hank and Archie worked together, helping each other with their crops and collecting lumber to begin building Archie's cabin. When the lumber arrived from Charleston, Archie wrote his father-in-law to tell him he had enough supplies to get back to building his house. Hank helped Archie continue raising the walls, but they needed Mr. Garrett's help with the roof work.

Meanwhile, they began chinking between the logs to protect from cold wind and rain. Chinking was a terrible job that no one enjoyed doing, but it had to be done for the cabin to be as secure as possible.

One afternoon, after the two had finished working on the cabin, Archie gathered vegetables to take into town to sell at the General Store. Hank asked him if he would take his as well, saving him a trip. The two had become fast friends, so after helping Hank gather his crops, Archie headed back to Clayton. During the ride, Archie pondered what it would be like for Hank to live in town while he and Maggie were two miles away. He was going to miss his friend.

Tom bought the vegetables from Archie and applied his portion of the sale to his mortgage. Hank's portion was put on his account to pay for supplies he had purchased earlier. Widow Henry had sold lumber to Archie at her cost, but it still took most of the money he had saved. Just before Archie returned to Widow Henry's, Tom gave him a letter he had gotten that afternoon.

The letter was from Mr. Garrett, saying he would be there next week to help with the cabin. It was great news. Archie would be able to finish the cabin before the cold of winter.

Walking into Widow Henry's house, Archie gave Maggie the letter from her father. She was glad he was coming back to Clayton to help Archie with their house. She wanted the two of them to get to know each other personally.

Widow Henry began buying supplies to prepare lunches for the men to enjoy while they worked at the cabin. She, of course, was going to make apple pies, but she wanted the lunches to be filling. Work like they were going to be doing was exhausting, and they needed all the nourishment they could get. Tom had just received a fresh shipment of Virginia hams. Widow Henry bought the largest he had to make sandwiches. She could bake bread and pie crust with the flour she had purchased. The tomatoes Archie had given her would make the ham sandwiches a perfect midday treat.

As she was paying her bill, Tom told her that Doctor David Smith would be in town this Saturday and Sunday. Tom suggested that Widow Henry and Doc join him and Nancy for dinner at the boardinghouse on Saturday evening. He and Doc were going to spend the day with the prospective doctor to show him Doc's place and discuss the patient demographics.

"I'll tell Sarah to expect us Saturday evening," said Tom.

Saturday morning, David Smith arrived from Charleston and was met by Tom at the boardinghouse. "Good morning, Doctor Smith; I'm Tom Campbell. Let me help you with your things."

The two men walked into the boardinghouse just as Sarah Adkins was cleaning a table one of her guests used.

"Good morning, you must be Doctor Smith; I'm Sarah Adkins," said Sarah, somewhat embarrassed by her ruffled appearance. "I'll show you to your room in just a minute," she said as she rushed to the back to put her washcloth away and wash her hands.

"This way, I'll take you to your room."

"Thank you, Miss Adkins," said David.

Once she left, Tom informed him that she was Mrs. Adkins. "Her husband died a few years ago."

"Oh, I must apologize," said the doctor. When David had freshened up, he came downstairs to begin his tour with Tom. Seeing Sarah on his way out the door, he smiled and said how much he looked forward to having dinner at the boardinghouse that evening.

Tom walked up the street to Doc's house and introduced them. Doc extended his hand and welcomed the young doctor.

"Welcome to Clayton, doctor; I'm glad to meet you. What can I show you first? I don't have much equipment or many examining tables, just some basic medicines and bandages."

"Thank you, Doc. I'm most interested in getting to know you and how you have cared for all of these people for so long."

Doc and David talked for over two hours about the people in Clay County, how Doc knew them, and what each of them was like. He shared some of the various illnesses he had helped with and the broken bones he had seen.

"Boys in these parts think nothing of climbing trees and building "forts or lookouts" when they play soldier. David could see in Doc's face how he cared for everyone in the area, more like a father than perhaps a physician.

After their discussion, Tom escorted David to the General Store to meet his wife.

"David, this is my wife, Nancy," said Tom proudly.

"I've heard a lot about you, Nancy. I understand you have been working with the pregnant women around here for years. Can you tell me what that has been like for you?"

Nancy explained that the women seemed more comfortable with her than Doc, "I'm sure it's because I'm a woman. Doc's a fine man; they're just shy for the most part."

They continued talking for an hour, and then Tom left to take David up the street to Widow Henry's house.

"I understand. I will be seeing you again this evening for dinner. I look forward to it," said the young doctor as they headed out the door.

Widow Henry was sitting on her front porch reading her Bible when she saw the men approaching. "Welcome, welcome, you must be Doctor David Smith," said the widow warmly.

"Nice to meet you, ma'am," said the doctor. "It's a beautiful day to enjoy your front porch; I see you read the Good Book."

As the men sat down, Widow Henry excused herself to bring fresh coffee for them to enjoy. "Have you enjoyed meeting some of the folks in town, Doctor?" she asked.

"Yes, I have, thank you. I understand you can tell me all about Clayton and its history," mentioned David as he added cream to his coffee. Widow Henry was never short on tales of days gone by in Clayton.

"Clayton has been my home for most of my life, so I've seen this community grow from a small store and church to what you see today. People who move to this area are good, hard-working folks who appreciate their independence but completely enjoy being part of a community that cares for one another. The closest thing I can think of is that it's like a family. With the population growing nationwide, people have also started moving here. At first, they live the way they always have, but with time, they begin to see a difference."

Changing the subject, she asked the doctor what he expected a small rural area like Clayton to be like. David was surprised by the question but quickly gathered his thoughts and replied," Any community reflects the attitude of the people living in it. From what I have seen, Clayton's strength comes from a common faith, shared by most but even more importantly lived by them."

"I think you have seen what I was talking about, Doctor," replied Widow Henry.

Tom looked at his watch and noticed it was late afternoon. He suggested they could continue their discussion over dinner in about an hour.

"I'm sure David wants to get freshened up before this evening; I know I do," said Tom.

With that, the two men excused themselves and headed down the street to the boardinghouse. "I'll be back with Nancy, Doctor; rest, and we will return shortly."

When Doctor Smith entered the boardinghouse, he saw Sarah setting up a table for their dinner later. Smelling the aroma of stew and blackberry cobbler, he stopped and said to Sarah, "Dinner smells incredible, Sarah. Thank you for going to so much trouble for all of us."

"It's no problem, Doctor Smith; I hope you enjoy it."

Smiling, David said goodbye and went to his room. He wanted to make notes of his visit and share some ideas he had been thinking about for the last couple of years. He couldn't wait to begin practicing medicine, and his heart for the poor made today's visit seem like a dream come true. The people here were different. They didn't have much money or worldly possessions, but he had never seen so many people genuinely connected.

As the guests gathered, Sarah brought a pitcher of water and glasses. Widow Henry was the last to arrive and apologized for making everyone wait.

"Not necessary, ma'am; we were a little early getting here. Who could resist the aroma of Mrs. Adkins's dinner?" said the young doctor.

When everyone was seated, Sarah informed them that dinner would be served shortly. David looked at Sarah and asked if he could help, but she quickly replied that Lizzy would be her assistant that evening.

"We're in for a treat," said Tom, "Lizzy is quite the little firecracker."

As dinner was being served, Lizzy introduced herself to Doctor Smith, very grownup-like, and welcomed him to the boardinghouse. Dinner was delicious, and the blackberry cobbler was, in the words of the young doctor, "the best he had ever eaten."

The dinner discussion was centered on everyone getting to know one another better. The brief time Doctor Smith had spent with each of them was highly informative, but he was more interested in knowing each of them on a more personal level. As the evening wore on, it became clear to the young doctor that this was where he wanted to settle down.

When the conversation slowed, Doctor Smith spoke to everyone confidently and sincerely, "I want to thank each of you for taking the time to talk with me today. I have enjoyed getting to know every one of you very much. I would consider it my privilege to be a doctor in this wonderful town, but on one condition: I want to work alongside Doc as my partner. Doc, you have loved the people in these parts for years and know more about them than anybody. Please stay in Clayton and help me become the doctor you have been for years?"

The idea of staying in Clayton made Doc extremely happy, and helping Doctor Smith gave him a purpose. Over the last few years, Doc had seen his ability to help everyone diminish. It was obvious that the town needed a new doctor. The problem was that being the town "doc" was all he had ever done, so his future was unclear. All he knew was that he wouldn't be needed, and that sad realization had been very depressing, causing him to think that he needed to move to remove himself from the pain.

He had thought of moving closer to his daughter in Ohio. She and her husband had moved away years ago because of her husband's work in Canton. Doc visited them every year and hoped living closer would help fill the void losing his work would create. When Doctor Smith asked him to work alongside him, he could not have been more surprised. He loved the people of Clay County and wanted to be there for them. His purpose was now obvious: he would help Doctor Smith improve the medical care of his neighbors for as long as he could.

When everyone got up from the table and began to leave, Doc approached Doctor Smith and shook his hand while thanking him. Only Doctor Smith noticed his lip quivering and the tear running down his cheek.

"Let's talk Sunday after church, Doc; I have a couple more ideas," said Doctor Smith with a warm smile.

CHAPTER 17

THE MORNING FOG covered the valley as Hank began his trip to Clayton. Earlier, he had loaded two bushels of vegetables from his garden to give to Widow Henry. It was the only means he had to express his thanks for her generous offer to have him run her new mill. Today, they were going to walk around the property to determine the best layout for the construction.

Hank's horse whinnied as they began their two-mile trip into town in the cool air. It had been an eventful year for Hank. The new friendship with Archie, meeting Widow Henry, the fire and attempted murder, and now a new job running the lumber mill, but what affected him the most was the brotherly love displayed by the people in the Clayton area. Most people around Clayton cared about their neighbors and would do whatever they could to help them.

What surprised Hank was that they considered him a friend and neighbor, a former slave. Hank had the physical and emotional scars from his teenage years that made being cared for hard to comprehend. A deep part of him still maintained a reserve about everything. He had learned not to trust anyone, making relaxing in his new friendships difficult. He knew Archie and a few others were genuine, but he was still cautious.

Riding into town, he saw Widow Henry returning from the General Store and offered her a ride. Once Hank had helped her onto his wagon, they rode toward her house, where Hank proudly showed her the vegetables he had brought for her. When the bushel baskets had been put on her front porch and her groceries put away, they headed to the other end of town to look at the property.

The land had a gentle slope from back to front, making locating the mill close to the street easier. The back of the property was a forest that could be cleared, but it wasn't necessary to complete the building.

When Widow Henry began to talk about where Hank's house should be, Hank asked if she would mind if he said something. Widow Henry looked at Hank, saddened that he still wasn't comfortable asking questions. She could only imagine what terrible things had been done to this poor man for him to be so meek.

"Hank, you don't ever have to ask my permission again; we are both the same, equal in God's eyes. The Bible says we're made in His image and that we're loved by Him so much that he was willing to free us from something much worse than slavery. He freed everyone who believes in His son, Jesus Christ, from sin.

"Sorry, I didn't mean to preach, but I want you to understand that so badly I couldn't help myself. OK, what was your question?"

It took Hank a minute to absorb what Widow Henry had just said, but then he said, "Ma'am, I don't need a house; just build me a room attached to the mill so I can keep an eye on it. That's all I need: a room to sleep in and a little kitchen to cook for myself. You've already done so much for me; I don't want to be a burden."

As they continued walking around the three-acre piece of property, Hank asked if there was room enough in the back to plant some crops.

Widow Henry said she thought having a vegetable garden behind the mill was a fine idea. Hank didn't tell Widow Henry, but he hoped to grow enough to give to the church so they could help the poor. He had never considered doing anything like that before, but from the generosity of his heart, he wanted to treat others just like they had been treating him.

After leaving the property, Widow Henry suggested they stop by the General Store to see Tom. When they entered the front door, Nancy was behind the counter, and Tom was organizing the shelves.

"Good morning, folks; how are you doing this fine day?" said a joyful Nancy Campbell.

"It's been a great morning, Nancy. We just finished looking at the property to see where the best place would be to build the new mill," said Widow Henry.

"Hank, what do you think about the property?" asked Tom.

"It's a fine piece of land, Tom; I can't wait to start building the mill," replied Hank.

"Widow Henry, did you tell Hank that the men from the church want to build his house when the mill is finished?" asked Tom.

"Well, Tom," said Widow Henry, "Hank has decided to save the money and space and just have a small place attached to the mill."

"Are you sure, Hank?" asked Tom. "The men in the church were looking forward to doing something to help you after what happened."

"Mr. Campbell, I have never been treated so nicely, but I don't need much. I'd rather see what the church men and I could do to help those new folks who moved out toward my place. They're really poor and need help. Maybe I can cut some trees down to make room for a garden and use the trees to make lumber for them."

Widow Henry looked at Tom and smiled.

Before Hank left for his place, Widow Henry asked if he wanted to stop by her house for a cold drink.

As the two sat on the front porch, Hank shyly looked at Widow Henry and asked if she could begin showing him how to read.

"Ever since you mentioned it, I can't stop thinking about it. I have always wanted to read."

That was all the encouragement Widow Henry needed. Grabbing her Bible, she sat beside Hank and started teaching him to read. Hank struggled but kept trying until he was able to read a verse from the Bible.

On his way out of the door, Widow Henry gave him an old book she had and told him to try to read the first paragraph before he came back into town in a couple of days.

The shipment of lumber from Charleston was due in two days. Widow Henry had ordered what was needed and hired a small construction crew to help Hank.

On the way home, Hank kept whistling an old song from his childhood, only this time it was with joy, not sorrow.

When Hank settled down that evening, he began repeating the letters of the alphabet from a list Widow Henry had given him. She had told him the name of each letter and listed underneath each one two words beginning with that letter. As he studied each letter, he started to understand how to say them. Before going to bed, he closed his eyes and tried remembering every letter and word from the list.

"This is so much fun," he thought to himself. "I'm not dumb like folks have told me; I can learn!"

On a rainy day, the supplies arrived from Charleston on two wagons loaded with building materials and a three-man construction crew. Hank was there to meet the men and direct them where to unload the wagons.

"Let's put everything over there, out of the way of the site, to make it easier for us to use later," said Hank.

"I don't take orders from no darky," said one of the men.

Hank knew he needed to establish who was in charge early or never expect the three of them to work together well, so he stared at Fred and said, "If you expect to work on this job, you will. Do you understand me?"

Fred was a twenty-three-year-old man from Charleston who had lived with his mother since he was a little boy. His father had left when he was only seven years old and never returned. The part of town he lived in was poor. His mother worked two jobs, trying to ensure the two had a roof over their heads and food on the table. Because of this, Fred was usually on his own growing up. His only friends were poor, uneducated guys like him. They had gotten into trouble with the law early in their lives and grew never to trust anyone; it was every man for himself.

There were many living in those same poor conditions, just surviving, not caring about school or, for that matter, anything else but just getting by. Often, there were gangs, each having their territory. Boys would join gangs to have somewhere they felt they belonged. They became what a family should have been. Loyalty to your gang was expected, and that loyalty often caused fights with rival gangs. It was necessary for every boy to feel superior to others, to be feared and respected. Also mixed in this subculture was a lingering hatred for blacks. Blacks were inferior to whites, and no self-respecting man would think otherwise.

Fred's other co-workers were also from Charleston. Finn was from Irish descendants and had seen his fair share of prejudice. Irish were treated as if they were sub-whites, just slightly better than blacks in this hate-filled part of society.

The other worker was Samuel, a black man about thirty years old who couldn't stand either of his co-workers but needed the job to help feed his family. Samuel's father had been a slave, like Hank, and had taught him that white folks were evil, sons of Satan.

Looking into Hank's eyes, Fred saw that he meant business and eventually backed down.

After the wagons were unloaded, Hank asked Fred to help him measure out the dimensions of the mill so that they could begin digging holes for footers. Hank wanted the mill up from the ground so there wouldn't be any problems should there ever be high water from the creek. The four men worked all day doing their work, barely speaking to one another.

The next few days didn't improve, but at least they made progress in placing boards on the footers to begin building the floor.

One evening, Fred opened a bottle of moonshine he had brought and had several drinks. Later, when Finn saw what he was doing, he scolded him, reminding him that they had been told explicitly there was to be no drinking.

Fred, now drunk, charged at Finn, tackling him, and started beating him in the face. Samuel heard a noise and ran over from his tent to find out what all the noise was. Jumping between them, he tried to break up the fight, only to be hit squarely in the nose and lip with a wild swing from Finn.

All the noise in the normally quiet town of Clayton awoke Sheriff Griffith, who ran down the street to see what was happening. Samuel was still trying to stop the fight when the sheriff arrived but could not keep them apart.

"What's going on here?" asked Sheriff Griffith. "I smell liquor! Who's been drinking?"

All three stopped what they were doing and began blaming each other for the fight. Fred and Finn said Samuel had started it, trying to steal their moonshine.

"Well then, if that's so, why were you two fighting each other? Sure, looked like this black fellow was trying to break up the fight," said Sheriff Griffith.

"What's your story?" asked the sheriff, looking at Samuel.

Samuel was afraid to tell the truth since he knew the other two would get back at him later, so he just shrugged and said, "I don't know what they're talking about. I'm just sick and tired of both of them, so after a few words, one thing led to another, and we started fighting."

"Why don't you come with me to the jail? What is your name, son?" asked Sheriff Griffith.

"Name's Fred," said Fred, slurring his words. "You two get to bed and keep it down. I'll see you in the morning."

"Why me, sheriff, why not the others?" cried Fred.

"The others aren't drunk," said the sheriff, "besides, I don't believe your story. Now get in that cell and be quiet!"

When Hank arrived from the boardinghouse the following morning, he saw the mess the three had created the night before and asked, "Where's Fred?"

"He's in jail, drunk," said Finn.

Hank stormed up the street to see Sheriff Griffith and find out what had happened. After talking with the sheriff, Hank asked if he could speak to Fred alone. Sheriff Griffith stepped out of his office as Hank walked back to the cell.

"Want some coffee?" asked Hank.

"Yeah, that would be good; I don't feel so good," said Fred.

Hank went to the front of the sheriff's office, poured a cup of coffee for Fred, and brought it to him, sitting down beside the cell.

"You know Fred, you don't like me because I'm black, but frankly, you don't seem to like much of anyone. Do you want to tell me why?"

"No, I'm not telling you anything!" yelled Fred.

"I expected that. You know Fred, hate is a terrible thing. Hate steals any real chance for you ever to be happy. It causes you to live alone, suspecting everybody feels the same about you. There's no joy in that, ever! Listen, I've known hate from both sides. I'm hated simply because I'm a different skin color than others, and I've hated because of the way white people have treated me. Hate only divides; it never brings peace or joy. The only way to find happiness in this life is brotherly love for everyone. It's not easy; there's a lot to forgive, but it's the only way. Drinking to get away from everything only makes things worse. Look, I don't expect you to care about what I am saying, but take it from someone learning to care for others; I can tell you there is real happiness to be found, Fred."

As he left Sheriff Griffith's office, he told the sheriff that he was sorry for the problems his crew had caused and that he would stay with them from now on until their work was finished.

"What happened, Sheriff?" asked Hank.

"My guess is this Fred fellow got drunk, and he and the other guy started fighting. It sure looked like the black guy was trying to break it up, but I couldn't get him to tell me what had gone on," replied Sheriff Griffith.

"I'm sure you are right, sheriff. Fred's full of anger, and the other two have their share, too, but he's the one I worry about most," said Hank.

The three men worked on the mill the rest of the day without saying much to one another until the day was almost done.

"I'll be staying with you men the remainder of the week," said Hank, and with that, he left to get his things at the boardinghouse.

When he finished dinner, he asked Sarah if she could make him three more meals for his men. After loading his things into his wagon, he put the meals on the seat and headed for the mill. Fred had just arrived from the sheriff's office and was grumbling about how hungry he was.

"Here, men, I've brought each of you dinner. I bet you're hungry after all your work today," said Hank. When the men had gotten their food, Hank suggested they should set together around a little fire Samuel had prepared to help keep the misquotes away. While no one thanked Hank for their food, each was grateful.

Talk around the little fire was strained, so Hank felt the need to share.

"You know, guys, we'll finish this job in a few days. Thank you for all your hard work; you have done an excellent job. I couldn't have asked for better workmanship. It's incredible how well you work together despite how you feel about each other. All of you share the same curse: you are angry at how your life has turned out. I'll give you that each of you has had it rough, but the question is, will you let the past control your future?

"Samuel, you were taught to hate white folks because your father was mistreated as a slave. Finn, you were disliked simply because you were Irish. You were made fun of, couldn't get a good job, and have lived in poverty your entire life, and Fred, you hate because you feel rejected. Am I right, fellows?"

"Who do you think you are?" asked Fred, "We are the way we are, and there's nothing we can do about it."

"You know Fred, you're wrong. You feel sorry for yourself just like the rest of you do. You think all you have is yourself to depend on, but you're mistaken. It's good to be strong and work hard, but what's it worth if that's all there is? Do you know how you were picked to work on this job?" asked Hank.

"All I know is some guy from the neighborhood came around and said he had a job for me, so I took it," said Finn.

"Yeah, that's what happened to me, too," said Samuel.

"So, let me get this straight: all three of you were doing nothing to better yourselves, just wasting your lives grumbling about how unfair you had been treated. Each of you has been given a gift, and instead of being thankful for the work, you complain. Listen, I know it's been hard, and you get caught up in your anger and don't see any way out; I get it. All people aren't mean. Some people want to help you, but you've got to want to help yourself, too.

"Do you know why that guy came into your neighborhoods and picked you for this job? Widow Henry asked the foreman at her Charleston mill to be on the lookout for three young men who needed encouragement. She wanted men from different cultures and backgrounds to have an opportunity to see they could make something of themselves, so you three were picked."

"I ain't no charity case," said Fred.

"This isn't charity. You are expected to work and work hard, but it's a chance for each of you to learn a trade. If it were charity, you would get something for doing nothing, and there would be no sense of accomplishment or pride, for that matter. This is your chance, and it's been given to you by an elderly white lady who understands your circumstances and cares enough about you that she took the risk of hiring you to do this work. She did the same thing for me. Widow Henry treats you like she would like to be treated if the roles were reversed."

"Why would she care about any of us?" asked Samuel.

"Widow Henry tries to live her life by her faith. She doesn't just read her Bible; she applies it to her life. It's all a matter of faith", said Hank.

"If I were you," said Hank," I would make the most of this opportunity. When we are done, Widow Henry will let her foreman know how well you did, and if you work hard and do a good job, there's a good chance he will offer you a full-time position. With all the construction going on in Charleston, there should be plenty of work for you.

"Look, it's an opportunity to make something of yourselves. Anger gets you nowhere, but brotherly love offers you a future. Widow Henry is showing you that brotherly love. There are good people in this world that genuinely care for other folks."

The following two days were hot, and the work was hard, but each man seemed not to care. They began talking to one another and occasionally helped each other out. It was incredible for Hank to see what caring does to the souls of men previously lost in their hate. He had felt the same way, but love's effect outweighs hate's anger.

When the job was finished, Fred, Finn, and Samuel left for Charleston on their wagons, thanking Hank for the opportunity.

"You will hear from Widow Henry's foreman in a couple of days," said Hank.

As Hank looked at the job the men had done, he could hear them joking and laughing. On the ground, he found Fred's moonshine bottle still half full. Picking it up, he poured it on the ground, remembering his promise to Sheriff Griffith. It had been a good week.

CHAPTER 18

ARCHIE AWOKE EARLY to prepare for his ride to Charleston to pick up his father-in-law, James Garrett. On his way out of Widow Henry's house, he grabbed an apple to eat along the way, but before he could leave, Widow Henry stopped him and gave him a bag with a sandwich for lunch and two hard-boiled eggs.

Archie quickly walked down the street to the General Store to hitch Buck to his wagon. Before he left, Archie went into the store and asked Tom if he needed anything in Charleston.

"Your windows arrived the other day," said Tom," but otherwise, I've got what I need. Say hi to Jim Hoffman for me." With that quick exchange, Archie left for Charleston.

Along the way to Charleston, Archie began thinking about what he would like to do to the cabin to make it special for Maggie. He knew she wanted an oversized mantel over the fireplace, but he wanted to do something else as a surprise. Suddenly, an idea came to him that he knew she would like. He could make their bedroom larger than they had discussed so there would be room for a rocking chair. She could rock their baby and feed it, but later, it could be her quiet place where she could read and relax.

Just then, Buck reared up and began running off the road, trying desperately to escape from the copperhead snake in the middle of the road. Quickly, Archie calmed him down, getting him away from any danger. After tying Buck to a tree, Archie walked over to the snake and shot it. Copperhead snakes are poisonous and had become a problem along the river of late. Buck was frightened by the gunshot but could not loosen himself from the tree. Archie ran over and petted his neck while whispering to him. When Archie untied Buck, it was clear he was anxious to escape the snake, so Archie slowly walked him further down the road while petting his neck.

The remainder of the trip was uneventful, though hot. The summer skies were clear, and the sun was bright. It had been a hot summer, and today was no exception. When Archie arrived at the train station, he tied Buck to a hitch and walked into the depot. As he stood waiting for Mr. Garrett, the ticket salesman yelled at him and motioned him to come over to the window.

"Are you the man who told me about those criminals a few months back?"

Archie was surprised that he recognized him but responded to his question, "Yes, I am, and thank you for letting the authorities know. In case you hadn't heard, they were captured in Huntington and have since been convicted. Thank you for what you did. They would never have been captured without your follow-through with the Charleston sheriff."

As the men finished their conversation about the Harless', the train from Huntington arrived. After a few minutes, James departed from the train, looking intently for Archie. Archie waved to get his attention as he ran over to greet him. Reaching for James' bag, Archie welcomed him and asked how his trip had been.

Archie informed James that he needed to stop at Hoffman's as the two men walked to the wagon to pick up his windows.

Hoffman's was busy when they arrived, but Jim Hoffman noticed Archie as he came into the store and motioned that he would be with him shortly. While the two waited, Archie noticed a rocking chair for sale and walked over to look at it and see how much it cost. James followed and, as Archie began looking intently at it, asked, "Are you thinking about buying a chair, Archie? You know, I could make one for you."

Archie explained that he wanted to surprise Maggie with the chair for their bedroom.

He wanted it to be special but now found himself in an awkward position. James' offer was a generous gesture, but could he make a good chair?

"That's a wonderful offer, sir, but it looks like it would be a lot of work," said Archie.

James smiled and said, "I've made rocking chairs before, so it shouldn't take me too long."

"Great. Knowing you had made it for her would be special to Maggie," said Archie.

"What can I do for you, gentlemen?" asked Jim Hoffman.

"Tom Campbell mentioned to me that my windows were ready to be picked up, and since I was in town to meet my father-in-law, I thought I would stop by and get them," said Archie, realizing he had forgotten to introduce James. "Oh, sorry, Mr. Hoffman, this is my father-in-law, James Garrett," said a somewhat embarrassed Archie.

After shaking hands, Jim led them to the windows and told Archie to drive his wagon to the loading dock.

As Archie got his wagon, Jim asked James how long he would be in town.

James explained that he had come to town to help Archie build his cabin and would be there for two weeks before he had to go back to Canton. Jim smiled and said, "Archie sure is a lucky man to have a father-in-law willing to spend that much time working on his cabin. I am sure you will have a good time working together."

When Archie pulled into the loading bay, Jim had two men put the windows in the wagon. Archie went with Jim to pay the bill when Jim said, "You sure have a nice father-in-law. I don't know many men who would spend their vacation working on a house with their son-in-law. Enjoy the time you have together."

As James and Archie pulled away, Jim yelled to Archie to tell Tom his new order would arrive next week.

Archie pulled his wagon up to the boardinghouse; Sarah was leaving with a basket of cookies for the general store. Quickly, Sarah went back inside to welcome her new guest.

"Mr. Garrett, how long will you be staying in Clayton?"

"Only tonight, Archie and I will go to his place for the rest of my visit. I will probably spend my last night here later next week," said James.

"I have room three ready for you; here is your key. I hope you and Archie enjoy working on the cabin. We're going to miss Maggie and Archie when they move", said Sarah.

As Archie carried James' bag to his room, Sarah left for the general store with her cookies.

James walked up to Widow Henry's to see Maggie. He loved his daughter and couldn't wait until morning to see her. "You're looking very pregnant, sweety, how are you feeling?" asked James.

"Other than feeling like I'm the size of a horse, I feel good," said Maggie.

When Archie arrived, the four talked briefly before James returned to the boardinghouse. "See you in the morning," said James, heading out the door.

Early the following day, James walked up the street to Widow Henry's to enjoy breakfast. When he walked up the front stairs, Maggie came out, hugged him, and escorted him to the dining room. Archie was helping Widow Henry bring things to the table for another one of her incredible breakfasts.

"Eat a big breakfast, men; you're going to need your strength," said Widow Henry. During breakfast, Widow Henry mentioned that the new doctor was moving into town this coming weekend, to the delight of Maggie, who, although her pregnancy had gone well, was still concerned about the lack of a doctor.

During breakfast, Maggie assured Archie and her father that she was feeling well and that they did not need to be concerned about her. Archie listened and knew she was doing much better, but he still didn't like leaving her.

After breakfast, Archie left James to continue visiting his daughter while he went to the general store to hitch Buck to the wagon and pick up a few tools that Tom was lending him. Before he left, Tom asked him if he would return to town in time to celebrate the Fourth of July.

Archie had forgotten entirely about the town picnic. The only thing on his mind had been getting his cabin finished before the cold weather began.

"I will try Tom, but I need to get as much done as possible while James is in town," said Archie. By the way, I heard the new doctor is moving into town this weekend." That sure gives me peace of mind. Thanks for everything you did to bring him here."

Archie loaded his wagon with some of the lumber delivered from Charleston and said he would return for the second load later in the week.

Riding up the street to Widow Henry's house, Seamus McConnell yelled to Archie, "Can you stop by my place for a few minutes?"

Turning Buck around, Archie rode toward the church to meet Reverend McConnell.

"What can I do for you, Seamus?" asked Archie.

In a quiet, almost whisper voice, Reverend McConnell asked Archie if he and Maggie would join him and Carol for dinner the evening after the Fourth of July picnic. "I'm a little nervous having dinner alone with her, Archie; I've never courted," said Seamus nervously.

"I hadn't planned on being in town, but if you need me, we'll take a break and return," said Archie.

As Archie rode to Widow Henry's, he remembered how Seamus had helped him when he wanted to propose to Maggie, calming him down. Now, the roles were reversed.

When Archie arrived at Widow Henry's, he went to Maggie and held and kissed her, for neither of them liked being apart. It would be over a week, but he promised her he would return for the Fourth of July picnic and that they would go out to dinner at the boardinghouse the following evening. With one final kiss goodbye, Archie pulled away with a basket of food for him and James to enjoy, along with a wagon full of lumber and new windows.

Widow Henry had been preparing food for the two of them over the last few days as her way of helping the young couple. As they were leaving, Archie thanked Widow Henry for breakfast and the basket full of food.

When they arrived at Hank's place, Archie stopped to see how his friend was doing and to ask if he still had the pulley he had used to raise the beams for the schoolhouse.

"I'll tell you what, Archie, I'll bring it out and help you and Mr. Garrett later today," said Hank.

"Great, thanks, Hank. Are you sure you have time? I know you are going into town to work on the mill," Archie asked.

"I wouldn't have it any other way, my friend," said Hank.

When James and Archie pulled up to the cabin, James was surprised at how much Archie had gotten done in the few weeks since he had been there. The outside walls were finished up to the level where the windows would go, and Archie had already built a door.

After the wood was unloaded and Buck was taken down to the creek to rest and cool off, Archie walked up to the cabin and told James about his surprise for Maggie.

"Do you think we could make the bedroom larger by moving it from the side of the house to the back and moving the second bedroom slightly?" asked Archie.

"Yes, I think that will work, but we could also remove the three feet of wall on that end of the house and extend the foundation. That way, the second bedroom can stay larger, and your bedroom will be much more private," said James.

It took most of the day to remove the exterior wall and extend the foundation with new rocks. The extension would also call for new logs to be cut for two walls. Around five o'clock, Hank arrived with the pulley. He had cut trees along the road to make it wider and easier to navigate and thought they would be suitable for the new walls.

"Already expanding the cabin, Archie," teased Hank, "you two planning on having a bunch of little ones?"

The following day, Hank set up his pulley and helped James and Archie place the support beams for the roof. The beams were heavy, but with Hank's help, they saved many hours of hard labor. With the roof beams in place, Hank said he needed to get to Clayton to start building the rest of the mill.

Archie and James worked the remainder of the week finishing the exterior walls and installing the windows and the door. They talked as they worked, telling funny stories. James shared memories of when he and Phoebe were first starting out. He wanted to encourage Archie and gently warn him that it's always hard initially.

In the evenings, when the work was finished for the day, the two men would settle down and enjoy the food Widow Henry had prepared for them. During these times, they began building a bond that would last all their lives. Archie felt comfortable enough to share his fears about being able to provide for his new family. He also told James how his life had changed over the last year.

"So many aspects of my life are different than they were just a year ago. I always hoped to marry and have a family, but I had no way of knowing how that would happen and then to meet the most wonderful, beautiful woman in the world; well, I can't put it into words. But there's been something else as well. Both Maggie and I have grown stronger in our faith. With the help of Widow Henry guiding us, we have started to understand how great God's love is for each of us.

"The other evening, we read how God has called us to represent him to everyone."

James listened intently to Archie and shared that he could see a difference in Maggie."

On our trip back to Canton, Phoebe and I discussed how Maggie had changed since she left to be with Carol. We knew she was overjoyed meeting you and falling in love, but there was something else. Maggie is at peace, living by faith instead of worrying about all the little details of life that can take away true happiness. You've certainly been a large part of that, but clearly, it's been a strong faith that directs how she approaches everything now. It's so wonderful to see, Archie," said James as his eyes reddened.

"It's all that a parent could ever want for their child."

With all the lumber installed and the Fourth only a day away, Archie and James agreed they should go back to Clayton to get the additional wood for the roof and enjoy the Fourth with family.

Pulling into Clayton, the red, white, and blue decorations were everywhere. The yard in front of the church had been set up for the picnic, and the tables were ready for pies and watermelon. When James entered the boardinghouse, Sarah greeted him, saying, "It's good to see you, Mr. Garrett. You came back sooner than I expected. Is everything all right?"

"Yes, thank you. Archie and I used all our supplies and thought we would come into town for the Fourth before going back out for a few more days," said James.

Archie took Buck to the general store to clean him and ensure he had food for the night. He planned on getting the remaining lumber on the fifth so that the next day, they could leave early. He hoped they could finish the roof before James returned to Canton, but he wanted more than anything to see Maggie.

After dinner, the four retired to the parlor that evening for Bible study. Holding Maggie's hand, Archie asked Widow Henry if she would introduce him and Maggie to the new doctor.

"He's heard about both of you from Tom and Nancy and mentioned that he would like to meet you, perhaps at the picnic," responded the widow. "He's staying at the boardinghouse for now."

The next day, people from all around came for the festivities, just like they did every year. Hank had invited his new neighbors and brought them in his wagon since they didn't have one of their own. Seeing how everyone welcomed them and made them feel at home was wonderful.

Like the year before, the children played games, the teenagers bobbed for apples, and the pie-baking contest was saved for after the picnic.

There was something different this year besides the new neighbors. Carol seemed happier than Maggie had seen her in years, but Seamus McConnell was fidgety and not being himself.

When the food had been eaten and the winners of the three-legged race had won their prizes, the pie-baking contest began. As usual, Widow Henry's pies were terrific, but this year Sarah won. She had never won anything before and was so surprised. Lizzy hugged her mother and jumped all around.

Widow Henry came over to Sarah and congratulated her. "I guess I met my match, Sarah," said the widow. "Sarah, I bet Tom will let you sell your pies at the store too. You know he's a good businessman, and having your pies for sale will surely draw more customers to the store."

Unknown to anyone, Widow Henry had intentionally changed some of the ingredients in her pies, hoping Sarah would win. She could see that Sarah needed encouragement as she struggled grieving her husband's loss. Her pride didn't want people to feel sorry for her, but as Widow Henry saw it, a little love from her community would go a long way in encouraging her.

The next day, Archie loaded the supplies into his wagon and did a few odd jobs around Widow Henry's place. After cleaning up, he walked down the street to the parsonage to see how his friend was doing.

"Hey, Seamus, how are you?" asked Archie. "Are you ready for tonight?"

The reverend was used to public speaking and private counseling but had difficulty thinking about courting. "I'll tell you something a wise man once told me, Seamus," said Archie," Just be yourself; if it's God's will, everything will be fine."

They both laughed as they recalled how nervous Archie had been the day Seamus had given him the same advice." Maggie and I will meet you at the restaurant at six thirty," said Archie as he left.

When Archie and Maggie entered the boardinghouse restaurant, they saw several people they knew. Hank was there with Doc and Doctor David Smith. James was having dinner while Lizzy was entertaining him with her stories.

Seeing Archie and Maggie, Dr. Smith rose and shook their hands. They had met briefly the day before, but talking with so many people coming up to the new doctor to introduce themselves had been challenging.

"I wish we could spend some time together; I've heard so much about both of you," said Doctor Smith. "I'm going out to our new home to finish working on it tomorrow, so it will have to wait until I return later this week," said Archie.

"Sure, I understand, Archie; I'll see you when you return. Maggie, if you would like, I would like to check your vital signs someday when you have time," said the young Doctor.

As they parted, Seamus McConnell and Aunt Carol walked into the restaurant. After the four sat down, Archie winked at his nervous friend and said they were glad they could have dinner together. Maggie always enjoyed being with Aunt Carol but could tell she, too, was a little nervous.

"Do you remember what happened a year ago?" asked Archie, trying to help start the conversation for his friend.

"I met Maggie at the picnic as she was escorting you from the boardinghouse."

"I remember, and all the children came running over to hug me," replied Carol.

"Yes, I remember that," said Seamus, "the children love you so much."

After that, the conversation became easy for both Seamus and Carol as they recalled the past year and how Maggie and Archie had fallen in love, gotten married, and now we're going to be parents.

When David Smith finished his meal, he asked Sarah if he could speak with her when she had time. Sipping on his fresh cup of coffee, he noticed Sarah seemed exhausted. She kept each room clean daily and prepared three meals daily for her guests and any town folks who came into the restaurant. It was clear to him that she needed help. Lizzy was too young to be of much assistance other than clearing off the tables when people left the restaurant.

After most of her dining guests left, she went over to talk with the new doctor, bringing a fresh pot of coffee.

"How was everything, Doctor Smith?" asked Sarah. "I hope you enjoyed your meal."

"Everything was wonderful; it couldn't have been better," said David. "You sure were busy tonight. Is it this way most evenings," asked the young doctor?"

"No, tonight was unusual; most of the time, there are five or six people, including guests," replied Sarah. "Why do you ask?"

"I noticed how tired you seemed and thought you were exhausted from working so hard," he replied.

"I'll be all right; I haven't slept very well lately," said Sarah.

"Well, I was just concerned for you, ma'am," replied David.

Changing the subject, Sarah asked how the move had gone this past weekend. Doctor Smith replied that he hadn't moved most of his things since he stayed in the boardinghouse. He left most of them at Doc's place until there was lumber for the addition to Doc's.

"I'm hoping to add on to Doc's and build a clinic where people can stay if they need to, so it will be easier for me to take care of them."

"A clinic?" responded Sarah, "Now that's a good idea. Folks around here are so spread out; it would be hard to take care of everybody if you needed to travel hours each day," said Sarah. "I'm glad you have decided to move to Clayton Doctor; you're just what we needed," said Sarah, gently smiling.

For the rest of the week, Archie and James placed boards across the roofing beams and then spread tar paper, sealing it with hot tar. After everything cooled, they put wooden shingles over the tar paper to protect it from the weather. By the week's end, both men were tired but very satisfied with everything they had accomplished.

In the late afternoons, James worked on the rocking chair, showing Archie how to make the pieces that he would assemble to finish the job. During that time, Archie saw James's deep emotion for his youngest daughter and how much he loved her.

The ride back to Clayton again seemed to take longer than usual since both of them wanted to see Maggie and get a good night's sleep. Looking at James as they approached Clayton, Archie said softly," I'll take care of her. Don't worry, I love her too."

That evening, James joined Maggie and Archie for dinner at Widow Henry's house. They shared a wonderful meal and told tales of their adventures at the cabin the last two weeks. They brought back several bushels of vegetables for Widow Henry. Looking at all the fresh food, Widow Henry suggested Archie take some of it to Sarah.

"Her restaurant could use more fresh vegetables. She has been busier than normal lately, and I am sure she will appreciate the gift."

CHAPTER 19

Monday morning, Doc, Tom, and Doctor Smith met at Doc's house to discuss Doctor Smith's ideas for adding a clinic to the property. Doc and David had seen a few folks the day he moved to Clayton for minor issues but still hadn't seen most of the people in the area.

"Gentlemen, with the population growing, there is a need to build a clinic to care for them in an isolated location to help prevent the spread of anything they may have that is contagious. Additionally, with the folks in the county spread out in so many different directions, it will be challenging to care for all of them if I have to spend most of my time traveling," said Doctor Smith.

"I agree; the population has grown much larger in the last three years. I couldn't get to everyone as soon as I liked. With a clinic, I can stay and care for the patients while Doctor Smith goes to see the sick," added Doc.

"What do you have in mind, David," asked Tom. "I would like to have six rooms for patients and two other rooms for examinations. In the back of the clinic, I would like to build a small house for me and hopefully a family someday," said Doctor Smith.

"I can convert my parlor to a reception area and keep my bedroom and kitchen for personal use. That will help keep the costs down and allow me to be close if someone needs my help during the evening. Someday, after I retire, it could be used by a second physician while he gets established," said Doc.

"That's quite a tall order," said Tom. "Perhaps we can break it down into phases while we raise the money for the project. I have to go into Charleston Wednesday; I'll check to see what can be done."

David had discussed a possible clinic with Tom when he interviewed in Clayton earlier, so Tom had already begun the process of starting the project. Howard McDougal was making preliminary drawings and was expecting to meet with Tom on Wednesday. Tom was finding it more challenging to keep the fact that he and Nancy, through their corporation, owned the property. He knew that a clinic like this would cost more money than the people in the area could afford, so funding the project would come from the owners unless some other entity wanted to participate.

"I have a friend in Charleston who may be able to get the board of General Hospital to build an annex in Clay County. It's worth a shot!" said David.

When the meeting broke up, it was decided that David would contact his friend, and Tom would see about the other details while he was in Charleston. On his way out the door, Tom turned to Doc, looking him squarely in the eye, and thanked him for helping develop the new clinic. Doc shrugged and said, "These are my friends; how could I do anything else?"

That evening, Tom and Nancy discussed what to do about the clinic and if the fact that they owned it should be made known. After talking about it for quite a long time, Nancy suggested that they create a separate company and donate the property to it; that way, other organizations and individuals could partner in building the clinic."

Upon arriving in Charleston Wednesday morning, Tom immediately went to Hoffman's to leave his wagon. While he was in town, Jim's employees would load the supplies he had ordered to construct the gazebo in the new town park. The drawings that Howard McDougal had completed had been delivered to Hoffman's earlier so that a millwork shop could make the trim and other delicate details. Most of the structure would be made from wood provided by Widow Henry's mill in Charleston since the Clayton mill was not open yet.

Leaving his wagon, Tom walked downtown to Howard's office to look at the preliminary drawings for the clinic.

"Good morning, Tom," said Howard as Tom entered his reception area, "I have your drawings spread out on my conference table."

Tom was excited to review the drawings and tell Howard what he and Doctor Smith had discussed during their meeting earlier that week.

"I've drawn a separate structure with six rooms and an office," said Howard. The building is basic but should allow for additions later if you need to expand."

Looking at the drawings, Tom could see the detail Howard had put into making them and hated to tell him they would need to be modified.

"Howard, this is great and certainly meets all my expectations; however, we decided to have six patient rooms and two examination rooms at our meeting earlier this week. Doc has also suggested we could use his parlor for a reception area and that he would live in the back of the house using the bedroom and kitchen, so we will need to build a connecting hallway from the house to the clinic. After this is completed, David wants to build a house on the back part of the property."

Picking up a notepad, Howard wrote down all the changes Tom had mentioned and then repeated them to him to be assured he had understood correctly.

"That shouldn't be too difficult to change, Tom," said Howard. The hallway from Doc's parlor to the clinic is an innovative idea. When we're done, I will talk with Doctor Smith to see what he wants for a house. It sounds like he is excited to be in Clayton and plans to stay for a long time," remarked Howard.

"Did Hoffman's get the gazebo pieces completed?" asked Howard.

"Yes, I'm picking them up today," replied Tom. "I've asked Widow Henry if she knows a carpenter who can construct it for us. She told me her foreman would send two men to build it next Monday. Nancy and I are so excited to do this for the community. We think it will allow us to have more community activities throughout the year. With the area growing so fast, we want to bring people together to enjoy themselves and build strong relationships," said Tom.

"How did you make out getting some property owners to contribute land for a park?" asked Tom.

"Well, Tom, this isn't Clayton, and property is more valuable than further out in the country, so getting them to see the vision was a little hard. I met with the city council to see if they could offer any benefits to the landowners if they contributed property. That made all the difference, and now we are having surveys done to see exactly how much of their land will be needed. We have decided to call the park Daniel Boone Park. He lived along the Kanawha River for two years, just east of Charleston. Naming it was important so that there would be no arguing between the property contributors. I am excited the community has come together on this; we need something to help bring us closer together," said Howard.

Tom left Howard's and headed for Thomas Franklin's office to discuss several matters. As Tom entered Thomas' reception area, Elizabeth greeted him and asked if he would like a cup of coffee while he waited.

"Thomas will be with you shortly; he's in a meeting," said Liz.

When Thomas' meeting concluded, three men left through the reception area. Tom looked up, and Thomas motioned for him to enter his office.

"Those were men from the coal operator's headquarters telling me that the miners were beginning to complain about working conditions and wages," explained Thomas. "I guess you were right, Tom; the miners are treated poorly. Although my client is the owner, I empathize with the miners and their families."

Tom could tell Thomas was bothered by what he knew and appeared to be holding back more than he told him.

"Client confidentiality, Tom, prevents me from telling you more than I have. Everything I told you has been in the newspaper. There's more to the story, but I can't share it for the moment," explained Thomas.

"What can I do for you, Tom?" asked Thomas.

"You always seem to have projects you and Nancy are working on." "Actually, Thomas, I have two things I need to discuss with you. I want to give the town park to Clayton, but since we are not an incorporated city, I don't know how to do it. The second project is the new clinic. As you know, Nancy and I own Doc's old house. We want to contribute that property to a new entity so that it can hopefully partner with some other entity or entities to help build the facility," explained Tom.

"I can handle the park situation working with the county, so should Clayton ever incorporate, it would be included as part of the city property. It will take a few months to accomplish, but it shouldn't be a problem. As you know, dealing with the government is always slow. As for the second project, I will need to set up a new entity with the state, complete all the necessary paperwork, and transfer the property from your corporation to the new one. This should take about a month, but there shouldn't be any problems. Who are you hoping will partner with you on the clinic?" asked Thomas.

"We're hoping that General Hospital will be interested; otherwise, we'll look at other hospitals in Charleston," answered Tom.

"Tom, I doubt General Hospital will be interested. Clayton is in a poor county, so the clinic's patients cannot pay that much for care. However, I can talk with a board member I know to see if they could give the clinic their used beds and equipment. If not, they may be able to order what you need, and since they are such large purchasers, they can get things at a much lower price than a startup clinic. I will write to you in a couple of days about it. I'm meeting with him on another issue tomorrow and will bring it up," said Thomas.

Disheartened, Tom left Thomas' office, unsure how the clinic could be financed. Walking up the street to Hoffman's, he ran into Howard, running to another late lunch. Seeing Tom, he invited him to come with him to grab a quick bite. Tom explained the dilemma the clinic faced after they had ordered. As their orders arrived, Howard asked Tom if he could say the blessing. Tom was slightly surprised since Howard had never asked him to pray before. Tom thanked God for all his blessings and the food He had provided them for lunch. As he finished his prayer, he asked for direction regarding the clinic.

"Thanks for asking me to pray, Howard. You know how important it is to me. I appreciate it," said Tom.

Howard looked at Tom and said, "You know me well enough to know that I am a believer as well, but the last couple of times we have been together, you have prayed over your meal even though we were in a public place. That impressed me, Tom; you were not timid, afraid of what others would say or think. I've been doing the same ever since, so thank you," said Howard, smiling.

During lunch, Howard suggested that if the hospitals didn't want to invest in the clinic, people could give whatever they could afford. Businesses could provide products or whatever they had to a community clinic.

"With the new park, more and more people will come into town so that you could hold fundraising events. It would be a terrific way for folks around Clayton to feel it was their clinic, not some outside business,' "said Howard. "I'll donate my fees for doing the drawings."

"Thank you, Howard, that is extremely generous," exclaimed Tom.

Tom returned to Clayton, anxious to hear from Thomas about his meeting with the hospital board member. On his way out of town, Tom picked up a newspaper to read when he got home. He liked keeping up with what was going on outside of Clayton.

When Tom rode into Clayton that early evening, he didn't unload his wagon but decided to keep it fully loaded in his outbuilding. He wanted to wait until the carpenters arrived next week, plus keeping it out of the weather would keep it dry should it rain. Hopefully, it could be built and painted within a week so the two bridges over the creek could be made the following week. The land would need to be leveled and pitched for drainage before construction could begin, so a great deal of work must be accomplished before they could start building.

The next day, Tom went to Doc's and met with Doctor Smith and Doc to let them know what he had accomplished. David said he had mailed a letter to his friend at General Hospital the day after they had met. All three of them were excited to see the final drawings for the clinic.

"Attorney Thomas Franklin will meet with a client on the board at General Hospital and write to me to let me know what he said about their possible involvement. If they aren't interested, we'll have to reach out to other people and businesses we know and raise the money for the project. Howard McDougal, the architect, has already donated his services for the clinic," said Tom.

"In the meantime, Doc and I will meet people and see what we can do for them, just like Doc has been doing for years. The new folks near Hank's place need us to stop by."

As Tom was walking back to the general store, he stopped by the boardinghouse to see if Sarah had anything for him to bring to the store. He walked into the restaurant just as Sarah covered up two of her pies and Lizzy was carrying a bag of fresh cookies.

"I'll get those for you, Sarah. Lizzy, come with me; you stay and care for your restaurant. We've got this, don't we, Lizzy?"

"Thanks, Tom," said Sarah, "I have some guests coming this afternoon."

When Tom entered the general store, Nancy grabbed one of the pies and showed Lizzy where to put the cookies.

"I've got something for you, Lizzy," said Nancy as she reached for a doll they had just put on the shelf.

"Maybe someday I can teach you how to sew a dress for her," said Nancy, smiling at little Lizzy.

"Thank you, ma'am. It's the most beautiful doll in the world," exclaimed Lizzy. As she left the store, skipping back to the restaurant, Nancy's heart was warmed. Lizzy's the little girl she never had. *I love her so much*, she thought.

Archie and James spent most of the day gathering stones for the fireplace. The roof was finished, the doors and windows had been installed, and Hank had found the perfect board for the hearth. Archie had added a small front porch and roof to protect it from the elements. The project was finished, and the two men had become more like father and son than father-in-law and son-in-law.

Gathering all the ripe vegetables they could from the field, they returned to Clayton. It had been a great two weeks!

Widow Henry greeted them at the front gate when they arrived in town. When Archie showed her all the vegetables, she couldn't believe how much food his garden produced.

"I'll take most of the beans to can and half of the tomatoes and the squash; the rest you can give to Sarah. It will go to waste before I can use it, Archie," said Widow Henry.

After unloading the food, Archie took James to the boardinghouse. The two of them brought in the vegetables for Sarah's restaurant.

"Thank you, Archie. I can use them. Let me get you some money," Sarah said.

"That won't be necessary, Mrs. Adkins; I had extra that would go to waste if you didn't use them. It's my pleasure," said Archie.

"Well, thank you, Archie, I appreciate it. Mr. Garrett, your room is ready for you," said Sarah, smiling.

Just then, Lizzy came running out yelling, "Mr. Garrett, Mr. Garrett, look at my doll. Her name is Molly. Isn't she the most beautiful doll in the world?"

James was glad to see his little friend. He picked her up in his arms and carefully looked at Molly. "She's almost as pretty as you, Lizzy," said James.

That evening at Widow Henry's, the stories about working on the house went on and on for hours as the two men laughed and laughed.

It was clear to Maggie that they had bonded during their time together. Nothing could have made her happier.

Later, Maggie informed them that she had gone to see Doctor Smith earlier that day, as he had asked, and that he had said that she was doing fine.

"He wants me to drink more water, but other than that, he said everything was fine."

As the night wore on, James realized he needed to return to the boardinghouse so he and Archie could get up early the following day to head for Charleston. Thanking Widow Henry, James walked back to the boardinghouse with a full stomach and a warm heart. He really enjoyed Archie.

CHAPTER 20

HANK MET WITH Widow Henry every evening on her porch, learning to read, and was slowly beginning to understand and had also begun spelling a few words. His excitement about this new skill was encouraging to Widow Henry. She couldn't help noticing that Hank was not only a quick learner but that he was very bright. He had mentioned several ideas about the mill she planned to incorporate in her Charleston mill. Hank had asked if he could have one assistant to help him with the truss work and moving lumber to storage shelves.

"Widow Henry, I would like to give Fred another chance. I think he could become a good carpenter someday."

"Hank, isn't that the fellow who was trouble the last time he was here? " Widow Henry asked.

Hank shook his head slowly and said, "Yes, he was a handful, but I want to see if I can help him overcome his past. Deep down, he's a good man, but life has been hard for him, and all he knows to do is fight for everything he wants. You've shown me that someone caring about you can give you confidence, not only in yourself but also in others."

"Why don't you take your wagon into town, pick up a load of lumber from the mill, and see if my foreman can help you find Fred?

That evening, as Tom and Nancy settled down, Tom picked up the newspaper he had gotten while he was in Charleston. The headline story was about coal mining safety and workers' conditions. Tom remembered reading about the history of coal mining in southern West Virginia one evening from a magazine Howard had given him. One hundred and fifty years ago, an English explorer, John Peter Salley, had discovered "great plenty of coals," as he wrote, south of Kanawha County in Boone County. His discovery later defined the future of the region.

The salt industry had been the region's first industry. Salt was used for preserving and shipping meat before refrigeration. It was produced by boiling brine found along the Kanawha River. Originally, salt manufacturers had used wood to fuel their furnaces, but when the wood supply dwindled, salt maker David Ruffner began using coal.

Ruffner's success prompted other salt makers to open small coal mines. By the mid-1800s, salt furnaces lined the Kanawha River, using narrow gauge railroads to haul coal from the nearby mountains.

The salt industry peaked just before the Civil War, and what salt works remained were destroyed by Union and Confederate troops. They left the coal mines that had just begun producing coal oil.

In the mid-1800s, indoor lamps for the wealthy in northern cities like New York, Boston, and Baltimore began using kerosene instead of animal fat, which, although burned brightly, produced a pungent odor. Steam engines also relied heavily on coal oil as a lubricant.

When distilled, coal produces oil. One of the cleanest burning types of coal is cannel coal, discovered in large quantities in Kanawha County. Charleston became a major refining center, manufacturing five thousand gallons of coal oil per day.

These coal mines from fifty years earlier and some newer mines had caused many issues. Originally, mines had been worked by slaves from Virginia and other areas from the South. Coal operators saw that investing in slave labor was costly, so they began enticing free workers to their mines. The working conditions were horrible. During the hand-loading era, an underground miner's workplace, usually called a "room," was only as high as the coal seam. "Rooms" in Kanawha County mines were usually only four feet. Boys under twelve often worked beside their fathers since this was often the only job available. Many workers died from gases in the mines, coal dust inhaled daily, or mine cave-ins.

Miners had begun to complain about working conditions and pay. The news story mentioned that coal operators had started bringing outside "help" to keep the miners working. There had been rumors of some being beaten for being what was considered "troublemakers." During an interview with local newspapers, Thomas Franklin, the attorney for the mine operators, said that operators were considering ways to improve mine safety and that the additional "help" was there to ensure non-interruption of production.

It was clear to Tom that his concerns about the area were well-founded. There was no interest in people, only profit, and while he understood that those taking financial risks should expect a return on their investment, it shouldn't come at the cost of the lives of their employees.

Hank rode into Charleston to meet with the Widow Henry's mill foreman to see if he thought Fred would be helpful and to pick up an additional load of lumber. Riding in his wagon along the streets of Charleston, he was suddenly stopped by a gang of young men, one of whom was carrying a whip. As the others watched, the whip wrapped around Hank's right arm, cutting it.

"What do you think you're doing riding around in this part of town, boy?" yelled another young man.

As two of them grabbed Hank's horse and were about to climb on the wagon, a loud yell sounded, "Stop it, I know him."

It was Fred, who had just gotten there after hearing the noise. Fred was from a different gang and knew he was taking a considerable risk, confronting a rival gang and defending a black man. When the group began to turn on Fred, a shot was fired in the air. Some of Fred's friends had followed him to see where he was running and, seeing their leader in trouble, had rushed to his defense. One of them had fired a shot in the air, getting everyone's attention.

"Leave him alone; he isn't bothering you," said Fred.

"Get out of here, now," yelled Fred's friend with the gun.

After everyone had disbursed, Hank looked at Fred and thanked him for standing up for him.

One of the men asked Fred, "Is this the guy you have been telling us about? You didn't tell me he was black."

Fred turned, looking his friend in the eye, saying, "What difference does that make? He's a good man." Another slightly older man with them asked Fred if this was the guy who had offered him a job.

After a while, Hank could tell that Fred had been talking about this guy in Clayton who had been nice to him and was trying to help him for no reason other than to give him a chance.

"Come on, sir, we'll get you out of this part of town. Where are you going?"

As Hank moved his wagon through the streets, Fred jumped on the seat with him. "Thanks, Fred; I thought I was in real trouble," said Hank.

"You were," said Fred.

When Hank got to the mill, he went inside and talked with the foreman as the crew began loading his order of lumber into the wagon.

"I want to take Fred to work with me for a while," said Hank.

When the foreman looked at Hank, he said, "I don't know what you did with him, but he has become one of my best workers. He cuts and loads orders all day without even taking a break unless I make him. I had to tell him to take today off. He only wants to work."

Just then, Hank had an idea." I want to use Fred so that I can continue teaching him about carpentry, but why don't you ask him to pick one of his friends to take his place while he's in Clayton? He seems to be the leader of this group, and if they begin to see the opportunity, maybe when Fred gets back, he can teach them what he learns from me."

"I'm not sure about that, Hank; it seems risky."

"If he doesn't do the job, I'll bring Fred back," said Hank.

"All right, but make sure Fred tells him not to mess up," said the foreman, still not confident in Hank's idea.

Fred talked with one of his friends and told him that he could work at the mill in his place for the next two weeks because Hank had vouched for him.

"Listen, this could be your chance, too. Just do everything you are told to do and stay out of trouble. Do you understand?" asked Fred.

After his friend assured him that he wouldn't let him down, Fred left with Hank.

While leaving Charleston, Hank noticed two men riding together in a wagon- Finn and Samuel. "You guys heading to Clayton? Why don't we ride together?" offered Hank.

All three men had been working for the mill since returning from Clayton, but none of them as hard nor as eagerly as Fred. As they rode along, Hank asked Fred if he was willing to learn more about carpentry.

"I will teach you everything that I know, and maybe you can show some of your friends when you return to Charleston. Who knows, maybe you could start your own carpentry business someday. I bet the mill would recommend you for jobs if you do good work," said Hank.

Fred shook his head and said, "Why are you doing this? I'm just a guy off the streets of Charleston. Why do you care what happens to me?"

"Fred, I have spent most of my life angry, hating almost everybody. After the war, I was called a free man, but nobody liked black people and treated us like we were less than human. All my friends were angry black folks who hated white people. That anger didn't go away with our new freedom; it grew. There was no work except doing what we had done before the war: picking crops or working in the mines. The pay was almost nothing, barely providing enough to eat most days. One day, this old black man saw me and stared at me for the longest time. I didn't know what he was looking at, but it bothered me. Finally, he walked over to me and reached out his hand, telling me his name. We stood there for a long time, getting to know one another, when I noticed his hand. Three fingers were missing, and when I asked him what had happened, all he would say was, hate, son, hate.

"What do you mean, hate?" Fred asked.

He went on to explain that he hated his boss-man and every other white man he saw because of the way he had been treated when he was a slave." I hate all white people, don't you ever trust them," he said, and with that, walked away.

"I thought he was right, so I just stayed out of the way as much as possible. Then, one night, I was in a bar drinking when this guy came in and started yelling at me, calling me names. I tried to ignore him, but he kept trying to start a fight. Finally, he pulled out a gun and pointed it at me, so I quickly threw my drink in his face and jumped on him. The fight didn't last long before the gun went off, and he lay on the floor dead. I was arrested and later convicted by an all-white jury. Fred, I spent ten years in jail for murder, and I only learned to hate more. I finally hired a young attorney to have my case looked at by a new judge in town. I was released from prison after it was decided that it had been self-defense—everything I owned I had to use to pay the attorney. So, there I was, free, not a penny to my name. I had spent ten years of my adult life in jail because of hate. Drinking had only made everything worse.

" I found this old farm in the woods outside Clayton that the owner said I could rent for nothing if I fixed it up. That's where I lived until a year ago, Fred. I was alone, getting old, and hating, just like the old man I had met years ago. What had hate gotten me?

"What happened?" asked Fred.

"First, I met this young white man named Archie, who had bought a little farm down the road from me. Over time, we got to know one another, and then I noticed he began to change. He started treating me like a friend. He helped me with my garden, and I helped him cut lumber for a cabin he wanted to build. One night, he saved my life when some guys tried to kill me and burn down my place. Then, he introduced me to someone he had gotten to know. Her name was Widow Henry, and after I met her, I began to understand why Archie had changed. Widow Henry cares about people. She does things for them, often without letting them know what she has done.

"As I have gotten to know her, I have started to understand why she is this way. I've never been a religious man, but I have been invited to her home with Archie and his wife to study the Bible. I have learned so much. Fred, Widow Henry tries to live every day the way God has shown her in the Bible. I know it sounds ridiculous, but it's the only explanation for how she treats everybody. She's the one who gave me the job of running her new mill, and now she's even teaching me to read.

"Once, she told me, "Hank, the good Lord told us we only have to do two things: love God more than anything or anybody and love people as much as we love ourselves. I guess that's what she is doing."

"Knowing Archie and Widow Henry has taught me that not all white people are alike. There are good white and black people, just like there are bad folk, too. We must try to care for all of them, even if we don't like them. Fred, I have decided to live the rest of my life like Widow Henry instead of that old man."

Arriving in Clayton, Fred helped unload the wagon. When they were done, Hank said he would get his bed roll, and they could stay at the mill. "Why don't you come to the boardinghouse with me after you clean up, and we can have dinner," said Hank.

CHAPTER 21

SEAMUS MCCONNELL WAS in the parsonage studying in preparation for his message Sunday when an idea came to him that he could only credit being from the Holy Spirit. Rather than spend all week in Clayton in the comfort of the parsonage, he should visit the people of Clay County and tend to their spiritual needs. Many were so poor that getting into town for worship was impossible, and others saw no need for God; they were getting by the best they could. He knew he needed to spend much time in prayer about this to be sure it was God's direction. He also knew this was something he needed to discuss with Carol. They had been having dinner two or three times a week at the boardinghouse and were enjoying getting to know one another. He looked forward to time with her more than he had ever imagined, but how could he manage their relationship and travel weekly throughout the county?

Archie and Hank went to their farms once a week to tend to their crops and bring back to Clayton what they harvested. Archie gave Widow Henry all the fresh vegetables she needed and the remainder to Sarah, even though he could have sold them to Tom. Archie had seen how hard Sarah worked at the restaurant, trying to make enough money to care for herself and Lizzy, and felt he should help her as best as he could. Hank gave most of his crops to Reverend McConnell, and whatever he didn't use was given to the needy on Sundays after church services.

That evening, Carol and Seamus had agreed to have dinner at the boardinghouse. Sarah had prepared an excellent dinner for her guests, but Seamus found eating challenging. Carol could tell something was bothering him and quietly asked what was on his mind.

"I need to share something with you, Carol," said Seamus.

As Seamus told Carol about his plans to travel during the week and only be in town on weekends, she could tell how much it troubled him.

"Carol, I feel a conflict in my heart. I love spending time with you and look forward to our dinners together, but I also know that I need to minister to the people in our community outside of Clayton."

Carol could see the deeply felt conviction in Seamus' eyes to reach out to those in need, but selfishly, she knew this would change their relationship and was saddened.

"Seamus, you are the most wonderful man I have ever known, and I have enjoyed our times together, but if you feel that strongly that God is calling you to do this, how could I stand in your way? We can have dinner together when you are in town," said Carol. "I would ask you one favor, though: when you are visiting families, would you please see if the children are being taught lessons? I believe many children live in the backwoods and are not being educated. Without schooling, how can they ever escape their poverty?"

Seamus reached out his hand to hold Carol's as he said, "Thank you for understanding, Carol."

Widow Henry had just finished helping Hank with his reading lesson when she saw Archie coming back from the general store.

"Archie, Hank is getting Fred to help him build the mill, but I think he could use another hand. Could you work with him?" asked Widow Henry. "I will pay you for your time."

"I would be glad to help, but I'm not so sure about getting paid. After all, Ma'am, you have taken care of me and Maggie all these months, and the only payment I have been able to give you are vegetables from my garden," said Archie.

"I never expected payment, Archie; I just wanted to help you two. I tell you what, you pay me two dollars a week and keep the rest. I'm sure Maggie will want a few things for your new house; this way, you can get them for her," said Widow Henry.

The following day, Seamus headed out to visit his distant neighbors. His old horse was slow but steady as he rode along the dusty roads. While riding along a small ridge, he noticed a boy fishing by a creek and rode down to say hello. Hearing the horse, the boy turned around to see what was making the noise.

He was about eight years old with bright red hair and freckles. His clothes were worn and dirty, but he was clean and outgoing.

"Hi, my name is Reverend McConnell; what's yours?" asked Seamus.

"My name is Rusty," said the little boy." What are you doing out here?"

"I'm from Clayton and came out to visit folks in the country. Where do you live, Rusty?" asked the Reverend.

"Our place is just up the holler a little bit."

Picking up his fishing pole and a stringer of four fish, he motioned for Seamus to follow him.

When they began walking along a narrow path, Seamus noticed the boy was limping and asked him if he was all right.

"I fell down the bank this morning and twisted my ankle pretty bad, but it'll be all right," said Rusty.

"Here, get on my old horse," said Seamus. When the two of them had worked their way back to the end of a hollow, Seamus saw the tiny rustic cabin that Rusty said he and his momma lived in.

"Look, Momma, I got four this time," exclaimed a proud Rusty. "This here is Reverend McConnell, Momma; he's from Clayton."

Rusty's mother looked up to see him on top of Seamus' horse and laughed at how little he looked.

"Hello, ma'am, my name is Reverend Seamus McConnell. As Rusty said, I'm from Clayton and am out meeting folks in the area," said Seamus as he looked around for Rusty's father.

"Nice to meet you, Reverend," said Rusty's mother. "My name is Mary, Mary Harless."

Mary was a thin woman in her late twenties with dark brown hair and beautiful blue eyes, though the dark circles underneath them emphasized her lack of rest and proper nutrition. The clothing she wore was tattered and stained from years of wear.

"It's a pleasure to meet you," said Seamus.

Seamus tied his horse to a tree nearby and sat on a stump to chat with Mary.

"Sure is nice here in the quiet woods, Mrs. Harless, real peaceful."

"Thank you," responded the young mother. We like it here, but honestly, with Rusty's father gone, it's all I can do to keep track of him, let alone feed him," said Mary with a forced smile.

Afraid to ask but knowing he needed to, Seamus asked, "Where is Mr. Harless?"

"He ran off with his younger brother. He used to send us money, but I haven't heard from him in almost a year. We get by eating whatever Rusty catches or what I can kill when I go hunting. We've got a little garden in the back that helps some. The winters are hard, but we get by," said Mary, trying her best to put a positive spin on their situation.

As they were talking, Mary noticed Rusty was limping badly. "What's wrong with your leg, son?"

"Fell this morning out by the creek. Twisted it pretty bad," said Rusty.

Looking closer at it, Seamus could see that it had begun to swell and was turning blue.

"You know, Ma'am, I could take him into town for the doctor to look at. It could be broken."

"I can't afford no doctor, Reverend; he'll just have to wait for the good Lord to fix it," said the embarrassed mother.

"Don't worry about the cost, Ma'am; I can take him into town and bring him back after Doctor Smith sees him," responded Seamus.

"Well, all right, if you're sure it won't cost me anything," said Mary hesitantly.

"Before I go, I would like to pray for you and Rusty if you don't mind, Ma'am," said Reverend McConnell.

"That would be nice," replied Mrs. Harless.

"Father, we ask for your blessing on this family. Please be with Mary while Rusty and I are gone. Give us safe travel. Father, thank you for bringing me to this home and these people. Amen"

After praying for the family, Seamus and Rusty headed toward Clayton. Along the way, Rusty pointed out different places where he and his mother had hunted and caught fish. Seamus asked him how long they had lived in their cabin and if he ever made his way into town.

"No, Momma doesn't like to be around other folks much. I think she is ashamed of how poor we are or something," said Rusty.

Seamus could tell the boy's ankle was beginning to hurt badly. Hoping on his horse, Seamus hurried him along so that he could get to Doctor Smith's as soon as possible.

When Seamus rode into town, Carol was leaving the general store and saw him with the little boy. Waving, she said hello but was quickly interrupted by Seamus.

"Where's Doctor Smith?"

"I just saw him over at Doc's place with Tom," said Carol.

Rushing to Doc's, Seamus helped Rusty down and carried him into his office. By now, the ankle had swollen so badly that he couldn't put any weight on it.

"What do we have here? " Doctor Smith asked in a calm voice. "Let me take a look at it. What's your name, son?"

As Rusty answered his question, Doctor Smith continued examining his ankle. "Looks like you twisted it pretty badly, Rusty."

After his examination, David Smith was sure it wasn't broken but badly sprained.

"You'll need to keep ice on it for a few days, and if you can, lay down and keep it raised a little. That should help the swelling to go down."

"But how will I be able to help Momma find food for us, doctor?" asked Rusty.

David turned to Doc and asked him to wrap the ankle and put some ice on it. He had just bought an ice box for the clinic and had ice delivered from Charleston the day before. "Reverend McConnell, may I have a word with you?" asked Doctor Smith.

"Seamus, I need to know where this boy lives; he's malnourished."

"I'll take you to his cabin, but there are a few things I must do before we go," replied Seamus.

With that, Seamus met Carol outside and, after telling her what had happened, asked her if she could go to the church and gather all the food Hank had left earlier. "I need to see Sherriff Griffith about something."

As Carol rushed to the church, Seamus saw Sheriff Griffith walking down the street.

"Sheriff, I need to talk with you for a minute," said Seamus.

"I was out meeting folks in the country and stumbled onto a Mary Harless and her son Rusty. From her explanation of her husband's disappearance, it sounds like this is Paul Harless' wife. He left her alone and ran off with his brother, and she hasn't heard from him in over a year."

"I heard Paul had a wife, but I didn't know they had children," replied the sheriff.

"They're poor, real poor. I honestly don't know how they're making it," said Seamus.

"I'll check with the Elkview sheriff to see if Paul had any money with him when he was sentenced. I think the judge can cause the land to be sold after having the attorneys get permission from Paul. I will ride to Elkview this afternoon to see if I can get things started."

Later that afternoon, Seamus and Doctor Smith started to the Harless cabin in the wagon they had borrowed from Hank. Carol asked if she could join them, saying, "I think Mrs. Harless will be more comfortable if there is a female visitor rather than two men."

Agreeing that it would make Mary more comfortable, they headed out of town. Carol had gotten two bushels of vegetables from the church and loaded them into the back of the wagon. Carol rode on the bench with Seamus; Doctor Smith sat in the back with Rusty as they headed out on the bumpy road leading to the Harless cabin. Rusty's ankle had begun feeling better, though it was still swollen and stiff.

He proudly showed Doctor Smith some of his favorite fishing holes along the way.

"What do you do in the winter, Rusty?" asked Doctor Smith, "Isn't the creek frozen?"

"Yeah, most of the time, we eat meat that Momma has killed, or there are always apples from a tree we found," said Rusty with a saddened look.

Taking the wagon was slower because the road was terrible in places, and several times, the men had to move fallen tree limbs so the wagon could pass.

Rounding the final knoll, Rusty yelled," There's my house." Seamus had also noticed it but was surprised at how excited Rusty was at being back.

When the wagon came to a stop, everyone waited for Mary Harless to welcome them before getting down. Rushing out the door, Mary ran to see Rusty, ignoring the others. Her son had never been away from her. Hugging Rusty, she looked at his ankle and asked how he felt.

"Doctor Smith said I will be fine in a few days; don't you worry, Momma," said Rusty in as mature a voice as he could muster.

Getting down from the wagon, Seamus went over to Mary to introduce Carol and Doctor Smith. "Mary, this is Doctor Smith, who has been caring for Rusty today." Looking at Carol, he said, "This is Carol McCombs."

"I'm sorry; I should have said hello when you rode up, but I was scared that my boy was hurt badly or something with all of you coming out here," Mary said.

"We understand," said Carol. "I would have thought the same thing. We just wanted to visit you to see if there was anything else we could do for you. We're neighbors, Mrs. Harless; that means something to us."

"Ma'am," said Doctor Smith," Rusty will be fine. He has a badly sprained ankle that must rest for a few days. The swelling will go down, but he will still need to keep his weight off it another week so that it can heal properly."

"We've brought you some vegetables we thought you could use," said Seamus.

"Well, I sure do appreciate it. Our crops didn't do so well this year," replied Mary.

"Mary, could I speak with you privately?" asked Seamus.

As they left the wagon, David carried Rusty into the cabin and laid him on a bed. David saw that there were two beds, and neither one of them looked very comfortable.

"Is this where you sleep, Rusty?" asked Carol.

"Yeah, me and my sisters used to sleep here," replied Rusty

"Where are your sisters now, Rusty?" asked Carol.

"They died last winter when it was so cold. Momma and I tried to keep them warm, but they got sick and died. Momma cried for days. Once it warmed up enough, we dug graves by the tree out back. It was really sad," said Rusty, trying not to cry.

When Seamus and Mary had gotten out of earshot, Seamus asked Mary if her husband was Paul Harless.

"Yes, that's my husband, and his brother is Jim. The two of them always seem to get into trouble with the law, so I never know when I will see Paul next. Paul and I never had a proper wedding," said Mary, looking down at the ground. "We just started having babies, always moving away from trouble.

"Deep down, I think he's a decent man, but he gets angry with me when he starts drinking his shine. The night he left, he beat me pretty bad and yelled at Rusty."

Seamus could tell that Mary was embarrassed and depressed about how her life had gone so far.

"Mary, Paul was caught trying to kill someone and is in prison. He had been selling moonshine and was almost caught by Sheriff Griffith in Clayton but escaped to Elkview, where he and Jim bought some land. When he learned that someone had told the sheriff what he was doing, he and Jim returned to Clayton for revenge. Only by God's grace they didn't kill the man. He had a visitor that evening that chased them away."

Mary cried as Seamus continued, "Sheriff Griffith is going to Elkview and meet with their sheriff and the county prosecutor to see if they can sell his property and get you some money. It will take a while, but hopefully, you can get enough to help."

Mary collapsed to the ground, unable to process everything she had just heard. Sobbing, she rocked back and forth uncontrollably. Carol looked out the cabin door as Doctor Smith continued talking with Rusty and saw what was happening.

"I'm going to see how Mary is," said Carol to Doctor Smith as she ran out the door. When Carol arrived, she quickly sat down next to Mary, put her arm around her, and began rocking back and forth with her as she spoke softly.

"Mary, everything will be fine. I know it's hard right now, but I know, somehow, by God's grace, everything will work out."

"What am I going to do? We barely survived last year; how can I raise Rusty proper? I've never had a job, never got an education, nobody will hire me. What am I going to do?" cried Mary.

Seamus knelt in front of the two ladies and quietly and confidently told Mary, "You are a child of a loving and caring God who will not abandon you. He has promised never to leave or forsake us, so rest, Mary, you are loved."

As he stood up, Seamus reached out his hand to Mary and helped her get up. Helping Carol as well, Seamus said, "Mary, please trust me; it will be all right."

When Mary calmed down, she began walking back to the cabin with Carol and Seamus. When they approached the cabin, Carol saw the two graves Rusty had told her and Doctor Smith about earlier. Her heart was broken for Mary. She could not imagine the grief she must have felt.

Coming out of the cabin, Doctor Smith noticed Mary had been crying. Mary went into her house to see Rusty, who also saw that she had been crying and asked, "Is everything all right, Momma?"

Looking squarely into his eyes, the frightened mother said, "Everything will be fine, honey, everything will be fine."

When Mary regained her composure, Seamus said he would return the next day to check on his new buddy's ankle. As the three of them rode away in the wagon, Carol turned and waved to Mary and said, "I'll come back too."

Mary smiled and mouthed, "Thank you."

Hank was working on the mill when Seamus brought back his wagon. "How did it go?" asked Hank.

"That family needs our help, Hank; they're in bad shape," said Seamus.

Seamus, Carol, and Doctor Smith were exhausted from the day's discovery. They decided to have dinner at the restaurant and discuss what they could do next.

"She's doing all she can, but I don't like what I see," said David earnestly.

Carol said she thought Mary was depressed before finding out about her husband. "Just the day-to-day strain of trying to do everything and not seeing an end in sight has worn her out. Seamus, we've got to find a way to help her."

Seamus sat quietly, listening to Carol and David, thinking about what they could do. "We need to pray tonight, asking God for His direction. We can try to help them, but if we follow what we are directed to do, we will be able to help them. God always shows the way, though sometimes it isn't what we think it will be. Let's meet for breakfast at eight-thirty and see where God leads us."

Sarah listened to some of their conversation while she served them their dinners but kept it to herself. She didn't want to get into another discussion about trusting God.

As the three of them were leaving the restaurant, Tom and Nancy were arriving for their weekly "date night."

"Hi folks, fancy seeing you here," said Tom.

"How's the little boy doing, David?" asked Nancy.

"His ankle will be fine, Nancy," said David. "We're all concerned about his family."

"We're going to meet here for breakfast at eight-thirty if you want to join us guys," said Seamus.

Seamus, David, Carol, and Tom met in the restaurant the following day. David started by stating the obvious problem," they need a place to stay in town. I'm new here, but the only place I can think of is the boardinghouse."

Carol spoke up and said that she had prayed about it and thought that maybe she could ask Mary to help Maggie with the little ones when school began. "She can help keep them under control while listening to what Maggie is teaching. She could learn and be helpful at the same time. I will pay her from my salary so that it won't cost the school committee any more money. Rusty needs to be in school, so if Mary is there, he may feel comfortable with the other children."

"The church collects food for people just like this, so there should be enough for them at least until winter," said Seamus.

"Nancy and I talked last night and decided that I will move into the boardinghouse, and they can move into our home with Nancy.

"Are you sure, Tom?" asked Seamus. "We don't know how long this will last. Even if they can sell Paul's property in Elkview, I don't know of any place close to town they could rent," said Seamus, concerned that Tom and Nancy were taking on considerable responsibility.

"I appreciate your concern, but God will provide. He always has," said Tom.

When Sarah had finished serving breakfast, she asked if she could say something.

"Of course, Sarah, of course," said Seamus.

"I'm sorry, but I couldn't help overhearing as you talked. If this lady helps Maggie at school, what will she do the rest of the day when school is out? You know, I am busy cleaning rooms and preparing meals all day and could use some help cleaning off tables and getting everything ready for the next day, after everyone has gone for the evening. Maybe she could work for me a few evenings a week. Lizzy helps, but there is only so much an eight-year-old can do. Maybe Lizzy can help her son with his schoolwork while she works with me."

Seamus looked at David while Sarah was talking and could see how moved he was by everyone's desire to help this stranger. He considered himself a believer but had never witnessed so many people willing to put their faith into action.

"Carol and I are heading out to see Mary later this morning; I'll let her know what we have discussed," said Seamus.

On their ride to the Harless cabin, Carol and Seamus discussed how important it was for Mary to know that her heavenly Father loved her.

"There's nothing more important for anyone than to know that God loves them," said Seamus.

"Mary needs to know that she can work and care for her family, surrounded by her new friends," added Carol.

When Carol and Seamus arrived, they saw no sign of Mary. Seamus went into the cabin to ask Rusty where his mother was but found him sleeping.

"Carol, Rusty is asleep, and there's no sign of Mary."

"You stay here," said Carol, "I'll look for her," said a worried Carol.

Running through the woods yelling for Mary, Carol imagined the worst. Mary had been overwhelmed the day before. She kept telling herself that Mary was a strong woman and would be all right, but she also knew Mary was at the end of her rope and felt hopeless.

Suddenly, Carol looked up a small hill and saw Mary holding a gun. Carol yelled as loud as she could as Mary raised the weapon.

"Stop, stop!" yelled Carol, running up the steep slope.

Just as Carol got to Mary, she fell to her knees, crying. Carol quickly took the gun from her hand and laid it beside her as she embraced Mary.

For over an hour, Carol and Mary talked. Mary had gone hunting, and the longer she looked for food, the more depressing her situation seemed. When she got to the spot where Carol found her, the hopelessness of her condition brought her to tears as she slowly raised the gun.

How can I keep living this way? Rusty will be better off with the people from Clayton.

"That's when you called from down the hill," said Mary, tears still rolling down her eyes.

"Carol, my twins died last winter. They were almost a year old, but I couldn't keep them fed enough. I needed more to eat, so my milk would be better for them. It was so cold. I couldn't keep the fire going and kill enough game to feed us. Day after day, I did everything I could. Rusty helped as much as he could, but there's only so much a little boy can do. Rusty and I slept with them to keep them warm, but it wasn't enough. I'm such a terrible mother."

Carol held Mary close and tried to comfort her while she wept.

After quite a while, Carol explained what her new friends wanted to do for her. She also explained that there were two jobs for her in town and how everyone was excited to welcome her to their community.

"You know, Mary, God loves you, and so do we," said Carol with tears streaming down her face.

As they returned to the cabin, Carol explained how everyone met and agreed to pray about her and Rusty.

"When we met for breakfast, each of us felt God had directed our thoughts to finding ways to help you. You see, Mary, God loves you; trusting is the hard part."

Mary couldn't believe what Carol said. People she had just met and others she had yet to be introduced to were willing to help her and her son.

"Why Carol, why? These folks don't know me. Why would they care about me and Rusty?"

"Mary," said Carol, "Christ told us to love our neighbors. As Christ followers, how could we turn our backs on you and Rusty and still claim to be Christians? "

"But I'm not a Christian," replied Mary.

"That doesn't matter, Mary; Christ said to love everyone, even those that reject him. He also told us to love God more than anything or anyone, so that's what we're doing; we're loving you just like Jesus told us to do!"

As the women returned to the cabin, Mary thought about what Carol had said and pondered what it would be like to love Jesus that much.

Rusty's ankle was sore but seemed to be healing. Seamus cut some firewood for the fireplace while Carol helped clean vegetables from the baskets they had brought the day before. Mary washed the one little rabbit she had managed to kill to put into the pot to make rabbit stew. As the little family settled for dinner, Seamus and Carol left, saying they would return in two days to bring them to their new home in Clayton.

When Carol looked at her new friend, she saw a smile and knew Mary would rest this evening better than she probably had in years.

CHAPTER 22

Sunday, Seamus taught from Luke 10: 27. "What does it mean to love your neighbor as yourself?" asked Seamus after reading the scriptures. To me, it's having compassion for those in need and doing something about it. In the parable, the Samaritan gave his time, belongings, and money to help a stranger. Christ told this parable to answer the Levite's question," Who is my neighbor?" The answer was clear: everyone is your neighbor, even people very different than you, even people you may not like."

After finishing his sermon, Seamus asked, "Who do you know who is so different from you that you can't imagine reaching out to in Godly love? Pray for that person, and then ask God to change your heart and teach you to love the way Christ did. Then help them when you can, in Christ's name."

Seamus had preached on this parable before, following the loving care he had received when he first came to Clayton, but this time, he wanted to challenge everyone to be more like Christ. He had seen many people in the backcountry who needed to know they were loved.

On his way out of the door from church, Hank saw Widow Henry. Walking over to her, he took her hand and thanked her for treating him like she had, saying, "God bless you, Ma'am, you have been God's example to me." Smiling as his lip quivered, Hank turned and left as tears filled his eyes.

That afternoon, Carol and Seamus enjoyed a picnic under the oak tree in front of the church. They laughed and talked away most of the afternoon. They knew their affections were growing, but neither wanted to admit it to the other or themselves. Carol loved how Seamus enjoyed his work, helping families grow in their faith, and she also noticed how he always reacted to little ones. It was easy to see how he and Rusty enjoyed one another.

Seamus, too, saw a different side of Carol than he had before. She clearly loved her schoolchildren, but her reaction to Mary, with a calming warmth that came easily, instinctively, like second nature, demonstrated her deeply felt love for the hurting. It had been her compassion that helped Mary cope with her situation. Carol was just like the Good Samaritan he had spoken of earlier.

Archie and Maggie decided to ride to their new house on Sunday afternoon. Archie wanted to show her everything that had been done since she was last there, especially the larger bedroom. Maggie had seen Doctor Smith after church service and asked him if it would be safe for her to travel to their home.

"Just take it slow, and you will be all right, Maggie," Doctor Smith warned.

Widow Henry had prepared a picnic for them to enjoy their first meal in their new home.

Buck seemed to understand that today, he was to pull the wagon slowly and steadily, occasionally looking back at Archie to see if everything was all right. The sun was hot, but the cool shade from the trees along the road kept it comfortable. Upon rounding the last bend and descending the hill toward the creek, Maggie first saw her new home.

"Archie," exclaimed Maggie, "it's beautiful!"

Maggie put her hands to her face, overjoyed by what she saw. Proudly, Archie helped Maggie down from the wagon and walked her onto their front porch. Opening the door, Maggie noticed the beautiful fireplace with an oversized mantel. The kitchen was everything she had hoped for. Archie showed her that he could put stairs up and make a loft if they needed more room.

Leading Maggie to their bedroom door, he opened it, showing her the enlarged room, complete with the rocking chair her father had made. The house was more than she had ever hoped for, and knowing that Archie had worked so hard building it made it even more special. With tears flowing down her cheeks, Maggie turned and hugged Archie, thanking him for the beautiful home he had built for them.

"It will be hard to leave Clayton, but having a beautiful house like this will make it easier," said Maggie.

Carol and Seamus walked back to the boardinghouse to have a cup of coffee and a piece of pie together. They planned on going to Mary Harless' cabin on Monday to bring her and Rusty to Clayton. Some details they discussed had to be taken care of before leaving. Most importantly, Tom and Nancy needed to let them know if they were prepared for the transition.

Since Hank was expecting lumber and a worker to arrive Monday, he let them use his wagon. Sarah was aware that Tom would be using a room in the boardinghouse and that she would need more supplies for meals since Hank told her that he would have a worker there as well as Tom's crew for dinner. It would be a busy week in Clayton, but the most important thing was helping a young, struggling family trust that everything would work out.

Saying good night, Seamus walked back to the parsonage, deep in thought about Carol. He knew that he was in love with her and wanted to tell her, but was concerned that perhaps she didn't feel as strongly for him. Praying before going to bed, he asked God for direction.

Monday morning, two wagons left from the Charleston mill carrying wood to construct the town park and the mill. On one wagon were Finn and Samuel, each tolerating the other but neither caring about anything but the work. Finding work was difficult unless you worked in the coal mines south of Charleston. The other wagon was full of lumber for the mill and was driven by Fred.

Since the last time Fred had been to Clayton, his life had changed drastically. He had been recommended for full-time work in Charleston by Hank and was proving to be a good, hard-working employee. Before leaving Charleston, his boss told him that Hank had requested him for the job.

Archie arrived at the mill just as the wagons were pulling into Clayton.

"Morning," said Archie. Reaching out his hand to Fred, Archie introduced himself.

"I guess we will be working together the next couple of weeks. Glad to meet you."

Fred nodded and mumbled, "Yeah, we've got a lot to do."

Archie and Fred began unloading the lumber as Hank went to the back of the job sight to find his pulley system so that they could raise the trusses for the roof.

Archie tried to engage Fred in conversation but was mostly unsuccessful. Fred was very focused on the work and cared little for small talk. He clearly understood that he was there to work his best to keep his job. His friends in Charleston had been giving him a hard time about working, calling him the mill "slave." Fred knew if he were to ever get out of the poverty he had grown up in, he would need to earn a living and move away from the influence of his "friends."

During their lunch break, Archie asked Fred if he had been working at the lumberyard very long.

Fred answered that he had only been there about a month.

"Do you like the work?" asked Archie.

Fred said he was glad to have a job but said little else. Hank came back and sat down with the two of them. "Are you two getting to know each other?"

"I guess," said Fred uncomfortably.

"Do you remember what I told you about how my life has changed this past year, Fred?" asked Hank. "It all started with Archie here, just being kind to me. He treated me like a neighbor; that's what I'm doing to you. Listen, I know this is strange to you. You probably think I'm up to something, that I'm going to get something out of this; I understand. Fred, you are just going to have to trust me."

Archie could see that Fred was confused and said to him, "Fred, I was a loner. I lived on my little farm, hoping to have a family someday but not knowing how that would ever happen. One day, this kind elderly lady encouraged me and told me she had someone she wanted me to meet. A few days later, she introduced me to the woman who became my wife, but more importantly, she started showing the two of us how to know God. I will never be able to thank Widow Henry enough for all she has done for me. Fred, Hank, and I are now trying to live differently. We want nothing from you, only that you trust that God has brought you into our lives for His purpose. Just trust Fred, that's all, trust."

※

Tom and Nancy had gathered a few of his things to take to the boardinghouse where he would sleep. They knew that this was the right thing to do for Mary, but they wondered what the long-term solution would be for Mary and, for that matter, other single mothers in the area.

Tom returned to the park property after taking his things to the boardinghouse. The men had unloaded the lumber they had brought and were waiting for instructions from Tom.

"We will need to clear a path along the creek for a walking trail, and after that, the land in the middle of the property needs to be leveled so that it will be easy to walk and play on. Draining it toward the creek would be best to prevent water from standing. I brought you saws and axes to clear a trail."

Samuel looked at Tom and said, "I thought we were going to build things with the wood we brought, not cut a trail."

"You will make two bridges to cross the creek, picnic tables, and a gazebo. I've marked where I want the trail to go. I know it's a lot of work, but I have been told that you two are hard workers."

Samuel and Finn grabbed Tom's tools and headed for the creek to begin cutting the walking trail.

On his way back to the general store, Tom saw Seamus hitching his horse to Hank's wagon and stopped to talk with him.

"Headed out to Mary's?" asked Tom.

"Yes, Carol and I are bringing them to town later this afternoon."

"You know, I have been reading the newspaper, and this problem of single mothers is becoming more of an issue than ever before. It used to be that they would move back home to live with their parents, but more and more, they are left to fend for themselves. Most of them lost their fathers or husbands in the war or are new to this country and have no family here. Why don't we have dinner tomorrow night at our place and talk more about it? Bring Carol," said Tom.

Seamus picked up Carol, and they began riding to the Harless cabin.

Carol looked at Seamus and said, "This is a big change for Mary; I think she will have trouble feeling comfortable. She's a poor, uneducated, abused young woman who sees the rest of the world as being better than her."

"I agree, but if I know Nancy, she will make her feel right at home. Mary will be surrounded by a love she probably has never known between the two of you. I watched how she reacted to you the other day, and without thinking about it, you comforted her, and you could see she felt safe. You could see it in her face, Carol. That's a gift."

"I just couldn't stand seeing her so sad and frightened. I don't know what I would do if it were me, Seamus, alone and with no hope. What would I do?"

As Carol was talking and showing such deep emotion for a lost stranger, without thinking, Seamus said, "You will never be alone, Carol." Reaching his hand to hold hers. They both knew they were in love.

When Rusty saw the wagon approaching, he limped to meet Seamus and Carol. Evidently, he enjoyed Seamus, but what was even more telling was that Mary came out of the cabin and headed straight for Carol, smiling.

"I've gathered what few things we have and rolled them in blankets," said Mary. "I hope that's all right."

Seamus got down from the wagon and loaded their things into the back. Carol and Mary rode on the seat. Seamus lifted Rusty onto his horse and walked alongside him as they headed to Clayton and their new life.

He knew Carol was right; it would be hard for Mary to adjust. She still had to take care of Rusty until school started, and the only work she could do was at the boardinghouse in the evenings. Walking slowly, Seamus prayed most of the way, asking for God's direction.

CHAPTER 23

THE WORK ON the mill progressed quickly. Archie and Hank had worked together on the schoolhouse and Archie's cabin, so each knew what needed to be done; however, Hank took the time to show Fred why he did each of the steps, hoping Fred would understand why things were done in a specific order.

After half of the building framework was done, Hank told Fred to take Archie's place. "Archie, you can begin building doors and laying the floor."

Fred made mistakes, but Hank patiently showed him what to do, and together, they finished the roof truss work and framed out the building.

It had been a hard week's work. Hank was happy with the progress they were making, but he knew that next week was going to be that much harder. The roof was difficult and dangerous, especially for someone who had never worked on one before.

That evening, Hank and Fred had dinner at the boardinghouse together as they had done all week, but this evening was different. Fred was more talkative than usual and kept asking Hank questions about building and carpentry. Fred was obviously proud of what he had helped build that week and wanted to know more.

Hank answered each of his questions slowly and completely. When Sarah brought out coffee and pie, Fred abruptly looked at Hank and said, "Thank you. I still don't understand why you are doing this for me, but thank you."

Finn and Samuel also had dinner at the restaurant and began talking about all they had accomplished that week at the park when Seamus and Carol arrived.

They hadn't seen each other since Monday when they had helped Mary and Rusty move into town. Sitting at a table near the window, they talked about all the people Seamus had met during his travels.

"Carol, there are so many destitute people in Clay County; it's hard to imagine. Most are honest, hardworking folks who understand only how to survive. Their children are not going to school, so I don't know how they will ever have a life different from their parents."

Carol could see Seamus' concern and understood the importance of learning, but how could they learn if no one could teach them?

"The problem is their parents were never taught, so they aren't able to teach their children any more than they know; it's a terrible, vicious cycle," said Carol.

As Seamus and Carol continued their conversation, Finn and Samuel began arguing. Seamus recognized the Irish accent and, to calm them down, got up and went over to their table.

"Excuse me, I couldn't help noticing your accent. Where are you from in Ireland?" asked Seamus.

Finn was surprised to hear someone speaking to him with an Irish accent. He looked up at Seamus and said, "A village outside Belfast."

"How long have you been in America?"

"I left home when I was eighteen and have been here for three years," replied Finn.

"You two are the work crew down at the south end of town, aren't you?" asked Seamus. "I'll come down there tomorrow and see you. Good day to you."

Returning to their table, Seamus told Carol that one of the men was from Ireland. "I haven't met many people from there in Clay County since I've been here. Most of the Irish I met before I came to Clayton worked in the coal mines if they could find work."

As dinner progressed, Seamus asked Carol how Mary and Rusty were doing. When she began to respond, he could see how concerned she was for her new friend.

"Seamus, she had never bathed in a bathtub before Nancy showed her what to do. She is a wonderful mother to Rusty but doesn't take care of herself. Nancy and I have been encouraging her gently, but as we discussed earlier, she feels everyone looks down on her. She seems to understand that we care about her but hasn't gotten comfortable around other people yet."

"It sounds like you and Nancy have your hands full. I'm sure with time she will adjust; it will just take patience," said Seamus. "She will respond to your love, Carol, and grow in confidence the longer you and Nancy are with her. You're amazing, Carol."

When dinner was finished, Seamus left for the parsonage as Carol started up the stairs for her room.

"Carol, could I speak with you before you go to bed?" asked Sarah.

"Sure, Sarah, what can I do for you?" asked Carol.

"It's none of my business, but I overheard you and Reverend McConnell talking about Mary. Maybe she needs to spend time with another single mother. You and Nancy are wonderful women, but neither of you are mothers. Being a mother takes all your energy, making it hard to think about yourself or your future. Some days, all I can do is survive. Working and being a mother is hard, Carol. When you feel it's the right time, why don't you bring her by, and she and I can get to know one another better? After all, she's going to start working here next week."

"Sarah, that's a wonderful idea. I hadn't thought about it, but you're right. I have no idea what it's like being a mother and trying to provide for my family. I'll bring her by tomorrow afternoon," said Carol. With that, Carol headed upstairs to her room but stopped and looked at Sarah, still working, cleaning her restaurant, and said, "Thank you, Sarah."

Nancy and Mary had breakfast while Rusty played outside. "I think tomorrow we should go to the general store for some new clothes for you and Rusty," Nancy said.

"I don't have any money, Nancy; I can't afford new clothes," Mary said.

"Don't worry about that, Mary; Tom and I want to help. The next time, you can pay, but this time, we want to give each of you clothes to begin your new life here in Clayton," replied Nancy.

"I've never shopped for clothes before," said Mary.

"Don't worry, Mary, we'll have a good time, you'll see."

That morning, Mary was treated like a Queen. Nancy had her try on every style of dress she had in stock until they found the ones they each thought were perfect. Rusty got new clothes for school and some play clothes. Nancy also gave each of them supplies they would need. By the time it was lunchtime, everyone was laughing and enjoying their new outfits. Looking at how happy Nancy was watching Rusty, Mary reached out and hugged her.

"Thank you, Nancy; Rusty's never had new clothes before. Thank you."

Carol came by midafternoon and was given a fashion show by both of them, showing her their new clothes. It meant a lot to them, perhaps even more to Nancy.

"Nancy, could you watch Rusty for a while?" asked Carol. "I want to introduce Mary to Sarah."

While walking down the street to the boardinghouse, Carol told Mary that Sarah was a single mother raising her daughter, Lizzy, and that she had offered her a job helping her clean the restaurant in the evenings.

"Oh, I remember," said Mary, "I wondered when I would meet her."

When Carol and Mary entered the restaurant, Hank was finishing his lunch and leaving for the mill.

"How's the mill coming, Hank?" asked Carol.

"That's just fine, Ma'am. We're getting a lot done. You'll have to stop by and see when you can," replied Hank.

After Hank was out of earshot, Mary asked, "What's a black man doing eating with white's Carol? I was taught never to trust them; you don't know what they'll do."

Carol was surprised at what Mary said and quickly responded, "Mary, we're all God's children. Hank is my brother in Christ and a good friend."

"I was never told anything like that before, Carol; I'm sorry. I didn't mean to upset you."

"I'm not upset, Mary; it's just what you were told growing up. Hank's a good man, you'll see, the longer you're in Clayton," said Carol.

When they had finished their short conversation, Sarah came out of the kitchen. Reaching out her hand, Sarah introduced herself and asked Mary if she would like to sit at one of the tables and have a cup of coffee.

While they began to get to know one another, Lizzy bounced into the room.

"Hi, my name is Elizabeth, but everyone calls me Lizzy. What's yours?" asked the excitable Lizzy."

"My name is Mary," replied Mary.

"I get to go to school next week. Maggie will be my teacher. I'm so excited. She's wonderful, and she's going to have a baby," continued Lizzy without taking a breath.

"Honey, I'm sure Mary is just as excited about school starting as you are, but could you do Mommy a favor and go in the back and finish your chores? I want to talk with Mary," said Sarah.

"Sorry, she gets a little excited sometimes," continued Sarah.

"School is starting next week?" asked Mary. Rusty had never been in a classroom and hadn't learned to read because Mary didn't know how. Mary was upset at the prospect of school learning because she couldn't help her child.

Sarah could tell something was bothering her, so she reached out and touched her forearm and said, "Being a mother is hard sometimes, isn't it?"

Mary was embarrassed and didn't know what to say. Once again, she couldn't provide her child with what he needed.

As they continued talking about the work Sarah had for Mary to do at the restaurant, Carol walked in and sat with them. It was easy to see that Mary was worried about something, but Sarah didn't want to say anything since she had just met Mary.

"Sarah has offered me a job in the evenings after dinner, helping her clean up the restaurant," said Mary.

"You'll love working with Sarah; she's wonderful," replied Carol.

After a short while, Carol and Mary left and walked to the church. Carol sat on the bench in the churchyard so that she and Mary could talk quietly.

"Mary, I know that you are going through many different situations right now and that it may seem like it's more than you can handle. I want you to know I will help; you're not alone. There are some things I cannot be as helpful with as others. Sarah is a single mother and can help you deal with those issues. As much as I care for you, I have never been blessed with children and don't completely understand what it is like. I will walk with you through everything else; you can trust me, Mary," said Carol humbly.

"Carol, I am afraid I don't know how to help Rusty with his schoolwork. I don't understand how to act around people, and I'm poor," cried Mary. "I need your help, but I don't want to stand between you and Reverend McConnell. I can see that you love each other, and I don't want to take you away from being with him," cried Mary.

Reaching out, putting her hand on Mary's hand, Carol said to Mary," You are a precious woman that God has put into my life to do what I can to help.

"I also have work for you during the day at the school. I need you to work with the little children along with Maggie. She is pregnant and won't be able to handle all the little ones in her class. You don't have to teach the children; just help her keep them in line. Rusty will be in my class."

"Carol, I've never been in a schoolhouse before; I don't know what to do," cried Mary.

"All right, come with me, Mary. We're going to school. I'll show you around so you will be more comfortable next week," said Carol.

Mary hesitated as Carol grabbed her hand and said, "Come on, Mary. I'm here with you."

When the women arrived at the schoolhouse, Carol unlocked the front door and entered the new building. She hadn't been there since it was dedicated after church one Sunday morning earlier that month.

"There are two classrooms; one I will teach in, and the other you and Maggie will work in. Maggie will be helping the children understand the alphabet and hopefully learn to count. When the children are tired in the afternoon, Maggie reads them books. It's fun to watch their little faces while they are listening to a story, imagining themselves as one of the characters. Back in the back is where they will hang their things. See, it's nothing to be afraid of, Mary, just a room full of children, and you are so good with children, you'll love it," said Carol.

Mary slowly looked around, touching a few of the desks, wondering what it would be like for her next week. "I'll try it, Carol, but only because you said I wouldn't have to teach," said Mary.

That evening, Seamus picked up Carol at the boardinghouse, and together, they walked down the street to the general store to have dinner with Tom and Nancy at their home next door. Mary and Rusty had gone to the boardinghouse to spend time with Sarah and Lizzy.

Nancy had prepared an excellent dinner for them, complete with one of Sarah's pies from the store. During dinner, Carol told everyone that Sarah had offered to help Mary, saying, "It's one thing for us to see the problem, but it's another thing to live through it. Sarah told me how hard it is to be a mother and the breadwinner for your family. It's physically and emotionally exhausting."

Nancy agreed with Carol, saying, "She and Sarah are typical young women without a husband to share life; they are both tired and overwhelmed, not to mention lonely."

Seamus noted that, in his experience, people who become overwhelmed with life's issues seldom can step out of their troubles. They can't see a future.

Tom looked at Nancy and said, "God has blessed Nancy and me with a comfortable life. We have never had children, but that doesn't mean we can't help those who do but are struggling. Nancy and I will do whatever we can to help Mary as long as she needs help."

With tears running down her face, Carol looked at Tom and Nancy and said in a hushed voice, "Bless you."

Seamus joined in, saying, "Thank you, my friend. God bless you."

Down the street, Mary was learning what needed to be done at the restaurant while Lizzy was getting to know Rusty. She taught him how to play tic-tac-toe and hide and seek outside before sunset, and then, just as the evening was ending, she asked her mother if they could have hot chocolate as a special treat.

It was a very special evening for Rusty. He had never had someone to play with, nor had he ever had hot chocolate.

Lizzy was so happy to have a new friend. She didn't have anyone to play with during the summer when school was out, and now, she and Rusty could play every day.

Mary and Sarah began to bond as they shared their love for children. When Carol and Seamus walked into the restaurant, everyone was laughing. It was clear that God was changing lives right before their eyes.

CHAPTER 24

Finn and Samuel finished clearing the path through the park along the creek. They could pull tree stumps using Tom's horse, making the pathway smooth and easy to stroll. Later that day, they began clearing the undeveloped area, removing more stumps, and grading the soil so that it would drain back to the creek.

As they worked, both realized how much they enjoyed being outside in the fresh air instead of in a big city with all the factory noise and smoke. While they continued working, they also began to enjoy one another, forgetting about any prejudices they may have had.

Stopping for lunch, Finn noticed Seamus walking down the street toward them with a bag.

"Hey guys, I thought you might enjoy a sandwich from Sarah's restaurant," said Seamus as he handed them a bag filled with bacon, lettuce, and tomato sandwiches.

"Thanks," said Samuel," I am getting tired of jerky and apples for lunch every day."

Seamus sat down to eat with them, but he asked if they minded if he gave thanks before eating.

"Sure," said Finn, "whatever you want."

Seamus prayed, thanking God for the food they were about to eat and for the opportunity to work.

When the men began eating, Seamus asked how the project was progressing. Both men started to answer, sharing that it was demanding work, but they enjoyed it.

"Finn and I are going to finish grading this afternoon, and then we can start building the bridges and picnic tables," said Samuel.

"Yeah, and when we finish that, we're going to build the gazebo and spread grass seed," said Finn.

"Wow, you two know what you're doing. I can't wait to see it all finished. Do you like doing landscaping work?" asked Seamus.

Finn looked at Samuel and said, "Yeah, it's fun taking a piece of land and helping shape it into something people will use."

"I never knew what you called what Finn and I are doing, living in the city, but, yeah, I enjoy it," said Samuel.

Seamus could see that both men had begun to see that perhaps they had a future doing this kind of work, so he asked, "What if you could find this kind of work around the county? Would you want to do it?"

"I suppose so," said Finn, "so long as we had enough help and the equipment to do the work."

"What did you and your family do back in Ireland?" asked Seamus.

"My father grew potatoes on the little piece of property we leased, and my mother did wash for a few families. We were poor, with few work opportunities, so I came to America to build a future. What I didn't know was how much Americans hated the Irish. I couldn't even apply for work at most places because I was Irish, so I decided to move further west. Most people still wouldn't hire me when I got to this area. The majority of people from Ireland end up working in the coal mines. It's a terrible life. The pay is low, and the conditions are terrible. I refused to go down a mine shaft and earn the little bit they were paying; I would rather starve," said Finn.

"Samuel, what about you?" asked Seamus, "What did you do before you came to Charleston?"

"Well, my daddy was a slave, and even though he worked hard, it was never enough. The boss man used to beat him til he bled and then laughed at him. My momma was raped by the boss man twice until she got the owner's daughter to let her work in the house. I was just a little boy, but after the war, my parents used to tell me stories. They hate white people because of the way they've been treated.

"After the war, my daddy kept doing what he had always done, only as a free man. He didn't make much money, just enough to buy what food we couldn't grow or kill. When I got older, I left, like Finn, to make a better life than the one I had. There's not much real work for black folks, either. I was loading and unloading train cars or working in the mines. My cousin was killed in one of the mine collapses last year. Maybe that's why I am enjoying this work. I get to use my hands and be outside. No one is standing over me, yelling, or pushing me. Mr. Campbell just lets us work. I like that," said Samuel.

"I'm sorry to hear that both of you have had such terrible lives. I can't imagine what it's been like for you. Most white people don't understand what it's like to be a minority in this country. Most, not all, are good people, working and taking care of their families without giving the condition of others a thought. Some, both black and white, are prejudiced, some for a reason, but most are taught to hate. I pray every night that God's people would set the example Christ gave them to love all people, even your enemies," said Seamus.

"Sorry, I didn't mean to preach. It seems obvious that a life full of hate can never be joyful, but if we put aside our differences and love each other like brothers, this world would be much better."

"Yeah, but people aren't like that," said Samuel.

"Yeah, I've never seen people think about anyone but themselves," continued Finn.

"Well, fellows, I think you are missing the obvious. Do you understand how you were picked to do this work? Do you know why?" asked Seamus.

"I know that the owner of the Charleston mill had the foreman find three guys to do some work for them and that the first job was to begin work on the mill. Hank tried to explain it to us one evening as we sat around the fire after work, but I didn't believe everything he said," said Samuel.

Getting up to leave, Seamus told Finn and Samuel that he would return Friday after visiting people in the backwoods.

Heading back to the parsonage to prepare for his journey the next day, Seamus prayed that God would open the eyes of these two men He had brought into his life.

Before leaving for the week, Seamus asked Carol if she would have dinner with him.

At around five thirty, Seamus came to the restaurant in his Sunday preaching suit, carrying flowers he had picked earlier. Carol came down the stairs and was completely surprised by the formality of the evening. When she reached the bottom of the stairs, Seamus gave her the flowers. Noticing what happened, Sarah ran to get a vase and water.

As Seamus helped Carol to her seat, Carol noticed he seemed nervous and asked him if everything was all right. Seamus reached across the table to hold Carol's hand and said, "Yes, Carol, everything is better than I ever imagined it could be.

"Carol, I have only been courting you for a short time, but I feel that I need to tell you something."

"What, Seamus, is everything all right?" asked Carol with concern.

"Carol, I am completely in love with you. I've never met anyone like you in my entire life. My only fear is if you feel the same way," said Seamus.

Gripping his hand tightly, Carol looked into Seamus' eyes and said," I have loved you since we first started courting. You are the answer to my many years of prayers, Seamus. Yes, I love you with all my heart!"

The happy couple enjoyed their meal, but years later, when they told their story, neither could tell anyone what they had eaten; they only knew that they had found the person God had always wanted them to be with, and nothing else mattered.

When Seamus left the following day, he couldn't remember ever feeling so happy. As he rode along the dusty road heading out to the backcountry, he thanked God for bringing this joy into his life.

Carol went to the schoolhouse early to prepare for Wednesday's first day of school. She dusted the desks and swept the floor to ensure the day started on a good note. Maggie came by later in the morning to see what else needed to be done. The two discussed what Carol wanted to accomplish with the split classes.

"Maggie, I want you to spend the first week making sure the children know how to behave in a classroom. Mary is going to be here to help you. By the end of the week, you should be able to start showing them a few letters from the alphabet and read them stories. Here is one of my favorite books for this age. Read whatever story you choose, but don't ask Mary to help with anything but controlling the children. Maggie, I don't think she knows how to read, and the last thing either of us wants to do is embarrass her."

Maggie understood everything Carol had said, but she also knew that Carol understood that she already knew what to do with the children. It was easy to see that Carol was very concerned for Mary.

"Carol, I want to help Mary just as much as you do; I just need to get to know her better. I think we'll get along nicely; she needs to know that I care about her," said Maggie.

"I know, Maggie, I'm sorry, I have a lot on my mind. I want everything to go well for the children and Mary. I don't know what I would do without you. Thank you for understanding my nervousness," said Carol.

"What is really bothering you, Carol?" asked Maggie. "You seem distracted."

"Maggie, I love these children, but Seamus has made me aware that many children don't attend school who live in the backcountry. What will happen to them? There are more uneducated children than I imagined. Perhaps in the past, people could get along just by being able to take care of themselves, but things are changing so fast, those days are gone, and these poor children will live a miserable life, unable to survive," cried Carol.

"Your love for other people is inspiring, Carol. Maybe you and I can devise a way to contact them and their families. Let's pray for direction and talk more about it after school Friday," said Maggie.

The first day of school was exciting for all the children, but even more so for Mary and Rusty. This was a new experience for them; going to the schoolhouse and entering their respective rooms was frightening.

Immediately, with Lizzy's help, Rusty was welcomed by his classmates. Rusty liked being around other children and getting to know them. He had never had friends to play with, so it was very exciting.

Mary helped Maggie with the little ones, assigning them a desk to sit in and holding the ones that had never been away from their parents before. Without thinking about it, Mary comforted almost all the younger children and helped them settle down for their first day of school.

Once the older children had calmed down and gotten to their desks, Carol told them she wanted to spend the week reviewing what they had learned the year before. She asked Lizzy to print the alphabet on the blackboard and one of her classmates to do some basic addition on the other end of the blackboard. When they were finished, she asked each student to spend the rest of the morning writing everything on the blackboard in their notepads.

"Your homework for this week will be to memorize everything you have written. If you have any questions, please see me after school."

Rusty tried to write everything on his notepad, but since he had never learned to write, it took him longer than the other children. Carol was concerned that Rusty would be discouraged, but at the same time, she wanted to push him to work hard.

When school was out for the day, Rusty came to Carol and showed her all that he had been able to copy.

"Rusty, I'm proud of how hard you worked today. I will help you with your writing to make it easier for you to copy the work."

In Maggie's class, the children took a while to understand that they needed to listen to their teacher and stay in their seats. Mary slowly walked around the room, touching them on the shoulder to help settle them down as Maggie began reading a story. Mary had never heard someone read a story before and was engrossed in the adventures of the little girl Maggie was reading about.

When the day was complete, Maggie thanked Mary for how wonderfully she had settled the children down and comforted those who missed their mommies.

Overall, it was a great day for everyone. Carol began to understand her students. Maggie could do what she needed to do with the younger ones, and Mary felt that she was helpful to Maggie. Perhaps more than anything, Mary was excited about learning to read, just like Maggie.

After school, Carol and Rusty sat together in her office. Carol showed Rusty how to hold his pencil and form the letters of the alphabet. Slowly, Rusty was able to copy each of the twenty-six letters. Carol praised Rusty and told him to practice making letters at home after going outside and playing with his new friend, Lizzy.

Carol was concerned that Rusty would be overwhelmed with schoolwork and not enjoy time out with his friends. Sitting still in a classroom all day was foreign to him. He had spent all his life outdoors, hunting and fishing, so going outside and playing meant more to Rusty than most children.

With the children outside playing, Mary wandered in to see Carol, despondent over her lack of education, once again feeling unable to provide for Rusty.

"Carol, I am completely lost. How can I help Rusty when I don't know how to read? I want to learn. Today was so exciting to me, listening to Maggie read a story from a book. I've never heard a story read before, and it was incredible; I could see the girl she read about and almost smell the flowers out by the pond where she played," said Mary.

Carol looked at Mary and could see fear and excitement all at once. "Mary, if you want to read, you must start at the beginning. Have Rusty show you everything I am teaching him after school, and you will be reading in no time," said Carol.

CHAPTER 25

FRIDAY, DOCTOR SMITH'S friend from Charleston arrived in Clayton for the first time since the young doctor began practicing. Jim Hunter had gotten to know David Smith while they worked at General Hospital. He was in his early thirties, tall for men of that time, and had an athletic build. Before attending medical school, he had worked on his family's farm in Kentucky, growing corn and raising dairy cattle.

Early mornings were nothing new to him. As he rode his horse into town, he noticed men working in the lumber mill and asked them where he might find Doctor Smith.

Archie looked up and said to him," You must be Jim Hunter. Doctor Smith told me you would be coming to town today. Let me take you to his clinic."

As the two men walked down the street to Doc's house, Sarah was sweeping the sidewalk in front of her boardinghouse. Archie noticed her looking at them and said good morning. Doctor Hunter nodded, gesturing good morning as Sarah waved back to the two men, smiling.

When David saw his old friend, he opened the front door and rushed out to shake his hand and welcome him to Clayton.

"You're sure here early; of course, you always were an early bird. Welcome, my friend; I'm glad you are here."

The two men enjoyed coffee as they caught up on what they had been doing the last two months.

When they finished their coffee, David asked Jim if he was ready to ride with him to visit some folks he had met this past week.

"Jim, I need your help. Reverend McConnell has taken me to several families that needed medical attention but couldn't afford to pay. These hills are full of destitute people just barely getting by."

"That's what I'm here for, David; I want to help," said Jim.

The two men were riding down a little dirt road to a small farmhouse when they saw Seamus McConnell riding his horse as fast as it could go back toward them.

" Praise God, I found you. Follow me. There's a woman in labor that's bleeding terribly," yelled Reverend McConnell.

Riding as fast as they could, the men arrived to find the young mother exhausted and weak from all the blood loss. Quickly, the two doctors moved her into position and began helping her deliver.

"David, this baby is breached. With all her blood loss, we need to do a Cesarean procedure; she's too weak to get through a normal delivery. I did one last week at the hospital," said Jim.

Quickly, David grabbed his bag and did what he could to prepare the area.

"Please bring us some boiling water and towels," yelled David to the scared husband.

David attended to the mother, giving her medication to help with the pain while Doctor Hunter prepared for the surgery. The young mother was terrified; this was her first child.

After a few minutes, the father returned to the room with hot water and some clothes. Doctor Smith grabbed them and began assisting Doctor Hunter with the delivery. Soon, the sound of a crying little girl filled the room and brought tears of complete joy to the new parents.

"David, we need to take the mother and her baby to town so that she can recover. This has been a rough delivery, and she is very weak," said

Jim. "I'll go into Charleston and get some medication for her if you don't have them."

"Seamus, can you go into town and get a wagon to transport our patients? Jim and I will stay and take care of her and the baby," asked David.

Seamus took off as fast as his old horse would go, headed for town while the two Doctors cared for the young mother and her baby. When the father returned to the room to hold his little girl, Doctor Smith told him they would take them to town for a few days to help his wife recover.

"I don't want them to leave here. I can take care of my wife," said the father defiantly.

"Sir, I know you mean well, but your wife has lost quite a bit of blood and is weak. We will nurse her back to health and bring them both back in a few days. We also need to ensure there is no infection from the surgery," said Doctor Smith.

Suddenly, David had an idea he hoped would help resolve the situation. "Sir, would you like to come with us too? You can stay at my place until everyone is healthy enough to travel."

The young man walked back and forth, unsure what to do. Then he looked at Doctor Smith and said, "I don't have any money to pay for all of this, Doc."

Putting his hand on the father's shoulder, David quietly said, "Don't worry about it; we just want to help your family."

His resistance gave way to his desire to ensure his wife was cared for, and he agreed.

Seamus rode as hard as he could, and when he tore into town, he headed straight for the general store. Rushing into the store, he saw Tom and blurted out," Can Doctor Smith use your wagon to move a patient to his place?"

Startled, Tom agreed and ran to the back to help Seamus hitch his horse to the wagon.

"Let me get you some blankets and pillows, Seamus, while you get a drink of water."

As Seamus pulled away, Tom yelled, "I'll let Doc know you're on your way to his place."

When the wagon slowly pulled up to Doc's house, Doc and Nancy came out to meet them. Nancy went directly to the frightened mother and assured her everything would be fine.

"Doctor Smith is excellent; he will take good care of you. I'll come by to be with you, too."

Seeing another woman seemed to calm her down. When she had been moved to one of the examination rooms, Nancy stayed with her while David showed the father where he could sleep. After clearing out his belongings and ensuring the father was all right, David returned to be with the mother.

"Jim, we have everything we need to care for her, but feel free to check. I brought everything I had when I moved from Charleston."

As the day turned into evening, the mother and her child slept calmly, and the father relaxed on the front porch with Doc.

"Young man, you need to get something to eat. Come with me; we'll get some dinner."

Doc took his guest down to the restaurant for dinner. It was easy to see that he was hungry as he devoured everything Sarah brought.

"When was the last time you had a meal, son," asked Doc.

"Oh, I get by on what I grow and kill," said the hungry father.

The two talked about hunting and fishing for a while, and then, before Doc had finished his dinner, he asked Sarah for three more dinners. After paying Sarah for the food, Doc walked back to his place with his new friend.

"I brought food for you three," said Doc, handing the two doctors their dinners. Nancy took the other meal and began feeding her patient.

"Thank you, Doc, we haven't eaten all day," said David.

As the week progressed, the young mother began regaining her strength. The baby had taken to her mother's breast well and ate every three hours while the father looked for something to do to help pay for all the kindness he and his family had received.

Seamus told him he would appreciate it if he would clean the church for Sunday's service, a job that needed to be done badly since he hadn't been able to do it since beginning to travel during the week.

At the end of the week, Seamus gave them all the food Hank had brought from his farm. Doctor Smith once again borrowed Tom's wagon and, along with Nancy, took the new family back to their home. Nancy sat in the wagon with mother and child as the men rode together in the front of the wagon. Nancy assured her that she or Carol would come by every day to check in on her.

After delivering the young family to their home, Nancy and David slowly rode back to Clayton. It had been a trying week. Carol and Nancy had alternated filling in as nurses after completing their day's work. David was acutely aware of the lack of supplies and beds, and Tom saw clearly that the time had come to begin construction of the clinic. He had hoped to use lumber supplied by the Clayton mill but saw that perhaps he needed to start the project earlier. This was something he and Nancy would need to fund. What little the local folks had given wouldn't go far, but it was all they could afford.

Doctor Smith wrote Doctor Hunter and asked him if he could bring much-needed supplies the next time he came to Clayton. David knew that he would need to pay for most of them with his own money since he hadn't been in the area long enough to have saved any money from services he had been able to collect for.

The next day, Seamus taught about "being the hands and feet of Christ" in the community. As he talked, he noticed Sarah slip into the back of the church, bringing Mary.

"As believers in Christ, we are told not to judge others but to love everyone, just like Christ did. After being beaten to the point that he was hardly recognizable and stripped and nailed to a cross to die, Christ asked his Father to forgive the people who had done these horrific things to him. If we are to love like Christ, we must live lives reflecting that deep brotherly love for everyone we are blessed to meet." The words were stronger than Reverend McConnel usually used in his messages, but he sensed God's prompting that someone in his audience needed to hear what was said.

As the congregation sang the closing hymn, Sarah and Mary slipped out of the church. After the service, most people mingled in the churchyard as usual. Seamus whispered to Carol that he wanted to have lunch at the restaurant later that day.

Widow Henry thanked the Reverend for his message: " I see God working in your life, Seamus. He is using you as an instrument of healing."

After everyone had left, Carol and Seamus straightened up the church and walked to the restaurant for lunch. They saw David talking to Tom and Nancy as they entered and stopped to say hello.

"David, you had quite a week. I hope we didn't scare Doctor Hunter off," said Seamus.

"No, he told me he had never seen so many people jump in to help someone they had never met. He loves it here and can't wait to return in two weeks."

Seamus helped Carol to her seat, and as they waited for their lunch, he asked her how school was going.

"The children are wonderful. Most are well-behaved and are learning, but no one is as eager to learn as Rusty. For someone who has never been in school, he is obviously way behind the other children, but instead of allowing that to upset him, he has come by my office every day learning to read and asking for more work to do each evening. I'm afraid he might put too much pressure on himself to catch up, but his attitude is great."

"Maybe I should take him up on his offer to go fishing this afternoon," said Seamus. "We can have dinner when I get back. Besides, you could use the rest after the hard week you had teaching and then spending the nights at Doc's with the new mother," said Seamus.

"How do you do that? " Carol asked. "I'm about to fall asleep sitting here. That's a great idea."

Sarah brought lunch to their table, looked at Seamus, and said, "Thank you for today; I needed to hear that. " Then she turned quickly and walked away.

When Carol had finished her lunch, Seamus escorted her up the stairs to her room. "I'll see you this evening," she said, smiling.

Seamus went back to his table to finish his coffee, and as he sat, Sarah walked over to him and asked if he minded if she had a seat.

"Of course, Sarah," replied Seamus.

"Reverend, I need to talk to you when you have time," said Sarah humbly.

"Now's as good a time as any if you're not too busy," said Seamus.

"As you know, I haven't been to church for a while, and like I said, today I appreciated what you said, but I have a question," said Sarah, biting her lip slightly.

"I have been angry with God since Charles died. Everybody did all they could to save him, but God let him die, leaving me alone with Lizzy. Life is hard, Reverend, and I can't understand why He let this happen."

Seamus knew that sometimes explaining why God does what He does is impossible. We only know that He is good and that His actions are always right.

"God has promised never to leave or forsake us, so even though it seems He has turned His back on our lives, we must trust that whatever He does is for good."

Sarah began to cry as Seamus spoke to her, so Seamus got up and took her by the arm to the back of the restaurant, away from the few people still eating.

"Sarah, do you believe in heaven? Do you think it is a better place than we can possibly imagine? Sarah, do you believe Charles is with the Lord in heaven right now? Then, if you believe that, you know Charles isn't suffering but living in Christ's presence. The hard part, Sarah, is letting him go. God is with him now; you will be there with him someday.

"I know it hurts. I can't imagine life without Carol, but you must trust that your hurt is for a reason.

"Your love for Charles was a gift, and your hurt is evidence of it. Imagine life if you had never known love, true love. Do you see how it was a gift? Charles, I am told, was very sick and suffering, but now there is no pain, only complete joy.

"You must share with Lizzy what real love is and help her see that even though you miss Charles, you have complete confidence that you will be together again when God takes you home. I know you are still hurting, Sarah, but trust in the One who gave you love and life and Lizzy to give you the strength to grow by faith through this tough time. I will always be here for you to talk with, as will Carol. Sarah, you must believe."

"I know, Reverend, it's just so hard sometimes. Thank you for talking with me; you're a good man," said Sarah as she wiped the tears from her eyes. "I have been blessed, and I still am."

As Seamus left the restaurant for the Campbell's house, he thanked God for helping him speak to Sarah. "Please, Father, watch over her," prayed Seamus walking up the street.

"Where's Rusty?" asked Seamus. "I want to go fishing," said Seamus loud enough for Rusty to hear.

Rusty was playing with Lizzy and turned with a huge smile and said, "Now? This afternoon?"

Rusty ran to tell his mother he was going fishing with Reverend McConnell while Seamus asked Tom if he had any fishing poles he could use.

"Sure, there's some in the back, next to the stable."

Seamus grabbed two poles after putting a saddle on his horse. When Rusty returned, Seamus put him on the horse and walked alongside, carrying the fishing poles.

"Where to Rusty, I'm ready for some fish," exclaimed Seamus.

That afternoon, Rusty and Seamus caught five trout in Rusty's favorite hole. On their way back into town, Rusty beamed with joy. He had missed fishing and being outdoors.

Today was "his favorite day ever!"

CHAPTER 26

Friday afternoon, as Seamus rode into town after spending the week visiting people around the county, he noticed that the mill was almost complete. He could hear Hank and Fred talking while Archie was carrying planks to the back of the building. The park looked good as well. Samuel and Finn had been working hard all week. The gazebo was finished, and he could see them building picnic tables. The schoolchildren were playing outside, and the aroma of dinner from the boardinghouse restaurant filled the air.

Seamus thought how grateful he was to live in this beautiful community.

After caring for his horse, Seamus walked to the schoolhouse to see Carol. He had missed her very much and couldn't wait to be with her. When he entered the room, she was sitting with Rusty, teaching him to read. Rusty turned to see who was there, and to everyone's surprise, he got up and ran to Seamus, hugging him.

With Rusty in his arms, Seamus smiled at Carol and asked, "How's my fishing buddy?"

Carol took the opportunity to brag about how well Rusty was doing with his schoolwork. "I don't think I have ever had a student that has worked as hard as Rusty. He's learning so much. I'm really proud of him."

Rusty thanked Miss Carol for helping him and saying such nice things about him and then left to go out with the other children.

"He is doing wonderfully. He's a very smart boy, Seamus," said Carol.

With no one in the room, Seamus and Carol hugged, and as they held each other, Carol said how glad she was that he was back.

"I've missed you so much. I know you were only gone four days, but I still missed you like you had been gone for months."

"I've missed you too, but if we are going to have more time together, I need to get back and prepare for Sunday. Why don't we have dinner this evening? See you around five thirty," asked Seamus, embarrassed about his appearance.

On his way to the parsonage, Seamus saw Tom walking down the street with Widow Henry.

"Good afternoon," said Seamus, "what a beautiful day."

Widow Henry looked at Tom and said, "Someone is in an awfully good mood. Good to see you, Reverend."

Everyone in town could see how much Carol and the young Reverend loved one another, and it was good to see. Both of them had lived lonely lives until recently.

Seamus asked them where they were headed, and Tom replied that he wanted to escort Widow Henry to the sawmill so that she could inspect the completed facility.

"I thought we would look at the new park while we were at it. Would you like to join us, Seamus?" asked Tom.

"Actually, I had other plans, but I had told Samuel and Finn I would come by and see them on Friday, so this works out perfectly," said Seamus.

Arriving at the sawmill, Widow Henry looked all around, checking the roof and the storage yard along with the saws that had been installed. It was evident by the look on her face that she was delighted, saying to the three men, "You have done a wonderful job. Your workmanship and attention to detail are obvious. Hank, you have exceeded my expectations."

Hank quickly said, "Ma'am, this was a group effort. Archie and Fred did most of the work."

"Well, Fred, Hank has told me quite a lot about you and how proud of you he is, and now I can see why. Do you enjoy carpentry work, Fred? It certainly looks like you take pride in doing excellent work."

"Well, Ma'am, I have never done anything like this, but Hank here taught me these last two weeks, and yeah, I do like doing it," said Fred proudly.

"What do you plan on doing with this newly learned skill, Fred," asked Widow Henry.

"I don't know, Ma'am; I guess I would like to learn more and maybe become a carpenter," replied Fred.

"Well, why don't you then," said Widow Henry.

Tom looked at Widow Henry and then turned toward Fred and said, "We need carpenters to build a clinic here in town, and I think you and Archie would be perfect. Hank, I want all the lumber to come from this mill. Do you think you can fill the order?"

"Yes, sir," said Hank, smiling ear to ear.

After conversing with the three men, Tom escorted Widow Henry to the new town park. As they approached, Samuel and Finn were finishing another picnic table.

"Good afternoon, fellows; I would like to introduce you to Widow Henry," said Tom.

Seamus spoke up, reminding them that he had promised them that he would be back today. "The last time we talked, you told me that you had never known anyone that really cared about anybody other than themselves and maybe their family. Is that correct, guys?" asked Seamus.

"Widow Henry is the person who cared enough to give you a job and help you learn a trade. She wanted to help you, so she had her foreman find three young men who needed a chance. This job has been that chance, and I have to say, it looks great to me."

Finn thanked Widow Henry for the work, and as he started to tell her how much he liked what they were doing, Samuel interrupted, saying, "I have never trusted white folk, never. Tom here seemed like a good man, and I have enjoyed the work, but Ma'am, you actually looked for a black man to help?"

"Yes, Samuel, I asked my foreman to find men from different backgrounds who needed a chance. I didn't care what color they were; I just wanted to give whomever he sent an opportunity to succeed."

Bowing his head, Samuel slowly reached out his hand to shake Widow Henry's, saying simply, "Thank you, Ma'am, thank you."

"How do you feel about your work?" asked Tom.

Finn and Samuel quickly started saying how much they enjoyed landscaping work, and then, to everyone's surprise, they both began telling Tom what else needed to be done.

"I noticed all the children playing after church Sunday and after school during the week. They need something to play on. Back in Charleston, I saw a playground with teeter-totters and swings," said Finn. "Samuel and I could build them, and maybe when we're finished, we can paint everything."

Tom laughed, saying, "Of course, build a playground and paint everything. I'll bring the paint over in the morning."

"Widow Henry," asked Samuel, "what makes you the way you are? Sure, wish there were more folks like you."

"Samuel, God has blessed me with money and, more importantly, His grace. All I do is try to live my life showing everyone that same kind of love."

When Tom and Widow Henry left, Samuel looked at Finn and said, "She's special."

Finn agreed and added, "Our lives will never be the same, friend."

That evening at dinner, Seamus told Carol about what had happened that afternoon.

"It's so good to see how Widow Henry lives her faith and how that affects everyone around her. Those three men now have an opportunity to make a good living and provide for their families someday, all because the Widow takes her faith seriously."

"I see the same in you, Seamus," said Carol. "You leave the comforts of Clayton to visit the lost and lonely people in Clay County, sleeping in a tent and eating dried meat and apples. You may not have the money to help others, but you give of yourself."

Seamus humbly thanked Carol and then changed the subject. He had never been comfortable with compliments.

"I stopped by to see that young family today, and everybody is doing well. The little girl is gaining weight, and they named her Nancy, after Nancy Campbell. They kept going on and on about how Nancy would come out to see them every day or so, and then on weekends when school was out, you came to see them. They are so appreciative and a little overwhelmed by all the care they received. I think they are planning to come into town Saturday to see Doctor Smith," added Seamus.

Hank, Archie, and Fred continued working on the mill until it was finished. They had worked six days a week for two weeks, and when everything was complete, Hank said, "Guys, let me treat you two to dinner this evening. I'm so proud of the work you have done. We should celebrate tonight."

"Thank you, Hank, but I miss Maggie and would like to spend the evening with her. Thank you for the invitation."

Samuel and Finn continued building the playground, and with the paint Tom supplied, they painted the gazebo, the bridges, and all eight picnic tables. The park looked great, but as they were wrapping up, Tom came by with a drawing of an arched entrance.

"I'm having Hank cut the lumber now, so you should be able to do it Saturday," said Tom.

Fred had never celebrated anything without drinking but wasn't drawn to do that this time. He and Hank ate a huge dinner and drank coffee until late evening.

"I can't believe how everything has changed in my life this last month and a half. I'm looking forward to what comes next. Building the clinic for Doctor Smith will be challenging, but I think I can do it, especially working with Archie. You were right, Hank; life is much better when you're not full of hate."

"All of this happened to you and, for that matter, me because of a simple act of love from a little old white lady who understands that all of us need hope and brotherly love," said Hank reflectively.

"She certainly has changed how I look at everything," replied Fred.

"Love is a powerful weapon," said Hank as the two men left the restaurant.

The following day, Samuel and Finn stopped by the sawmill to get the lumber Tom had mentioned. Both measured where Tom had told them to put the arch and began digging holes for the posts that would hold it. Around ten o'clock, the posts were securely positioned. Finn and Samuel climbed up on separate ladders to hold the arch in place, realizing they needed a third hand to attach it to the posts. Samuel ran up to the mill to see if Fred could help.

"Fred, can you come down to the park? We need your help?"

"Sure, I'm just cleaning up," replied Fred.

When the two men arrived, Fred stopped at the new park. "Wow, you guys did an amazing job. This is great!"

With Fred's help, Samuel and Finn erected the arch.

After Fred left, they both climbed up their ladders and painted the entry arch to Clayton Park.

Later that day, when Tom came by, he couldn't believe what a professional job they had done.

"Thank you, guys, you have worked so hard to make this park special for the people of Clayton. I'm sure the entire town will feel the same way. I want both of you to come to the grand opening on Sunday. You could join me and my wife, Nancy, if you want, at church. We would be proud to have you."

Both men fumbled around with what to say. Finn thanked Tom for the invitation but said he didn't have any church clothes, and Samuel said while shaking his head, "Black folk like me can come to your church? Are you sure?"

Tom approached Samuel and, putting his hand on his shoulder, said, "I am sorry, Samuel if you have ever felt unwelcome in a Christ-believing house of worship, which is not what Christ would have ever wanted. I understand if you are uncomfortable, but in this town, in our church, all people are welcome."

"If you say it's all right, then I will be there, but I have to warn you: I don't have anything else to wear but the clothes on my back," Samuel replied with a smile.

Later that day, after visiting Doctor Smith, the young couple and their little girl walked across the street to the general store to see Nancy. When the door opened, Nancy saw them walk in and immediately ran from behind the counter to see the baby. When Nancy had the baby in her arms, the father told her they had named it after her.

"We couldn't think of anyone more loving and caring than you have been to us, and so we wanted our little girl to always know about you."

When Tom arrived from talking with Reverend McConnell, Nancy showed him the little girl. He had never seen her so happy. Not knowing, Tom asked, "What's her name?"

"Nancy, Tom, they named her after me," said Nancy.

When they started to leave, Tom asked them if he could give them a ride in his wagon.

"Tom, can you stay and watch the store instead? I want to take them home one more time," asked Nancy.

When Nancy returned a few hours later, she was moved by the experience of helping this young couple and their little daughter. As they went from the store to their house, Nancy said, "This has changed my life, Tom."

Sunday morning, Tom and Nancy arrived at church and, seeing Samuel, reached out their hands to welcome him as they entered the front door. Hank was there, and for the first time in his life, Fred came to church services with his new friend. Sarah arrived early and brought Lizzy and her new friend, Mary, along with Rusty. Archie and Maggie came with Widow Henry while David Smith sat beside Carol.

When Reverend McConnell began speaking, his new Irish mate snuck in the back.

"Today, we want to consider all that we have to be thankful for. It has been an exciting couple of weeks for our little community. A baby was born and cared for by several of you. The new sawmill is finished and now open for business, and thanks to Tom and Nancy Campbell, we have a new town park to enjoy. We will have the grand opening following our service today.

"While all these changes are tremendous, what we have most to be thankful for is God's grace. It is His grace that has changed every one of us, and it is grace that will continue growing us to live lives that reflect God's love.

"Last week, I asked you to reach out to someone in brotherly love, regardless of whether you liked them or even knew them. I see several new faces in our congregation this morning, and in each case, it is because someone loved someone they didn't know in the name of Christ. This, my friends, is our purpose."

When Seamus finished his message, people began to leave the church. Many new folks could be seen talking with their "caregivers," shaking hands and hugging. Clayton had always been a loving community, but as new people came to the area, that love was reaching out and changing lives.

After the service, most people walked down the street to the new park. Tom and Nancy had brought several of Sarah's pies, cookies, and cold water for everyone to enjoy. Standing in front of the crowd, Tom welcomed everyone to Clayton Park, and as everyone cheered, Tom raised his hands and gestured that he wanted to say something.

"The park has been given to the community of Clayton for all to enjoy. Nancy and I hope everyone here will have many wonderful times here. I also want to thank Samuel and Finn for the amazing work they did to build our park."

After the applause died down, Tom continued. There's something else that needs to be done. I have spoken to everyone who lives in town except for one person, and everybody has agreed that the name of the street leading to Clayton Park should be changed. There's not a person here who has not been affected in some way by Widow Henry, and so with great joy, we, the people of Clayton, have agreed to change the name of Main Street to Henry Way."

Everyone cheered louder than anyone could ever remember hearing in Clayton as Widow Henry approached the front between Nancy and Tom.

"Thank you all so much for this honor. All that I may have done has been my way of honoring God, who loves me far more than I deserve. I pray this community becomes a beacon of light in a dark world. Thank you," said Widow Henry humbly.

For the remainder of the afternoon, children played in the playground, and couples walked along the path enjoying the creek. Standing off to the side were Samuel and Finn, both proud of what they had accomplished. Turning to Finn, Samuel asked, "Finn, would you like to work together on other projects?"

Finn replied quickly, "Yeah, I sure would."

CHAPTER 27

DOCTOR HUNTER STOPPED by General Hospital after completing his rounds on Friday to get the supplies Doctor Smith had ordered and to pick up some much-needed equipment. He had borrowed a wagon from his new friend Jim Hoffman.

The two had met one afternoon when Mrs. Hoffman came by for a checkup. It was supposed to be a regular checkup, but after talking with her, Doctor Hunter told her that her fatigue and upset stomach were due to her pregnancy. It was a day the Hoffmans would never forget. They had wanted children but had been unable to get pregnant.

Doctor Hunter told them he would see them again in two weeks and casually mentioned that he was going to Clayton to help at their new clinic this coming weekend. Jim Hoffman quickly said that he had some supplies that Tom Campbell had ordered for the fall picnic and that Jim could borrow his wagon. Doctor Hunter was pleased to use the wagon because it would allow him to bring the equipment the hospital was donating to the clinic.

Saturday, the sky was blue, and the air was fresh as it often is in the fall. It was Jim Hunter's favorite time of year, and with a wagon full of equipment and supplies, he enjoyed the slower travel. Working in the hospital was very fast-paced, and by the end of the week, he was ready for a break.

As Jim rode by the Elk River, he saw a group of boys fishing along the bank and immediately remembered when he was young. He and his father would go fishing together when the work on the farm was finished for the day. When he was older, he hunted deer with his father and sometimes his uncles. Those were special memories that he hoped to someday share with a son of his own. For now, however, he had to get to Clayton; there were people to help.

When he arrived in Clayton, Jim went to the general store to bring Tom his order and, while unloading, noticed Sarah carrying a load of pies. Quickly, he ran over to her to help her with the awkward load.

Sarah nervously handed him two pies and a bag full of cookies.

"Thank you, Doctor Hunter; I needed a little help," said Sarah.

"Glad I was here to help," replied Jim.

David Smith was happy to see his friend and surprised to know that he had been able to bring some equipment along with the supplies.

"Jim, I'm so glad you could be here this weekend. I've been visiting people around the countryside and noticed many hungry people needing medical help."

Jim could see David's sincerity, and knowing that people were in serious need bothered him.

"Let's go, David, that's why I came," said Jim, smiling.

David told Jim about the clinic construction on their way to the backcountry.

"Tom's friend, Howard McDougal, is the architect he has used to do the renderings. I understand he will come to town later today to review everything with the construction crew."

"With winter just around the corner, how much do you think they will be able to finish?" asked Jim.

"It's my understanding that they are going to do all of the foundation work now so that they are ready as soon as warmer weather returns in the spring," replied David.

Jim could see the excitement on David's face as he continued telling him about the future clinic. As a doctor, Jim easily saw the need for the clinic, but another need was more significant. The people he had met the last time he was in the area were lost. The world was changing very quickly. Many had immigrated from Europe in hopes of finding a better life but had failed to see the changes that were overtaking everyone, regardless of where on the globe they lived.

The economy was expanding, and people needed to learn new skills. It seemed to him that education had never been as crucial to the survival of people as it was now. Jim's education ideas were displayed when the two doctors rode up to a small cabin in the woods. Doctor Smith introduced himself and his companion and asked if the family minded if they asked them a few questions. As was usually the case, they were hesitant to talk, but as Doctor Smith assured them they were there to help them if needed, they began to relax.

Many of the people they met used old treatments of salves made from berries and roots. Others applied leaves to wounds, claiming that this was how their parents had always taken care of any ailments. The two doctors slowly and carefully began to introduce medicines. In this case, the little boy had cut his leg climbing a tree, and the wound had become infected. Doctor Smith treated the wound and covered it with a bandage.

"Apply this cream to it every day for a week, and it should heal just fine," said Doctor Smith.

As they left, the family thanked the doctors for helping them.

"Whenever you need help, please come into town and see me," said David.

The doctors treated several people for anything from rashes to broken bones for the remainder of the day. It was clear that Jim's belief was correct. People didn't know what to do and feared strangers, let alone the cost of good medical care.

After the long day, Jim and David went to the boardinghouse for dinner. As they sat at a table near the window, Jim noticed Sarah serving someone across the room.

"Who is she?" asked Jim.

"Oh, that's Sarah Adkins. She owns the boardinghouse and this restaurant," replied David.

"I noticed her the first time I came to Clayton, and then this morning, I helped her deliver pies to the general store."

"I understand she's had it pretty rough the last few years. Her husband died after being ill for some time. She's running the boardinghouse and the restaurant and raising her daughter, Lizzy," said David.

Just then, Lizzy came into the restaurant excited to see Doctor Smith. Lizzy ran over to their table and introduced herself. After telling Doctor Smith all about school and her new friends in her usual non-stop way, she left and began clearing dishes for her mother.

When Sarah came by their table, she shyly said hello to Doctor Hunter.

"It's good to see you again. Thank you again for helping me this morning. You came just in time; I was about to drop one of the pies. I guess I tried to carry too many."

"It was entirely my pleasure, ma'am," said Jim.

"Oh, please call me Sarah," said Sarah, hoping she hadn't been too forward.

"Thank you, and you can call me Jim," replied the young doctor.

"Jim comes to Clayton every two weeks to help me see patients living in the countryside," said David.

"It's a pleasure to meet you formally," said Sarah, "What can I get you two for dinner?"

As the two enjoyed dinner, David noticed Jim occasionally looking at Sarah. "She's a special woman. She works long, hard hours every day to ensure she provides a good home for her daughter," said David.

"Yes, I can see that she's special," replied Jim.

As they finished dinner, Tom and Nancy walked into the restaurant with their friend, Howard McDougal. Howard hadn't been to Clayton in a while, and as they sat at their table, he was telling Nancy how much everything had changed.

"Tom took me by the park earlier this afternoon. It's beautiful! I hope I can get our committee to use the men you used to build some of the new park in Charleston," said Howard.

David guessed that the Campbell's guest must be the architect and walked over to introduce himself.

"It's a pleasure to meet you, Doctor Smith; I've heard many good things about you from the Campbells. Perhaps you could join us tomorrow afternoon to review the plans," said Howard.

"I wouldn't miss it for the world. I'll see you then," said David, excusing himself and returning to his friend.

That evening, as the two friends enjoyed a piece of pie, they discussed the need for education for the folks they had met and others like them.

"I don't know how to address the problem short of having a school built closer to where they live," said David.

"I remember when I was in school, my mother would sit me down at the kitchen table after school while she made dinner and make sure I did my schoolwork. When my father returned from the fields, he would go over everything with me and make sure I understood what I had been working on that day," continued Jim.

"My parents did the same thing for me."

"So, just as big a problem is adult education. It helps the parents find better-paying jobs and help their children with schoolwork," said Jim.

While the two men were talking, Mary overheard their conversation. At first, her reaction was to realize that she had failed to support her son's learning adequately, but she quickly began to understand that the problem was cultural. There were many people like her, and she wondered if she could be part of a solution for the first time in her life. Until then, the only concern she had ever had was ensuring her children were well-fed and had a home where they felt safe, never having the time or energy to consider others in the same situation.

Sunday was a beautiful fall day with a hint of frost on the ground, followed by bright sun and clear skies. Reverend McConnell's sermon was intense and seemed to awaken everyone in attendance. Everyone had a role to play in sharing what they knew about their heavenly Father's love for all mankind. After service, the Campbells, Doctor Smith, and Howard McDougal went to Doc's place, where they met Archie and Fred.

Together, they all reviewed the plans for the clinic and established a timeline for the project.

While they were meeting, Mary and Rusty saw Sarah and Lizzy. As the children played outside, Sarah and Mary began preparing the food to be served later that day. When the work was completed and everything was ready, Mary asked if Sarah minded if she went to see Carol for a few minutes. Sarah encouraged her to go and continued putting together pies to be baked.

Carol was in her room getting ready to meet Seamus when she heard a knock on her door.

"Good afternoon, Mary, it's good to see you."

"May I come in for a minute? I won't take very long," said Mary.

"You take as long as you want, my friend," replied Carol.

As Mary tried to put the right words together, Carol looked her in the eyes and said, "I am here for you, Mary; just say whatever is on your mind."

"Well, I heard the doctors discussing how country folks need education. They're just like me, so I thought maybe I could help. I know a lot of the folks out in the country. We used to trade for food and things so I could talk with them and teach them what I'm learning."

Carol slowly sat down on the edge of her bed. The need for education had bothered her ever since Seamus started telling her about what he discovered during his travels.

"Mary, I think that is a wonderful idea. I've been praying about the problem since I first met you. Reverend McConnell has told me about many people he has met in the countryside. My heart for them has caused me to pray daily about what I can do to help them. Mary, you are an answer to those prayers," said Carol with deep emotion.

"Let's talk with Reverend McConnell when he gets back in town next Friday; in the meantime, you and I can devise a plan. Thank you, Mary; you have no idea what impact you have had on me," said Carol as they left the room.

Carol and Seamus met and took a walk in the park that afternoon. They wanted to spend as much time together as possible before Seamus left. Carol shared with Seamus her conversation with Mary and that, for some time, she had wanted to teach missionally, much like Seamus was doing.

"My heart was changed the first time you took me with you, and I saw the condition so many people live in. I don't know how I can teach and be somewhere else simultaneously," said Carol.

"Our situations are different since I preach on Sunday and you teach all week, but there is a solution. Rather than following our plan, let's agree to pray about it this week and see where God directs us," said Seamus.

Both Carol and Seamus could feel that their relationship was deepening and that, without saying so, they were making long-term plans as a couple. Holding hands and walking back to the boardinghouse, Seamus knew the time had come for him to ask Carol to be his life partner.

Turning to face Carol, Seamus asked her if they could go to Charleston next Saturday for a treat.

"Let's have an adventure and go to the big city for the day," said Seamus, unable to hide his excitement.

"I haven't been to Charleston in a long time. Why do you want to go?" asked Carol.

At that moment, Seamus knew that now was the moment he had hoped for the last few months.

"Will you come to the church with me, Carol?" asked Seamus.

Walking across the street to the bench in front of the church, Seamus sat down with Carol and, looking her in the eyes, got down on his knee and said, "I've never known anyone like you, Carol. I've never felt so much in love. You have been in my thoughts and prayers ever since our first date. Carol, I love you, will you marry me" asked Seamus as tears ran down his cheek.

"Yes, yes, I'll marry you," Carol said loudly.

At that moment, they both heard cheering from down the street. Tom and Nancy were walking to the restaurant with Mary and Rusty for a special dinner. When they heard Carol laughing and smiling as she said, "Yes, yes," they knew what had just happened, and everyone began cheering. Carol was embarrassed but waved to her friends as she and Seamus hugged.

Carol and Seamus held one another for the longest time, absorbing the complete joy of their special moment.

It was another excellent weekend in Clayton. Doctor Hunter had seen firsthand the poverty of the people in the area, which caused him to ponder its solution. He had also met a woman that shook him to the core. Mary had seen that she could be part of a solution rather than a part of the problem. Carol and Seamus had committed themselves to one another, and lastly, Doctor Smith could see the beginnings of the clinic take place. It was a weekend that would change Clayton for many years.

CHAPTER 28

This year's fall picnic was going to be the first official event to be held in the new town park. Tom had rented a large tent to cover the picnic tables to be used for the pie-baking contest. In addition, the Campbells had acquired some baseballs, bats, gloves, and bases. Archie lined the field for the game along with lines for the tug-of-war and the sack race. Pumpkins were brought in by local farmers, along with baskets full of fresh apples. It would be a grand time for everyone who attended.

When Saturday arrived, the sky was a little cloudy, but the temperature had risen to the mid-sixties, making it very comfortable. People from all around began pouring into town. Samuel and Finn rode in from Charleston, and the young couple with baby Nancy also came. Mary and Rusty, along with Sarah and Lizzy, came early to help set up for the pie-baking contest. Walking slowly down Henry Way came Sheriff Griffith with his longtime friend, Doc. Widow Henry arrived with Archie and Maggie, who looked exhausted but happy to be with everyone. Her advanced pregnancy slowed her average quick pace, and to everyone's applause, Carol and Reverend McConnell came arm in arm. Others came as well—people that Reverend McConnell had met and still others Doctor Smith had treated.

The new, expanded community had come together to enjoy each other, many for the first time. As people greeted one another, children played in the playground. The teenagers bobbed for apples while the young men gathered for the tug-of-war contest. Everyone was having a great time, and to top it off, the sun appeared. It was a perfect late fall day.

At three o'clock, the food most people brought was set out for all to enjoy. Hank and Fred had been cooking chicken over an open fire pit all day, filling the air with the aroma of the burning wood. Before eating, the crowd stopped while Reverend McConnell asked the blessing, thanking God for all He was doing in the community. Everyone enjoyed their meal, but the word went out to save room for pie. Again, this year, Sarah won the pie-baking contest. All that was left to do was eat the pies that people from all over the county had supplied. When dinner was done and dessert eaten, the young men suggested a baseball game. It was the first time baseball had been played at the picnic, but it seemed everyone enjoyed either playing or watching the shortened game. It had begun getting dark, so a full nine-inning game was limited to four.

As darkness began, most folks gathered their children and left for home. Nancy Campbell was forced to give baby Nancy back to her mother and promised to be out to visit soon. When some country folks began leaving, Tom suggested they hop in his wagon and let him take them home since it probably would be dark before they arrived. Seeing what Tom was doing, Archie did the same thing with another family, but before leaving, Tom and Archie ensured that all the leftover food was given to those in need.

When Archie arrived back at Widow Henry's that evening, they sat in the parlor drinking hot tea and talked about the day.

"It was so wonderful to see how people in our community have reached out to others and made them feel welcome. Just because we're growing doesn't mean we can't still be good neighbors to one another," said Widow Henry.

Down the street, Tom and Nancy were also enjoying a cup of tea with Mary as Rusty settled down.

"What a big picnic," said Mary. "Is it always like this?"

Nancy replied, "Yes, Clayton picnics are always fun, with people from all around coming, but this year it was larger than ever. I'm so glad folks feel welcome in their new community."

Tom had a look on his face that indicated he was thinking about something.

"You know, I should have had Samuel and Finn build three or four shelters so people could enjoy the park regardless of the weather. I will write them and see if they can build one or two before winter."

Nancy knew what Tom was doing. He wanted to make sure they had work when there were few landscaping projects. Tom had grown to like Samuel and Finn and wanted to ensure they had plenty of work.

"Did you see how big Nancy is getting?" said Nancy." She seems healthy, and her parents were so proud to bring her today."

Carol and Seamus were enjoying a cup of coffee at the restaurant when Carol said, "Did you notice how Maggie seemed exhausted? I think I will stop in to see her after church service tomorrow and make sure she is doing all right."

"She looked just like a woman about to have a baby to me," said Seamus with a smile.

The following day, Hank read the scriptures. It was the first time he had read in public. Widow Henry was so proud of him; he had worked hard to learn to read, and now he was reading to the congregation.

Walking to the front of the church, Hank nervously turned to the scripture Seamus had asked him to read and read with such emotion that several people had tears in their eyes.

It was a massive accomplishment for Hank, and as he left to go to his seat, he, too, had tears running down his face. He understood that he only learned to read because Widow Henry cared enough to live out her faith. His soul was forever changed.

The cool Sunday afternoon kept most people indoors; however, Rusty and Lizzy went to the park with their mothers to enjoy the playground.

Mary and Sarah talked about the picnic and Sunday service, but Sarah could tell something was on Mary's mind. Finally, Mary turned to Sarah and asked her how she got through all the times she must have felt lonely and afraid.

"I've been alone with Rusty for three and a half years, and although everything is much better now, I still feel like I'm just barely hanging on. The Campbells can't continue letting us stay with them. What am I supposed to do?"

Sarah knew all too well what Mary was feeling. The loneliness sometimes was more than she could bear as well. Reaching out and putting her hand on Mary's arm, Sarah gently said, "Mary, I understand how you feel. Sometimes, I ache for someone to love me, not just a companion, but someone I know in my soul loves me completely.

"When I talked with Reverend McConnell about this, he reminded me that Christ loves me more than I can imagine, and I think I understand that, but I yearn for someone to hold me. What I have learned to do these last few months is something that Reverend McConnell told me. He said that each of our lives is our own individual journey that God, who loves us, is walking through with us. When I don't understand why things are the way they are, I remind myself that this is all part of that journey with God. I don't have to understand why; I have to trust Who I'm traveling with."

Mary smiled and asked Sarah how she could have such strong faith.

"I have struggled ever since Charles died, and frankly, I stopped believing for a long time. It's only been lately that I have learned to let my plan for life go and trust in God's plan for me. I have no idea what's coming next, but I trust that, in the end, God will be there with me."

"I've noticed many people around Clayton act differently than most. I wish I could have that kind of strong faith, but life has been hard, Sarah, and like I said, I don't see any future," said Mary.

"Look, Mary, these things take time; just try to see life as an adventure.

"Regarding work, I could use you for more hours daily, especially during Christmas. People like to have dinner at the restaurant, and sometimes there are small parties. You could move into two of the rooms, one for you and the other for Rusty, and then Tom could move back to his home with Nancy. With the extra work, you could more than cover the cost of the rooms. I don't usually have that many people stay during the winter, so it wouldn't be a problem; plus, I'd like having you and Rusty around."

Smiling, Mary thanked Sarah. Just feeling that she was paying her way and not living on handouts encouraged Mary, and she liked working more with her new friend.

Her common-law husband was not the kind of person who thought about anyone other than himself. They lived together, each in their own world, enjoying physical intimacy but never emotional closeness.

Sheriff Griffith had talked with her last week about how things were coming in trying to sell the property in Elkview. He was hopeful everything would be settled by late January. That would help financially, but her lack of a lifetime companion to share life with weighed heavily on her heart.

Carol and Seamus visited Widow Henry, and while the men talked, Carol, Widow Henry, and Maggie went to Maggie's bedroom to chat.

Widow Henry had supplied everyone with coffee and had just settled down when Maggie began telling Carol how she felt.

"Most days, I'm fine. Perhaps it's the children at school that help take my mind off how tired I am, I don't know, but some days I can barely get out of bed."

"Well, Honey, it's almost time for your little one to come into this world. You're using most of your energy on your baby, so it's no wonder you get tired," said Widow Henry.

"If you can't teach at school, I can always work with both rooms. I will have Mary stay with the children when I'm in the other room. She'll make sure they are doing their work. It will be fine. Why don't you stay home and rest until the baby comes?" said Carol.

Maggie was grateful for the additional rest time but felt she was letting Carol down.

"I'll come in when I'm feeling better; I don't want to leave you alone," replied Maggie.

As Carol and Seamus were leaving, Archie thanked them for coming by to visit. Archie knew that after the baby was born, they would move to their home and miss times like this when friends easily stopped by to see how you were.

Monday morning came fast for Seamus. He had a few people he needed to see before the weather turned and weekly trips would end for the season. He had promised Archie he would stop by his place to check on everything, so he saddled up his horse and headed out.

Before leaving town, Seamus stopped by the boardinghouse to say goodbye to Carol. They had decided to postpone their trip to Charleston to the following weekend, so he planned to get back into town early Friday afternoon so that he could have his message prepared before leaving Saturday morning.

Seeing Carol one last time before leaving warmed his heart. Carol had just finished getting ready for school and was waiting for Seamus as he entered the boardinghouse. When they kissed goodbye, Carol handed Seamus a note. "Here, I wrote this for you. I hope what I said brightens your day while you are alone."

When they parted, Sarah sighed, having overheard their passionate farewell. Remembering what she and Mary had discussed the day before, she had to remind herself that this was only a season in her life. "Who knows what God has in store for me? Someday, maybe I will find love again."

Before going to Archie's cabin, Seamus stopped by Hank's old place. When he arrived, he saw the destruction from the fire and how close it had come to spreading to the cabin. Everything looked in order inside the cabin when suddenly he had an idea. Since Hank lived in town and the cabin wasn't being used, he could stay there in the summer and hold meetings outside. There was plenty of room, so all that was needed was for a shelter to be built. Carol could use the shelter to teach during the daytime. He could hardly wait to tell Carol. When he returned to Clayton, he would try to find out who owned the cabin and see what they could work out.

Leaving Hank's, Seamus traveled down the road until he reached Archie and Maggie's house. Everything was still closed up tightly, and there were no signs of anyone having been around. Seamus gathered what late vegetables he could find and put them in his saddle bag.

The remainder of the week, Seamus met four different families, shared his Sunday message with them, and ensured they knew they were always welcome to come to services in Clayton when they were in town. He had begun getting to know the folks more personally and easily understood their desperation. Their physical plight, along with their spiritual condition, deeply affected Seamus.

On his ride back to Clayton on Friday, Seamus was deep in thought about what he could do to help the poor when he noticed that he was only a short distance from the young couple he had met a month or so ago. Approaching their little cabin, he saw the mother hanging laundry out to dry while the husband chopped wood for the long winter months.

Getting down from his horse, he said hello and asked how Nancy was doing.

"She's doing great," said the mother.

"She's napping now; would you like to see her," asked the father.

Peeking his head into the cabin, Seamus saw little Nancy sleeping, hardly stirring. He also noticed there was very little food stored on the shelves.

"How have you two been doing?"

He knew they would do all they could to care for little Nancy but was concerned for their health.

"We're just fine, Reverend. I've gathered all the crops our little garden had left, and we should be fine for the winter," said the father.

Seamus doubted they had enough to sustain them for the long, cold winter but smiled and said, "Listen, I've got some vegetables I dug up the other day at an old farmhouse. Would you like what I found?"

"Sure, said the young father, we could always use more. Thanks."

As Seamus rode away, he was convinced there was something that could be done for poor folks like this.

At dinner that night, Seamus shared with Carol the idea he had about Hank's old place, and just as he expected, Carol was very excited.

Ever since she had gone out with Seamus into the countryside and met the poor folks living in the wilderness, her compassion for them kept her awake, thinking about what she could do to help them. She knew God was calling her but didn't know what to do. Seamus' idea must have been God speaking to his heart because now it was clear to her what she would do.

As Seamus continued sharing what he had witnessed at the houses he had visited, Carol realized that there was something they could do to help. "Seamus, we don't need an expensive engagement ring. Why don't we use most of the money to buy food for these people?"

Mary was clearing the table next to Carol, and she began to cry when she overheard what Carol had said. Setting her tray down, Mary turned around to face Carol and Seamus, tears pouring down her face, and said, "You have no idea how horrifying it can be during the winter. There's very little to eat if anything, and the cold never goes away. You hope and pray every morning that the fire didn't go out overnight."

Carol reached out to Mary and motioned for her to sit with them. "I can't imagine how terrible it must have been for you and your little ones, Mary," said Carol.

As the three of them talked about the horrors of winter, Mary reached into her pocket and handed Seamus six dollars and fifty cents. "It isn't much, but it's all that I have. If this can help someone, please, take it; I have all I need."

When dinner was finished, and Carol had gone up to her room, Seamus headed for the Campbells to see about borrowing their wagon. After telling Tom what he and Carol wanted to do, Tom asked him to wait while he wrote a note to Jim Hoffman.

"Take this to Hoffman's and give it to the owner, Jim Hoffman. He's a good man; I'm sure he will have what you need."

The trip to Charleston was different than Seamus had imagined it would be. He had pictured going there with his bride-to-be and finding the perfect engagement ring, but instead, he realized that their trip was a mission to help the poor. Their engagement was very important, but sharing a vision and mission with Carol caused today to be much more significant than anything he had ever dreamed.

Jim Hoffman noticed the young couple drive up in Tom's wagon and went to meet them. Introducing himself, Jim asked what they needed. After telling Jim what they hoped to do, they gave him Tom's note. Reading the note, Jim asked them if they had time to wait for his crew to fill the wagon.

"Actually, we were headed to a jeweler to discuss buying an engagement ring," said Seamus.

"Well, well," said Jim. "Congratulations! The best jeweler in town is down the street three blocks. Tell him I sent you, and he'll take good care of you," said Jim.

"Thank you for the directions, Jim, but we didn't bring enough money to buy food to fill the wagon," said Seamus, somewhat embarrassed.

"Oh, that's not a problem. Tom told me that the Clayton food pantry needed supplies and that I could take it out of his account. You see, every year about this time, Tom, Nancy, and Widow Henry buy food, clothing, and toys for the poor people of Clayton. Tom said the need would be greater this year because of all the new people you and Doctor Smith have met. See, right here in his note," said Jim, showing Seamus Tom's note.

Carol remembered helping Widow Henry the year before, so she was aware of the help the Widow had provided to many around town, but she wasn't aware that Nancy and Tom were also part of it.

"I don't know what to say. I never knew about any of this," said Seamus. Reaching into his pocket, he handed Jim the money he had, along with the six dollars and fifty cents Mary had given them at dinner Friday night.

"There is what we have; please use it too," said Carol as she hugged Seamus' arm.

When Carol and Seamus entered the jewelry store, they felt a little awkward. They knew they didn't have much money, and everything looked expensive. Seeing the two of them looking closely at engagement rings, the shopkeeper came over and asked if he could help them.

"Well, we hope so. Jim Hoffman told us this was the best place in town."

"Jim's a nice fellow; he sends quite a few people here. Now, what can I help you with today?"

As the two of them looked at rings, Carol spotted one she liked very much but tried not to get her hopes up since it would probably be more than they could afford.

"Can I see that one?" asked Carol.

Carol beamed excitedly as the jeweler pulled the ring from the case. She was engaged to the most wonderful man she had ever met, and they were looking at engagement rings together. It all seemed like a dream that she hoped would never end.

"It's beautiful!" exclaimed Carol.

"May I ask how much does the ring cost?" asked Seamus.

To their extreme disappointment, the ring was more than they could afford.

"Do you have anything a little less expensive?" asked Seamus.

"Of course, follow me," said the shopkeeper.

Going to the back of the store, the shopkeeper pulled out a tray of rings and asked if any of them appealed to Carol. Looking carefully at each of the rings, Carol suddenly gasped. "That one is just like the one my mother had. May I please see it?"

"Oh, Seamus, this is perfect. I always hoped for a ring just like my mother's," said Carol.

"Take your time, Carol; if you want to keep looking, we can," said Seamus.

"No, No, this is exactly the ring I want, Seamus," said Carol.

After the shopkeeper sized Carol's finger, he didn't think any adjustments needed to be made and asked Seamus if he could have a minute to find a box. When he returned, he looked at Seamus with a gleam in his eye and said, "You know, this ring just happens to be on sale today for ten percent off the normal price."

Seamus thanked the shopkeeper and paid him for the ring. Putting the box into his pocket, Seamus and Carol headed out of the store, knowing that today their lives had changed forever. As they were halfway out of the door, the shopkeeper shook Seamus' hand and gently said to both of them, "God bless you."

CHAPTER 29

MARY CONSIDERED SARAH'S offer for several days before discussing it with the Campbells. After Rusty had gone to bed Thursday evening, Mary approached Tom and Nancy as they sat in the parlor talking. Tom was about to leave for the boardinghouse for the evening but stopped when Mary entered the room.

"What can we do for you, Mary?" asked Tom.

"I need to talk with both of you if you have time," said Mary quietly.

Tom settled back into his chair to listen to Mary. It was clear that whatever Mary wanted to talk about was important.

"Both of you have been more generous than anyone I have ever known. Tom, you have given up your evenings with Nancy so my family could be together. And Nancy, you have been so loving to me, and Rusty, you've become like a sister to me. Both of you have given us food to eat and clothing to wear. I don't know how we would have survived without your help. I don't know how I will ever be able to thank you enough. You have saved my family," said Mary as she began to cry.

"Mary, we only want the best for you and Rusty," said Nancy as she reached out to hug Mary.

"I know," said Mary, "but it's not right that I continue burdening the two of you. Sarah has offered me more work in the evenings after school and said we could stay at the boardinghouse. She says there aren't many visitors in the winter, so she could spare the extra room. This way, Tom could move back. I hope I don't sound ungrateful because I truly am, but I need to know that I am paying my way and not living off your generosity. I can pay for the rooms and food with the extra work, plus what I make at the school. I've never been one that doesn't do what I can to take care of myself and my family, and now I have a chance."

Tom understood the need Mary had to take care of her family. People lose their self-respect when they aren't providing for themselves. When Mary was finished sharing, Tom got up from his chair and walked across the room, putting his hand on Mary's shoulder, saying, "Mary, you and Rusty will always be a part of our new family. Nancy and I will be here for you. Promise me that you will not be too afraid to ask for help if you need it. We respect you, Mary. You have done an incredible job raising Rusty. Please allow Nancy and me always to be a part of your family. We love you."

"I'll leave now so that you and Nancy can talk. This weekend, I will help you move to the boardinghouse," said Tom as he picked up his coat. "God bless you, Mary."

The next day at school, Carol asked Mary to watch the older children while she taught the younger ones. Anxiously, Mary went to the classroom, not knowing what she would face. The children tried to test her a little to see what they could get away with, but soon, they learned that Mary would not let them get the best of her.

"Miss Carol has given you work to do, and I expect each of you to do your best; nothing less than that will be tolerated," Mary firmly but lovingly said.

Rusty looked at his mother and was proud of her. *She's a real teacher,* he thought to himself.

After school that day, Carol told Mary she did an excellent job with the children, just as she expected. "You have a special way with children, Mary," said Carol. "Thank you for your help."

That evening, Seamus and Carol went to the restaurant for dinner. Seamus had asked Sarah if they could have the table in the corner where it was quieter and more private. While the two walked to their seats, Sarah brought them some tea and biscuits.

"Thank you, Sarah, the warm tea will help warm our hands," said Carol.

Seamus looked into Carol's eyes and told her how much he loved her.

"From the beginning, your heart has attracted me to you, and the more I've gotten to know you, the more I see how much you reflect Christ's love to everyone you meet. So, you see, it's not just you, but Christ in you, that makes you irresistible to me. I can't imagine spending my life with anyone but you."

With that, Seamus got down on one knee and formally asked Carol to be his wife. When Carol said yes, Seamus pulled the ring from his pocket, placed it on her finger, and gently leaned over to kiss her.

To their surprise, everyone in the restaurant cheered. Neither of them had noticed how everyone had stopped talking and started intently watching them.

With tears running down her face, Carol turned and smiled at everyone in the restaurant, including Mary, Sarah, and Lizzy, who had come out from the kitchen to celebrate with Carol and Reverend McConnell.

Saturday morning, Tom paid Sarah for his stay at the boardinghouse and brought his things to his house. Mary and Rusty gathered what they had and began heading for the boardinghouse when Nancy stopped Mary and hugged her.

"I'll miss you, Mary; you mean so much to Tom and me."

As they said goodbye, Tom walked into the house with his things. "Let me help you, Mary."

When they arrived at the boardinghouse, Sarah was working in the kitchen preparing food for her guests. Tom stuck his head in the back and asked Sarah where she wanted Mary to put her things.

"Oh, sorry, I didn't hear you come in. Could you please put everything in rooms two and three?" said Sarah. "Thanks, Tom, for your help; I'm a little swamped this morning."

After Mary settled into their rooms, Rusty went to the park to play at the playground while Mary cleaned the restaurant. The lunch patrons would be there shortly, and she wanted everything to look its best. When she finished, she went into the kitchen to see what else Sarah needed her to do.

"You could help me deliver the pies to the general store," said Sarah.

As Mary gathered the pies, she asked Sarah if the restaurant had many guests for Thanksgiving. To her surprise, Sarah said it was one of the slowest days of the year.

"People around here like to fix their dinner for Thanksgiving, but that doesn't mean we're not busy. Widow Henry has me prepare dinners for several neighbors and then has Carol deliver them. We've been doing it for the last three years," said Sarah, proud that she could be part of helping others.

"When everything has been delivered, we have our feast here in the restaurant. This year, you and Rusty will be included. Carol and Reverend McConnell will also be here, along with Tom, Nancy, and, of course, Widow Henry. It's always such a good time," explained Sarah.

"Do you think I could help Carol this year?" Mary asked. I know several of the folks who will probably receive dinners."

"I'll ask Widow Henry," said Sarah, "I'm sure she would appreciate your help."

Just then, Doctor Hunter walked through the door. "Good morning, Sarah, it's good to see you. I'll be in town today and Sunday to help Doctor Smith. Where can I leave my bag?"

"I'll have you in room four, but the room isn't ready yet. You can leave your things here behind the counter, and I'll take them up later this afternoon," said Sarah.

After Doctor Hunter left, Mary asked if Sarah would like her to prepare the room, but before going upstairs, she said to Sarah, "You sure looked excited to see Doctor Hunter," smiling at her friend.

"He's a nice man that stays here at the boardinghouse every other weekend when he's in town helping Doctor Smith," said Sarah somewhat evasively.

"I know that, Sarah. You seemed to perk up when he walked into the room. Are you sweet on the Doctor?" Mary asked teasingly.

"Don't be silly, Mary, I hardly know him," replied Sarah.

"Whatever you say, Sarah, whatever you say," said Mary as she headed upstairs.

When Doctor Hunter arrived at Doctor Smith's, he saw how Fred and Archie had begun staking the project, preparing to build the footers so that they could hopefully get the subflooring done before winter's cold weather.

"Looks good," said Jim to Fred as he headed inside to see his friend.

David greeted Jim when he entered the house and asked if he was ready for a long day.

"We've got several people with bad colds or influenza that we need to see."

"Let's get going then," said Jim, "That's what I'm here for."

David was right; it was a long day. Both doctors returned in the late afternoon tired. They had seen thirty people suffering from cold-like symptoms. As they sat down in David's office area to fill out paperwork describing each person they had treated that day, Jim commented on how quickly the clinic was coming along.

"The men are working as hard as they can, trying to get to a logical stopping place before we start getting snow. I think they will be able to do it, but only because of how hard they work," said David.

"How are things in Charleston?" asked David.

"Not as good as I would like," said Jim. "We have had to treat several miners from beatings and a few broken bones. It seems things are heating up between the miners and the operators," said Jim.

Industry had shifted after the Civil War from coal to the oil industry. However, there were still hundreds of thousands of tons shipped down the Kanawha River every year as had been done fifty years earlier, but with the C&O Railroad having tracks from western West Virginia's new town, Huntington, east to the Atlantic, moving coal to the east was much quicker and less expensive using the railroad. The demand for coal brought investors from the east to operate mines in southern West Virginia. Labor costs had historically been kept low, initially by using slaves. Later, freed slaves and immigrants were enticed to work in the area. The pay was meager, and working conditions worsened, causing miners to demand better pay and safer mines. The situation only worsened with time. Neither side was willing to give, so the operators brought in enforcement crews of men whose job was to stop the troublemakers and keep production at its maximum.

Jim had seen enough injured workers to know that the operators did not care about their safety. He feared things would worsen if someone didn't step in and stop it.

David found their discussion troubling. He had known a few men who had worked briefly in the mines, and their descriptions of what it was like confirmed everything Jim said.

When the paperwork was complete, Jim headed for the boardinghouse to clean up before dinner. "I'll see you in about an hour," said David as Jim headed out the door.

When Doctor Hunter arrived at the boardinghouse, he rushed to his room. He didn't want Sarah to see him dirty from his long day.

After cleaning up for the evening, Jim came downstairs, hoping to see Sarah before David arrived.

Seeing Sarah behind the counter, he asked where he should sit.

"Why don't you sit at that table in the corner? It's quieter and more private. I'll bring you some coffee while you wait," said Sarah with a spring to her step.

When she returned with the coffee, Sarah asked how his day had gone and made small talk for as long as possible.

She had been waiting all day for Doctor Hunter to return to town. Not knowing if she would see him again due to the coming cold weather, she blurted out, "Do you have any plans for Thanksgiving?"

She knew her question was awkwardly asked and felt a little embarrassed.

"We are having the Reverend and his fiancée, Carol, along with Mary, Rusty, and some other folks from town. It's fine if you don't want to; I know it's a long way to come, but if you're in town, I just wanted you to know you are invited," continued Sarah.

"Thanksgiving is earlier than I would normally return to town, but your invitation is enticing me to think that perhaps I can come for the long weekend to help David if that's all right with you," said Jim, eager to spend more time with Sarah.

"Of course, it's all right with me," said Sarah.

With that, the two parted ways. Sarah to complete dinner for her guests, and Jim to greet Doctor Smith.

That evening after dinner, Jim lay in bed reviewing everything Sarah had said and began anxiously looking forward to Thanksgiving weekend. Sarah closed up the restaurant for the evening and collapsed in bed. Lizzy was long asleep, so as she lay in bed in the quiet of the night, she also reviewed every word of her meeting with Doctor Hunter. She resisted the urge to get ahead of herself and dream of them as a couple, but she wasn't always successful.

The next day, Sarah, Mary, and their children walked across the street to Sunday worship service, where they met Widow Henry, Archie, and Maggie. It was clear that Maggie was not feeling well as she climbed the four stairs to the church's front door.

The usual crowd was there: Doc, Sheriff Griffith, Hank, the Campbells, David Smith with his friend Jim Hunter, and many new people from the area.

The message this Sunday, after Hank read scripture, was on Thanksgiving. Reverend McConnell reminded everyone that the apostle Paul said that we are to give thanks always, not just for the good things that happen in our lives, but also for the times things are more difficult. Everything we have is a gift from God.

As the sermon ended, Reverend McConnell also reminded everyone how blessed they were to live in a community that cared for one another. He stopped and looked around the church and saw many faces of people new to the area. He thanked God for the people who had given their time, some their money, but most of all, their hearts to the new people they had just met.

"Your witness for Christ is changing the lives of many folks who need to know they are loved. Thank you for being the people you are."

In his heart, he could tell that the Holy Spirit was moving in this little part of the world, and as he closed in prayer, he thanked God for allowing him to be a part of this change.

When people were leaving, Maggie struggled to stay on her feet, feeling very weak. Archie yelled for Doctor Smith, who came running back into the church. Close behind him followed Doctor Hunter, who told Doctor Smith he would be back with his medical bag.

Turning, he dashed out of the door to the clinic to get the bag. As he ran back, he saw Sarah heading into the boardinghouse and asked her to have someone help Widow Henry back home. When Jim returned to the church, Maggie was lying on the floor as Doctor Smith took her pulse. With his bag opened, he reached for his stethoscope to listen to her and her child's heartbeats to be sure both were all right.

"Maggie, you are to rest in bed until the baby is born. Everything is fine with both of you, except that you are exhausted. Archie and Doctor Hunter helped Maggie to her feet and escorted her outside to Tom Campbell's wagon to be driven back to Widow Henry's.

Tom had seen the commotion and rushed to his house to get his wagon if needed. Once Maggie was safely home and in bed, she slept most of the afternoon. Archie was very concerned but tried to keep his feelings from her so she wouldn't be more anxious.

Maggie did as the doctor ordered and stayed in bed, and Doctor Smith checked on her every afternoon.

On Thanksgiving, Carol and Mary traveled all over the countryside, delivering food to the poor and sharing some of Sarah's cookies with the children.

Both were weary from being out in the cold weather. Despite how tired they were, their hearts were full of joy, knowing that they had been able to help Widow Henry love their neighbors. Carol's trips with Seamus and today caused her to want to be part of changing the lives of the needy, not just with food but with education. She was excited about the possibility of the summer school and church that she and Seamus had discussed but told no one until all the details had been worked out.

That evening, Seamus and Carol came to the restaurant and were greeted by Mary, Rusty, and Lizzy. Sarah was in the kitchen and had asked Mary to greet people as they came. Carol excused herself to go in the back and see Sarah to find out if she could help.

"Sarah, your cookies brought so many smiles to the children we gave them to today, most of whom said it was the only sweet they had had all year."

Sarah was pleased to learn that her cookies were a hit with the children but insisted that Carol return to the others.

"Thanks for telling me, Carol, but you're my guest this evening, so you just go out there and be with your fiancé."

Just after Sarah and Mary finished bringing all the food to the table and everyone was about to sit down, Jim Hunter opened the door. Sarah couldn't help lighting up. She thought he wouldn't make it since it was so late.

"Sorry, I'm late," said Doctor Hunter, "I had a last-minute emergency I had to take care of before I could leave."

"No problem, we're just glad you are here," said Sarah. "Now, let's sit down before our dinner gets cold."

The night was one of those that everyone in attendance remembered for years. People enjoying a wonderful meal, sharing stories and a little news, too. Carol and Seamus announced that they hoped to be married in the spring and would have their wedding at Clayton Park. Doctor Smith talked about what a fantastic job Archie and Fred were doing on the new clinic and that he hoped it would be open by late spring or early summer.

As the evening was ending, Mary said that she had something she wanted to say. The room came to a hush as Mary, looking around at every face, said, "I cannot believe all that has happened to me this year. Instead of foraging in the forest to find something to eat, I am here with people I didn't know a few months ago, enjoying a feast. Although the food was delicious, this night is about each of you to me. When we were hungry, you fed Rusty and me. When we were wearing rags as clothes, you gave us clothing to wear. When I had no place to live, you opened your home to us. When I was without love or hope, you gave me both. I can't imagine ever having a Thanksgiving again where I am as thankful for the love you have given to me and Rusty."

When she had finished, tears were streaming down her face and several others. She picked up a Bible she had brought with her and read John 3:16. "For God so loved the world that he gave His only son, that whosoever believed in Him would not perish but have eternal life."

Sarah rose from her chair to comfort her friend when Mary said, "Today, I accepted God's gift of salvation, demonstrated to me by each of you. Each of you has helped me understand how dear I am to God."

Everyone got up to hug Mary that night, but none more tightly or longer than Rusty.

CHAPTER 30

THE DAYS FOLLOWING Thanksgiving were colder than usual. There wasn't snow, but the temperatures were indeed cold enough. Maggie continued to stay in bed, following Doctor Smith's direction, and the good doctor continued checking in on her every afternoon.

Today, December 1, Doctor Smith told Maggie he felt their child would be born within twenty-four hours. Widow Henry stayed with Maggie while Doctor Smith went to his office to let Doc know where he would be for the remainder of the evening. Before leaving to go back to Widow Henry's house, Doctor Smith went outside to where Archie and Fred were finishing their work for the day.

"Archie, I'll stay with you and Maggie tonight to help with your child's birth. Your baby will be born within the next few hours."

Archie ran to get his lunch, which he had not eaten, and went off with the doctor. Hank, who had stopped by the clinic to see his friends, looked at Fred and said, "We need to pray, Fred; I've never seen the doctor that upset."

In the middle of the work site, Hank knelt and asked God to be with the Doctor and Maggie. "I'm not sure what is going on, Father, but the Doctor seemed worried. If it's your will, please show your hand to everyone looking out for this new life. Keep the baby safe and the mother well. Thank you, Father, in Christ's name I pray."

Fred wasn't sure what to do, so he said, "Amen." It was the closest he had ever come to praying, and oddly, he felt at peace, a comfort he didn't know how to explain.

"What should we do?" asked Fred.

"We've done the most important thing we can do, Fred; now we must trust the Lord. It's in His hands now," said Hank, smiling at his new friend.

The two men went to the boardinghouse as usual for dinner. Both were excited for Archie and Maggie and found it hard to keep their excitement to themselves.

"You two sure look happy, especially on such a dreadful day," said Sarah.

"Doc Smith just came to get Archie. Maggie is having her baby," exploded Fred.

"That's wonderful," exclaimed Sarah. Who is with her?"

"Doctor Smith, Archie, and Widow Henry are all there," said Hank.

"After you finish your dinners, will you take some food to the widow's house? Everyone will need to eat, and Widow Henry will be too busy helping the doctor to have prepared anything," said Sarah.

The contractions were getting worse but still were too far apart for delivery. Doctor Smith talked with Maggie, explaining what was happening, while Archie kept a fresh, cool cloth on her forehead. Finally, when the pain was too much for Maggie, she started screaming at the top of her lungs; Doctor Smith asked Archie to leave the room.

"Archie, please go to the general store and see if Nancy is available?"

After Archie left, Doctor Smith looked at Widow Henry and asked if she could prepare some boiling water. "It won't be long now," he said with a hint of concern in his voice.

The contractions continued throughout the evening and into the late night. Shortly after midnight, they began coming closer together, and Widow Henry could see the relief on Doctor Smith's face.

With Archie in the parlor and Widow Henry beside him, comforting the soon-to-be father, Nancy and Doctor Smith helped Maggie give birth to a beautiful girl. When Archie heard the cry of his newborn child, he could hardly control his excitement. Widow Henry assured him the doctor would ask him to come into the bedroom when the time was right. "Just be patient, son; you'll see your child soon," said the wise widow.

Doctor Smith opened the door, entered the parlor, and asked Archie, "Would you like to meet your daughter Archie?"

When Archie entered the room, Nancy handed the child to Maggie, wrapped warmly in clothes with a little cover on her head. Maggie looked exhausted, but Archie had never seen her happier.

"Look at our daughter," said Maggie.

Archie reached down to pull the wrapping away from her little face as Maggie handed her to him.

When Archie picked her up from Maggie's hands, he couldn't believe how light she was. "I almost threw her up in the air," he said. "She is so much lighter than I expected. She looks just like her beautiful mother," were the first words out of Archie's mouth as he held his newborn daughter, closely looking at her beautiful face.

Nancy and Widow Henry looked at the young family. Widow Henry couldn't help but think how God had completely changed their lives in the last year and a half. She silently prayed, thanking God for all He had done and for allowing her to witness His work.

When everyone left the bedroom so that Maggie and the baby could rest, they found food on the kitchen table from the boardinghouse. They had been in the back of the house when Hank had arrived. Hank knew where to take everything since he had been there many times when Widow Henry taught him to read.

He still came by occasionally to visit and read scripture with her. The two of them had bonded as close friends during their scripture reading. Often, Hank thought to himself how incredible it was for a former slave to have close friends who were white.

This all happened because Widow Henry lovingly shared her relationship with Christ with everyone she met. Most people wouldn't understand how transforming life can be when you are full of a holy love for one another rather than living your life as if you were the center of everything around you. It's not about giving up so much; it's a life full of mystery and love.

When Hank arrived at the boardinghouse, he told Sarah that he had left the food on the dining room table and told her he could hear Maggie crying in pain. Hearing her cry brought back memories of his childhood and the horror of those years.

"I'm sorry," he said to Sarah. I don't usually tear up, but for some reason, thinking about all of the changes that have happened to me and Archie this last year and a half, I am overwhelmed."

With that, Sarah reached out to hug Hank and comfort him, but instead, she was comforted. She, too, had begun noticing that she was changing in ways she couldn't put into words.

The next day, the town was a-buzz with excitement about the birth. Nancy and Tom talked over their morning coffee about how difficult the delivery had been but that Doctor Smith had handled it very confidently.

Tom asked Nancy if she had heard when Archie and Maggie planned to move to their cabin. Nancy said the last she had heard was that it would be shortly after the birth. "Maggie told me they wanted to wait until Doctor Smith told them it would be all right to move. Probably in a week or so," said Nancy.

"Why?" asked Nancy.

"Oh, I think a few of us want to do something for them. They have become such an important part of our community that not having them around daily will be hard," said Tom.

With that, Tom excused himself and went to the store to open up. Nancy stayed to rest from her long night.

As the week progressed, the little girl ate more and seemed healthy. Doctor Smith checked in on her every day and then asked if he might speak to the two of them before they moved.

Saturday, Archie and Maggie brought the child to the doctor's office to see what he wanted to tell them. They were a little anxious but didn't say so to one another. As they entered the clinic reception area, Doc welcomed them and asked to look at their little girl.

"She's beautiful," he exclaimed, "just like her parents."

Doctor Smith walked into the room and welcomed them as well. Turning to the side, he motioned them into his office. After everyone was seated, Doctor Smith said, "I, again, want to congratulate you on having a beautiful little girl. She has begun to put on weight, and her color is good, but there is one thing I wanted to talk with you about.

"During this past week, I have been paying close attention to her heartbeat and noticed a slight irregularity. I don't think it's anything to worry about, but I want you to pay attention to her as she grows up. I want to know if she gets winded easily or has dizzy spells. Usually, these things take care of themselves, but we will want to get her to a specialist if it doesn't.

"I'm sorry, I don't mean to worry you. As I said, most of the time, these problems heal themselves. I just wanted you to be aware. From everything else I see, she is a perfectly healthy little girl who will live a normal life. I am comfortable with you taking her to your new home. Please let me know if you have any questions or need anything. I will be out next week to see how all three of you are doing."

On the way back to Widow Henry's, both Maggie and Archie were shaken by what Doctor Smith had told them. When they arrived, Widow Henry could tell something was bothering them.

After putting the baby to bed, the three entered the parlor, where Widow Henry brought hot coffee to enjoy. Almost before they had settled into their chairs, Archie asked Widow Henry if they could pray, explaining what the doctor had told them.

They prayed for quite some time, with Widow Henry finishing their time by praying, "God, this is your child that you have given Archie and Maggie to raise; we ask that you help them as parents to trust you with her. You love her more than they do and will always do what is right, so we ask you to watch over her all her days, and if it is your will, Father, please allow her to live a long and healthy life following you in all that she does."

When they had finished praying, Archie noticed Widow Henry was trying to hide the fact that she was shaking as she wiped tears from her eyes.

The widow had not told anyone that when she was a young bride, she had lost her only child just months after giving birth. The loss took her years to recover from. It wasn't until she and her husband began reading and studying the Bible together in the parlor every evening that she was healed from her loss. Knowing God's love gave her the peace that her child was taken from her to be with her heavenly Father, where she would flourish in his care. Though she didn't understand why, she realized Who loved her daughter.

Finally, the day arrived for Archie and Maggie to move to their cabin, but before doing so, they wanted to attend worship service. Before Reverend McConnell began his sermon, everyone was oohing at the newborn. When Reverend McConnell approached the podium, he welcomed the newest member of their church community.

Archie and Maggie stood up to the applause of the entire congregation. When the applause had settled down, Seamus asked if the couple had chosen a name for their little girl. Archie proudly said, "Yes, her name will be Alma Gay."

"That's a wonderful name. Would you join me in praying for Alma Gay?" As the congregation bowed their heads, Archie, holding his little girl in one arm and grasping Maggie's hand with the other, joined in prayer.

"Father, you have blessed Archie and Maggie with Alma Gay, and together they become a family. We all pray, Lord, for their health, happiness, and safety. Father, more than anything else, we pray that Alma Gay will come to know you personally as her Lord and Savior. As sweet as she is, she, like the rest of us, is born with a sin nature that separates her from a relationship with you. But you, through Jesus Christ, have provided each of us a way to have those sins forgiven so that we may be reconciled with you. Thank you, Father, for doing everything possible to bring us to a relationship with you. Knowing you on a deep, personal basis directs our lives in ways we would never go without your indwelling spirit. Be with Alma Gay, that she will understand this and live the life you want all your children to live, loving You and loving others with your Holy love. It is in the name of your son, Jesus Christ, I pray. Amen."

After the service, Seamus and Carol caught up with Archie and Maggie and said they would gladly help them move to their cabin. Seamus had arranged to borrow Tom's wagon for the trip.

Archie had packed most of their things during the week after work while Maggie and Widow Henry gathered some additional kitchen supplies and utensils. Almost everyone came by to say their goodbyes and offered to help. Sarah brought food for their first few days, while Nancy brought a present from her and Tom. Surprisingly, Archie didn't see Tom or Hank and wondered where they might be, but he was so busy packing the wagons that he didn't have time to think about it.

When the packing was finished and the wagons filled, it was time to say goodbye to Widow Henry. Archie held her with his hands on her shoulders, looked into her eyes, and said, "From the first time I met you, I have felt a peace I have never known. You gave me a job when I was down and out, and you gave Maggie and me a place to live while we were building our cabin, but more than anything else, you slowly shared, day in and day out, the peace that you have. Thank you for introducing us to Jesus and showing us his love. I will never be able to thank you enough for all you have done. You have completely changed my life."

When Archie finished speaking, the two hugged as a mother and her beloved son would.

Trying unsuccessfully to hold back her tears, Maggie hugged the Widow and said, "Oh, and let's not forget, you introduced me to this wonderful man. You're a life changer, Widow Henry. To everyone who meets you, you're a life changer."

Widow Henry gently whispered to Maggie, "I don't change lives; I just introduce you to the One that does."

Waving goodbye, the four of them and little Alma Gay rode off to the cabin. The ride was more emotional for Maggie as she knew she wouldn't be in town as often as Archie, who was still working at the clinic. She would miss the children at school and quiet afternoons cooking with Widow Henry, but there was something else she was only just now realizing. She would miss the community. Even though it was a small town, it was filled with people she considered friends. People that she often visited or talked with as she walked around town. It was a spirit of togetherness that would take her months to adjust to losing. Looking down at her little girl as she pondered these things, she smiled, knowing deep in her soul that there was a purpose bigger than her that she was going to discover in the years to come.

Thanking God in silent prayer, the young mother put her arm through her husband's as the wagon rocked gently along the road to their new home.

CHAPTER 31

Traveling along the road to their cabin, Archie began to smell the familiar aroma of wood burning. Rounding the final curve in the road, Archie and Maggie couldn't believe their eyes. People from town were at their cabin waiting for them.

Hank and Tom had stacked enough firewood on the side of the cabin for the rest of winter. Tom had started a fire in the fireplace so that the house would be warm when they arrived. Sarah had brought dinner and the other food she had given Maggie the day before.

Above the door, Hank had hung a sign that read, "Our Home, Established December 1893." The cellar was filled with vegetables from the general store that Tom and Nancy brought. It couldn't have been a better welcome home. Maggie's fears about not having neighbors were softened, especially when Mary told her she planned on coming out at least once a week to help with the baby and see how she was doing living out in the woods.

As Archie and Maggie settled in their cabin, folks bid them goodbye and left for town, understanding that they needed to unpack their things. Seamus and Carol stayed on for several hours to help unload their belongings. When the last boxes were stacked in the back bedroom, Seamus asked if he could pray over them before he and Carol left for town.

Kneeling, Seamus removed his hat and prayed for blessings on the home. When he finished, Carol handed Maggie and Archie a gift from her and Seamus. Opening the box, Archie saw it was a Bible.

Looking at Carol and Seamus, his lower lip began to reveal the deep emotion he was feeling; he said, "Thank you so much. I have been using Mr. Henry's Bible since I didn't have one."

"I'm sure she would have given his to you, but I'm sure it's a very treasured memory for her. I've been told that she and Colonel Henry sat in their parlor every evening and read their Bibles together. It's an important keepsake for her," said Seamus.

"I learned so much using it. The Colonel had underlined many passages and made notes in the margins that helped me learn," said Archie.

"Well, Archie, now you can do the same with your Bible and teach Alma Gay," said Seamus.

Carol looked at Maggie and told her how much she and the children would miss her at school. With that, Carol reached into her purse and pulled out a card the children had made. On the card, the children from the older class wrote messages to Maggie, telling her how much they loved her. Then Carol gave Maggie a second card from the little ones she and Mary had been teaching. Each child drew a small picture of themselves. On the bottom of the card, Mary had written, "The children didn't want you to forget them, so they drew pictures of themselves. Love Mary."

After hugging goodbye, Seamus and Carol left for town just as Alma Gay woke up from her nap. It had been an emotional day but a perfect day. Saying goodbye is always hard, but it was apparent to both Archie and Maggie that many people loved them, people they didn't know a little over a year ago.

That night after dinner, even though so much needed to be done, Archie and Maggie sat by the fire and began reading their Bible together. It was the first time the two had studied without Widow Henry.

As they read, they discussed what they understood about the passage and how it applied to their lives, just as they had done every night at Widow Henry's.

Monday morning came quickly for Archie. He had to get up earlier than he was used to so that he could make the trek into town to work at the clinic. After he left, the quietness of the woods was frightening and peaceful at the same time to Maggie. She had never lived away from a community where she was accustomed to the noises of others.

The quiet made her a little jumpy, not knowing what she was hearing or who or what caused it, but it was also peaceful. She found herself meditating on scripture she and Archie had read the night before as Alma Gay rested. She also prayed more, continuously asking God for direction. She knew that raising children was a full-time job, but in her heart, she felt that she had more to do to help little ones begin to love to learn. She had no idea how her desire and being the mother of an infant would go together.

Maggie prayed about this yearning to help other children daily until Mary came by to visit one day.

Mary was still working at the school, helping keep the children focused on the lesson Carol had given them to do. Now that she could read, she could help them with more schoolwork than ever before. Her confidence began to grow, as well as her friendship with Sarah.

She left Rusty with Sarah to help clean the restaurant. Mary wanted to be alone with Maggie to help her feel more comfortable living in the woods, and she didn't want Rusty to wake Alma Gay.

"I'm going to walk outside for a little while, Maggie. I want to see what critters have been around. Maybe I can put your mind at ease," said Mary.

Mary went outside and walked along the ridge and down to the creek. She saw prints in the snow that she easily identified. She also saw some scratching in the dirt next to some bushes. Her walk brought back memories of when she had to find food during the winter to feed her family and how she was always afraid she wouldn't be able to find enough. She loved the outdoors, but those haunting memories took away her joy.

As she walked, she also thought about how Carol had rescued her when she was at a very low point. A stranger who cared enough to run through the woods in city clothes, looking for her, she would never forget how Carol held and comforted her as she cried. A lot had changed since she and Seamus found them in their little shack- a lot!

Knocking the snow off her boots, Mary entered the cabin to find Maggie rocking Alma Gay in the rocking chair Maggie's father had made.

"Well, you've got a very busy rabbit that's been digging around the garden and a small flock of turkeys that have been scratching for berries down next to the creek," said Mary softly so she wouldn't wake the baby.

Maggie motioned for Mary to have a seat as she slowly got up and carried Alma Gay to her crib.

"What can I get you to drink, Mary?" asked Maggie, hoping Mary would stay for a while.

"Water will be fine," replied Mary.

As the two friends sat near the fireplace, Maggie asked how school was going. Mary told her several stories about the children but seemed to want to discuss something else. Finally, Mary stopped talking about the students and said, "Maggie, I could be a better helper if I knew math. Could you teach me?"

Somewhat surprised by Mary's request, Maggie quickly responded that she would love to help her. "You'll pick it up quickly, Mary; you're a very smart woman. I can't believe how quickly you learned to read."

Mary blushed slightly as Maggie complimented her.

"When would you like to start?" asked Maggie.

"I need to get back to town, so how about in two days, after school?" replied Mary, excited at the opportunity to learn.

With that, Mary finished her water, buttoned her coat, and headed out the door for their trip back to town.

After Mary left, Maggie reflected on the need people in the backwoods had to learn some of the basic skills taught in school. How would they ever help their children with schoolwork if they didn't understand themselves? Maybe, she thought, if the parents learn, they will encourage their children to attend school.

Suddenly, ideas about how to solve this education problem flooded her mind. Where could they meet, and how would they find out about the classes and what about supplies? Thoughts kept coming until she stopped and remembered that she needed to pray. If this was God's will for her, then He would give her answers to all her questions and others that she hadn't thought about. Maggie grabbed a pencil and paper and began making notes of her thoughts to pray about them specifically.

Before she knew it, she heard Archie putting their horse away. The afternoon had flown by for Maggie. Perhaps this was the answer to her prayer. "What would you have me do, Father?"

As she and Archie read scripture that evening, Maggie told him what had happened that afternoon. Archie could hear the excitement in her voice, but he also knew that this was something that would have to wait a while until Alma Gay was a little older and she had a better idea of how God wanted her to handle all that would be required to take on a project like this.

As the weeks passed, Mary continued to travel to Maggie's to learn mathematics and help her with Alma Gay. One day, Maggie mentioned her idea of helping backwoods parents understand some basic skills to empower them to help their children learn. Mary told Maggie that she and Carol had been discussing the same idea.

"Carol said that Reverend McConnell has noticed that many of the folks he visits can't read or write. Both of them have prayed about what they could do to help. Maybe when you and Alma Gay are in town, we could meet and talk about it."

Maggie was encouraged that her friends had seen the same problem and were wanting to do something to help.

"Please tell Carol and Reverend McConnell that Archie and I will be in town for worship service this Sunday and that maybe, if their schedule permits, we could get together and talk about what can be done," said an excited Maggie.

Sunday at worship, Reverend McConnell's sermon was about giving, but unlike most sermons on giving, it wasn't about money. The people of Clay County who attended his church were poor, yet they gave freely of what they had. The sermon was on giving time.

"As all of you know, many neighbors around this area need our time. Some need help with long overdue chores, some with repairs, and others need a neighbor to sit with them and listen. If we give of our time and talents as we get to know these people, we can help them understand that their neighbors and their heavenly Father love them. Please pray about what you and your family could do. I pray that our church becomes a light in this dark world."

As people were leaving, Maggie noticed several of them talking with one another about working together to help folks.

With most of the folks leaving, Archie saw his dear friend, Widow Henry, and asked if she would like a ride to her house.

"Yes, I would, Archie, thank you very much," she said warmly. "How have you and Maggie been?" she asked sincerely.

She knew that Maggie was weak after the delivery, and as a first-time mother, she would probably be exhausted by the end of every day.

"We're doing fine," said Archie. I do have a question, though," he said hesitantly. Could Maggie and I visit you on Sundays after church services? I want to make sure we understand everything we are reading in our evening Bible studies."

Widow Henry was glad to hear they had continued studying despite being tired. "Of course, I would love for you to come by and visit Archie."

"I do not want you to make any food or anything like that," insisted Archie. We want to make sure we're not getting off track, plus we miss seeing you," he said, smiling.

As Widow Henry was getting out of the wagon, Archie told her about the meeting he was going to. He explained how Maggie had felt a calling to help the people in the backwoods begin learning basic educational skills so that, hopefully, they would encourage their children to learn.

Turning back towards Archie as he pulled away, Widow Henry said, "Let me know what happens at your meeting, Archie. I think that is a wonderful idea, wonderful!" As she walked toward her house, she thought, *Thank you, Father, for letting me see your mighty hand at work.*

Carol, Seamus, Mary, Archie, and Maggie decided to have lunch at Sarah's restaurant to talk. That way, if Sarah needed any help, Mary could excuse herself for a while to do what was required. After lunch, Mary got up to help Sarah clear the dishes and began washing them when Sarah asked her what they were discussing. When Mary told her, Sarah asked if it would be all right for her to join their discussion.

"Of course, Sarah, that would be great," said Mary.

Seamus began by sharing what he had seen during his travels throughout the county.

"I see so many families trying to live off what little land they have settled on, growing food in the summer and hunting and fishing year-round just to have enough food to survive."

Mary told them what it was like trying to get by. "There's no time for learning. Everybody pitches in to help gather as much food as possible."

Carol spoke about what she had seen when she traveled with Seamus and that the widespread problem, besides the incredible poverty, was the lack of education. She understood what Mary said about available time for learning but knew that without education, there was little hope for them.

As he listened to everyone, Archie began thinking of ways the entire community could help.

"Based on what Mary and Carol have said, it seems that if these families were either helped with their farming or simply given food to eat from us, they would have some available time to be taught lessons."

Maggie jumped in, unable to control her excitement," We need a traveling schoolhouse so several families can join us and learn together. When I helped the little ones at the school with Mary, once you helped the children learn to sit still and pay attention, they were like little sponges. They couldn't learn fast enough."

"I can vouch for what Maggie said. When I first began helping, I didn't know how to read, but just listening to Maggie read stories from a book made me want to learn to read more than anything," said Mary.

"I do think that there is a problem, though," said Mary hesitantly, "It will take a long time to earn these folks' trust, and until you do, they will never accept any food from you. These are proud people, and taking something from someone they don't know isn't something they will do. They have to earn what they get."

As the afternoon began to slip away, it was evident that everyone wanted to do something about the problem. Still, the solution would be much more complicated than initially thought. While everyone gathered their things, Sarah spoke up for the first time all afternoon.

"What if we planted a huge vegetable garden just outside town near Hank's old place? Working with these folks, we could grow more food than they all need. We could share with them enough food to fill their cellars and then take the excess to Charleston and sell it at the farmer's market. Any money we receive would be shared by those who worked the farm, based on a method they agree to."

"I think that's a great idea, Sarah," said Seamus. "Why don't we think and pray about the issue and meet in two weeks? In the meantime, I will find out who owns the property you mentioned, Sarah. Folks, this problem needs all our sincere prayers; people's lives depend on this."

Everyone left Mary and Sarah at the restaurant and headed to their homes. It had been a great first meeting, but as Seamus shared with Carol on their way home, "What Mary said about gaining their trust is the most significant issue we have to solve."

Monday morning, Seamus went to see Tom Campbell shortly after the store opened. Seamus explained what the group had discussed Sunday and asked if he knew who owned Hank's old place. Tom hesitated to answer but realized the time had come for him to be honest about his real estate holdings.

"I do," said Tom, "along with the ten acres next to it."

Seamus looked at Tom and said, "I will keep that between us, my friend. I see now how much you and Nancy have had your hand in helping so many people around here."

"What we have is a gift from God, so we try to help people without them feeling embarrassed or beholding to us," said Tom.

"I like the idea of a vegetable garden to feed the poor, but how will you get them to work on it when they are busy with their places?" asked Tom.

"We hope to get everyone involved in the plowing and planting, but after that, our hope is when people have time away from their gardens, they can work for a few hours a week. With enough people helping, there shouldn't be too much for anyone to do. At harvest, we will set a date, and everybody will come and harvest everything that is ripe. Each person will get their share based on how much they worked, and anything not taken will be sold at the farmers market in Charleston, and the money will be divided between them.

"I'm sure men from the church will help, too," said Seamus.

When Seamus was about to leave, he remembered what he and Carol had discussed. "Tom, Carol, and I discussed building a sheltered area where the current garden is to hold summer school and, hopefully, church services, and if it's not too much trouble, could we stay there in the summer rather than living in a tent? I will gladly pay rent."

Tom smiled and said he would talk with Nancy and get back to Seamus shortly. Seamus thanked Tom for all he and Nancy had done for their community, and as he walked back to the church, his thoughts again went back to the parable about the Good Samaritan.

Archie and Fred's work at the clinic was almost complete. The internal walls and doors had been installed. The next few days would be spent painting the inside and moving the furniture and equipment into the clinic. The exterior would also be painted once the weather was consistently warm enough.

Doctor Hunter will be in town to assist Doctor Smith this weekend. He hadn't been to Clayton for the last few months due to his work in Charleston. The city continued to grow with new industry, which brought people from the east looking for work. His career was rewarding, but he found himself missing quiet little Clayton. Perhaps it was the slower pace, or just maybe it was the boardinghouse owner.

CHAPTER 32

ARCHIE AWOKE TO an early Spring snow, and as he was getting ready to leave for town, he asked Maggie if there was anything she wanted him to bring home after work. Maggie responded that she had everything she needed, but Archie detected a slight hesitancy in her voice. Warmer weather would soon be here, and Maggie could spend time outside with Alma Gay. It had been a long winter, and cabin fever was taking its toll.

On his way into town, Archie stopped by Widow Henry's house to ask his friend about the scripture he and Maggie had read the night before. As he was leaving, she said she had been thinking about them and wondered if he and Maggie would join her for dinner on Sunday.

"Of course, that would be wonderful. What can we bring?" asked Archie.

"Tell Maggie I would love for her to bring her delicious cornbread," replied Widow Henry.

"See you Sunday," said Archie as he rode off.

Fred and Archie continued the finishing work inside the clinic, and by noon, they were ready to move the remainder of the equipment and supplies. While the two men sat eating their lunches, Archie asked Fred what he would do now that the clinic was complete.

"Unless there is more work for me, I'm going back to Charleston and see if I can find carpentry work. Maybe I can teach a couple of my friends what I've learned. Who knows, maybe I really can start a business someday," answered Fred.

"What about you?" asked Fred.

"With Spring coming, I'll be busy preparing my field for planting later, but I don't know what to do for a job. I might have to go to Charleston a few days a week," replied Archie.

Later that afternoon, Archie and Fred went to see Tom at the general store to ask him to come by the clinic to inspect their work. Tom was anxious to open the clinic and was very pleased with how hard the two men had worked, finishing the interior as quickly as they did, even though they had no other work lined up.

"Guys, this is top-notch work you have done. Everything looks perfect! Let's go next door and tell Doctor Smith; I want him to see the finished product," said Tom.

As the three entered the front of the house, something was obviously wrong.

"Doc has fallen, Tom!" yelled Doctor Smith. "Help me get him on the table so that I can examine him."

After waiting about a half hour, David came out and told Tom that he needed to borrow his wagon to take Doc to Charleston, where he was better equipped to care for him. Tom rushed across the street to his stable along with Archie to ready the wagon. When the two men returned, Fred and Doctor Smith loaded Doc onto the back of the wagon and covered him with blankets to keep him warm.

"I'm going to go with them," said Fred, quickly running over to get his things.

"I'll be back in the morning," added Doctor Smith, "I think he has had a stroke!"

As the three rode out of town, Tom headed over to see Seamus to tell him what had happened. Archie gathered his things and rode back to his cabin, concerned for Doc and also bothered by his lack of steady employment. Now, with a family to support, he had to find something more reliable.

When Archie arrived at his home, he noticed Mary's horse was tied to the post outside his small barn. When he entered the room, Mary and Maggie were working on some mathematics problems.

Mary had kept her promise and came to see Maggie every week, sometime twice a week. She had been very helpful to Maggie, answering questions about Alma Gay. Maggie was glad to have the company and truly enjoyed teaching Mary mathematics. Mary's desire to learn was evident, and the results were amazing. In just a few months, she had learned addition, subtraction, and multiplication tables. They had been working on applying this knowledge to practical situations.

After Mary completed the last problem, she rose from her chair and began putting on her coat to go back to town. Archie told them what had happened to Doc earlier and suggested they pray for their dear friend.

Mary asked if she could pray before she left. Bending down on her knees, Mary prayed fervently for God to bless their friend and to give him peace during his recovery.

After praying, Mary got up and thanked Maggie again for helping her. As she rode off, Archie put his things away and sat down. Alma Gay had just awoken, and he quickly went into her room to pick her up to hold her closely.

When he and Alma Gay came into the front room, he sat in the rocking chair and, holding Alma Gay, began to rock back and forth gently. The look on his face told Maggie he was deep in thought, so she left to finish preparing dinner.

When Doctor Smith arrived at the hospital in Charleston, Doc was weak and needed medical attention. Doctor Smith had Doc admitted to the hospital, where he began undergoing a series of tests to determine the extent of the damage. While waiting in the hospital for the test results, Jim Hunter happened to walk by and, seeing David, ran over to see what was wrong.

"Doc has had a stroke. They are running tests now," replied David, obviously shaken.

"I'll see what I can do," said Jim as he rushed down the hall.

While David waited, Jim met with the attending physicians and learned that they believed Doc had had a stroke followed by a mild heart attack. His heart seemed to be fine now, but the damage from the stroke would take time to heal if it ever did.

"We'll know more in a day or two after we observe him for a while. The medication we have given him will help him rest," said the attending doctor.

When Jim came out to the waiting room, he told David what he had learned and suggested they get something to eat and go to his place for the night.

"There's nothing we can do for him tonight. He will rest and be cared for by the staff. We can return in the morning and see how he is doing."

That evening, David began wondering what could have been done differently. Should he have persuaded Doc to have a physical? Perhaps he would have been able to help prevent the stroke if he had only done an exam.

Jim could see how David was affected and wanted to say something to him to help him feel better because he knew exactly how he felt. He had been late for Thanksgiving dinner because of a very similar situation with one of his patients; only his patient died.

The grief many doctors suffer when people they are responsible for die is something the public doesn't comprehend. Doctors spend years learning the most up-to-date information to help their patients. Sometimes, all that knowledge isn't enough to save them. If this kind of loss isn't dealt with correctly, a doctor can lose his effectiveness in dealing with people.

Jim slowly walked across the room, sat beside David, and calmly said, "You did all he would allow you to do. You are an excellent doctor, David, but you must understand we will lose all our patients eventually. It's our job to make their lives as healthy and comfortable as we possibly can, that's all."

The following morning, the two doctors went to the hospital and learned that Doc was doing much better. The heart problem had been mild, probably caused by the stress of the stroke. Doc's stroke had been on the right side of his brain, causing him to lose control of his left hand and leg. Over time, his leg and hand would improve, but the drooping left side of his face was another story. After going through therapy, he would get better, but his speech would always be affected.

When David was able to visit Doc in his room, he shared the prognosis with him. Doc shook his head, acknowledging that he understood. David asked him if he wanted him to contact his daughter in Ohio to let her know what had happened, and with a nod of his head, Doc gave him permission.

"Doc," said David, "I will send her a telegraph before I return to Clayton. I'll come back this weekend when Jim is covering for me to see how you are doing. We'll have you back in town with your friends in a few weeks; rest and do what the doctors tell you to do."

David left the hospital and headed for Western Union to telegraph Doc's daughter.

On his way out of the hospital, David ran into Jim and told him what he had told Doc.

"I'll keep an eye on him this week. I'll be in Clayton Saturday morning to help out where I can," said Jim as he rushed down the hall to see another patient.

David went to the city stable and got Tom's wagon, but before he left for Clayton, he stopped by Hoffman's to see if Jim had anything for Tom.

"Hi, Doctor Smith; what brings you to town?" asked Jim Hoffman.

After explaining why he was in Charleston, he asked if there were any orders he could pick up for Tom.

"It just so happens I got something for Tom this morning," said Jim. "I'll have my men load it on the wagon."

Two men carried a large box out of the warehouse a few minutes later and put it in the wagon.

"Wow," David said, "what's in the box?" "I think it's for the clinic, but I'm not sure," Jim said.

"That's odd; I don't remember asking Tom for anything," said David, and with that, he said goodbye and headed for Clayton.

The ride back was beautiful. Some of the trees had begun blooming, along with wildflowers. The maple trees were starting to show their leaves as the river rushed by quicker than usual due to the melting snow in the mountains. David kept thinking about Doc and wondering what he could have done differently. Jim Hunter's advice had been very helpful, but he still believed there was something else he should have done.

When he arrived in Clayton, he took Tom's wagon back to his barn and, after taking care of Tom's horse, walked around to the front of the general store to talk with Tom.

"How's Doc," asked Tom.

"He's resting at the hospital. He had a stroke and will be there for a few weeks until he can travel. I've sent a telegram to his daughter to let her know," said David.

"Tom, I left your wagon in the back. Hoffman's had a large box for you that I left in the back since it will take two men to unload it."

"Great, I was hoping that would arrive soon. It's a chair for your office. I'll ask Archie and Hank to unload it and put it in your office."

David was subdued the remainder of the week, often contemplating what he could have done differently. Doc had opened his home to David, treating him like a son, and yet he hadn't been given a physical that perhaps could have prevented him from having the stroke.

Friday, after seeing his last patient for the day, there was a knock on the door. Archie and Hank were delivering the chair Tom had ordered.

"Thank you for bringing it, guys."

Archie could tell something was bothering Doctor Smith and asked if he could talk with him for a minute.

After Hank left, Doctor Smith asked, "What's on your mind, Archie?"

"Doctor, you don't seem yourself lately. Is there something bothering you?"

"Oh, I'll be all right, Archie; I'm feeling bad about Doc and just wondering if I could have prevented him from having the stroke," replied David.

"Well, David, I'm not a doctor, but it seems that all you can do is help people; God is the one who gives them life and takes it away when He chooses. You are a wonderful doctor who cares about the people in Clay County. What could you have done differently? If Doc wasn't complaining about something, how would you know to examine him?" asked Archie. With that, Archie said he needed to head home before it got dark.

That evening, David thought about all that Archie had said, and suddenly, an idea came to him that he couldn't wait to share with Jim Hunter on Saturday morning.

Jim got up very early, knowing that David wanted to go to Charleston to visit Doc. When he arrived in town, David was waiting for him at the boardinghouse. After checking in with Sarah and taking his things to his room, he and David sat at a table for breakfast.

" Jim, I have been thinking all week about what I could have done differently, and I think I've come up with an idea that will affect everyone in the Clayton area. I want to advertise free medical examinations. It has occurred to me that no one around here comes to see me unless they are sick. What if they were ill and didn't know it? An examination could possibly detect it, and I could see that they received proper treatment. I want to emphasize preventative healthcare for everyone."

Jim sat back in his chair and thought about what this would entail.

"David, once this is accepted, you will be very busy doing exams and prescribing treatment for folks, but there is a problem. Who will take care of your other patients? You will need another doctor to do what you have been doing, and since Doc isn't here to help at the front desk, you will need that position filled as well."

"You're right, Jim, if people respond to this offer, I won't be able to do what I normally do, at least for several months," said David.

As the two men ate their breakfast, they recognized that more time was needed to consider all the ramifications. When they were finished, David thanked Jim for covering for him and left to get his horse for the trip to Charleston.

"No problem, my friend, I'm glad I can help; besides, I like being here," said Jim with a smile.

The day was long for both doctors. Jim saw people from all over the county suffering from a bad cold to broken bones. When he was done for the day, he headed down the street to the restaurant to have dinner before turning in. He was exhausted.

The hospital in Charleston was overcrowded and understaffed. The hospital administration pushed the doctors to work more hours but made little effort to find additional staff. Several doctors had already given notice, along with a few nurses. Profit was apparently more important than good medicine. While Jim enjoyed his dinner, he thought about his discussion with David earlier that day. Deep in thought and exhausted, he hadn't noticed Sarah walking up to his table.

"May I get you some pie?" asked Sarah.

Jim jumped, startled and embarrassed by not having seen Sarah, and replied, " That would be wonderful, Sarah."

When Sarah brought the pie, Jim asked if she would like to sit with him for a little while.

Sarah looked around to ensure no one needed her and said, "I would like to very much, Doctor Hunter."

"My name is Jim, Sarah. You don't need to call me Doctor."

They enjoyed their brief time together. Both were shy, which caused their discussion to be a little strained, that is until Lizzy ran into the room from the kitchen.

"Hi, Doctor Hunter; I'm so happy to see you and Mommy talking. I think she likes you!"

Quickly, Sarah asked Lizzy to quiet down and told her to go in the back and help Mary.

"Bye, Doctor Hunter; I hope you and Mommy have a good talk."

Sarah was embarrassed, but Jim handled the situation calmly. "Lizzy is such a wonderful little girl, so full of energy and very observant."

Doctor Smith returned to Clayton Sunday afternoon, tired from the trip and the long weekend with Doc. After he had stabled his horse, he and Jim went to the restaurant for dinner before Jim headed back to Charleston.

As the two men sat enjoying their meal, David couldn't help noticing how he and Sarah kept looking at one another fondly.

"She's a fine person, Jim," said David. "It's my understanding that she has been through some really tough times but has kept her head up, taking care of Lizzy and her business."

Jim heard every word David said, but his mind was somewhere else. He and Sarah had briefly talked about her husband's death, the struggles she had gone through, and the difficulties of raising a child on her own, but all of that served as a backdrop to how they were feeling about one another now.

"I know David; she's an incredible woman," said Jim.

"I wanted to talk with you about something you said the other day," said Jim. "Your idea of preventative medicine is wonderful, but the problem is you will need a female to go with you. The women you want to examine will not let you, nor will their husbands, for that matter, unless a woman is present. I know a nurse who is looking for a job that would be wonderful. She left the hospital because of how they have treated us all. I've worked with her, and I can tell you that she is very good at what she does. And as for the doctor you will need, I think I know someone very interested in being in Clayton," he said, smiling.

"Are you sure, Jim? You have an outstanding position at the hospital, something you have worked for your whole life," said an excited David.

"You're right, David. I have a good position at the largest hospital in Charleston, but that's all I have. My life is empty. I have no one to share it with, nothing to work for, no family, no love, only me. I like it here. The people are good, hard-working folk who deserve good medical attention. Besides, a certain lady is becoming very special to me."

The trip back to Charleston went slower than usual as Jim continued to think about his future.

For the first time in his life, he felt truly alive. The early spring flowers and the budding trees had been there two days ago, but today, he noticed. He knew moving to Clayton was right for him, but he also felt responsible for his patients. This transition would take a while, but he knew it was right for him.

Tom had stopped by the clinic to see Jim on Saturday and asked him if he would give Fred a letter he had written asking him to come back to Clayton to help build a shelter at Hank's old place. He also asked if he saw Samuel and Finn to ask them to come as well to clear ten acres of land.

When Archie came by to collect what was owed him for his work at the clinic, Tom asked him if he would work with Fred to build a shelter at Hank's.

"I want to get the property ready as soon as possible so we can hopefully plant the community garden and have summer school in the hills."

"Thanks, Tom; I appreciate the work. Things are a little tight, and the extra money will come in handy," said Archie, reaching out to pay Tom half of his wages against Tom's mortgage on the farm.

"Archie, I can wait on payment; no need to put yourself in a bind," said Tom.

"No, Tom, I promised to pay you every cent I owe you, and I am a man of my word," said Archie humbly.

That Sunday, while Archie and Maggie shared a meal with their dear friend, Widow Henry, Seamus and Carol met at the restaurant to plan their wedding. It wouldn't be long before warmer weather came, and the park would be full of spring flowers, the perfect time for a wedding. Seamus told Carol he had already written a pastor friend in Elkview to preside over the ceremony and that he had agreed to do it any time in the spring.

Their plans would be simple but beautiful. Both wanted their wedding to honor God, who had brought them together. Seamus felt that a ceremony of thanksgiving for the blessing of their love would make the service more God-honoring than one that focused on them.

"We are blessed, and I know our friends are happy for us, but I feel the ceremony should be about praising God," said Seamus.

Carol looked into his eyes and saw the man she loved and knew their lives together would be spent on mission, sharing the truth of Jesus.

"Seamus, I love you" was all that Carol could say before she began to cry.

CHAPTER 33

Mary was working in the kitchen with Sarah after school when Sheriff Griffith entered the restaurant. "Good afternoon, Sheriff. Can I get you some pie and coffee?" asked Sarah.

"A cup of coffee would be fine, Sarah. Could I speak with Mary when she's free?" Sheriff Griffith asked solemnly.

Mary came from the back of the restaurant shortly after his coffee had been served.

"Sarah said you wanted to see me, Sheriff," said Mary.

"Have a seat, Mary; I've got some news I want to share with you. Mary, remember last year when I told you we would get Paul to sell his property and give you half of the money to help you and Rusty?"

"Yes, I remember," said Mary calmly.

"Well, I've been in contact with the county judge, and he has spoken with an attorney Paul hired and found out that common law marriages aren't recognized in West Virginia. Even if Paul were to sell his land, he would not be obligated to give you any money. I'm sorry, Mary; I didn't mean to give you false hope; I hoped he would do the right thing, regardless of the law."

Mary could see that Sheriff Griffith was distraught. Mary was disappointed, but her newfound faith kept her from being upset. Reaching out her hand and putting it on Sheriff Griffith's arm, she looked at him and said, "I appreciate all the effort you have made to help me and Rusty. You're a good man, Sheriff Griffith, you're a good man. Having some financial security would have been nice, but my real security is Christ. Money can only buy things that will eventually be destroyed, but no one can take my faith away. It will be all right. I'm richer today than I ever hoped to be, and it has nothing to do with money," said Mary with a gentle smile.

"Could you do me a favor, Sheriff?" asked Mary.

"Sure, Mary, what can I do for you."

"I want to write Paul a letter, but I don't know how to get it to him in prison. Could you see to it that he gets it for me?"

"I'd be happy to Mary," responded the Sheriff.

When Sheriff Griffith got up to leave the restaurant, he couldn't believe how this impoverished, single mother reacted to the news he had shared with her. There was something about her, some inner strength, that he had seldom seen.

Doctor Hunter met with the hospital administration to tell them he planned to leave the hospital staff but would honor his current contract, which extended until the end of June. When asked why he would give up a promising career, he responded, "I hope you will understand, but all I have here is a medical practice that provides me with an excellent income, but something is missing. I am passionate about caring for my patients, and I will miss them, but that's all I have. Life is meant to be shared with people you love. I know what I am giving up, but I also know what I am getting."

As Doctor Hunter was leaving the meeting, he turned and added, "If there is ever a time that the hospital finds itself overwhelmed and in need of a doctor, I will be happy to help out on a short-term basis."

That relatively short meeting changed Doctor Jim Hunter's life forever.

The following Saturday, Jim Hunter rode to Clayton in a wagon he had borrowed from his new friend, Jim Hoffman, along with Peggy Wallace, a nurse he had worked with at the hospital for the past two years.

Peggy had been a nurse for ten years at General Hospital, but the recent changes had caused her and others to resign. She was a good nurse whom Doctor Hunter thought might be just what the Clayton clinic needed. The lack of a female professional often created problems with David's ability to provide some of his patients with the best care.

As they rode into town, Tom was leaving the restaurant after bringing Sarah the money he owed her from selling her cookies and pies. Doctor Hunter stopped the wagon, introduced Peggy to Tom, and explained that Tom and his wife, Nancy, owned the general store across the street.

Peggy smiled politely, but it was clear that she was all business. She had only agreed to come to Clayton to see if her expertise was needed and if the clinic was up to her standards.

"Nice to meet you, sir," said Peggy, and with that, Jim Hunter continued the ride to the clinic.

Jim tied the horse up and assisted Peggy from the wagon. He then escorted her to the clinic. Just as he was about to open the door, Doctor Smith came out of the door, heading over to get a block of ice Tom had delivered from Charleston.

"Well, well," said David Smith, "it's nice to finally meet the nurse Jim has been talking about for the last few weeks."

"David, please meet my former associate, Peggy Wallace," said Jim.

David welcomed Peggy to the clinic and suggested he could show her around when she was settled from the trip from Charleston. Peggy replied that she could wait to straighten up and would appreciate a tour of the facility now rather than wait.

Proudly, Doctor Smith showed her the examination rooms, his office, and the equipment they had gotten from the hospital earlier that year. When he was done, he asked her if she would like to come to his office to discuss his expectations and learn of hers. After both were seated,

David offered Peggy a cold drink of water, which she gladly accepted. Doctor Smith explained that he would need her help with all the female patients and that, in addition, she would need to travel with him in the backwoods to help the poor.

Peggy was not sure about all that Doctor Smith desired. "Why do I need to go into the backcountry? Why don't your patients come to the clinic?"

David smiled as he explained that many people come into town for help but that he had found many didn't take the time to travel to Clayton or were frightened of the city. "These are good people that barely have a cent to their names, so the thought of incurring medical care costs scares most of them. You'll see, we're going out for a few hours this afternoon."

"Well, for my part," began Peggy, "First of all, I think it would be better if I am involved in all your examinations so that I am better prepared to assist you when you are busy. Secondly, I am uncomfortable with going into the backwoods, but I will wait to see what it is like. I didn't ask Doctor Hunter where I would be staying, but I assumed it would be at the boardinghouse we passed on the way into town. Do you know if there are any homes for rent in the area? I can imagine boarding houses can get noisy in the evenings. I prefer to keep to myself and read when I'm not working.

"I want to keep up with all the latest medical practices to be the best nurse I can be," said Nurse Wallace.

"Let's see how you like visiting the backwoods folks first, and if it interests you, I will see if I can find a rental property for you. I think you will find the people in Clayton to be very welcoming. You'll like it here, Nurse Wallace, I am sure of that," said David, somewhat surprised by the stand-offish attitude Peggy projected.

Seamus and Carol went to the general store to discuss a few things they wanted to get for their wedding with Nancy. Carol had planned on using flowers she found in the meadows outside of town to decorate the trellis in the park.

Their biggest concern was seating. Nancy told them about a place in Charleston where she could rent folding chairs and an altar. "I will send them a letter this afternoon and explain what you want and when you need it," said Nancy, hardly able to control her excitement.

"What are you doing for wedding rings?" asked Nancy. "

"We're going to wait until we have the money to buy rings," said Seamus humbly.

"How about I have a couple of rings sent to the store to accompany your beautiful engagement ring? You can purchase them from us on credit," said Nancy.

"That would be wonderful, Nancy," said Carol," but we don't want to be a burden."

"Nonsense, Carol, it will be my pleasure to help you two."

After they had finished shopping, Seamus said he wanted to go to the church and complete his sermon preparation. Carol could tell something was bothering him, so she reached out and grabbed his arm. "Hey, what's wrong?" asked Carol.

"I feel like I can't provide for you what you deserve, and I don't see that changing. I guess I'm feeling inadequate."

Carol reached up and, touching his cheek, said, "Seamus, I thought you knew me better than that. I don't want things; I want you. I see us working together in ministry, being and doing all that God calls us to be. I want to share my life with you; that's everything I have ever wanted. I love you."

Seamus smiled as the two hugged goodbye.

The roads were muddy, what roads there were, and the wind made an otherwise beautiful day challenging. Doctor Smith and Nurse Wallace visited four families to see how they were doing. During each visit, Doctor Smith introduced Peggy as his nurse and explained that she would be with him during all female examinations.

"I want to ensure you have good quality health care," said David. "I am going to start providing free examinations next week. This way, we can track you through the years and know better what to do if there are any changes. Feel free to tell everyone you know."

After their last visit to the young couple and their baby, David described the delivery and how Nancy had helped.

"This is how it is in this part of the world, Peggy. I hope you will grow to share my enthusiasm for caring for the poor," said David. Hesitating, he continued, "I can imagine that today has been eye-opening to you, maybe even overwhelming, but I wanted you to know what life in the mountains is like. These people live the only way they know how; they are poor and have little, if any, education. They're good people, Peggy. If you decide to stay, you will grow to care for them."

"It was very interesting, I'll say that," replied Nurse Wallace.

"Are they always as nice when you show up? I imagined them to be more protective."

"They were at first, but I've been making my rounds for the last few months, and they have started to trust me. You'll see, it takes time for them to believe you only want to help.

" I also wanted to mention that you may not be allowed by the men to help with their examinations. If they will permit it, fine, but my guess is most will not want a woman around they do not know to know their private business. Again, you have to learn to be patient with these folks."

As the day ended, Nurse Wallace was escorted to the boardinghouse and treated to dinner by Doctor Smith. When Sarah brought their meals to their table, Doctor Smith introduced her. Once again, Peggy was polite but could have been more friendly.

That evening, Peggy settled into her room and took out her journal to write about the day. Writing in her journal was something she had been doing ever since she began practicing. In many ways, this was the only place she felt she could express her feelings.

The entry for today was one of the most interesting she could remember. As she wrote, she began to realize that this position would require her to do more than practice her medical skills; it would need her to make personal connections with very simple people that, if she were honest with herself, frightened her.

Doctor Smith was more personable with his patients than she was used to, which caused her some concern. To her, medicine was science, and it wasn't necessary to know your patients as much as Doctor Smith seemed to want to.

The following day, Peggy came downstairs for breakfast. Mary came to her table to see what she would like.

"Two hard-boiled eggs with toast will be fine," said Peggy.

"Would you like some coffee?" asked Mary.

"No, thank you. I want some tea if you have any," replied Peggy.

"Sure thing, I'll be back with your tea shortly. By the way, my name is Mary. You must be the new nurse I've heard about. Welcome to Clayton," said Mary, returning to the kitchen.

As Peggy sipped her tea, she tried to imagine living in this little town. She had always lived in the city and enjoyed being "invisible" when she wasn't working. In Clayton, it seemed everyone knew each other on a much more personal level than she thought she would like. However, she also knew that she needed to work. Leaving the hospital in Charleston had been difficult, but she could no longer work in an environment that treated professionals like uneducated help.

Peggy had worked very hard to obtain her nursing certificate, working full-time while taking classes. She was overly proud of her accomplishment because of all she had to endure. As she continued, deep in thought, Mary came with her breakfast and asked if she needed anything else. Motioning for more tea, Peggy looked at Mary for the first time. She seemed to be a happy sort, but something about her was different.

After breakfast, Peggy went to the clinic to talk with Doctor Smith. During their conversation, she mentioned that she wasn't comfortable going into the backwoods to check in on people.

"They make me very anxious. They stare at you, and who knows what they are thinking? I also think you get too close with your patients for a professional.

"Well, that's what I think, so if you don't want me to stay, I will understand; otherwise, I'll give it six months and then decide for the long term."

David was surprised to hear all that Peggy said, but he could see how someone from a large city might feel like she did.

"You stay just as long as you want, Nurse Wallace. All that I ask is that should you decide to leave, you let me know in advance so that I can find a replacement. I don't want these folks to lack any medical help they might need."

With that exchange, Doctor Smith and Nurse Wallace began working together at the Clayton Medical Clinic.

Doctor Hunter began coming to Clayton every weekend to help at the clinic. Sometimes, he would visit people he had met from the backcountry, but most days, he stayed in town, freeing Doctor Smith to travel. Being in town more often allowed him to see Sarah regularly. He knew he had strong feelings for her but wanted to take everything slowly. He understood that she had more to deal with than just how she might feel about him.

They talked about how deeply she loved her late husband and that a part of her wasn't sure she could ever be that vulnerable again. Then there was Lizzy. Sarah was very protective of her daughter, always keeping her from anything or anyone that could bring back those dark days following her husband's death.

On Saturday, as Sarah prepared food for the dinner crowd, Lizzy asked if she was in love with Doctor Hunter. The question surprised Sarah. Putting her cooking aside, she sat down and asked Lizzy to sit on her lap.

"Doctor Hunter is a very nice man, honey, and I enjoy spending time with him, but I don't know if I love him. Ever since your daddy went home to be with the Lord, I've missed him very much. I think about him every day. Doctor Hunter is very nice, but he isn't your father."

Lizzy hugged her mother and softly said, "Daddy would want you to be happy, Mommy. It's all right if you love Doctor Hunter; I think he is really nice. Daddy would like him too."

Hopping down from Sarah's lap, Lizzy kissed her on the cheek and said, "It's going to be fine, Mommy. God loves you."

Nurse Wallace had grown up in Richmond, Virginia. Her father was a well-respected attorney in the area. They lived in a lovely home in the Richmond Hills area. Her mother was very involved in local society, often hosting tea parties for her friends. Peggy attended a small private school that provided her with a quality education, but something was always missing. Her parents were very involved in their lives and seldom did anything with her other than attend church on occasion. Her father's legal practice consumed most of his time. He was a good man but not overly affectionate.

As the years went on, Peggy became increasingly isolated; her friends at school were more interested in flirting with boys and going to dances. Peggy never felt she belonged. Being a good student didn't help. Her classmates teased her about being the teacher's pet and never included her in their parties.

She begged her father to attend nursing school in Baltimore when she graduated. She wanted to leave Richmond and discover life on her terms. After graduating from nursing school, she moved west to a new hospital she had learned about from one of her teachers. Striking out on her own had been exciting, but she soon discovered that she didn't have many friends again. She had grown to distrust people and felt more comfortable keeping to herself.

She had gotten to know Doctor Hunter during her years at the Charleston hospital. He was different than anyone she had ever known. He was an excellent doctor, always full of energy. He had been raised on a farm in Kentucky and still had some of the characteristics of a countryman. He ignored her shyness and talked with her throughout the day as they did their rounds together.

When things began to get difficult at the hospital, Doctor Hunter tried to comfort her. Finally, she realized that she could no longer stay. It was then that Jim told her about this little town a couple of hours away that needed a nurse. She never knew why, but she told him she would go when he suggested it to her, even though it was nothing she ever thought she wanted.

With the spring flowers coming into full bloom and the tree leaves opening to a fresh bright green, many things were about to change in Clayton besides the season.

CHAPTER 34

EASTER IN CLAYTON was always the most glorious Sunday of the year. The return from a dormant winter season to the beauty of spring flowers and warmer temperatures only served to emphasize the celebration of Christ's resurrection. This season of new life was a reminder of what Easter is about.

Seamus McConnell had spent the last few weeks reflecting on what he needed to say in his sermon. Still, it wasn't until Rusty knocked on his door on Saturday that he realized exactly what had been in the undercurrents of his mind during this time of reflection.

"Reverend McConnell, can we go fishing?" asked Rusty.

"The springtime is the best fishing all year long."

Looking at his little buddy, Seamus realized how much he had missed spending time with his new friend.

"Let's go see if it's all right with your mother, "said Seamus.

Mary was thrilled that Rusty was comfortable with Reverend McConnell. She wanted him to have a Godly example of a man rather than the father who had abandoned them. Quickly, they rushed to get Seamus' horse ready and gathered the fishing poles. Standing next to Seamus, Rusty held out his arms, waiting to be picked up and put on the horse.

Smiling from ear to ear, Rusty headed out with his adopted father to his favorite fishing hole. That day was special for each of them. For Seamus, the peaceful joy of being with this little boy brought a desire to be Rusty's surrogate father and to help teach him about being a man of God. On Rusty's part, there was comfort in being with Reverend McConnell, a fatherly security that he had never known.

That afternoon, they caught eight trout and laughed at the funny stories they shared, but more importantly, that day, they bonded. Rusty knew that he could trust Seamus, and Seamus discovered how much he loved Rusty. From that day on, Rusty and Seamus would go fishing on Saturday afternoons for the rest of the summer through the fall.

As the church filled with folks from all over the county, the sun shone through the windows, filling the sanctuary with the brightness of spring. The flowers the Campbells had supplied from a Charleston florist gave the sanctuary a sweet aroma. After singing two opening hymns, Hank walked to the podium.

Hank read the scriptures most Sundays, but this was the first Easter he had gotten the honor. Opening his Bible, Hank read about the resurrection of Jesus Christ and began trembling. When he finished reading, tears dripped on his Bible from his cheeks. In a soft voice, he said, "Thank you Jesus."

When Hank had settled into his seat, Reverend McConnell rose and came to the podium. Before opening his Bible or looking at his notes, he looked at Hank and said, "Amen, my dear brother, amen."

Beginning his sermon, Seamus slowly looked out into the audience, noticing Mary, Hank, and Fred and then looking at his little friend Rusty, and was overwhelmed.

"I have spoken at many Easter morning services, but today, as I look out at each of you, I see many people who weren't here a year ago and am again reminded of the power of Easter. The resurrection is the most crucial event in history, yet it is taken far too lightly if we are not careful. Most of the world doesn't believe that it happened. Most of the people of the world, if they're honest, don't think that God exists. The resurrection did happen because God loves us so much that He was willing to sacrifice His only Son to pay the price for our failures. Without the resurrection, none of what Christ did in his life would have mattered, but with His resurrection, if we completely believe in Jesus as our Savior, we will live eternally with God.

"Yesterday, a friend knocked on my door, and I immediately opened it and asked him to come in. The rest of the day, I kept thinking of what Christ said about how he is standing at the door of our hearts, knocking. Will you open your heart or continue going about your lives, ignoring His cry for your peace in Him? My friend knocked on my door because he wanted something only I could give him. When I opened my door, we were filled with happiness, knowing how much we had missed one another. He knocked, wanting me to spend time with him, just like Christ knocks on the door of your heart, simply wanting to spend time with you. Today, he is knocking. Will you open your heart and welcome Him into your life? Your life will never be the same."

As the congregation sang a closing hymn, Rusty put down his hymnal and walked to the front of the church, tears rolling down his face. Seamus held out his arms and grabbed his little friend while they knelt at the altar together and prayed. Soon, others came. Mary joined her son, crying out to the Lord a prayer of thanksgiving. Hank came and, laying his hands on the shoulders of Mary and Seamus, fervently prayed while many others came forward in support of this new believer.

When the service ended and most people left, Widow Henry sat in a pew talking with Hank. Both of them were wiping tears from their eyes.

Hank had shared with Widow Henry that he was going to leave Clayton and move to a former slave community at the mouth of Cabin Creek.

"I heard about these folks and felt God calling me to go to them and share the peace I have received from Christ. These folks are in the same place I was before I met you, Ma'am; they are poor and angry. They hate people just because they are white. I know how they have suffered and how hard forgiveness is, but a life full of hate isn't worth living. Please pray that I can share with them what you have shared with me in a way that reaches their souls."

In a gentle voice, Widow Henry said, "Hank, I will miss you. I have grown very fond of you as a dear friend, yet I know that what you are doing is just what Christ told us to do: share the good news. I hope you'll stay for a little while longer; I'm sure the people of Clayton will want to say their goodbyes."

"I plan on staying until the end of May so that I can make sure you have plenty of inventory at the mill," said Hank. "I'm sure going to miss you, Ma'am."

When Widow Henry and Hank finished their conversation, Seamus and Carol came over to see if everything was all right. Widow Henry shared that Hank was going to leave Clayton as a disciple, going to a new community to share the good news.

Seamus reached out to shake Hank's hand, but the two men hugged when Hank stood.

"I am going to miss you, my friend. You have encouraged me many times this past year with your loving heart for others. How long are you going to be with us?"

"I'll be here until the end of May. You know, Reverend, I would sure like to spend some time with you before I go. I need your help knowing how to reach these folks," said Hank.

When Mary and Rusty returned to the boardinghouse, Sarah was with Lizzy. "What a great day!" exclaimed Sarah. "Rusty, I'm so happy for you."

Mary started to speak, but tears of joy filled her eyes again. Putting her hand on Mary's arm, Sarah said, "Why don't we make a picnic lunch and take the children to the park? It's such a beautiful day."

That afternoon, the residents of Clayton shared Easter with one another. Widow Henry had Archie, Maggie, and little Alma Gay over to her home for dinner. Sarah, Mary, and their children spent the afternoon at the park. The Campbells had Hank and Fred over for the afternoon. Carol and Seamus had a small dinner at Seamus's home and began making final plans for their upcoming wedding while Doctor Smith returned from Charleston with Doc.

Doc's recovery was moving along very slowly. He had limited use of his left side, and his speech was difficult to understand. He was learning how to form words using the right side of his mouth. All in all, he was doing as well as could have been expected. His daughter had spent a week with him in Charleston but couldn't convince him to move to Ohio to be with her.

Doc slowly explained that he wanted her to enjoy her life with her family.

"We've been apart for a long time, and I don't think now would be a good time to be together. I want you to remember how I was, not how I am now. I want to spend whatever time I have left with my friends in Clayton."

The ride back to Clayton seemed to encourage Doc. He loved this little town and the people that lived there. As they rode along River Road, he remembered when he was a little boy and how he used to fish along the riverbank. He saw trails in the woods that he used to hike.

"How's Sherriff?" asked Doc. "I miss that old cuss."

Doctor Smith saw the change in Doc's countenance as the wagon slowly made its way home. He had a gentle smile on his face, only marred by the effects of the stroke.

As the two rode up Henry Way, Mary and Sarah saw the wagon and ran from the park to say hello. Seamus and Carol had just left to go to the park to talk about seating and saw Doc. They, too, ran to greet him. As his friends surrounded him, Sheriff Griffith noticed everyone running and came out of his office. Seeing Doc, he began running, yelling, "Welcome home, you old goat!"

During all this beautiful day, Nurse Wallace stayed in her room. She hadn't gone to church or out to enjoy the beautiful spring day, nor had she said so much as a word to anyone. While she thought her solitude brought her comfort, she subconsciously longed to have friends, someone whom she could share life with, but her fear kept her from reaching out. Hearing all the commotion, she went to her window to see what was happening. To her amazement, people were coming from all over town to welcome the man Doctor Smith had with him.

"There he goes again, making friends with his patients," she said to herself as she headed back to her chair to continue reading.

That night, as Peggy was lying in bed, she thought about what she had seen earlier. *What would it be like to have so many people glad to see you?*

When morning came, Peggy went downstairs to the restaurant for breakfast. When Mary came over to bring her tea, she asked, "Who was that man everyone was coming out to see yesterday?"

"Oh, that was Doc. He used to care for people in these parts before Doctor Smith came to town," replied Mary. "He's been in Charleston recovering from a stroke. Doctor Smith goes to see him every weekend."

While Peggy ate her breakfast, she couldn't help thinking about the considerable effort going to Charleston every weekend must have been for Doctor Smith. By the end of the week, he must be exhausted, yet he still traveled all that way."

As the work week began, Archie started plowing his field, preparing it for the growing season. Hank brought in several logs to cut for lumber, and Sarah began to clean rooms that had been used during the weekend. Mary and Carol taught their classes at the school, and Seamus gathered his things to make a trip into the backwoods. Nothing looked different, yet everything had changed.

Doctor Smith and Nurse Wallace met to discuss Doc's care schedule.

Nurse Wallace was to be Doc's primary caregiver, while Doctor Smith cared for patients as they came to the clinic. Peggy knew that Doc would need close attention for the next few weeks. Doc was slowly recovering, but it would be a long time before he could do most of the tasks he had done before his stroke. The first time Peggy came into the room, she told him that she would be helping take care of him. Doc looked confused at this revelation. In a very slow, slurred voice, he told Nurse Wallace that he didn't think he would need much help, but soon, he discovered just how much support he did need.

Peggy wasn't prepared for the visitors he had every day. Most brought food and, after leaving it in the kitchen, would sit beside his bed telling stories, most of which were about episodes they had had with Doc during their lives. Peggy noticed they enjoyed the time with Doc as much, if not more, than Doc.

Most evenings before going to bed, Peggy would think about that day's stories and the people who took time to be with Doc. They all were busy, but whatever they had to do wasn't as important as being with their friend.

Tom had agreed to help Carol and Seamus with Hank's old place, so he rode out to see Archie one afternoon. As Tom rounded the last curve in the road, he saw Archie hard at work, plowing his garden. Archie looked up and, seeing Tom, stopped what he was doing and walked over to see him.

"Let's take your horse down to the creek for a drink," said Archie.

As the two men walked the short distance to the creek, Tom told Archie he needed help.

"Remember our meeting about trying to reach out to the folks in the backwoods? With the weather warming up, let's get started. I've contacted Fred, who agreed to help you build the shelter we mentioned. Also, I would like you two, Samuel and Finn, to clear as much of the ten acres next to the cabin as possible; that's where I want to plant the community vegetable garden. Archie, it will be a lot of work, but we need to get started before too long. Do you have the time?" asked Tom.

"Sure, I'd be glad to work for you, Tom. Let's go over to the property, and you can show me what you want done," said Archie with a sense of relief in his voice. He knew if something didn't come along, he would have to look for work in Charleston soon.

Tom and Archie rode to Hank's old place, and Tom showed Archie the boundaries of the ten acres. As they were about to leave, Tom asked Archie if he thought he could get to the work soon. Archie told Tom he needed to finish getting his garden ready but thought he could start by the following week.

"Sure, you get done what you need to do and get started as soon as you possibly can," replied Tom," I'll let Finn and Samuel know."

As Tom was about to ride back to Clayton, Archie looked at him and said, "Thank you, Tom, I needed the work."

Tom knew the next few weeks would be a very busy time for this little community, affecting many people in the months ahead.

CHAPTER 35

Early Friday morning, Tom hitched his horse onto the wagon and left for Charleston. He had several things he had to tend to, so he left just after sunrise. As the light of day began filtering through the hills to his left, Tom could see two Dogwood trees with beautiful white blooms in the otherwise dormant forest. It wouldn't be long before the other trees would spread open their leaves.

The river was running fast with melting snow and rainwater from the storm on Tuesday. Just before he got to Elkview, Tom noticed some houses being built on the west side of the river overlooking a small waterfall. As the population was expanding from the growing industry in and around Charleston, it made sense that people needed houses to live in. He knew new housing was also required in Clay County since most old farmhouses were now occupied.

About three miles outside Charleston, the sky darkened from the smoke spewing from the factories. He couldn't help remembering simpler times when the river was crystal clear and the sky as bright as anywhere he could imagine.

As usual, Tom's first stop was at Hoffman's. Seeing Tom, Jim ran out to meet him, but it seemed to Tom that something was wrong.

"Hey, Tom, it's good to see you," said Jim, with less enthusiasm than usual. Before they discussed Tom's order, Tom looked at his friend and asked, "Is everything all right, Jim?"

Jim's head dropped, and Tom could tell something was terribly wrong. "Can you come to my office?" asked Jim.

Putting his hand on Jim's shoulder, Tom walked into the office. When Jim closed the door, Tom noticed he had tears in his eyes. "What is it, Jim," asked Tom.

"We lost the baby," said Jim with a trembling voice. "She was fine for the first month but then began getting weaker and weaker. The doctors told us that her heart was very weak, and they couldn't do anything for her. She died in her sleep earlier this week."

"How's your wife doing, Jim? " Tom asked.

"Not very well at all, Tom. Both of us are overcome with grief I can't begin to explain. It hurts, Tom, it really hurts!"

As the two friends sat in Jim's office, Tom felt it was better to listen than to try to offer advice. He knew the pain of not being able to have children, but to have a daughter and lose her was more than he could imagine. After listening to Jim for a long time, Tom said that he needed to leave for the time being and return the next day.

" You can wait to fill my order, Jim; take whatever time you need."

Tom didn't know what to do. He could offer Jim and his wife to come to Clayton and stay with him and Nancy for a while, but Jim needed to be at his store. Walking downtown, deep in thought, Tom walked into Howard McDougal's office.

Tom had written to Howard earlier to let him know he needed to speak with him for a few minutes. As Howard greeted him, he could tell something was bothering Tom.

"Come into my office, Tom. What can I do for you today?" asked Howard.

"Sorry, I'm having trouble gathering myself, Howard. I just found out Jim Hoffman and his wife lost their baby girl."

"Vivian and I stopped by his place a couple of weekends ago to see what he carried. It's a nice place, not your normal supply store. He thanked us for stopping by as we left, but I could tell something was bothering him. I can't imagine what they must be going through. I will stop by this evening and see what we can do."

"Thanks, Howard, that would be nice," said Tom.

"Why don't we go to the diner and have an early lunch, Tom? We can talk there," suggested Howard.

After the short walk, Tom had gathered himself. The two men ordered lunch, and when the waitress brought their food, Howard asked her if there was anything she would like him to pray for as they were about to pray over their food. Looking puzzled, the waitress shook her head and said, "I don't believe all that stuff about prayer."

"Well then, I'll pray that someday you do," said Howard boldly.

After the waitress left, Howard prayed for Jim and his wife, thanked God for providing their food, and then asked God to open the eyes and heart of their waitress. Tom was pleasantly surprised. He remembered the days when Howard felt awkward praying in public, but now, he was bold with his faith.

As they enjoyed their food, Tom told Howard how he and Nancy wanted to build four houses on the south end of Clayton, next to the park.

"Howard, I want you to do the house's architectural renderings. We would like each of them to be different. One with one bedroom and a guest room, two with an additional bedroom, and the fourth one to have four bedrooms. We want to have available housing for new people moving to our area, regardless of the size of their families."

"Well, well," said Howard, "things must be changing in Clayton."

"They are Howard, just like everywhere else. We want to have houses that welcome our new neighbors and make them feel at home from the first day they move to town," said Tom.

"I'll get right on it, Tom," said Howard. "Are you staying in town tonight, or are you headed back this afternoon?" asked Howard.

"I thought I would stay at the hotel and go back tomorrow. I have a few other stops to make."

"Nonsense, you stay at our place. Vivian would love to see you and discover what has been happening in your world. I insist," said Howard with a broad smile on his face.

"If it's not a bother, that would be wonderful. I always enjoy visiting with you two. I'll be by around six."

After lunch, Howard returned to his office while Tom headed for the teacher's college. The time had come for Clayton to find two new schoolteachers—the growing number of children coming to the local school required two qualified teachers. Carol had told him that she wanted to start a school for the backwoods folks in the county, but Tom could tell there was more to it than just a school. She and Seamus were looking to do mission work in the mountains to reach people who were lost. Carol had told their committee that she would stay on at the school as long as they needed her, understanding the custom that married women didn't teach. It was a custom that often cost communities good teachers, but for now, that's how it would be.

Tom met with the head of placement services at the teacher's college and told him about Clayton.

"Our population is growing, and therefore, so is our school. Up until now, we have had one certified teacher and two teacher aids that work with the younger children. The teacher we currently have is getting married but has agreed to stay until her replacement can be found," said Tom with a sense of pride in his community.

Tom explained the area and the type of people that lived there. "They're good people, hardworking, but they lack formal education. Carol, our current teacher, has done a wonderful job working with the children, teaching them the joy and excitement of learning."

As Tom finished, he could tell the administrator had something on his mind. "Who pays for your current teacher since Clayton is an unincorporated town?"

"Up until now, the community has paid the teacher's salary and built the schoolhouse," replied Tom."

Incorporated cities allocate a portion of their real estate taxes to their local schools, and I would guess that since Clayton will now require more teachers, the county will demand tax revenue to cover the cost. I will contact the Clay County Education Commissioner to see how much they will pay for these positions and then get back to you with any candidates we may have."

This small private teachers' college only wanted to place their students in well-paying positions, often in large cities. Tom left the meeting a little discouraged but still hopeful something would work out.

As the afternoon was ending, Tom realized he still hadn't seen Thomas Franklin. The meeting at the college had gone longer than he had expected, so he rushed uptown to Thomas' office, arriving there just before they were about to close for the day.

Opening the door, Tom was breathing heavily as Thomas walked into the reception area.

"I wondered if you would make it," said Thomas. "I know you try to get a lot done when you come to town."

"I'm sorry, Thomas. I got stuck at the teachers' college talking with their placement administrator."

"How did that go?" asked Thomas.

The look on Tom's face told Thomas all that he needed to know.

"It's tough to find any employees nowadays. The need is outpacing the supply. With industry taking off, people are moving here in droves, so teachers are in high demand. I told you before I would check around, and I have; that's why I know what's going on out there. I'll keep looking, but I'm not overly optimistic. Now, what else can I do for you, Tom?"

"Nancy and I want to parcel off the property we own next to the park to build houses. We will start with four houses and, as they sell, build more. Clayton is growing, and all the old houses are either being used or aren't in good enough condition to be lived in."

"So, you will need some of the property for a street and then divide it into lots. I assume the standard city style lot size as opposed to some larger tracts the older homes have."

"Yes, that's correct, only I would like the lots to be wider so that the houses aren't so close together," said Tom.

Tom explained that their vision was to build a street of welcoming houses, not overcrowded, to complement the other homes in Clayton.

"I'll take care of it for you, Tom, and send you preliminary drawings before going to the county board."

As the two men were saying their goodbyes, Tom asked what had happened to Thomas' role as legal representative for the coal mine operators. With a somewhat guilty look, Thomas said, " It was too hard to pass up the money they pay Tom. I know they are not the kind of people I like doing business with, but sometimes you have to do what you don't like."

"I was just wondering," said Tom, trying not to show his disappointment.

"Thanks for all of your help, Thomas," said Tom on his way out the door.

When Tom finally reached Howard's home, Vivian met him at the front door.

"Howard will be back in a minute, Tom; he said something about having to go to Hoffman's for a while."

That evening, Tom told Howard and Vivian about all the changes in Clayton.

"We need to come visit you and Nancy Tom. We're so busy with work, and now, on weekends, Vivian and I work in a food pantry our church has for the needy. I love helping people, but we must skip one Saturday and come out to Clayton. When I finish the drawings, we will contact you and plan our visit?"

The evening was as fun as always, full of laughter and news from their different worlds. It was clear that Howard and Vivian were very different from what Tom remembered. It seemed that most of their stories centered around work they were doing with their church in the lower-income communities of Charleston.

As they headed for bed, Howard told Tom about his visit with Jim Hoffman.

"He's hurting, as you saw, so I did all I could. I shared some scripture and then prayed with him. I don't think he was used to anyone praying outside of church. He seemed surprised that I bowed my head and prayed for him and his wife in his office. Anyway, I plan to stop by to see him as often as possible. I think Vivian and I will have them over for dinner next week. Thanks for letting me know, Tom; he's a good person that needs our help."

When Tom lay down that evening, he couldn't help thinking about the changes he saw in his friend. He had always been a good guy, but now he took faith more seriously. Drifting off to sleep after a very long day, he asked God to guide him in finding teachers for Clayton.

The next morning, Vivian had breakfast ready for Tom and Howard, and as they ate, Vivian mentioned that she was going to Hoffman's to see if she could visit Jim's wife.

Leaving, Tom thanked his hosts for a beautiful time and headed to Hoffman's. When Tom arrived, his wagon was filled with his order, including folding chairs and an altar. "Thanks for having everything ready, Jim; I was hoping to get on the road this morning," said Tom.

"No problem," said Jim, "I'll see you next time you're in town."

It seemed odd to Tom how quickly Jim rushed off, so he followed him into his office before leaving. "Hey Jim, is everything all right?"

"Sorry, I was a little upset that you told Mr. McDougal about our baby. We were keeping it to ourselves," replied Jim.

"Well, my friend, I didn't mean to upset you, but honestly, this isn't the time to withdraw from people. Howard and Vivian are two of the nicest people I know in Charleston. We all need someone to share our burdens with occasionally. I'm sorry if I offended you," said Tom.

"Oh, it's okay; I know you meant well," said Jim.

As Tom began his ride back to Clayton, he thought about Jim and his wife and how they were trying to handle their grief independently, without any faith or community to support them. Once again, he thanked God for the small town he was privileged to live in and, more importantly, the trust he and Nancy shared in Christ.

Seamus helped Tom unload the folding chairs and the altar into one of the park shelters. That evening, he and Carol went to the park to determine where they wanted the chairs set up. With the placement determined, Carol and Seamus went to the general store to see the rings Nancy had ordered. With much excitement, each tried on the rings and quickly concluded which ones they wanted.

"I thought those would be the ones you would choose. You can pay for them when you can, no hurry. Now you two can enjoy this time getting ready for your wedding," said an excited Nancy.

As Saturday ended, Tom and Nancy shared iced tea and discussed the business Tom had been able to accomplish while in Charleston. Nancy told Tom how Doc was doing. She had gone by to see him after the store closed Friday.

"After the wedding, I will host a small group of women for tea. Nurse Wallace is very quiet, but if you ask me, I think she's lonely and could use some new friends."

"She sure is very efficient," said Tom, "but doesn't seem very comfortable with people."

"Yes, she's very good at what she does, but she's all business. I want to help her if I can."

After worship Sunday, as the final hymn was being sung, Carol joined Seamus at the podium. Holding hands, Seamus told everyone they were invited to their wedding on Saturday.

" If the Lord provides, we will have the ceremony at Clayton Park. Our only request is that you not bring any gifts, but if you can, please help us resupply the food pantry. After going into the backwoods this past week, I can assure you that there is a great need. Thank you. Hope we see you Saturday at two o'clock."

The next day, Fred came back to Clayton with Samuel. Finn had left Charleston one night, and Samuel wasn't sure where he was going.

"He said something about going back east for a bit, but when I asked him where he just said he had something he needed to do. It seemed strange, but he didn't want to tell me, so I let it go; he acted upset," said Samuel.

After Fred and Samuel had dinner at the restaurant, they got rooms in the boardinghouse and called it a night.

Archie finished preparing his field for the growing season Monday and went into town to order lumber from Hank. Seeing his old friend,

Archie couldn't help but hug him. "I'm going to miss you, Hank. You and I have done a lot together and had a few laughs, too."

"I know. I'm going to miss this place and the people who have treated me like family, especially you, but I've been praying about it for a long time, and it just wouldn't be right for me to learn about real freedom and not tell others just like me. They need to know what I know and feel the joy in true freedom," said Hank enthusiastically.

After telling Hank how much lumber he needed and what he and the guys would build, Archie bid farewell to his friend and headed back to his cabin. Before leaving town, he stopped by to see Fred and Samuel to let them know Hank would begin their order tomorrow and that, in the meantime, they should get what equipment Tom had and meet him at Hank's old place at nine the following morning.

CHAPTER 36

This was the week Carol and Seamus had looked forward to for months. It was hard to believe that in just a few short days, they would be husband and wife, but along with the excitement came the anxiety of making sure each of the details were taken care of. Seamus had arranged for his pastor friend from Elkview to officiate the ceremony and to preach Sunday's sermon; he didn't feel he would have the time to prepare a message. Carol was busy at school during the day and handling wedding details in the evenings.

On Wednesday, Nancy came by the schoolhouse after the children had been dismissed to see Carol.

"How are you doing, Carol?" began Nancy.

Carol replied that she was almost finished with the wedding planning. "I have asked Sarah to prepare our wedding cake, and Widow Henry will bring drinks for the reception. Sarah and Mary are making little sandwiches for the guests, and I've asked Lizzy and Rusty to help me pick wildflowers on Saturday morning. We have rings and wedding clothes, thanks to you, so I think everything is handled."

"Well, there is one thing that you didn't mention. Friday evening, I have invited several women to our home for a dinner party in your honor," said Nancy, smiling from ear to ear. Carol had known about the possibility of getting together with her friends, but with everything she was handling, she had forgotten.

Hank initially came to see Seamus to discuss his ideas about sharing his faith. Seamus assured him that he didn't need to preach to people, live a life honoring Christ, and get to know the people God puts in his path." You will know when and what to say if you pray about it. The Holy Spirit will direct you, walk by faith my friend, and words will flow like living water," said Seamus. The two men continued talking for over an hour about Hank's challenges in a community that has known so much hate and poverty.

"One of the hardest issues you will face from those that come to a relationship with Christ is forgiveness. Be patient; God will slowly lead them," counseled Seamus.

As Hank was leaving, he asked Seamus if he would like to have dinner at the restaurant Friday evening "before you get hitched."

Laughing, Seamus agreed as the two men hugged goodbye.

Rain on Thursday helped brighten all the new leaves on the trees. The Dogwoods were now in full bloom, along with many of the wildflowers. Hank had been able to cut all the lumber ordered by Tom for the shelter, and Archie had picked it up on Wednesday.

As Archie, Samuel, and Fred worked on the shelter, Hank came to see how they were doing. It was the first time he had returned to the place since he had moved to Clayton, and he knew this would be the last time he would see his old home.

He had gone through quite a lot there. He remembered the solitude and distrust that defined his life back then. He also remembered how he became best friends with a young white man who, one night, saved his life.

"Hey, guys, that looks good," yelled Hank.

Turning to see his old friend, Archie replied, "Thanks, Hank. What brings you out to this place?"

"Oh, I just wanted to see how everything was coming along and help if possible. I am waiting on some logs to be delivered and had time," said Hank as he rushed over to help Fred lift a large support beam.

The men worked all afternoon into the early evening. When work was done for the day, they headed back into town.

"You know guys, I'm having dinner at the restaurant with Reverend McConnell Friday; maybe you could join us? We could enjoy being with him before his big day."

"That sounds good," said Archie. "I'll let Tom know when I stop by to see him about how we're coming on the shelter."

Friday began like most Fridays, everyone busily working on whatever project they had taken on. Archie and his friends continued building the shelter; Carol was teaching school while Sarah began making side dishes for the men having dinner at the restaurant that evening. Sarah and Mary would have to be late for Nancy's dinner party, which was all part of running a business. Tom and Nancy were busy preparing their house for the evening dinner party while Seamus ensured the seats and altar were placed just right. At the end of the day, Doctor Hunter arrived from Charleston.

When Jim was getting his room key, he asked Sarah if she was busy that evening. When Sarah told him about the dinner party at Nancy and Tom's, he asked who would cover for her at the restaurant. After telling him her plan, he immediately said he would clear all the tables for her and Mary so they could get to their event as soon as possible. Sarah modestly attempted to decline Jim's offer, but when he insisted, she accepted, thrilled that she could go so much earlier.

Women from all over town began arriving at Nancy's home. Carol was escorted by Lizzy, who would return to the restaurant to help her mother and Mary. Lizzy was very excited about the honor of escorting her teacher to the party.

When they arrived, Lizzy told Carol, "I will see you at the meadow at ten o'clock tomorrow morning to help pick flowers, Miss Carol." With that announcement, Lizzy turned and ran back to the boardinghouse, skipping all the way.

The men also arrived at the restaurant around the same time. When Tom realized what was happening, he asked Sarah, "Why don't you put the food in large bowls so the men can serve themselves? That way, you and Mary can get to the dinner party?"

The other men joined in, encouraging Sarah to do as Tom had suggested. When Mary and Sarah finished bringing all the food out, everyone insisted that she and Mary leave. Sarah was not comfortable going. She had always served individual plates and tended to her guests as they enjoyed their meals. Leaving a group of men and bowls of food was strange to her until Jim Hunter told her he would ensure everyone had an enjoyable evening. Oddly, Jim's assurance brought Sarah comfort, and she agreed. Without thinking, Sarah quickly kissed Jim's cheek and left to get Mary.

The other men mercilessly teased Jim for the remainder of the evening while everyone had a great time. Seamus laughed at the nonstop stories. Everyone enjoyed their time together, but as they were about to leave, Archie noticed Doctor Hunter gathering the dirty dishes and taking them to the kitchen to be washed.

"Hey guys, let's help Jim out; he'll never get everything cleaned up before Sarah returns."

Everyone picked up their dishes and took them to the kitchen. As men always do, they made a production out of it. Tom and Jim washed, and four others dried and put the dishes back on the shelves where they belonged. Seamus and Hank swept the restaurant floor as they talked about how to be good shepherds to the people God would put into Hank's life.

Nancy had invited Nurse Wallace, but it was evident that she felt uncomfortable, saying she didn't want to interfere with the festivities since she didn't know anyone. As she was going to get her coat, Nancy followed her to the closet and asked her to stay.

" Nurse Wallace, you can't get to know people if you don't spend time with them. I'm sure we will tell some stories and maybe play some games. I think it will be an excellent way for you to get to know some of the ladies. Won't you please stay?"

Uncomfortable but appropriately challenged, Peggy agreed to stay for a little while. Just as Nancy had said, many stories were shared. Most of the time, there was laughter, but a few tales also brought tears. As

Peggy Wallace listened, she couldn't help noticing how close everyone was, though they were very different from one another. She coveted relationships like these women had with one another, yet risking rejection had always kept her from attempting friendships.

While everyone laughed and eventually played games, Widow Henry kept noticing the look on her face. When all the guests began to leave, Peggy got up from her chair to get her coat when Widow Henry stopped her.

"Would you mind escorting me back to my house, Peggy?"

Surprised, Peggy agreed.

When Carol approached the door, Nancy hugged her and whispered, "You're going to be a gorgeous bride." Carol blushed a little as she thanked Nancy for complimenting her and hosting such a wonderful evening.

Walking slower than she needed to, Widow Henry asked Peggy if she had enjoyed herself.

"Yes, it was a nice time. I didn't have much to say since I'm new here, but it was nice," replied Peggy.

"Well, my dear, I can think of no better way to get to know people than to hear them share stories from their past. You know, Maggie and Mary didn't know anyone until about a year or so ago. Maggie came to town to help Carol at the school, and Mary, well, Mary, has found a new life here that she never dreamed of before. I'm sure you will, too," said Widow Henry soothingly.

Saturday morning, Carol, Lizzy, and Rusty met at the meadow where the day's flowers were opening. Carol brought two baskets to fill so there would be plenty for the trellis and her bouquet. Spending time with the children was special to Carol; even though she taught school and was with children daily, she loved how joyful and inquisitive they were.

It was Rusty who had inspired her to teach the underprivileged children of the backwoods. Even though he knew almost nothing taught in school, he was a very bright boy and had caught up with the others his age very quickly. As they headed to the park, the children held the baskets in one hand and Carol's hand in the other. Even though this was her wedding day, Carol would remember this time with Lizzy and Rusty for the rest of her life.

After collecting the flowers, the children yelled, "See you later, Miss Carol," as they ran off chasing one another. Carol and Seamus had asked them to be ring bearers at their wedding.

When Sarah returned to the restaurant Friday evening, she was surprised to find everything clean and put where it belonged, so when Jim came down for breakfast Saturday, she brought him extra biscuits, knowing they were his favorite.

"Thanks for your help last night, Jim; I appreciate it," said Sarah.

Jim looked at Sarah and said, "Anything for you."

Around one o'clock, everyone was finalizing their preparations for the wedding. Drinks were set out, only waiting for the snacks. The wedding cake was placed on the table in the corner, along with plates and serving utensils. The preacher came into town and visited Seamus before the service, but unfortunately, he told Seamus that he had to be in town on Sunday for a funeral. Seamus understood and was confident that God would provide direction.

Around two o'clock, people began making their way to the park. It was a beautiful, sunny, late spring day, perfect for an outdoor wedding.

Hank was helping Widow Henry. Archie and Maggie rode in their wagon with Alma Gay. Tom and Nancy closed the general store and walked down to the park. Everyone was leaving their places and heading to the wedding. Nurse Wallace and Doctor Hunter worked at the clinic, having seen some people during the day. Most of their time had been spent updating files from notes Doctor Smith had left. Doc was doing much better and hoped to attend the wedding, but Nurse Wallace didn't think it was a good idea.

Seeing everyone headed for the wedding, Peggy said to Doctor Hunter, "People around here are very friendly. It's not at all like the city."

Jim smiled and said, "Most people's worlds get smaller when they are around so many people they don't know, but here, people know and care for each other, regardless of their differences. It's a different place, that's for sure."

As Jim's words were still resonating with Nurse Wallace, a loud yell came from Doc's room. Doctor Hunter and Nurse Wallace rushed into the room to see what was the matter.

In a slow, methodical voice, Doc pleaded, "I want to go to the wedding. Please!"

Jim looked around for the wheelchair and, seeing it, said, "Well, let's go!"

"I think he's too weak to go, Doctor," said Nurse Wallace.

"Sometimes people need people to regain their strength. Doc needs his friends, and today, he's going to be with them," replied Doctor Hunter.

Rolling Doc down the street, Jim could see the smile on Doc's face. Being outside and seeing people he had known all their lives was the best day Doc had had since returning to Clayton. Jim quietly rolled Doc to the park, just behind the last row of chairs.

Together, they watched the wedding ceremony. Jim smiled, seeing Lizzy and Rusty carrying the rings to the altar.

Seamus and Carol never looked happier. As they shared their vows, kissed, and walked to the back of the audience, they stopped and knelt to hug their old friend. The ceremony had been just like Carol had imagined, surrounded by friends, and now, seeing Doc, she couldn't imagine how it could get any better, but just then, all the school children, who had been hiding in the church, came running to hug their teacher that they loved so very much. As tears ran down her face, Seamus knew asking the parents to bring their children to the church was the best surprise he could have given her, especially on this perfect day.

At the reception, everyone congratulated the newlyweds and enjoyed talking with one another. Jim brought Doc back to his house to warm up from the cool spring air. Nurse Wallace made sure he was comfortable and brought him soup. As she did her best to take care of him, Doc reached out and grabbed her arm.

"Thank you for letting me go," as tears of joy ran down his cheeks.

Not knowing what to say, she said, "I'm glad you had a good time, Doc; now get your rest."

As the sun was setting, people started leaving the reception. Rusty stood close to his buddy, wearing a flower on his shirt. He knew things would be different now that Seamus was married, but he wanted to stay close for one more night.

When the clinic closed, Nurse Wallace went to the boardinghouse and quietly tried to sneak up the stairs to her room. Seeing her, Nancy asked her to stay for a while to get to know folks. Hesitantly, Peggy allowed Nancy to take her to the women she had met the night before and introduce her to their husbands and children. Being very polite, Peggy met several people but was uncomfortable.

"I'm exhausted, Nancy; I think I should go upstairs for the evening if you don't mind," said Peggy very formally.

Before everyone left, Seamus caught up with Hank to ask him a favor. "Hank, after you read the scripture tomorrow, would you mind saying a few words? You could tell everyone what God is calling you to do. You don't have to preach; just share from your heart."

"Oh, I don't know. I don't think I'm ready, Seamus. I don't have much learning, so I can't say all those nice words like you say."

Putting his hand on Hanks's shoulder, Seamus looked Hank in the eye and said, "I don't want you to preach; just tell people why you want to go and see where the Holy Spirit leads you. I'll be there if you need me, but I don't think you will."

The newlyweds came to church Sunday morning and sat in the front row with Hank and Widow Henry. Hank looked exhausted; he hadn't slept much that evening.

Slowly, after the last song was sung, Hank made his way to the podium. When he tried to open his Bible, his hands shook so hard he couldn't find the page he wanted to read from. Looking down at Carol and Seamus, Hank suddenly felt the warmth of their friendship. His hand stopped shaking as he searched the scriptures for the text he wanted to read.

"Before I begin, I would like to introduce our good friends, Mr. and Mrs. McConnell."

Standing, everyone applauded, and as they were clapping, Widow Henry looked at Hank and mouthed, "Let God lead you."

Hank shared how he had once been a slave and had seen many terrible things done to friends and family." My big brother was sold, my mother raped, and my daddy beaten. When I was finally freed, no one would hire me; most people treated me like I was still a slave. I did some terrible things in my days. I drank too much, got in fights often, and spent many years in jail for a crime I didn't commit. When I finally was let out of prison, I came to this little place to get away from people. I had no money and a bad attitude. I stumbled onto this little run-down cabin in the woods and decided to stay there. A couple of days later, Tom Campbell came by and asked me what I was doing in his cabin. When I told him he did something I had never seen before, he put his hand on my shoulder and asked me if I would like to stay there, to settle down. I told him I didn't have any money, and he smiled and said, "I have an idea: you fix this place up and run this old mill, and you can stay here for free." That was the first time in my life that a white man had ever been nice to me, and I didn't know what to make of it, but I sure did need a place, so I said sure.

"I fixed everything as he asked me to, but I still didn't trust him. I thought he would come out someday and kick me off his property, but until he did, I had a place to stay. Then, one day, this white guy came by while I was plowing my field and asked me if I could use some help. From that day on, Archie has been my best friend, someone I would do anything for. One night, Archie saved my life when the Harless brothers attacked me. They burned the barn and shot me. I'll never forget it; a white man saved my life. Oh, brother, hallelujah!

"Archie brings me to town, where Doc fixes my leg up and takes care of me, just like I was his son or something. Later, Archie introduces me to Widow Henry. Folks, if there are angels among us, she is one of them.

She took the time to get to know me, gave me a job at her new mill, and, most importantly, taught me to read using the Bible.

"I have told you all this to show how living our lives like Christ affects everyone you meet. Tom gave me shelter and work. Archie became the friend I never had. Doc treated my wounds, and Widow Henry cared for me, sharing God's word as she taught me how to read. We are all told to love God with all our hearts and to love others like Christ loved us.

"One night, Widow Henry and I talked about what that means. Christ loved us so much that he was willing to be tortured to death to save us from all the wrong we have done, and then he rose from the dead to conquer death. What He did reconciled us to our heavenly Father if we believe in Him and obey his commands to love others as He did. To me, this means to love other people so much that you would be willing to die for them so that they may have a relationship with God Almighty. I'm not perfect; I still struggle, but I have learned that these temptations can help me grow closer to God if I trust Him to get me through them. His strength builds me up and draws me closer to Him.

"As most of you know, I am leaving Clayton and going to a community of former slaves that live a few hours from here. I am going to share the love that each of you has shared with me. I will show them that a life full of hate is no life at all, but a life full of love is the life God wants for each of us. Please pray for me as I try to teach my brothers and sisters that they must forgive people, regardless of what some may have done to them. It won't be easy, but neither was dying on a cross. Thank you for all you have done for me; I love you."

As Hank started to leave the podium, Seamus came to the front and put his arm around his friend.

Holding him tightly, Seamus looked at everyone in the audience and said, "We all must ask for forgiveness for the wrong we have done to our African brothers and sisters. Maybe we didn't own slaves or beat them, or for that matter, we may not have known any black people, but what all of us did do was not stand up against their plight. Hank, please forgive me. I can't imagine what your life has been like."

"People caring for people, regardless of skin color, can show them God's love," said Hank.

It was a powerful day. Most people didn't think they were part of the problem, but they were saddened to realize their silence had contributed to the growth of hate and segregation. After church, everyone approached Hank and asked for forgiveness, and many prayed with him for his success in reaching the hurt and poor.

After everyone except Carol and Seamus had gone, Mary approached Hank, sobbing. "I'm so sorry, Hank. When I first met you, I was terrible to you, but by God's grace, He has opened my eyes to see you as a warm, humble man of God. Please forgive me."

Looking down, Mary told Hank that this was the first time she heard that it was Paul who tried to kill him."

As she stood there weeping, not knowing what to say, Hank grabbed her hand and said, "Mary, you're my sister in Christ. Through our hardships, He opened our eyes to His truth, and now we can share that truth with others. Of course, I forgive you."

CHAPTER 37

HANK SPENT HIS final week in Clayton visiting with Widow Henry and Reverend McConnell. He was sad to leave Clayton, where he had so many friends.

He and Archie met every day that week. The relationship they shared was very special. They hunted, worked, and laughed together many times, yet what he remembered most was that Archie was always there for him. Reverend McConnell had taught him many things about trying to live his life as a follower of Christ. It wasn't easy; many, if not most, would make fun of you or even persecute you for your faith.

Hank knew it wouldn't be easy moving into a new community, even though all of them were blacks, and telling them to forgive their former enslavers. Teaching that not all white people were evil would take much time and prayer.

Saying goodbye to Widow Henry was like saying goodbye to his mother. She had opened his eyes to how living the way Christ had told believers to live changes everything. Widow Henry hugged her friend goodbye with a confident look on her face. She knew he was ready to take on the challenge, but as Hank turned to leave, she handed him a box. Opening it, Hank burst into tears.

Inside was Colonel Henry's Bible, along with pages of notes he had made. A note read, "Go in peace, my dear friend; the Lord will always be with you. I will pray for you every morning when I wake and in the evening before I sleep."

Hank packed what little clothing and supplies he owned in bags, his tools, and the special box Widow Henry had given him. As he rode out of town in his wagon, everyone came out to wave goodbye; even the school children cheered for their big, strong friend. Hank prayed as he left Clayton, a prayer of thanksgiving for his time in this small town in the mountains of West Virginia.

At the mouth of Cabin Creek was an African-American community populated by many former slaves and their families. Life there was hard. Most of the men and young boys worked in the coal mines. Although the pay was terrible, at least it was steady. The women cleaned what clothes they had in the creek and cooked vegetables from their gardens. Their very existence was always in jeopardy. Winter was the most challenging time.

Their small shacks did not protect them from the cold wind that seemed to blow all day and night. When they could find old newspapers, they would make glue and attach the paper to the walls to help keep out the wind. Children slept together in their beds to help keep each other warm. Like the poor mountain folks in Clay County, they survived. As bad as it was, life was still much better than thirty years ago on the plantations.

On Sundays, many people went to an old, abandoned shed on the outskirts of the village, to church meetin', to hear an old former slave preach about how great it will be someday when they are in heaven. Blacks worship differently than their white counterparts. They sing louder and longer while shouting praises to God. The old preacher was sure their suffering would be rewarded in heaven, and the white owners would all be burning in hell. "Judgement is mine, says the Lord," the preacher would quote from the Bible, and all the people would leave with a hope for tomorrow in their hearts and a desire for God's judgment on their former owners.

It was easy to understand why they felt the way they did about white people; after all, they had been the ones who captured their parents and grandparents in Africa and brought them to America to be sold to the highest bidder. They were treated terribly; their families were separated and sold like cattle. Most didn't know what to do or where to go when the war ended. News of work in the hills, mining coal, brought these men and their families to this little village on the bank of Cabin Creek, where it emptied into the Kanawha River.

When Hank rode into the settlement, he asked if there was a boardinghouse where he could stay for a while. An old man, walking with the help of a handmade cane, laughed and shook his head. "The Only place you can stay is in a tent out by the riverbank. If you come to make any trouble, leave, or you'll wish you had never stopped here," the old man continued suspiciously.

"Thank you, sir," said Hank as he turned his wagon toward the river. He searched for a while to find a place that was level and dry, on a high bluff overlooking the river.

Hank pulled his tent from the wagon and began pitching it on a flat spot. It reminded him of the time he first found Clayton. He had slept in his tent for a few nights before discovering the old cabin he later lived in. With his tent set up and his horse grazing on the grass nearby, he began building a fire from sticks and wood he found in the area. Just as the fire started to burn well, two men wandered over to see what he was up to.

"Hello," said Hank.

The two men didn't say anything until they got next to Hank's fire when one of them asked, "What are you doing in these parts?"

"Well, I heard about this settlement and thought I would stop by and see what it was like," replied Hank.

"Where are you from?" asked the taller man.

"I have lived in Clayton the last couple of years, but before that, I was in Virginia," replied Hank.

"Ain't never heard of Clayton, but most of us came from Virginia after we was freed to work in the mines."

Hank asked if they would care to join him for a cup of coffee, and both agreed. While Hank ground the little bit of coffee he had, the men looked at him like he was rich. They had never seen a black with a coffee grinder.

"Where did you get that thing?" asked one of the men.

"I bought it in Clayton," said Hank.

As the three men sat around the campfire, it was clear that they were trying to figure out why Hank had come to their little village. Reaching out his hand to shake theirs, Hank, once again, introduced himself, and the men told him their names. Jonna was from Roanoke, Virginia, and Henry was from Richmond. Both had been slaves, and the scars of that time were very evident. They continued to talk sparingly, but at least they stayed long enough for Hank to learn a little about them.

When Jonna and Henry left, Hank could tell that it would take a long time before anyone would trust him. Seamus had warned him about that, so as he laid down for the night, he prayed for God to guide everything he said and did in the months ahead.

The next day, Hank walked around the village, observing how the people lived. He noticed that there wasn't a school and that the children stayed close to their houses, protected by their mothers. The women all worked cleaning what clothing they had and cooked outside on open fires. The houses were barely shacks: four walls, no floor, and no indoor fireplace. They were trying to get by, and it was hard. Without education, little food, and only low-paying jobs, how could anyone escape this culture unless something changed?

On Sunday, Hank found the old shed that served as the church building. Sitting on a rustic bench made from a split log, he noticed how few men were in attendance. When the service began, everyone sang praises to the Lord from memorized songs they had sung while still slaves. There were no hymnals, just singing from the heart, songs they could remember, most focusing on their hard life and the hope of better days.

When the singing was over, the old preacher went to the front to begin his sermon. When he announced what scripture he would speak from, Hank opened his Bible to follow along. A quiet filled the room, and when Hank looked up to see what was happening, he saw everyone looking at him.

"You know how to read?" asked the preacher.

"Sure do," replied Hank.

"Would you mind reading to everyone before I begin?" asked the preacher.

Hank was a little nervous since he didn't know anyone, but he felt the prompting of the Holy Spirit to "speak." Hank stood up and read the parable about the talents given to men to manage while the owner was away, and as he read, he became more and more passionate. When he finished reading, he quietly sat down on the log. The old preacher looked at the people and said," This man knows God; I can see it. What's your name?"

"My name is Hank," replied Hank.

Hank explained that a woman back in Clayton had taught him to read. He hesitated to say more, sensing it wasn't time yet. "If anybody would like, I'd be glad to teach them what I know," said Hank, hoping someone would step forward, but to his disappointment, no one indicated they wanted to learn. It was understandable since slaves were not permitted to learn to read or write before the war, and now most were still afraid of what might happen to them if they tried.

When the service was over, Hank returned to his tent. Setting on a log beside his fire, he read Colonel Henry's notes for most of the afternoon, stopping to remember the many times he had spent reading and talking with Widow Henry. Closing his Bible and putting his notes away, Hank prayed that God would bring someone into his life that he could teach to read and share the Bible with, the same as Widow Henry had done with him.

On Monday, Hank began cutting trees to build a small cabin. He had most of his tools from the sawmill, including a log splitter. By Friday, there was enough rough lumber to build the walls and roof braces. He would begin building on Monday.

Saturday afternoon, as Hank had finished placing three-foot logs in the ground to serve as footers for the cabin, it began to rain. The storm continued for hours, and the creek overflowed its banks and caused damage to two of the shacks. When the sun finally came out on Monday, Hank felt that rather than build his cabin, he would help some of his new neighbors repair their homes.

One of the shacks was owned by a widow with a twelve-year-old boy. He later discovered that her husband and four other men had died in a mining accident. She survived by washing people's clothes and caring for their children so their parents could work in the mines. She would buy meat from the men who hunted in the backwoods with her money. She had a rough life but was determined that her son would escape this camp-like environment and make something of himself.

The other shack that was damaged was where Jonna lived. Working all day at the mine didn't give him much time to repair his place. That evening, Hank waited for Jonna to come home from work. Walking down the path from the mine, Jonna looked exhausted, barely able to stand up straight.

Most of the mine shafts were only four feet high, and the constant stooping was extremely hard on the men's backs. When Jonna finally reached his shack, Hank greeted him and said he wanted to talk briefly. As Jonna drank a cup of water his wife brought him, Hank told him what he wanted.

"Look, Jonna, you work all day and don't have the time or energy to repair your home. What if I fixed it for you? The only repayment I want is your help repairing the widow's place. You can help me on Saturdays until we get it done. How does that sound to you?"

Jonna sat on the log, shaking his head, and slowly asked Hank, "Why would you do this for me? You hardly know me?"

Hank looked into Jonna's eyes and said, "I know you need help, and I know how to build; that's all I need to know."

Smiling, Jonna said, "Sure, if you want to, that's fine with me."

"Good, I'll be here first thing in the morning," said Hank as he reached out to shake Jonna's hand.

On his way back to his tent, Hank stopped by the widow's shack to ask her if she would mind if he repaired her home. Before the conversation had gone very far, Hank realized he didn't know her name.

"I'm sorry. I should have introduced myself."

As Hank started to tell her his name, she said, "Hank, right? I was at worship the other Sunday, so I know your name. My name is Liz Jones. Nice to meet you in person. Now, why do you want to help me? I don't have any money to pay you, so don't come around here expecting to make anything."

Liz was a tough woman. Her parents had been slaves, along with her husband's parents, so she didn't trust anyone. She was very protective of her son and was not sure she wanted a stranger around her house.

"Mrs. Jones, I know you don't know me, so I understand you have no reason to trust me, but I assure you my only intention is to help you. Do you remember the scripture I read last week? Well, ma'am, I take the word of God seriously, so in my own little way, I'm trying to help you out because I know how to build. I don't expect anything in return. If you want, I can try to teach your son a few things about carpentry while we work on your home."

Liz looked at Hank, and though she was overwhelmed with grateful emotion in her heart, her rough, defensive persona responded, "No, I'll be just fine. I don't want no stranger, regardless of how he can read the Bible, comin round my house, and I sure don't want you near my boy. Do you understand?"

Walking back to his tent, Hank felt dejected. All he wanted to do was help Liz, yet she rejected him.

That night, he prayed, asking God for direction. He remembered that Christ had come to offer more than to repair storm damage, yet he, too, was rejected.

CHAPTER 38

ARCHIE AND FRED worked on the shelter every day so that Carol and Seamus could use it in their mission work when the school year ended. While they were there, Archie thought they should also replace all the burned wood. Working long days, he and Fred completed everything sooner than Tom expected.

Samuel worked on the ten-acre property while Archie and Fred finished the shelter. The trees he cut were used to build the shelter. Archie and Samuel's horses helped pull stumps so that, slowly, the land began to look more like a garden suitable for planting vegetables.

Fortunately, about half of the property had been cleared and farmed sometime in the past, making the project much more manageable. Probably, Native Americans had planted the field. There were native burial mounds along the Kanawha River valley that attested to the original inhabitants in the area. When Archie and Fred were finished, they joined Samuel, working hard since it needed to be ready for planting season. The work on the garden continued for three weeks after the shelter was completed, but finally, everything was prepared for planting.

Tom and Seamus rode out to see the finished property and were delighted. "I will make an announcement at church service next Sunday that the community vegetable farm is ready for planting and ask for donations of seed and labor. While I am out during the week, I'll tell all the folks I meet about the garden and encourage them to come and help plant. It may take a while for them to trust that we are doing this for them, but eventually, they will come around," said Seamus excitedly.

"I will provide whatever seed you still need after the donations, and of course, my horse and I will be here too," said Tom.

"Archie, Fred, and Samuel, you have done a tremendous job with this property. I can't thank you enough for working hard to finish it before planting season. Do you have any more work lined up, guys?"

Samuel said he would go back to Charleston to find work, but Fred and Archie didn't know where they might find a job.

"Widow Henry told me to ask each of you to stop by her place when you were finished," said Tom with a hint of a smile.

The three men rode back into town with Seamus and Tom. On their way back, Seamus remembered that he was going fishing with Rusty down by the creek they were passing. When he mentioned this to the others, they all noticed how excited he was to spend time with his little friend.

"I think it's wonderful how you are taking your time to be with Rusty; he needs a father figure in his life. Mary works so hard to take care of him, but a boy needs time with a man to learn what being a man means," said Archie.

"And what a Godly example you're showing him, Seamus," said Tom.

Seamus and Tom left for their homes when they arrived in town, while the others rode over to Widow Henry's house. Widow Henry saw them as they came up her front walk and opened the door, motioning them to come in, but Archie said they were too dirty from a long day's work to go inside. Pointing to the chairs on the front porch, Widow Henry went inside to get a pitcher of iced tea and glasses.

"Here, you all look like you could use a nice cold glass of tea," said Widow Henry.

After pouring their drinks, she asked how they felt about helping the community.

"Ma'am, I needed the work, to be honest, but the more I saw it coming together, the more I felt proud of what we were doing. Reverend McConnell told us that he and his wife would live there during the summer and help tutor children and, hopefully, some of their parents to read and write. He also said they would have services there each week on Wednesday nights. I think that's awesome. Nobody ever taught me to read. I picked up enough to get by, but for them to spend all their time trying to teach those folks is special," said Fred.

"I'm so proud to be part of this community. People here care about one another, so it only makes sense that we would try to help our backwoods neighbors learn and grow more food so they can eat better during the cold winter, but most importantly is sharing God's love for them," said Archie.

Samuel sat quietly, a little shy. He had never been in a white person's home before and felt a little awkward. "Ma'am, thank you for the cold drink; I sure do like it. I guess all of this makes me shake my head. Like Hank, I grew up hating white folks, but since you brought me here to work and me getting to know folks around here, I see that it's not skin color that makes the difference; it's the love of God in folks. I sure do wish I had grown up in a place like this. Thank you, ma'am; you gave me a job when I was down and out. Nobody would hire me cause I was black, but it didn't matter to you. So, when you asked how I feel about working on the community farm project, I can tell you that every night when I went to bed, I thanked God I could do somthin for this town," said Samuel with emotion.

Widow Henry smiled and thanked them for all their demanding work. "I'm happy to have each of you as friends."

In her heart, Widow Henry could see how God was working in each of these men's lives, and nothing gave her more joy.

"Well, gentlemen, I need your help. Samuel, I understand you are returning to Charleston to be with your family. Is that correct?" asked the Widow.

"Yes, ma'am," replied Samuel.

"Well, it so happens that I need someone at my Charleston lumber mill to work full time. Now I know you enjoy landscaping work, so I've told my manager that he should begin telling our customers that we offer those services, along with lumber. Would you be interested in the job, Samuel?"

" Yes, ma'am, I sure would. Thank you, ma'am, thank you."

"Now Fred and Archie, as you know, Hank is gone, and I need two men to run my sawmill and lumber yard, at least until you find a job in carpentry, Fred. Would the two of you be interested?"

Fred was ecstatic; he never dreamed of a full-time job. "Yes, ma'am, thank you."

Archie looked at his dear friend, knowing that everything she did was to help people, and quietly thanked her, smiling. "Once again, you have helped me and Maggie out."

As the day ended, Widow Henry could see how the future looked bright even though Clayton was changing. A community with the vision and desire to reach out to their less fortunate neighbors was a sign of the Holy Spirit working in their lives. Oh, she knew many weren't believers, but the attractiveness of love, instead of selfishness, drew them together as one community.

When Archie arrived at his cabin that night, he shared what Widow Henry had said, and they both were beyond happy. Though they loved living in the small town, they didn't have much hope of finding work other than farming, with occasional jobs that would give them enough money to pay their mortgage and buy a few necessities. The stress of not having a regular income would now be gone, and their lives would change.

Fred knew he wanted to work full-time, so working at the mill would provide him with the needed income. He still wanted to build, but until there was an opportunity, it would have to be put on hold.

The following day, Samuel packed his belongings and headed for Charleston. Before leaving, he rode by Widow Henry's to thank her once again.

As usual, the widow was sitting on her front porch, drinking her morning coffee and reading her Bible. "Samuel, will you join me for coffee before you leave?" asked the widow.

Samuel humbly got off his horse, tied it to the fence, and walked up to the porch. "Why, thank you, ma'am. I'd like that," said Samuel.

While the two enjoyed their coffee, Widow Henry asked Samuel to tell her about his plans.

Samuel had never given his future much thought; he just wanted to be able to provide for his family.

"I understand," said Widow Henry.

"Most people see only a short distance and seldom look beyond their current situation. Samuel, do you have any children?" Widow Henry asked.

"Yes, ma'am, I have an eight-year-old boy and a ten-year-old daughter. My wife has been caring for them while she cleans houses for the rich folks in the South Hills section of Charleston. It's pretty rough, ma'am. She's still at work when the little ones get home from school. Sometimes, I worry about what all they might get into with her not there, but we need the money."

Samuel realized he may have said more than he should and felt a little embarrassed.

"Hopefully, with your income, she will be able only to work while the children are in school so that she can be there when they get home," said Widow Henry.

"That would be nice, ma'am; I sure don't want my children to get in trouble like most of the rest of the young folks in our part of town do," replied Samuel.

"Before you go, I'd like to pray for you and your family, Samuel," said the widow.

"That sure would be nice, ma'am," replied Samuel.

Bowing their heads, Widow Henry asked for safety for Samuel as he traveled and fervently pleaded with God to protect Samuel's children from temptation and to give his wife the courage to fight for her little one's souls.

As Samuel left and headed out of town, he felt more encouraged than he could ever remember. Somehow, when Widow Henry prayed, he knew that God would protect his family.

Howard McDougal and his wife, Vivian, were in the audience at worship that Sunday. They spent the weekend with their friends while reviewing the plans for the homes the Campbells would build. On their way back to Tom and Nancy's house, Howard told Tom it had been a long time since he had attended a service where the Spirit had been so evident. "Is it like this every Sunday?" asked Howard.

"Every Sunday, the message is challenging, which is why I see such transformation happening in Clayton. Did you see people signing the notice attached to the bulletin board? Those were people volunteering to help with a new community garden we are starting in a couple of weeks. The food we grow there will be used to help feed the poor. People are beginning to see their role in being committed to Christ," said Tom.

When Howard and Vivian left for Charleston, they were excited to tell their pastor about the community garden. Many people in the city were hungry and needed help. A community garden would go a long way in feeding struggling people while also bringing the community together.

While many relaxed at Clayton Park that afternoon, Mary wrote to Paul. She had thought about what she wanted to say, but when she sat down to write, she had trouble. Only after praying about it for the last week was she able to calmly say what she knew needed to be said.

Dear Paul:

I wanted to let you know that Rusty is doing well. Our daughters died the first winter after you left, leaving a void that will never be filled. Rusty and I have learned to read and write and enjoy our new lives here in Clayton. Your selfishness caused both him and me tremendous suffering. Many days, we had no food or hope for a better tomorrow, but something extraordinary happened. We started attending church after new friends took us in and cared for us. Over time, we both could see how God was working in the lives of our new friends and how that godly love affected everyone around them. Both Rusty and I have accepted Christ as our lord and savior. We are both very different people now. When Sherriff Griffith told me you refused to give us any money, I was sad for you, not us. We have Christ, and that's all that we need. I don't want anything from you, but I pray that you will someday accept the gift of salvation through Christ that God so freely gives. Without it, your life will never be what it could be. Repent Paul, humble yourself, and repent of all the evil you have done in your life. I believe that deep inside, you are a good man, but you are entirely lost.

Paul, I forgive you for all you have done to me and Rusty.

Signing the letter, Mary felt a burden lifted from her shoulders and strangely a sadness. She didn't love Paul but longed for him to be saved, much like others she had met. True believers want others to know the joy and freedom they have experienced. It was what Christ talked about when he said to love your neighbors like you love yourself.

When Samuel arrived in Charleston, he told his wife about the new full-time job he had at the sawmill. They both cried. They decided to save as much money as possible to buy a house someday or, if they qualified, help their children get a college education. They both laughed as they lay in bed at the dreams they now had, dreams they had never thought possible.

The next day, Samuel reported to work and was assigned to a group to work with that was responsible for moving the logs from the yard to the mill to be cut. When lumber was cut, they transported the boards to the warehouse. It was hard work, but Samuel loved that he got to be outdoors most of the time.

The three other men he worked with seemed all right to Samuel but not as welcoming as he had hoped. Samuel tried to start a conversation during their lunch break, hoping to get to know them, but there was very little response to his questions. The men didn't like that a black was given a job when plenty of white guys they knew could have used the work.

On his way home from work, Samuel thought about the prison of hate and prejudice these men lived in. They saw the world just like they used to until someone gave them a chance and honestly cared for him and his family. He knew it would take a long time, but he would get to know these fellows and tell them how to live a life full of joy.

CHAPTER 39

Nurse Wallace came down the stairs of the boardinghouse, muttering to herself about having to go with Doctor Smith into the backcountry. She didn't like being away from the clinic. More honestly, she didn't like being outdoors, around people she disliked or trusted. Growing up in Richmond, though her parents were less attentive, her life was reformed and predictable. She never knew what she would have to deal with in the country, let alone who. As she sat at her usual table, Mary brought her tea and asked if she wanted her typical breakfast.

"Yes, of course," snapped the frustrated nurse. Mary just smiled and went to get her food.

When Peggy finished her breakfast, Mary cleared her table and brought her more tea. "Is there anything else I can do for you?" asked Mary.

"No, that will be all," replied the annoyed nurse.

Mary could see something was bothering her, so she put the teapot on the table next to her, turned gently, and asked, "Are you all right, Miss Wallace? You seem upset?"

"I am upset. Doctor Smith takes me out in the middle of God knows where to see people who didn't even ask to see a doctor. Somehow, he thinks he's a good doctor, helping people like that. I don't like it out in the woods. The people are ignorant, and they smell. They look at you like you're from the moon or something. Who knows what they're thinking? They just stare at you. It's very frightening."

Realizing that she had said too much, she quickly stopped talking. Mary felt hurt and angry at Nurse Wallace's attitude about the less fortunate and was strongly tempted to lash out at her but caught herself. Some still, small voice said to be patient and try to understand why she might feel the way she does.

"What bothers you most, if you don't mind me asking?" asked Mary.

"I don't know; I'm just very uncomfortable and frightened, I suppose," Peggy replied.

"I can understand that it can be scary riding up to strangers. You grew up in the city, right?" asked Mary.

"Yes, Richmond," replied Peggy.

"Well then, I completely understand your feelings. In the city, you can choose who you want to be around. There are so many people that all you need to do is stay at your office, and there will always be people that come to see you, right?"

"Yes, we were always busy," replied Peggy.

"Did you ever wonder about the poor living in the city who needed your help but didn't come to the hospital? I think that Doctor Smith thinks about everyone the same, rich or poor; they all need medical help occasionally. Sickness affects everyone, educated or not, clean or smelly, and I think Doctor Smith wants to care for all of his neighbors, regardless of their circumstances."

"I'm sure you're right, but that doesn't mean I have to like going in the woods to see people that frighten me," retorted Nurse Wallace.

"No, you don't have to like it, ma'am, but perhaps you will grow more comfortable the more time you spend with them. Well, I've said too much. I just wanted to see if I could help," said Mary as she picked up the tea pitcher and headed for the kitchen.

That day, as Doctor Smith and Nurse Wallace traveled throughout the backcountry, Mary's words kept coming to her. She didn't want to get to know them. All she wanted was to do her job and stay to herself. She didn't need anyone.

That evening, as Peggy lay in bed, she began thinking about telling Doctor Smith that she didn't think this arrangement would work out.

As she walked up the street to the clinic the following day, Nancy stopped and asked if she would like to come to dinner the next evening. "I've invited Widow Henry to join us. How about around six thirty?"

Nurse Wallace didn't want to go but thought she should be polite since Nancy had been so helpful when she first came to town. "Yes, I can be there," replied Peggy.

As Peggy wrote in her journal that evening, she wondered why she had accepted the invitation since she planned to leave in the next couple of weeks. She hadn't mentioned anything to Doctor Smith but thought she would tell him Friday after work.

Thursday evening came, and after leaving her things in her room and freshening up a little, Peggy went across the street to Nancy's home. Widow Henry was already there when Peggy arrived. She and Nancy were sitting in the parlor drinking iced tea.

"Can I get you some iced tea, Nurse Wallace?" asked Nancy.

"That would be nice," replied Peggy.

The women talked while dinner was cooking in the oven. When everything was ready, Tom put all the food on the table and entered the parlor to tell them that dinner was ready.

"Aren't you staying?" asked Widow Henry.

"No, I am taking this opportunity to have dinner with Doctor Smith this evening; we have a few things to discuss about the clinic."

Widow Henry and Nancy discussed things happening in the community and the vegetable garden project during dinner. More people than expected had signed up to help plant the garden. Nancy said Tom was excited to see everyone come together to help those in need. As they continued to eat and visit, Widow Henry couldn't help noticing Peggy had very little to say. Trying to draw Peggy into the conversation, Widow Henry asked how things were going at the clinic.

Somewhat surprised, Peggy said everything was going fine but didn't attempt to continue any conversation. Finally, Nancy asked Peggy if she was getting to know people in the area.

"I have met people who have come into the clinic, but otherwise, I've kept to myself. Honestly, I'm still trying to decide if I want to live in a small town," replied the timid nurse.

"You've always lived in larger cities, haven't you?" asked Widow Henry.

"Yes," answered Peggy.

"It's very different living in a smaller community. In Clayton, like in most smaller towns, everybody knows almost everybody else, and in those towns that are primarily Christ followers, care for one another, much like siblings rather than just neighbors. I suppose in a larger city, most people are more focused on themselves and don't pay much attention to the needs of their neighbors. I'm sure some reach out to the less fortunate, but most only live for themselves and their friends. Is that right, Peggy?" asked Widow Henry.

Peggy thought for a while before answering. "I've never seen the need to get to know the people around me more than to say hello. To me, everybody is busy with their own life and doesn't need, or want, for that matter, to know everything going on in someone else's life. I've always tried to be the best nurse I can be so that patients know I will take proper care of them. I don't need to know anything more than that about people. Just be a nurse they can count on."

When Tom returned from dinner with Doctor Smith, he saw the women talking and noticed they hadn't had dessert yet. Cutting three pieces of Widow Henry's apple pie, he quietly brought them into the room and served them.

"You're going to love this pie, Peggy. Widow Henry's apple pie is the best you've ever had."

The interruption had come at a perfect time. It gave them time to consider what needed to be said next.

"Thank you, Tom, you know how I love to bake," said Widow Henry.

"Do you cook, Peggy?" asked the widow.

"No, I've never had to. My parents had a cook, and when I worked in Charleston, I always ate at the restaurant just down the street from the hospital," replied Miss Wallace.

"Would you like me to teach you how to bake?" asked Widow Henry.

"I don't see the need," responded Peggy.

"Well, my dear, some things you do just for fun. I grow vegetables in my little garden behind my house but don't need to. I could get all I needed at the general store or from Archie. I enjoy watching the plants grow and produce food I can eat," said Widow Henry, laughing. "It's work, but the joy is the result."

"I can see that, I guess. I've never taken the time to do anything unproductive," said Nurse Wallace.

"Well, what do you say? Do you want to try it?" asked the persistent Widow Henry.

Though she didn't know why, Nurse Wallace agreed to come over to Widow Henry's house on Saturday and learn to bake an apple pie.

That evening, after her house guests had gone home, Nancy told Tom about their conversation. Tom said he wasn't surprised by what Nancy told him. He had met with Doctor Smith to discuss Nurse Wallace.

"David said that he has never seen anyone as gifted at being a nurse, but her attitude is purely technical. She doesn't attempt to comfort anyone. All she does is apply whatever medical treatment is required. He's not sure how long she will stay. She seems very unhappy to him, and those feelings pour over to her patients," related Tom.

When they were ready for bed, Nancy knelt beside Tom, as they had done every night since they were married. Holding Tom's hand, Nancy prayed specifically for Peggy Wallace, asking that whatever was keeping her from living a peaceful and joyous life would be revealed and that she would see that she was meant to live her life consumed by God's love for her.

With summer on the way, more people would be coming to Clayton. A construction company would arrive in town to work on the Campbell's houses, and while most of them stayed in a large tent, the company provided the supervisors and foremen rooms in the boardinghouse. Tom had suggested that Mary and Rusty could return to his and Nancy's home, but Mary didn't want to impose.

One day after school, Mary asked Carol if she thought Widow Henry would like to rent her room to her and Rusty.

"I'm sure she would, but I have a better idea. Why don't you move into our place while we're gone this summer? We'll be back on the weekends, but I'm sure Seamus could stay in the room at the church Archie had previously stayed in," replied Carol.

"That seems like a lot to ask of Seamus," retorted Mary.

"He will probably be spending most of his Saturdays at the church preparing for Sunday, so it wouldn't be any trouble at all," Carol replied.

A few days later, Carol told Mary that she had told Seamus about her idea, and "he was excited about it. He reminded me that he would be spending Saturday mornings fishing with Rusty so that it would work out just fine."

That evening, after all the dishes had been cleaned and put where they belonged and the restaurant cleaned, Mary approached Sarah and told her about her plans to move out during the summer.

"You're going to need those rooms for the workers that will be in town all summer, so I am going to stay at Seamus and Carol's house while they're out of town."

Mary's thoughtfulness touched Sarah. The two had grown to love spending time together after work, simply sitting and enjoying tea after a long day. They shared everything, and that support and friendship encouraged each of them.

Tom had met with the owner of the construction company before they came to town. He requested that he use Samuel to help with the development work and that Fred be used as a carpenter apprentice so that both could learn more about their new skills.

The crew entered town early on Monday morning and established the office and sleeping quarters for the workers. After spending the day setting everything up, the foreman met with Tom to go over the plans.

A few weeks earlier, Howard had sent his crew out to stake off the property according to his drawings. The county had been made aware of the project, and all required permits had been drawn up to allow them to proceed. All seemed well until Samuel came into town from Charleston.

The crew had a real problem with Samuel being black. They began by hurling insult after insult at him, and when that didn't have its intended effect, one of the workers started shoving him around, trying to pick a fight.

Samuel had faced this kind of harassment before and knew he could do nothing. Looking his attacker in the eyes, Samuel asked him, "Do you know me?"

"Of course I don't know you, stupid. I don't hang around your kind."

The reply was predictable, but Samuel kept on. "So, you don't want me around because you don't like the color of my skin? Did you get to pick the color of your skin when you were born? You don't have to care for me, but at least make it because of something I did or said, not because of something neither of us had any control over."

Samuel turned and walked away, leaving the bully even more frustrated and confused.

Tom and the foreman were at the work site and witnessed everything that had transpired. Looking at Tom, the foreman said, "I can't help how these guys feel; that's just who they are."

"Well, sir," replied Tom, "around here, we respect people for who they are, so if you can't or won't respect my friend, I'll have to get a different company to do this work."

The construction foreman tried to argue with Tom that that was just how it was as they walked up to the boardinghouse where the job manager was staying. After explaining what happened, Tom asked the two men if they would take a ride with him. "I've got something to show you," Tom said firmly.

After hitching his horse to the wagon, Tom stopped by the boardinghouse to get the men. A short while later, they arrived at Hank's old place. "Come with me," said Tom. "Do you see that field? Men, we will plant a community garden on those ten acres of land. About half of it was covered with trees until Samuel cleared it with a little help toward the end from a couple of his friends. Samuel is a good man and will work harder than any of your crew, but you don't want him on your job because he is black."

Shaking his head, Tom looked both men in the eyes and said, "I feel sorry for both of you."

He returned to the wagon and took them back to town. As they were getting out of the wagon, he said, "You can pack up your crew and go back to Charleston. You're fired."

Tom knew that this would set his project back a few weeks, if not longer, but he couldn't, in all good consciousness, turn his back on this issue. As he headed back to the general store to unhitch his horse, he saw Samuel coming from the sawmill where he had stopped to see his friends.

"Samuel, can I see you for a minute?"

The two men entered Tom's house. After Tom poured them a glass of iced tea, he pointed to the front porch, where they could sit and enjoy the breeze while they talked.

"Samuel, I'm very sorry for what happened to you today. I don't understand people like that. I want you to know that I have fired them. That type of attitude cannot be permitted."

Samuel was surprised by what Tom said. Every other time in his life, white folks said that that was just how it was and went on like nothing ever happened.

"Sir, you don't have to do that. That's just the way it is if you're black. People don't like you because you're a different color than they are, but frankly, I used to be the same way. If you were white, I didn't like you, that is, until I came to Clayton. You folks are sure different."

"Samuel, do you know some men in Charleston that would like to work with you preparing this land? I'll still have to get someone to run the project since you don't have the experience on a project of this size, but I would like you to work alongside whoever I bring in so that you can learn more about land development work."

"I know a few men I think will work hard and do a good job for you, sir," replied Samuel.

"Great, I'll go to Charleston tomorrow and start finding someone to work with you. Maybe we can ride together. I want to get to know you better, and oh, by the way, it's Tom. No more of this Sir stuff," laughed Tom, slapping Samuel on the back.

CHAPTER 40

Finn woke up from a long night riding in a boxcar headed east. When he left Charleston, he only brought a couple of apples and a jar of water; he hadn't counted on the train stopping for as long as it had to load on more boxcars—the extra time caused him to be out of food and water. Tired and hungry, Finn tried to make himself comfortable enough to sleep, hoping sleep would make the time pass quicker. He had carefully hidden the money he had saved from the work he had done for Tom in his socks to keep any thieves he might come across from finding it.

In the boxcar with him were some cattle headed for a meat packing plant and an older black man who hadn't said anything the entire trip. He looked to be in his early fifties, with gray hair and beard. On his cheek was a terrible scar. He looked hungry and exhausted. Finn didn't know how he would have the strength to jump from the train when it began to slow down as it approached Baltimore.

The old man began waking up as the train slowed, grumbling about how he ached and how badly the car smelled. Finn asked him where he was from, but he didn't answer, preferring to keep to himself.

The day grew hotter, and the boxcar became almost unbearable. The heat and the odor from the cows were suffocating. At this point, Finn's jar of water was nearly gone. He knew he had to jump soon, if for no other reason than to find something to drink. Seeing the old man sweating and having trouble, Finn offered him what was left of his water. The old man grabbed the water and drank it all without saying a word to Finn.

Wiping his lips with his shirt sleeve, the old man looked at Finn and asked, "Why'd you give me your water?"

"You needed it," said Finn. With that short interaction, the two men began talking. Finn told him he was from Charleston and was going east to see his sick mother. The old man said he was trying to find a place where he could live in peace, without people always fighting. "I can't do much work these days, but I can do enough to keep food on the table."

"What's your name?" asked Finn.

"Name's George, or least that's what the white man called me back when I was a slave."

"George, where're you from?" asked Finn.

"My family was all slaves in Richmond before I was sold to a man in Lexington, Virginia," replied George. "Lexington, of all places. That's where General Lee and Stonewall Jackson moved to after the war started. I worked at a tobacco plantation just outside town. Bossman was the devil. He beat us all the time," said George as his voice faded off as though he had gone back there in his mind.

"Richmond? I know a man who used to live there. He was a slave, too. The big guy runs the sawmill in Clayton. I worked with him for a while. He's a nice guy. He told me his older brother was sold and that he hadn't been able to find out where he was. His name is Hank. Do you know him?" asked Finn.

"Does he have a scar on his arm?" asked George. "Yes, a big old ugly scar right here," Finn pointed to his forearm.

"That's my younger brother!! I haven't seen him in thirty years," said George as he began to weep. He thought he would never see his brother again.

"Where's Clayton? Is it far from here?"

"It's a couple of hours north of Charleston along the Elk River," replied Finn.

"I'm going back there after I see my mother in Washington. You could come with me if you want," said Finn."

"You sure?" asked George.

"Come on, let's get off this stinking boxcar and find a creek or river to wash in," said Finn.

When the train slowed down to unload some of its cars, Finn jumped off and waited for George. It took him a little longer, and although the train was moving slower by then, George landed on the edge of a rock and turned his ankle badly. Finn ran over to help him and saw the scar on his left cheek. It was a brand burned onto his cheek.

George saw Finn looking at it and said, "Life was hell in those days."

The two men wandered around for a while until they noticed a train bridge that had been built over a small river. Doing the best they could, they washed themselves and most of their clothing. The stench from the boxcar lingered in their senses for over an hour, but finally, it, like the train, left.

After resting that afternoon, the two slowly headed east to a road Finn had noticed. George's ankle had continued to swell from the fall. Finn knew he needed to stay off it and keep it as cold as possible.

"Why don't we go back down the hill and rest your ankle in the water to keep the swelling down? I'll see if I can find some food," said Finn.

Groaning, George agreed and turned to go back to the river. When they finally arrived, George lay back on a sunny rock while dangling his foot in the water.

"I'll be back," said Finn as he scurried up the small hill toward the road. Lying on the rock, George doubted he would ever see Finn again; after all, he was a white man, but at least he had found out where his brother was living.

Finn discovered a little village just a short distance from where he had left George. He had taken four dollars from his sock before getting on the road in case someone saw him. There was a small general store he hoped would have something to eat, but when he walked in the door, he quickly could tell this was different from the store in Clayton. Seeing a lady behind the counter, he asked where he might find some food he could buy. Looking at his unkept appearance, the lady pointed at a small restaurant across the street.

Finn saw canteens and bought two to bring water for him and George.

The restaurant wasn't as nice as the one in Clayton, but at least they had some sandwiches he could buy and a glass of water. His Irish accent gave away his ethnicity, so the owner quickly took his money and told him to leave the glass on the table on his way out. People still didn't want Irish Catholics in their country and didn't mind saying so. Thirty-one years later, Congress would pass laws limiting immigrants from Western and Southern Europe, but for now, they were despised by almost everyone.

Finn found a water pump outside and filled the two canteens before leaving town.

George was awakened by a rustling in the bushes. Rolling over, he found a good-sized stick he hoped to use to defend himself. At this point in his life, he didn't care if he lived or died, but finding out about his younger brother's whereabouts gave him a purpose to live. Raising the stick, ready to hit whatever was coming, he stopped quickly when the noise turned out to be Finn.

"Hey, what are you doing? I'm bringing you a sandwich," said Finn a little nervously.

"Sorry, I thought you were a bear or someone coming to rob me," said George.

"A bear! Do you really think you would stop a bear with that little stick?" laughed Finn.

Both men laughed as George ate his food. It had been a long day, so they agreed to rest for the evening and decide what to do next in the morning, hoping that George's ankle would be better.

When morning came, George's ankle was in no condition to walk, so Finn said he would bring him food and drink and head for Washington.

"I'll come back this way and get you. Your ankle should be fine by then," said Finn, hiding his concern that it might be broken.

George could tell Finn was worried and, laughing, said, "I've sure had worse to deal with. Don't worry about me. Go see your momma; I'll be all right."

After getting food and more water at the restaurant, Finn took them to George and headed for Washington.

Washington was the largest city Finn had ever seen. People were riding and walking everywhere. Some were yelling at one another to move out of their way. The streets were dusty, causing clouds of dirt to fill the air. After asking several people, a lovely elderly lady pointed Finn to where the hospital was located.

When Finn arrived, he was hot and covered by dust from the city streets. His mother was in a ward with eight other people. Most looked helpless, just lying around waiting to die. Finn's mother had pneumonia and was not doing very well. Her breathing was shallow, and she struggled to stay awake.

Finn had left when he received a letter from the hospital that a nurse had written for his mother, asking him to come to Washington. Holding her hand, Finn told her how much he loved her. With all her strength, she smiled and mouthed, "I love you, son."

Finn told her he had found work and was learning a new trade. "Mother, I've brought money to help you with your expenses once you get out of here. I'll be sending more after I get back. You can count on me, mother." As the last words were still in the air, Finn's mother loosened her grip on her son's hand and died.

"Nurse, nurse, come quickly!" yelled Finn. When the nurse came to the bedside, she checked for vital signs of life. Pulling the sheet over her face, she whispered to Finn, "I'm sorry, she's gone."

There were no belongings or anything left from the little Finn's mother had brought with her from Ireland. Finn found a picture and her necklace with a small picture of him as a little boy. The photo was taken in better times when his father was still living. Looking at it, Finn felt the pain again of his father dying, and now, his mother was also gone. Finn fell into a chair in his mother's apartment and wept for a long time. Life had been a struggle for as long as he could remember. An hour or so later, Finn left for Clayton and a better life.

That night was a blur. With no place to stay and nowhere to go, Finn wandered the streets of Washington, heartbroken. His mother had always been there for him. She had been the one who insisted they leave Ireland and go to America.

Around eleven o'clock, Finn wandered into a bar and ordered a glass of whiskey. Perhaps this would take away the pain, but as he took his first sip, he thought, "I can't go back to what I used to be; it leads to nowhere."

Years later, Finn would tell people he had no idea where that thought came from because "all I wanted to do was get drunk." After eating his food, Finn paid his bill and left the bar, looking for the train station. It took him a long time to find it since there weren't many people out at night to ask for directions.

A few hours later, Finn discovered the train yard and began looking for a train that looked like it was headed west. Keeping out of sight, he listened as some train workers talked. He found the train he thought the men were talking about and jumped into a boxcar, thinking it was headed west toward West Virginia. Exhausted from the long, terrible day, Finn fell asleep. Several hours later, he was awakened by the jerking of the car as the train started to pull out from the station. When the train headed out of town, it dawned on him that this train was headed north, not west.

Cattle and coal were shipped from the west to the east and disbursed throughout the northern states. Before the train had gotten too far, Finn jumped from the car and ran away from the tracks. Since it was early morning, it was easy to tell which way was west, and finding a track headed in that direction was all he needed to make his way back to George.

Finn walked all day and into the night. Stopping near the train tracks, he leaned against a tree and slept for the night.

By midmorning the next day, Finn noticed a small town just ahead. The closer he got, he could tell it was where he had bought food a few days earlier. Again, he bought food and filled his canteen with water, but this time, before he left, he turned to the woman who had previously been so curt with him and said, "Thank you for the food and your help," and as he left, he put a dollar bill under the empty glass of water.

It didn't take him long to find George, although this time, as he approached, he sang an old Irish song to warn him of his arrival.

To Finn's surprise, George was much better. Although his ankle was still stiff, the swelling had gone down considerably.

"Brought you some food," announced Finn.

George grabbed his sandwich but stopped this time and thanked Finn. "I never thought you would come back," he said.

"I guess you don't know me very well," replied Finn.

"How was your trip?" asked George.

Finn told him about his mother dying, and as tears began to form in his eyes, he turned his head and stood up, announcing that he thought they needed to get on the road as soon as they had finished eating.

George had never seen a white man crying. He didn't think they did; he just thought they were different from black people. Oddly, Finn's sadness helped George to see that there were similarities between the two races.

The trip back to Charleston took longer than either of them had wanted, but two weeks later, they were in Charleston.

"Let's head to the lumberyard; I've got a friend that works there." When they arrived, the foreman informed Finn that Samuel was working in Clayton on a project for Mr. Campbell.

"Well, it's a two-hour horse ride, so if we leave now, we should be there by late this afternoon," said Finn.

Heading out, they stopped to get something to eat. Finn discovered that George wasn't permitted in the restaurant, something Finn hadn't known about before. Apparently, this was how it had always been. Finn was surprised and disappointed that people still acted like this, although if he was honest with himself, he too never wanted anything to do with blacks, that is, before he came to Clayton. Getting food for both of them, the odd twosome headed for Clayton.

The walk along the Elk River was pleasant. The breeze helped cool the hot air as the river flowed south toward the Kanawha River. When Finn could see Clayton in the distance, he felt relief and a peace he couldn't explain. Somehow, this little town was where he felt at home, and for the first time, he realized it.

Heading into town, Finn first took George to the sawmill. While working at the mill, cutting boards for the Campbell order, Archie noticed Finn walking up and stopped what he was doing.

"Hey, buddy, where have you been?"

"I'll tell you later; where's Hank?" asked Finn excitedly.

"Oh, Hank doesn't live in Clayton any longer. He moved to a little settlement west of Charleston, near Cabin Creek."

The disappointment was very evident on both Finn's and George's faces.

"Archie, this is Hank's brother," said Finn.

Archie jumped down from the sawing platform and ran to shake George's hand. "Wow, I can't believe it. He talks about you all the time. Wow!" exclaimed Archie.

As the three men stood talking, Tom came to see how his order was coming along.

"Tom, this is Hank's brother," said an overjoyed Archie.

"Finn met him as he was going to Washington."

Tom quickly approached George and shook his hand firmly. "I am so happy to meet you."

George was taken aback by all these white folks welcoming him to their little town.

"Hank went to a settlement about three hours from here to share Christ's love with the people there. I haven't heard from him since he left," said Tom."

George, let's get you and Finn over to the boardinghouse to get settled. When you're all cleaned up from your trip, Nancy and I will meet you at the restaurant for dinner."

"Sir, I don't have any money, and these are all the clothes I own," said George humbly.

"Well, I tell you what. You come over to the general store with me, and I'll take care of that. By the way, don't worry about the boardinghouse either. We're just so happy you're here," said Tom.

When George came down for dinner, he smiled from ear to ear. He hadn't had an actual bath in a long time, and this was the first time he had ever had brand-new clothes. When Sarah brought dinner, he couldn't believe how much food was on his plate.

"You all are sure treating me awfully nice. I appreciate it," said George as he started to dig into his meal.

"Pardon me, George; I would like to thank God for all this food and the honor of meeting you," said Tom.

After Tom finished his prayer, George dug in and ate like he hadn't eaten for a long time. Looking over at Finn, he said, "You're right, this place is different."

Before dinner was finished, Tom said that he would take George to see Hank in the morning.

Leaving the restaurant, Finn saw Samuel and ran down the street to see him.

"How have you been?" asked Samuel as Finn approached.

"I'll tell you later," said Finn. "Come meet Hank's brother."

After talking for a while, the three men headed to their rooms. Stopping, Samuel asked Finn if he would be interested in working with him on the Campbell project. Relieved and happy to work alongside his friend, Finn said he would love to.

This was George's first time on an actual mattress with springs. He couldn't believe how comfortable the bed was and how tired he was from the long journey. As he fell asleep, a tear ran down his face.

CHAPTER 41

After packing his office belongings in a box, Doctor Jim Hunter said farewell to the General Hospital staff he had worked with. He didn't have many items of interest, only his diploma, pictures of family in Kentucky, and a stethoscope given to him by his favorite college professor.

He had met Doctor Stephenson in his first year of medical school. Struggling with his assignments, the professor took him under his wing and helped him understand what was expected of him, but more importantly, he encouraged him. They had remained close throughout medical school and Jim's internship. Doctor Stephenson presented him with his diploma at his graduation ceremony and, later, privately, the stethoscope. Doctor Stephenson provided solid references to General Hospital when he interviewed them.

Jim had written Doctor Stephenson to tell him that he was going to leave the hospital to work with the poor in Clay County. As he was headed out of the hospital door, the mailroom clerk ran up to him with a letter. The return address was Doctor Stephenson's. Stopping what he was doing, Jim quickly opened the letter.

"Dear Doctor Hunter: (Jim)

I received your letter today and wanted to reply as soon as possible. I am honored that you would let me know of your decision. I am not surprised. You always had a heart for people. Your technical skills were always excellent, but there was something more you gave to your patients:

confidence that you would do your best to care for them and, even more importantly, that you genuinely cared about them. I am proud of you, Jim, for you have made the hard choice to serve all people, regardless of their ability to pay. You are a true physician.

God Bless.

Your Friend, Doctor James Stephenson"

Jim filled his wagon with his belongings the following day and headed for his future. He knew the change would be enormous, but the satisfaction of helping folks live healthier lives couldn't be measured. He also knew that Sarah cared greatly for him, and he was willing to wait as long as it took for her to feel comfortable moving their relationship deeper.

Riding along the Elk River in early summer, Jim saw boys fishing with their fathers and, further upstream, a group of people swimming and playing on one of the sandier places along the river's edge. Jim hoped he might enjoy time along the river with his family someday. The daydreaming had caused the time to go by quickly; before he knew it, he was in Clayton.

Tying his horse up in front of the boardinghouse, he went inside to get a room and, more importantly, see Sarah. When Sarah saw Jim walk into the boardinghouse, her face lit up. "Good morning, Jim; I have a room prepared for you. May I help you with your things?" said Sarah, pretending to be formal.

"Oh, I can get them. There isn't much, but I would like to have lunch before I go to the clinic," said Jim with a hint of invitation to his request.

When Jim had put everything away and taken his horse and wagon to the general store stable, he returned to the restaurant. Sarah pointed to the table in the corner, away from the others, as she went to get his lunch. After taking care of her other guests, she stopped by his table, asked how it had gone in Charleston, and made other small talk, hoping Jim would ask to see her that evening.

When he finished his meal, Jim got up, walked over to the counter, and softly asked Sarah if she would like to go to the park after work that evening. "We can star gaze and catch up."

The invitation was exactly what she had hoped for. "That sounds wonderful," Sarah responded.

Jim smiled as he left for the clinic to see David.

Walking into the clinic, Jim could see how organized everything had become. Nurse Wallace had arranged everything very neatly. All the patient's records were alphabetized and filed away, with only the current day's patient files out on the reception desk.

"Everything looks great, Miss Wallace; looks like you're keeping David in line," joked Jim.

"Doctor Smith is with a patient now," said Peggy.

"That's fine; I wanted to see Doc anyway," said Jim as he walked toward the room where Doc was recovering.

Jim could see that Doc was better than when he had seen him the last time, but the recovery was slow. Jim stayed with Doc for over an hour until it was obvious that Doc was tiring. Leaving, Jim said he would be back tomorrow. Little did Jim know that Doc would not survive the night. Around three in the morning, Doc had a heart attack and passed away.

Three days later, the entire town came for Doc's funeral. His daughter, her husband, and Doc's two grandchildren had arrived the evening before from Ohio. The church was overflowing with folks from all over the county. So many people loved Doc, people he had helped and others he had encouraged when needed. In many ways, Doc was a father to the people of Clay County.

Reverend McConnell's eulogy shared many of the stories he had heard from others about how Doc had been there for them. Several people stood up and shared how Doc had helped and cared for them. The last person to speak was Doctor Smith.

"When I came to town to be the physician for this area, Doc could have resented my being here, but instead, he welcomed me into his home; he went over every patient file and traveled with me to visit every one of them. During those weeks, it was obvious how much he cared for each of you. We have all been blessed to have known Doc."

Solemnly, Doctor Smith returned to his seat, tears running down his cheeks.

As the service ended, many people cried; they would miss their old friend.

In the back of the room stood Nurse Wallace. The service had impacted her significantly. She had never seen someone so loved by so many people; as she surveyed those who had been able to get into the church, the entire churchyard and the street in front of the church were packed with people. She saw many people she recognized from her travels with Doctor Smith. These ignorant, smelly, dirty people had come a long way to say goodbye to Doc.

Slowly, Peggy felt her heart warm at the thought of reaching out to others to let them know they mattered. It was an uncomfortable idea, but she could see firsthand its effects.

The crowd headed for the cemetery beside the church where Archie and Fred had dug the grave the day before. Setting beside the grave were Doc's daughter and her family. She saw why Doc wanted to stay in Clayton rather than live with her and her family. These people were his family. He cared for them the best he knew how, but she realized on that day that these people gave her father the love he desired.

He had been a good father as she was growing up, but when the war came, he felt strongly that he needed to defend the country against the traitors who had rebelled against it. After the war, she noticed her father was different. He talked little about what had happened. He was quiet and would often walk in the woods outside Clayton, contemplating his purpose in life.

After her marriage, she moved to Ohio to her husband's family's hometown, where her husband worked as an accountant for a local hospital. Though they were close when she was young, Doc understood that she needed to live independently of him. They had seen one another every few years, but as time passed, Doc visited less and less. Today, it was apparent why.

The burial lasted for another hour, as mourners struggled to leave, knowing this would be their final goodbye to their old friend, but as people began going, something odd happened. Nurse Wallace ran over to Doctor Smith and asked him if he thought it would be a good idea if they gave some of the folks a ride in his wagon.

Filling the wagon with women and children, they headed out into the country. The men walked alongside, sharing stories about Doc like the women did in the wagon. By the time everyone was home, nurse Wallace felt she knew the man that everyone loved. The stories were told with both sadness and humor. Doc had quite the sense of humor, but what was clear that day to Peggy Wallace was that he loved his neighbors, and they loved him.

That weekend, when Peggy went to Widow Henry's house to bake an apple pie, this time on her own with Widow Henry only watching, she opened up more than she had in the past.

"Mrs. Henry, how long did you know Doc?" asked Peggy.

"Well," said Widow Henry as she paused, "I knew Doc back when we were both teenagers. We liked one another, if you know what I mean. We never courted, but he was more than just another boy in my class. When my James moved into town, I only had eyes for him, but before that, I had thought that maybe someday Doc and I would court."

"What happened when he returned from the war?" asked the nurse.

"Well, like most of the men that did survive, they came back different. They had witnessed how evil men can be to one another. All the killing and blood tears away at the very spirit of men. Doc was one of them. For over a year, he seemed lost, as if wandering around in his own war. He didn't talk very often, and when he did, he seemed unengaged. Then, one day, a man came riding into town on his horse, yelling for help. He lived with his wife out in the backwoods, and a snake had bitten his wife.

Like most days, Doc was sitting on his porch and heard the man. Something clicked, and suddenly, Doc jumped to his feet and yelled for the man to show him the way. Grabbing his old army medical bag and jumping on his horse bareback, the two men rushed off into the woods.

That day, Doc saved that young woman's life and found his own. After that, Doc made it a habit to be available for anyone needing his skills. As people began talking, Doc started to have more and more people needing his help. Eventually, helping folks around these parts filled his days. You might say that Doc found his purpose, and I had never seen him happier."

When the pie came out of the oven, they tried a piece; to Peggy's surprise, it was terrific. Maybe the biggest surprise was how much she enjoyed doing it for fun!

"What do you want to do with it?" asked Widow Henry.

"Maybe I can take it with me Monday when Doctor Smith and I visit people in the backwoods," replied Peggy.

For the first time, she wanted to share something with someone she didn't know, just for fun.

Tom's trip to Charleston had been delayed because of Doc's funeral, meaning George had spent a few extra days in Clayton. George didn't trust people easily like his younger brother, so he stayed to himself. Sitting in the restaurant, sipping on a glass of iced tea, he had seen everyone going to Doc's funeral but guessed he must have been someone important.

As Finn returned from the funeral, he saw George sitting there and went inside to see how he was doing.

"We're going to leave in the morning. I hope you understand, we couldn't leave town before Doc's funeral. He was a really good man."

"He must have been important for that many people to come," said George.

"Oh, Doc was important, all right, but not the way you're thinking," said Finn." From what I've learned, while I've been around these parts, he cared for everybody, like a doctor, but it was more than that. He cared about every person he came across. He was the one who took care of Hank when he was shot. He patched him up and had him stay in his house until he was well enough to go home."

"My brother stayed in an old white man's house," asked George.

"Sure did. Doc cared for his wound, fed him, and sat and listened while your brother told him stories. Archie was telling me that before Hank left town, he went by to see Doc every day that week," said Finn.

George just sat there, not believing what he was hearing, for he had never known a white person who didn't look down on black people like they weren't human. Finn was the first white that had ever been nice to him. He slowly began to realize that not all white folks were terrible. It was a lot for him to deal with, given his history. He decided he would talk about it with his brother when they finally got to see one another.

The following day, Nancy filled a picnic basket with food for the men and took it to the stable, where Tom was hitching his horse to the wagon. George was there early, anxiously pacing back and forth, waiting for Tom to leave.

After saying goodbye to Nancy, Tom and George headed for Charleston. Finn decided to stay to help Samuel with his project.

"I'll be back tomorrow. I'm going to spend the night with Howard and stop by Hoffman's before I leave," said Tom as the wagon pulled away.

George kept asking how much further it would be before they got to the settlement, unable to hide his excitement.

Crossing the Kanawha River on the Patrick Street Bridge was exciting for George. Riding in Tom's wagon, high above the grand river, was a thrill. During their trip, Tom and George discussed how Tom met Hank and other stories from Hank's time in Clayton.

"You say that Hank went to this place to be a witness to these folks? Boy, something sure has changed. When Hank was a little feller, he was always gettin' in trouble. There was hardly a day went by; he wasn't gettin' into a fight or something," said George, shaking his head.

Tom smiled and said quietly, "You'll have to have him tell you what has changed; I'm sure he can't wait to tell you."

Taking the road east, along the southern side of the river, the men slowly made their way toward Cabin Creek. Tom had only been near this area when he rode over to look at the property Thomas Franklin wanted him to buy. As the road began making its way up into the hills along the creek, Tom noticed a small road turning left toward the river.

"Let's follow this road," said Tom, "it looks like it's headed downstream toward the river."

Rounding a sharp curve on the side of the hill, the road was poorly rutted from wagon wheels turning and sliding in the mud. Then, just as the road flattened, both men saw the settlement. Small shacks lined the road while smoke from fires filled the air. Tom began feeling very uncomfortable. It seemed everyone was staring at him. It was evident that he wasn't welcomed in their village. George saw a woman cooking and shouted, "Do you know where Hank lives?"

Looking at George and then Tom, the woman said, "Down the road a bit. You'll see it. He lives in a tent." With that, she turned back to what she was doing, clearly not wanting to talk further.

When the little road turned to the right and up a small knoll, George saw a tent. His heart was about to burst out of his chest in anticipation. Tom stopped the wagon, George jumped down and ran to the tent. To George's surprise, he saw his little brother sitting against a log reading. "Hank!" yelled George as he rushed to hug his brother.

Tossing his papers, Hank jumped to his feet, "George, is that you?"

"Yes, Hank. I can't believe I found you!" The two brothers ran towards each other and hugged, rocking back and forth, crying.

"I thought I would never see you again," said Hank. Their reunion was something Hank had prayed for every day since he became a believer, knowing that if it was God's will, he would someday find his big brother.

A few minutes later, Hank realized that Tom was there and yelled for him to come to his tent. Looking at George, Hank said," Big brother, you have no idea how this man changed my life," as he reached out to give Tom a bear hug.

As the men visited, Tom asked Hank what he had been doing since he moved there. "Well, I've been helping folks repair their places after it flooded. I cut down trees and do my best to cut the logs to replace what was destroyed. It's slow work since I don't have any help. The men work in the coal mines, and by the time they come home in the evenings, they're too tired to help much," Hank replied meekly.

"You know, that doesn't surprise me. I knew you would find a way to help people, but this seems like a huge project."

"Well, the Lord gives me the strength to do whatever He puts in front of me to do, so I don't mind," said Hank with a big smile.

Tom realized he needed to leave to be on time for his appointment with Howard and got up to go. Before he left, though, he stopped and hugged George. "It's been great getting to know you, George. I hope you enjoy time with your brother; he's one of the best men I have ever known."

"Wait, Tom. It might be better if I rode with you to the edge of town. These folks are a suspicious group and probably aren't too happy a white fellow is around," said Hank." George, wait here a little while; I'll be back."

Riding out of the settlement, folks looked at both men suspiciously. No one smiled or attempted to say hello. "You'll have to forgive them, Tom; they've all had a rough life, and frankly, things aren't much better here."

"I understand. I guess they live under the false impression that we're all alike, kind of how most white folks think about blacks. It's okay; I would probably feel the same way if I had been through what they have," said Tom.

When Hank felt Tom would be safe, he told Tom to stop his wagon, and he began to get down, but before he could walk away, Tom said, "Hank, what if some of your friends from Clayton came to visit you?"

"I think it might be a little too soon for anything like that, Tom; these people are in no place to deal with whites, not yet."

"But don't they work with white folks every day? Maybe if they see people different looking than them, wanting to help them, they may begin to understand white people aren't the same just because their skin is the same color," said Tom.

As the two friends said their goodbyes, there were a few men from the settlement who had followed to make sure Tom left.

When Hank walked back to his tent, men emerged from the trees they had been hiding behind and came toward Hank.

"What do you mean bringing a white man here?" yelled one man. "We don't want their kind around here," shouted another.

"Settle down, guys; he's a good friend of mine," said Hank. "All he wanted to do was bring my brother to me. Don't worry, he's a good guy."

"We're going to keep an eye on you, Hank; you better not be bringing white folk here again, or you'll pay the price," said the third man.

Walking back to his tent, Hank was filled with mixed emotions. He was overjoyed to finally be together with his brother, but the sadness of seeing how much he was still distrusted broke his heart.

CHAPTER 42

ARRIVING AT HOWARD McDougal's office just as it was closing, Tom asked if he could quickly go over an idea he had about some houses.

"Sure, Tom, come on in. I was headed home to help Vivian with dinner," said Howard.

"Howard, I don't know if you know, but Hank moved from Clayton to help the folks in the former slave settlement along the riverbank where Cabin Creek runs into the Kanawha River. I'll share the long story with you later, but his brother discovered where Hank was living and came to Clayton to see him. After Doc's funeral, I took him to the little settlement. It was so great to see them together. They hadn't seen one another for thirty years. While there, I couldn't help noticing what deplorable conditions these poor people were living in, and I had an idea of what could be done.

"As you probably remember, I sold Thomas my part of the land in Cabin Creek that was going to be used for mining. I could not be part of what was going on in the mines. The piece I kept has never been mined, but I thought that Nancy and I could build houses for the folks in this little settlement. They will work with Hank to cut trees that Widow Henry will have made into boards at her sawmill in Charleston. When the wood has properly dried, the homeowner and anyone from the community will work with Hank to construct it. Hopefully, on the next house, the new homeowner will help his neighbor and Hank build the second house, and so on, until the entire community works together to build their village. Could you create a simple plan for houses with a living area, kitchen, two bedrooms, and a bathroom? These poor people live in shacks without heat, floors, or kitchens.

I have to help Howard; it's terrible the way they're having to live."

Howard could see the despair in Tom's eyes. "I'll get on it tomorrow, my friend. Let's head home; I know what Vivian has prepared for dinner," said Howard, smiling.

After having another wonderful visit with his friends, Tom headed for Hoffman's to pick up a few things he needed for the store. On his trip back to Clayton, he wondered how to help Hank's new neighbors when he wasn't welcomed in their settlement. He knew he needed to talk with Widow Henry about making the boards for the construction, but it just seemed somehow something else could be done.

That evening, he and Nancy discussed his discovery during his trip with George.

"I don't know how they survive," said Tom. "The men work in the coal mines and have little time or energy to help Hank with any work that needs to be done. Years ago, the freed slaves worked in the salt works in Malden, West Virginia, but now that industry has almost closed down, so their only choice is to work in the mines."

In one of the newspapers Tom had brought from Charleston, Nancy had read that the white miners were provided housing in the mining camps and were paid with company money, which they could only use to buy food and supplies at the company store. The prices at these stores were very high, keeping the miners in debt to the coal mining companies.

Based on what Tom had seen, the black workers lived in even worse conditions, without any store to buy necessities.

"Maybe we can build a small store to provide necessary supplies. We would need someone to run it, but I think this would be as much of a service for them as better housing," said Nancy.

"That's a great idea. We would sell everything at our cost to help them out.

The next day, Tom stopped by Widow Henry's to discuss the use of her Charleston sawmill with her.

"My idea is that if Hank can get the logs to the mill, they can be cut into boards without affecting the lumber yard's inventory," said Tom.

Widow Henry slowly considered how this could be done to benefit Hank and his new neighbors without putting Hank in a bad position with them.

"You know Tom, I own land in that area, too. Maybe we could begin to clear some of it, in addition to your land, to get lumber to build houses and other buildings, including a school, a church, and the general store you mentioned. It would make sense to open a new sawmill there to do all of this.

"People could cut the trees needed to build their houses, and we could cut them into boards. After they dry, a construction crew could help build the houses, but only with the help of the neighborhood people."

"We could employ some men and get them out of the mines," said Widow Henry.

Tom hadn't seen Widow Henry this excited in a long time.

"We'll have to find them a schoolteacher since blacks aren't allowed in schools with white children," said Tom.

"Wow, we've got a lot to do, but I can't wait to get things going. I will go over to my housing project and see how Samuel and his team are doing. We could use them to help with the land when they're finished," said Tom, realizing he was as excited as Widow Henry.

Samuel and his small team of men were making good progress, but there was at least another two or three weeks of work left to do.

"Samuel, I have another project for you to do when you finish. If possible, I want to finish both projects before late fall," said Tom.

"We're doing our best, but last week's rain has slowed us down a bit," said Samuel.

"Samuel, I would like you and me to go to Charleston and upriver to Cabin Creek. I'll fill you in on the way," said Tom.

That evening, as Tom and Nancy were having dinner, they heard a knock on their front door. Going to the door, Tom saw that it was Widow Henry.

"Hello, ma'am. Please come in and join us; we're just about to have dessert," said Tom inquisitively.

"No, no, I don't have time for that this evening, though I am sure it's wonderful. Tom, I would like to ride with you when you go to Charleston. I want to talk with my manager about our plans. He may know of someone that could help us, plus it gives me a chance to see my old friend, Hank," said the widow with a smile.

"You're welcome to come, but I'm not sure about seeing Hank. That's a pretty rough place he's living in," said Tom in a concerned voice.

"I'm not afraid, Tom," said Widow Henry confidently.

The following day, the threesome headed out for Charleston. Tom told Samuel what he and Widow Henry wanted to do for the black miners. Listening to Tom, Widow Henry could see how driven he was to get this done sooner rather than later.

When they arrived in Charleston, they stopped by the sawmill, and Widow Henry talked with her manager. "Until we can get a mill built, I want you to see that Hank's wood gets cut and stored for drying," Widow Henry instructed the manager.

Samuel was glad to be back in town to see his family again.

"Ma'am, would it be all right with you if I went to my house to see my family for a few hours?" asked Samuel.

"Of course," said Widow Henry. Tom and I have some business to take care of, so why don't you meet us back here at three o'clock?"

Just as Samuel was leaving, Widow Henry asked him to wait. "Would you take me there too? I would love to meet your wife and children."

"I will be at Thomas' office working on some legal matters, so you can meet me there if you have time. Otherwise, I'll see you here at three o'clock," said Tom.

Widow Henry scooted over, took Tom's reins, and told Samuel to jump up front on the bench.

Samuel was so proud to ride in his neighborhood in a nice wagon. When they arrived, Samuel quickly got down, tied the horse to the front post, and helped Widow Henry down from the wagon. Samuel's wife and daughter ran to see him as they approached the door.

Samuel had been away for several weeks, and it was clear to Widow Henry that they missed him. After they hugged and kissed, Samuel embarrassingly stepped back and said, "Excuse me, ma'am. I should have introduced you."

"Nonsense, Samuel, I would have done the same thing."

Samuel introduced Widow Henry to his wife and daughter. Shortly, his son came out, shyly hiding behind his momma.

"It's all right, honey, this is the nice lady I told you about. This is Widow Henry from Clayton."

Samuel's wife and children didn't know how to act or what to say. Sensing their awkwardness, Widow Henry reached out her hand to shake theirs.

Kneeling to the children's level, she asked them if they had missed their daddy.

Slowly, the tension left, and everyone began relaxing and talking freely.

"Ma'am, when does school begin?" asked Widow Henry.

"Our little school begins in early September," replied Samuel's wife.

"Well, I was wondering if you and the girls would like to stay with me while Samuel is finishing the project he is working on in Clayton. When he's done with that, he has another project east of Charleston, so he should be able to come home on weekends, but until then, please, be my house guests."

"Oh, ma'am, that would be wonderful, but I don't think people would like that, you being white and all," said Samuel's wife, Ruth.

"Well, Ruth, once you get to know me, you'll find out that I don't care much about what other people might say, but just so you'll feel comfortable, you also need to know that nobody in Clayton would think anything about it."

Samuel felt the need to support what Widow Henry had just said. "Honey, these folks are different. People in this little town don't see skin color; they see the person you are. It's different there."

It was settled, and Samuel's family went into their house to gather their things to meet at seven thirty that evening for the ride to Clayton. Since it was June, the daylight stayed longer, allowing for evening travel.

At three o'clock, the threesome met at the sawmill and headed for Hank's settlement. Tom was very uncomfortable, but Widow Henry had a very determined look on her face.

As they rode into the village, no men except those unable to work due to injury or age were there. The women were cooking over their campfires what they had as their children ran to hide. When they were almost at Hank's tent, Tom noticed George and Hank working on the cabin they were building. Looking up, Hank saw Widow Henry and ran out to meet her. He wanted to give her one of his bear hugs but cautioned her about his sweaty, dirty shirt.

"I don't care about that; hug me. I've missed you, Hank."

"Take me to your place, Hank; we've have much to discuss."

Widow Henry and Tom talked with Hank for over an hour about how they wanted to help his neighbors. "Hank, I'm going to have a mill built not far from here on property I've owned for years. I want you to build it and hire two other men to help you in addition to George. I don't want him working too hard," she laughed.

If we can get trees cut this summer and fall that can dry over winter, we could begin construction in the spring. They will have to work helping build their houses, but we will provide a crew to help with the first one. As they learn how it's done, they can help build the next house, so the longer the project goes, the faster the homes will be built since more and more people will be helping. For now, the important thing is to get the sawmill built and lumber drying."

Hank had never seen Widow Henry so in charge before. His quiet, elderly friend envisioned what must be done, and nothing would get in her way.

"One last thing, Hank, before we go. You and all your neighbors need to pray for this project. It will only work if it is what the Lord wants us to do."

Samuel and his family put their things in Tom's wagon and rode along with Widow Henry while Tom walked beside his horse. The trip was slower due to the extra load and Tom's walking, but Widow Henry saw it as an opportunity to get to know Ruth and the children.

Once the little ones realized they could relax around these strangers, they began talking nonstop. Liza had never seen white people and was very curious. "Your hair is funny," said Liza, to her mother's embarrassment.

"I'm sure it does seem strange to you, Liza. You can touch it if you want," said Widow Henry.

"It is so soft," said the little girl. Samuel's daughter was shy but curious.

Widow Henry asked her if she had a doll to play with, and when she said she didn't, Widow Henry said, "Well, I'm going to take care of that just as soon as we have breakfast in the morning."

As the ride continued, Ruth and Widow Henry began discussing cooking. "My mamma was a cook on a plantation in Virginia before the war. She worked all day making food for the master and his family. I remember how tired she would be in the evenings after finishing her work," said Ruth.

"What was her favorite thing to make?" asked Widow Henry.

"Oh, that's easy," replied Ruth. "Chicken and dumplings."

"You'll have to show me how to make them," said Widow Henry, smiling at her new friend.

When they arrived in Clayton, Ruth and the children couldn't believe how lovely Widow Henry's house was.

"I've got some cots out back in the barn that you can set up for the little ones," said Widow Henry. "You can either put them in the room with you or in the hall outside your room, whatever you're comfortable with."

Since it was so late, Widow Henry knew she wouldn't have time to prepare dinner, so she took everyone to Sarah's restaurant. They had never been to a restaurant. As they looked around, it was clear to Widow Henry that she needed to direct them to a table.

Just as they were sitting down, Sarah came rushing over. "I'm sorry, I was busy with another guest. Please have a seat. I'll get you some iced tea."

When Sarah returned with the tea, Widow Henry asked what she was serving that evening. "I have meatloaf, mashed potatoes, and green beans tonight."

"Does that sound good to everyone?" asked Widow Henry.

"Yes, ma'am," said Samuel.

Everyone enjoyed their dinner, and as they left, Sarah thanked them for coming.

Walking back to Widow Henry's house, Ruth wasn't sure what to believe. She had never been treated so nicely by white people, but her tough nature caused her to doubt everything was as it seemed.

Widow Henry tried to imagine how her guests were dealing with their new circumstances but kept these things to herself, at least for the time being.

Samuel left for work the next day as his family sat down for breakfast. "I hope you like eggs, bacon, grits with biscuits," said Widow Henry.

"Everything is wonderful, ma'am; you didn't need to bother with all of this," said Ruth as she buttered her biscuit.

"I love to make my house guests feel welcomed, and I always believed that good food was one of the best ways," continued Widow Henry.

"How about we go to the general store and see about a doll after breakfast," said the widow, "and after that, I'll take you to see what your daddy has been doing."

The children were very excited to get toys. They didn't have any of their own. One of their friends at school had a doll that Liza sometimes borrowed to play with. Walking into the store, the children rushed to where Nancy kept all the toys. As Liza looked at the dolls, her face showed something was wrong.

"Ma'am, all the dolls are white. I don't see any like us," said Liza.

Nancy looked at Widow Henry and shook her head, "I'm sorry, we've never had anyone ask for a black doll before, but I'll tell you what: I'm sure I can make one for you."

Looking at Ruth, Widow Henry could tell she was disappointed and quickly said, "Nancy is a wonderful seamstress; I'm sure the doll will be perfect."

"I will start on them immediately and have it for you in about an hour," said Nancy.

"That will be wonderful," said Widow Henry, "we're going to see all of the work Samuel has been doing and then go to the park so that the children can play in the playground."

Leaving the general store, Ruth said she understood why they didn't have any black dolls. "I guess there have never been any black children living in Clayton," said Ruth.

"You're right; Hank and Samuel have been the only blacks to live here for any amount of time," replied Widow Henry.

Widow Henry walked down the street and saw Rusty and Lizzy exit the restaurant and head to the park. Seeing the children, they rushed over, excited to have other children to play with. "Hi, my name is Lizzy, and this is Rusty. What's your name?" asked Lizzy.

Her forwardness initially surprised the children, but then, at Widow Henry's encouragement, they told Lizzy their names. "Do you want to come to the park and play? Rusty and I are headed there now," asked Lizzy.

Ruth knew playing would be more interesting to the children than looking at a work site, even if their daddy worked there. "You can go ahead; we'll stop by after seeing Daddy," said Ruth.

With that, all four children ran down the street to Clayton Park.

A few minutes later, Widow Henry and Ruth arrived at the new development that Samuel and Finn were working at. Standing there, looking at all the work her husband had done, Ruth was shocked. "I knew he said he was working on some land, getting it ready to build houses, but I had no idea how much he was doing."

Widow Henry waved to Samuel, who came over to say hello. By the time he got to them, his wife had tears in her eyes. "Honey, I knew you worked hard because you were tired when you got home, but I never knew how much you were doing. This looks amazing," exclaimed the proud wife.

"Wait until you see the park," said Widow Henry. "Samuel and Finn developed the land and built everything there."

Ruth looked at her husband, reaching out her hands to hold him. "I'm so proud of you."

Leaving Samuel, the two walked to the park to see the girls. Rounding the corner, Ruth couldn't believe what she saw. Her children were playing on the swings with the other children, laughing uncontrollably. Then, as if she had forgotten, she noticed the park. "Samuel built this?"

"Oh yes, he cleared all of the land, built the path along the creek, along with the bridges, play equipment, shelters, picnic tables, and the gazebo," said Widow Henry. "He's very good."

Ruth and Widow Henry left the children playing at the park so long as Lizzy and Rusty would return them when they were finished. It was clear that everyone was having a great time. When they reached the general store, Nancy was putting her sewing materials away as they walked into the store. Handing the doll to Ruth, Nancy again apologized for not having one in stock, but shaking her head, Ruth said, "It's all right; you've never had black children living in town, so why would you have them."

Looking at the doll, Ruth could see how much detailed work Nancy had put into making it and thanked her for her attention to detail. "Liza will love it just as much as Willie loves the baseball," said Ruth.

When Widow Henry reached into her bag, Nancy stopped her and said, "No charge; tell Liza that I have some clothes for the doll if she wants."

After arriving home, Widow Henry suggested they sit in the parlor and get to know one another. "I'll get some iced tea; you just make yourself comfortable."

The two women talked all afternoon. Ruth told her about growing up as a little girl on a plantation where both her parents were slaves and how she was always afraid of being sold and separated from her family. As she listened, Widow Henry couldn't imagine what living like that must have been like. Finally, Ruth gained enough confidence to ask Widow Henry why she was helping her husband.

"Everything my husband and I have was given to us by the Lord, so I have tried to use it like I think He would have. If someone is willing to work and I can help them get a start, I am happy to do it. When my foreman sent Samuel, Finn, and Fred here to work for me, they didn't like each other. In fact, Finn and Fred got into a fight one night, but Samuel stepped in to break it up. He's a good man and has proven to be an excellent worker. That park was a huge job, yet he and Finn were able to get it done, just like Tom had asked.

"Tom is Nancy's husband. They own the general store. It is Tom that Samuel is working for now. They're going to build a new part of town so that when people want to move here, homes are available for them."

"Is everybody in Clayton white?" asked Ruth.

"Yes, now at least. Hank used to run the sawmill, and he was black, but he left a while back to go to a former slave community east of Charleston. He wanted to share Christ's love with those folks and felt strongly that God was calling him there."

"I've heard about that place. It's pretty rough, so I hear like the old salt works plant in Malden years back. You know that Negro school there had a fella named Booker T. Washington. I hear he is headin' up the Tuskegee Institute someplace in Alabama. But the folks where your fellow moved to don't have a school. I don't want anything to do with that place," said Ruth, surprised someone would leave Clayton to go there.

"It's not for everyone, but Hank isn't like most people. He's big and strong but with a tender heart for people," said Widow Henry.

"Sounds like you know him pretty well," replied Ruth.

"Oh, Hank and I are good friends. He used to come here and sit right where you are, and I would teach him to read. He learned reading from my husband's old Bible. I'm very proud of Hank; he's a good man," said the widow.

Just then, the children came running up the sidewalk with Rusty and Lizzy. "Oh, Mommy, we had a great time at the park," yelled Liza.

After saying goodbye to their new friends, the children talked about all they had done that afternoon. By the looks of their clothes, they had been playing hard.

"Why don't I draw up a nice bath so they can clean up, and we can talk after dinner," said Widow Henry as she got up to head for the bathroom.

That evening, after the children were fast asleep, Samuel, Ruth, and Widow Henry sat in the parlor. "It's the custom in my house to read the Bible every evening and talk about what we have read. Would you like to join me?" asked Widow Henry.

That evening, they enjoyed discussing Jonah and the whale and what it meant to each of them. It was clear to Widow Henry that neither Ruth nor Samuel read very well. When they were finished discussing the Bible story, Widow Henry prayed for Samuel and his family, and as they were about to head off to bed, she offered to teach them to read if they wanted to learn.

"I know you won't be here that long, but I think we can get a lot done when you are here," said the Widow, hoping she hadn't overstepped.

"You would," exclaimed Samuel," I have always wanted to read better than I do."

Ruth sat in her chair, shaking her head yes as tears filled her eyes. These last two days were starting to overwhelm her. For the first time in her life, she began to feel like a human being instead of someone's piece of property. Freedom from slavery hadn't meant real freedom at all. Like most blacks, she was treated the same way she had always been, only now they had to find a way to fend for themselves.

As she got up from her chair, Ruth reached out her hands to hold Widow Henry's and whispered through her tears, "Thank you."

CHAPTER 43

MEN AND WOMEN from Clayton, along with some of the folks from the backwoods, came to help plant the community garden. Seamus explained that all the produce would be given to the people who had helped, and any leftovers would be sold at the farmers market in Charleston. The money from the sale would be given to those who had helped during the summer, weeding, tying up the beans and peas, and watering, if needed.

Just as Mary had warned, most of the backwoods folks didn't believe the garden would be helpful to them and chose not to help. Those that did went about planting and hoeing on their own, feeling they didn't know any other people until Carol and Seamus asked everyone to stop what they were doing for a minute.

"I want to thank everyone who came today to help with this garden. We hope that it will be useful in raising food for everyone in the area. My wife, Carol, and I will live in that cabin this summer. I will still travel around the countryside during the week but preach at the shelter on Wednesday evenings. Those of you who can't make it to Clayton on Sundays can come and enjoy the fellowship of others while we study God's word. Also, Carol will teach school at the shelter during the week."

Seamus noticed most were not paying much attention. Carol stood up to explain what she planned to do over the summer.

"I am the schoolteacher from Clayton. I will teach anyone, children or adults, reading and basic mathematics. I want to help each of you learn so that you have skills that will help you find employment. With the world changing as fast as it is, you will no longer be able to survive doing what your ancestors did. There's nothing wrong with hunting and farming, but it will not be enough. Being able to read will help each of you, but none more than your children. Please tell your friends that I will be here every day to help anyone that comes."

As Carol sat down, the few men from the backwoods began talking among themselves.

When the garden was planted and watered as well as possible, folks began leaving. The people from Clayton patted Seamus on the back and told him they thought this was a promising idea.

When Carol and Seamus were finishing tying the strings for the green beans and peas to climb, Carol felt a tap on her shoulder. It was the young farmer and his wife, along with little Nancy.

"Ma'am, when are you going to start teaching? I need to learn to read and do numbers, " the young man said humbly.

"We can start Monday morning at nine o'clock. That should give you time to tend to your garden or whatever chores you need to do first," said Carol, pleasantly surprised.

The following Monday, after riding to Hank's old place, Seamus headed out for his visitations. Meanwhile, Carol put some of her things in the cabin and tried to make it as comfortable as possible. After organizing the old cabin, she headed to the creek to get two buckets of water when she heard someone walking down the road. Looking up, she saw Clyde, the young farmer she had gotten to know when his little girl was born.

"Good morning, Clyde; I'm glad you could make it," said Carol enthusiastically. As they settled under the shelter, Carol brought out her chalkboard from the cabin and sat across from Clyde.

"Tell me, Clyde, have you ever tried to read, or is this your first time?" asked Carol.

"Oh, I started learning when I was little, but momma said I needed to help her take care of my brothers and sister. My daddy died from the fever when I was eight, and my three brothers and sister were all younger than me. Momma worked hard, but she needed help, so I became the man of the house," said Clyde a little shamefully.

"I understand, Clyde. The fever has taken a lot of folks and left families struggling. Where are they now?" Carol asked.

"The boys have all left home to find work, mostly in the mines. They send money to my momma when they can. She lives with my little sister outside Charleston in a little cabin close to the Elk River. Sometimes momma gets work doing laundry or cleaning houses, but not very often."

"Well, Clyde, I will help you learn to read, but I can only do so much. You must want to learn and work hard on your own. It will be hard at first, but after a while, you will begin seeing that you are learning, and it will encourage you to keep at it," said Carol, trying to encourage Clyde.

That day, Clyde was shown the first half of the alphabet and taught how to pronounce each letter. Later, Carol gave him a piece of paper and a pencil and had him write each letter seven times. Under each letter, she had him draw something that began with that letter to help him understand how to sound each one.

When they finished, Carol asked Clyde if he would mind if she read to him. As Carol began reading, she saw how Clyde was enjoying the story. As with her students at school, he found himself immersed in the story, and when Carol stopped, he quietly hoped she would continue. He had never considered how interesting reading could be.

"It's getting late, so we better stop for the day. Tomorrow, we'll work on the second half of the alphabet.

"Will you read too?" asked Clyde hopefully.

"Yes, I will read," said Carol, "but someday, if you work hard, you will read to me."

The day had gone wonderfully, but Carol couldn't help being disappointed that more hadn't shown up.

The first few weeks of the summer had gone by quietly, with only one student and only two or three coming to Wednesday services. Discouraged, Seamus reminded Carol that they must "wait on the Lord." Then, one day, Clyde brought his wife, Meg, and Nancy.

"I hope you don't mind, but I want to learn too. Clyde has been so excited. He's been working every evening on the assignments you have given him. I'll keep Nancy as quiet as possible," said Meg.

"I'm glad you're here, Meg. Don't worry about Nancy; I love little ones."

Carol started with Meg, teaching the same way she had Clyde, but as she got further into the lesson, she noticed how Clyde kept helping his wife. Clyde was excited for her to learn. Carol decided to give Meg some memory work to do while she taught Clyde.

Clyde, Meg, and little Nancy were always there on Wednesday evenings. Clyde had mentioned what he and his wife were doing at the shelter to a hunting friend of his, hoping he would come as well. When he didn't make the trip, the disappointment was evident on Clyde's face.

Seamus talked with him about planting seeds. "You know, Clyde, all you are responsible for is to share what you know. You never know what will happen. Some days, you plant a bean seed, which grows quickly, but other days, it might be an acorn that takes years to become an oak tree. Just do your part and leave the rest to God."

From time to time, Carol noticed men and sometimes their wives tending to the garden. The people from Clayton came on a more regular basis. These people truly wanted to help their neighbors, but it would take longer for the backwoods folks to trust the "city folks."

One Saturday, Mary and Rusty came out to see their friends. Mary could tell that Carol was discouraged by the lack of people coming to learn.

"You know, I know some of these folks. Maybe I can help. Let me talk with Sarah and see if I can travel with Seamus on Mondays and tell them to at least come and see for themselves," said Mary.

As Mary and Carol sat talking, Seamus returned to the cabin. It had been an unusually wet week, raining for three days. He had helped two families weed their gardens as he talked with them. He thought this would allow him to share God's word while helping them with work that needed to be done.

Seeing Rusty, Seamus quickly got a burst of energy. "Hey, Rusty, how would you like to go fishing?" Rusty couldn't have been happier as they headed off to one of Rusty's favorite fishing holes.

Shortly after Seamus and Rusty left, Clyde and Meg walked up to the cabin. Mary remembered them from the time Nancy was born.

"Afternoon, folks; glad to see you," said Mary. "How's that little one?"

Gushing with pride, Meg showed Mary Nancy.

"Wow, she's growing quickly," said Mary.

As the four of them caught up, Mary realized that she needed to back out of the conversation so that they could get to their lessons. "Why don't you let me take care of Nancy so you two can concentrate on your work? You know, Carol taught me how to read," said Mary in a supportive way. It's work, but it's worth it. I love to read!"

With that, Mary took Nancy from Meg and walked over to inspect the crops in the garden.

Later that day, some people came to the garden Mary knew from the backwoods.

"Hey guys, you all coming to work the garden?" asked Mary.

"Yeah, I thought we'd see if anything needed to be done. Seems like people keep everything pretty cleaned up, so there usually isn't much to do," said the old friend.

"I came out to visit Carol and Seamus and ended up babysitting while some people are learning to read," said Mary.

"I heard about that, but it sounds too hard. I'm just fine the way I am."

Mary thought about what she wanted to say and humbly said," Earl, I know you have always gotten along, but times are changing. You will have to get a paying job to care for your family, and you can't get a very good job if you can't read. It's not that hard," said Mary.

"How would you know?" asked Earl.

"Why, Carol over there taught me how to read, and another friend taught me mathematics. You'll catch on in no time, Earl. Give it a try," encouraged Mary.

Earl said he might try it as they pulled weeds through the garden. "I could use a paying job now that the wife is pregnant with our fifth one," said Earl.

That day, after Clyde and Meg completed their lessons and took Nancy home, Mary introduced Earl to Carol. "Carol, I've known Earl for many years. He's hard-working and says he wants to try to learn to read."

Carol asked Earl to sit at the picnic table under the shelter so that they could talk. Mary took her cue and wandered out into the forest, for old times' sake.

After about an hour, Earl left with his first lesson. He agreed to work on it over the weekend and return on Monday around eleven o'clock. Seamus returned with Rusty and four trout they had caught.

"Let me get these fish cleaned, and then we can put them in a bucket of chilly water before you head back to Clayton," said Seamus.

Rusty and Seamus cleaned the fish and filled an old bucket in the creek with cool water before hitching up the horse to the wagon. Seamus helped Carol and Mary to the front bench and his little buddy on the horse while he walked, holding the reins. Rusty was all smiles!

It had been a wonderful day. Seamus had spent time with Rusty, and Carol had a new student. Unknown to any of them, Mary's involvement would be one of the most critical factors in educating the people in the backwoods around Clayton.

That Sunday, Seamus spoke on the parable of the sown seeds. Finishing his sermon, Seamus concluded, "It's not our job to grow the seeds; that's God's; it's our responsibility to plant as many as possible."

As Clyde and Meg headed out of church, Seamus caught up with them and thanked them for making the trip into town. It was clear that changes were beginning to happen in this little family.

That Sunday, sitting with Widow Henry was Samuel and his family. After speaking with Clyde, Seamus met Ruth and the children. Widow Henry watched as Seamus and Carol talked with them. Carol asked the children about school and if they were excited for the new year to begin in the fall.

Ruth again was reserved, wondering if they were sincere or just polite. Widow Henry explained to Carol that they were her house guests while Samuel was working on the development project for Tom.

"This afternoon, we're all going to the park for a picnic. Archie and Maggie normally come by on Sundays to talk about scripture, so all eight of us are going to go to the park. Would you like to join us?" asked Widow Henry.

"We would love to. I'll cook the fish Seamus and Rusty caught yesterday and bring them along with some green beans I picked," said Carol.

Setting down on the pew so that she could be at eye level with the children, Carol asked them if they would bring their toys. Liza explained that she took her doll everywhere she went, and Willie pulled his new baseball out of his pocket, smiling.

The afternoon went by quickly. After lunch, the children played, and the adults sat at one of the picnic tables under a shelter and talked about what Archie and Maggie had been reading in their nightly Bible study time.

"You two read your Bible together every evening?" asked Ruth.

Maggie explained that when she and Archie lived with Widow Henry, they learned how important it was to have daily time with God. Ruth shook her head and said, "Samuel is so tired when he comes home; even if we had a Bible, I don't think he would be able to read much before he fell to sleep."

"I know what you mean," said Archie, "but as tired as I was in the evenings, I looked forward to reading the Bible. It is my favorite time of the day."

Alma Gay woke up from her nap and was hungry. As Maggie fed her, Ruth couldn't resist asking if she could hold her. Ruth loved children and loved caring for them. Carefully, Ruth took Alma Gay from Maggie's arms and cuddled her close to her chest. "She's so beautiful," exclaimed Ruth.

Taking her usual Sunday walk, Peggy Wallace walked down the street to the park. She hadn't baked with Widow Henry on Saturday since the widow had guests. The real reason was that she felt very uncomfortable being around blacks. In Richmond, her family had always had black housekeepers and cooks. She had always thought that they were not as intelligent as white people and that they were lazy. These feelings were learned from her father, who always stressed the importance of hard work and education, often boasting of his accomplishments.

Seeing everyone sitting under the shelter, Peggy walked their way. When she saw Samuel and his wife there, she began to feel awkward but knew she needed to at least stop by since she had made eye contact with Widow Henry.

"Good afternoon, Peggy," said Widow Henry. This is Ruth, Samuel's wife. His two children are playing on the swings behind you. Would you like to join us for some iced tea?"

"No, thank you," said Peggy," I usually take a walk on Sundays when the weather is nice, and today, I thought I would walk along the creek path. It's such a peaceful place, but thanks anyway." Wishing them well, Nurse Wallace left to continue her walk.

After Alma Gay fell asleep, Ruth returned her to Maggie so she and Archie could leave for their cabin. Maggie wanted to begin preparing dinner, and Archie had hoped to have some quiet time reading.

Samuel and Ruth enjoyed their afternoon, relaxing and talking with everyone. Ruth slowly began to see that these were good people, and her fear began to ease.

When the children returned from playing, Widow Henry suggested they leave so she could prepare dinner. On the way back, Ruth asked if she minded if she helped. "I would like that very much, Ruth, thank you," said Widow Henry softly.

CHAPTER 44

MARY WAS READY to ride into the backcountry with Seamus on Monday morning. She had borrowed Tom's horse for the day. His horse wasn't used to being ridden since he pulled Tom's wagon most of the time. However, Mary was skilled at riding and quickly calmed the horse down and rode with Seamus.

That day, Mary took Seamus to places he had never been to see people she knew from living in the woods. As they rode over a ridge, Mary saw an old friend's cabin and headed down the hollow. Suddenly, a gun was fired at the tree above them.

"Don't y'all come any closer!" yelled an old crusty man. He looked to be in his sixties, but he was only forty-five. The years in the mountains had been hard on him, as it was on most folks.

Mary yelled," Amos, stop shooting, it's me, Mary."

Amos lowered his gun slowly as Mary and Seamus descended the hollow. When they got close enough for Amos to see it was Mary, he put his gun down, signaling that it was all right for them to come closer.

"What brings you to these parts, Mary?" asked Amos.

"I'm showing Reverend McConnell around the mountains so he can get to know the people who live here," Mary replied.

"Why?" asked Amos, unsure why anyone would come to where he lived.

"Well, sir, I want to share God's love with everybody I can, so during the week, I travel into the mountains to visit folks," replied Seamus.

"Well, that's nice, Reverend, but I don't need all that church stuff; I'm doing just fine on my own," said Amos defiantly.

"Amos, everybody thinks they're doing fine until they learn the truth, and that's what I'm here for, to tell you the truth," said Seamus gently.

"Well, I ain't got no money to give your church, so don't go expectin' anything," said Amos, beginning to soften a little.

"Amos, God doesn't need your money or any of your stuff; all He wants is your heart."

After a few minutes of going back and forth, it was clear that, at least for today, Amos wasn't having anything to do with what Seamus was trying to share with him, so Seamus asked, "Is there anything I can do for you, Amos?"

Surprised by the question, Amos shook his head and said, "No, I don't need anything."

Seamus slowly reached into his saddle bag and pulled some carrots and collard greens out. "Could you use these? I just picked them Saturday from my garden."

"Sure, okay, I could always use food," said Amos as he took the vegetables from Seamus.

"Thanks," said Amos slowly.

Turning his horse around to leave, Seamus said, "It was good to meet you, Amos. Would you mind if I'm in the area if I stopped by again?"

"Sure, but I don't want no preachin'," replied Amos as Mary and Seamus rode away.

After they were well on their way, Mary began apologizing for how difficult Amos had been when Seamus stopped her and said, "Most people I meet react the same way, Mary. People don't ever want to think they need to know Jesus, never, until they witness His love. Sometimes, that happens quickly, but most of the time, it takes patience. I'll stop by to see him in a few weeks and bring more food."

That day, Mary introduced Seamus to five different families. Some, not all, were glad that he came to see them. It had been a long time since they had seen anyone new, so having the preacher stop by was special. One thing was clear to Seamus: they all needed food, and most needed to know the Lord.

When Mary and Seamus returned to the cabin, Carol was teaching Earl. He had been getting there later than planned because his wife wasn't feeling well. The longer Carol talked with him, the more she became concerned about his wife. "Earl, would you mind if Doctor Smith came to your place tomorrow to check on your wife? He makes rounds in the country during the week."

"How's he gonna know where to find us?" asked Earl.

Mary overheard the conversation and said, "I can tell him how to find you, Earl. Don't worry."

"Well, I guess that would be all right. We've never had a doctor visit before, but she sure was doing poorly this morning, not like any of the other times she was pregnant."

After Earl left, Mary described to Seamus and Carol where he lived in case Doctor Smith had trouble finding his place. Seamus thought he knew the area she mentioned and said he would accompany him.

When Mary arrived in Clayton, she took Tom's horse back to the stable, washed it down, and gave it fresh food. She remembered how much she loved to ride when she was a little girl and owned a horse.

Walking down the street, Mary entered the clinic to see Doctor Smith. Nurse Wallace was at the front desk filling out patient records. When she looked up, she was surprised to see Mary. "Is there something you need? I'm not used to seeing you anywhere but the restaurant."

"Yes, I need to talk with Doctor Smith," said Mary.

"Oh, he's out visiting some people in the woods. Can I help you?" replied Peggy.

"There's a pregnant woman that needs to see him. I'm afraid he'll have trouble finding where she and her husband live. I told Reverend McConnell how to get there, and he agreed to go with him, so could you please see that he goes out to their cabin first thing in the morning?" asked Mary.

"No problem. I will need to go too. It's always easier when a woman is helping in these situations," replied Nurse Wallace.

"Thanks," said Mary as she headed out of the door.

It had been a long day, and Mary was tired. She loved being outdoors, riding Tom's horse, and introducing folks to Reverend McConnell, but it was exhausting. When she had freshened up at Carol's place, she walked across the street to see if Sarah needed anything.

When she arrived, she saw Lizzy and Rusty setting plates on the tables and asked where Sarah was. "She's not feeling so good today," said Lizzy. "We're trying to help out, but I think she needs someone to cook for tonight's guests," said Lizzy.

Mary went to Sarah's apartment and found her lying in bed with a cool washcloth on her forehead.

"Oh, Mary, I'm so glad to see you. I'm not feeling very well. I started getting a fever this morning, and I haven't been able to prepare dinner for this evening."

"Don't worry, I'll get started on it right now," replied Mary.

The rest of the early evening, Mary did her best to prepare food for everyone who came to the restaurant, but she had never cooked for so many people and found it very hard to keep up with the orders.

Tom and Nancy went into the restaurant for their regular Monday date night and saw what was happening. Nancy went into the kitchen and asked if she could help while Tom helped Lizzy and Rusty clear tables and wash dishes. As the last guest left for the evening, everyone was exhausted.

Doctor Hunter and Nurse Wallace had gone into Sarah's apartment to check on her.

"Sarah, you've got a bad cold and suffering from exhaustion. You need to stay in bed for a week. Nurse Wallace or I will check on you daily, but you must stay in bed. Exhaustion is nothing to take lightly," said a concerned doctor.

The following morning, Widow Henry brought the children to the general store to look at clothes for their doll and a baseball mitt for Willie. While she was there, Nancy told her about Sarah. "I don't know how the restaurant can keep going without her. Mary did her best, but she's never cooked for so many people," exclaimed Nancy.

"I have an idea," said Widow Henry, "let me see what I can do."

When Widow Henry returned with the children and their new toys, she told Ruth she would like to talk with her for a minute. Widow Henry explained the problem at the restaurant and asked if Ruth would like a job working at the restaurant with Mary and her while Sarah recovered.

"We stick together here in Clayton, so I will help as much as possible, but I will need some help. I'm sure those chicken and dumplings we had the other night would be perfect for serving. It's totally up to you. I didn't invite you to be my guest to work, but I thought you might enjoy the extra money, especially knowing the children are nearby."

"Ma'am, you and everybody in this town have been so nice to me; I'd be glad to help out if it's all right with Sarah," said Ruth, realizing how her feelings were so very different from just a few days ago.

The next day, Mary cleaned all the rooms in the boardinghouse as usual and ensured everything was in order in the restaurant. When she entered the kitchen to prepare food for the evening guests, she was surprised to find Widow Henry and Ruth busily cooking. Ruth made chicken and dumplings, while Widow Henry made apple pie. Mary began stringing the beans to get them ready to cook.

That evening, all the guests were served timely, and everyone said the chicken and dumplings were the best they had ever had. When Jim Hunter came from the clinic, he washed dishes and cleared tables. Samuel and the children came by for dinner, and when they finished their meals, Samuel helped Jim put everything back in its place. As the last guest left, the kitchen was spotless and ready for the next day.

Sarah was grateful that her neighbors had come to the rescue, keeping her restaurant open; she didn't know what to say.

After Widow Henry and Ruth said goodbye, they returned to her house along with Samuel and the children.

The following day, Nancy pitched in to help Ruth while Widow Henry made pies and cookies so that there would be enough to restock the general store. By the end of the week, everybody in town had done something to ensure Sarah's restaurant stayed open.

On Tuesday, Nurse Wallace and Doctor Smith saw Earl's wife. She suffered from malnutrition and could not supply enough nourishment for her unborn child. While Doctor Smith and Nurse Wallace tended to her, Seamus rushed back to the garden next to the cabin, pulled a basket full of vegetables, and took them along with some meat he and Carol had planned on having that evening.

"She has to eat three to four times daily, sir, "said Doctor Smith. "If she doesn't, I'm afraid she will lose the baby."

Peggy saw the fear in both Earl's and his wife's eyes and quickly said, without giving it a second thought, "I will come out to see you every day until you begin feeling better."

That assurance calmed them down, and for the first time in her life, Peggy Wallace knew how vital her help was to someone. It wasn't her education but her caring.

While most of the town folks were helping at the restaurant, from time to time, Nurse Wallace went into the woodlands by herself to help a family she didn't know. By the end of the week, Sarah was much better, and the pregnant mother had regained her strength. On Friday, Peggy stopped by the garden and picked vegetables to bring to Earl and his family, along with an apple pie she had made in the restaurant kitchen Thursday evening.

By now, Ruth's children were good friends with Lizzy and Rusty. Every day, while their mother worked in the kitchen, they played in the park after helping place silverware, napkins, and glasses on each table.

After three weeks, Samuel's work at the Campbell development was completed, and it was time for him to return to Charleston. Liza and her little brother, Willie, cried, not wanting to leave Clayton and their friends. Ruth was very sad about leaving, too. These last few weeks, she had an experience she could never have imagined. She would later tell people that it was the first time she felt free. Widow Henry, Nancy, and Sarah had become good friends she trusted and enjoyed. Going back to Charleston and their life there would be difficult.

As they rode in Tom's wagon, Ruth thought how grateful she was for Samuel's full-time job, but she also realized how much having good friends meant to her. She didn't have anybody she considered a good friend in Charleston; only a few people she would say hello to if she saw them, but they were not real friends. People just tried to get by as best as they could, with little time for relationships. While the wagon continued toward Charleston, Ruth remembered something Widow Henry had said one evening as they walked back to her house after working at the restaurant, "you have to be a friend to have a friend."

Ruth's time in Clayton had changed her personally, and her heart wanted the same for her children. Life in her neighborhood of Charleston was about to change, and Ruth would be the reason.

CHAPTER 45

HANK AND GEORGE continued to work on the cabin Hank had begun before the flood. Since Liz wouldn't allow him to repair her shack nor teach her son carpentry, he decided to build a cabin for them but not tell Liz until it was finished. The damage from the flood had made living in her place very difficult, and even though she needed help, she didn't trust Hank or, for that matter, any man.

Before being killed in the mining accident, Liz's husband had been very abusive, and now that he was gone, she didn't trust men. Liz's life was consumed by trying to provide the best she could for her son, hoping he would have a better future.

Hank had gone to Charleston one day after Tom and Widow Henry had visited and brought back boards that he and George used as flooring. They also applied whitewash to the exterior walls to help repel wind and rain.

One early afternoon, as Hank and George were finishing the fireplace mantel, Liz walked by on her way up from the creek. Hank had just stepped outside to sit on the stairs to rest when Liz noticed him.

"Sure is a nice looking place, Hank."

Hank thought momentarily and decided that this was as good a time as any to tell her what he and his brother had been doing the last few weeks. "I'm glad you like it, Liz, 'cause George and I made it for you and your son. I wanted to honor your wishes and stay away from your place, but I just couldn't let you continue to live where you are now. George and I will move into your place as soon as you are settled here. Is that okay with you, ma'am?"

Liz couldn't believe her ears. "Why, Hank, why would you work so hard for a stranger?"

While wiping the sweat from his face, Hank looked at Liz and said," You needed a place, and I know how to build, so why wouldn't I help you."

Liz began to cry; no one had ever treated her with such kindness.

"Go get your son and show him your new home," said Hank with a big smile on his face.

The cabin had two small bedrooms and one larger room that served as a living/dining room. Two windows allowed natural light to make the house brighter, but what Liz loved most of all was an indoor fireplace. She repeatedly thanked Hank and George until Hank said, "Let's get your things moved in so you can spend your first night in your new home."

Hank felt good that he had been able to help this poor, struggling mother. Still, he was also aware that people in the village might think he did it for other reasons, so as he was leaving, he mentioned to Liz that he felt it appropriate not to do anything that might cause others to gossip.

That night, as George and Hank settled into Liz's old shack, George quietly said to Hank, "You're not the same person I knew growing up. I wish I had what you have, little brother."

Hank was setting up his tools to work on Jonna's place the following day when some men approached.

"I thought we told you to keep white folk away from here," said one of them in a threatening voice. George began getting angry at them. He didn't like anybody talking to his little brother that way, but Hank put his hand on George's arm and motioned for him to sit down.

Slowly, Hank walked toward the two men and began speaking to them in a soothing tone. "Fellows, I'm sure that in your lifetime, you have had white people treat you like you were nothing but animals. I understand; my brother and I were treated real bad, too. Look at George's cheek. See the brand his owner scarred him with? So, I know why you feel the way you do, but not all white people are alike.

"That man, Tom, is his name; he gave me a place to live when I had nothing. I figured he would kick me out after I fixed it up, but he didn't. Instead, he treated me just like everybody else. And the lady, well, that's Widow Henry. She taught me how to read using her late husband's Bible. Later, she gave me a full-time job working in a sawmill and lumber yard that she owned. Those two close friends came to tell me how they wanted to help everybody in this settlement. So, you see, you can't look at all white people the same."

As Hank finished speaking, one of the men said, "Well, that's good for you, but we've never seen a good white."

"I'll tell you what, "said Hank, "you get the other men together at the shed Sunday after worship, and I'll tell you what we're going to do. If you still feel the same way, I'll never bring them back here. Is that a deal?"

The two men shook their heads and said they would get everyone together on Sunday, but as they left, one of them said, "This better be good!"

Liz had watched all this unfolding from her new place and was impressed with how Hank firmly but gently handled the situation. She was surprised by how passionate he was about helping everyone.

"Hank, why are you so upset?" asked Liz. George was just as interested in Hank's answer as Liz; even though he had experienced a few days with Hank's friends in Clayton, he still didn't grasp all Hank understood.

"Liz, I know you have only known me for a few months, so I'm sure I'm a little hard to understand, but I used to be just like those guys, probably worse." George smiled, remembering the troublemaker his little brother used to be. "I want everyone I meet to feel what it's like to be completely and totally free. To enjoy your life the way it was meant to be, but we can't do it without changing."

When Sunday came, Hank went to worship as he usually did. George said he didn't feel like going but would attend the meeting afterward. Ironically, the morning sermon was about growing in Christ, and while most everyone in attendance shook their heads that they knew it was essential to try to live the way Christ had, few, if any, thought they needed to do much more than they were already doing. After all, they had survived slavery and extreme poverty yet still loved the Lord; what else could they do?

After the service, as everyone was leaving the shed, several men stood outside, none of whom had attended worship. Hank could tell they weren't pleased to be there.

When Hank began to speak, everyone who had been to the church service also stayed.

"I'm glad everyone is here today," started Hank. "A few of you have told me that you didn't like the white folks that have come here to see me these past couple of weeks. I understand, I do. My brother and I were once slaves, just like some of you, but you have to realize that not every white is a slave master. These two people are friends of mine who have helped me for the last two years.

"When George, my brother, came to find me and I had moved here, they took him in. They gave him a place to stay, some new clothes, and fed him. Knowing George, they fed him a lot," laughed Hank! "My point is you must treat people as individuals. They're all different. Some will be unlikable, but others will be someone you could call a friend.

"These two have seen how you have to live and want to help you. They will clear land up the creek on a level area they have already marked off. They will send two men, and we will clear that land with the help of as many of you as possible. The trees will be hauled into Charleston to be cut into lumber that we will use to build a sawmill and houses next spring. Right now, it is important to get the trees cut, and the lumber made so it can dry over winter."

"How do we know they're not just using us as free labor to clear their land?" yelled Jonna.

"I understand your hesitation, Jonna; you'll just have to trust me. I thought something like that when Mr. Campbell had me fix up his place, but as I told you, instead of kicking me out, he allowed me to live there and open a little sawmill to make some money. If I'm wrong, Jonna, I'll give you my horse and wagon."

That promise from Hank seemed to calm everyone down, but Hank felt they needed to have a bigger picture of the entire plan. "This spring, we will build a sawmill and lumber yard after the wood has dried. George and I will run it, but we will need two more men to work there, too. Widow Henry will hire them, hopefully, someone who's been working in the mines.

"Tom's construction crew will work with me and any of you that come to help. After the sawmill is built, I plan to build a house for you, Jonna. The next home will be for whoever helps me the most. When that house is finished, I want that person and whoever helped build the second house to get the next, and so forth, until the entire community is working together to help build one another's homes.

"So, the more trees we cut, the better; plus, I hope to use as many of the logs your current homes are made from as possible to help speed up the process. That's the plan, folks. They want to help, that's all. But there's more!

"Widow Henry and Tom Campbell will help the community build a church and a schoolhouse when everyone has their houses built. You provide the labor, and they provide the material and whatever additional workers are needed."

"Hank, we all work in the mines; we don't have time or energy to help out much," said Jonna.

"I know, my friend, but if everyone can work on Saturdays, you will be surprised how much we can get done. After that, we will need someone to help load the logs on the wagon and haul them to Charleston. Until the sawmill is finished, Widow Henry will have them cut at her mill in Charleston and stored in her lumber yard."

"How you goin' to get the logs to Charleston," asked Liz's son, George?"

"Great question, George. Widow Henry is loaning me one of her wagons and a team of horses to take the logs down the Kanawha Turnpike to Charleston. Look, I know there is a lot of work to do, but if we work together, we can finish everything by this time next year. My brother and I will start cutting trees tomorrow; whoever can come by and help, even if it's for only an hour or two a day, would be greatly appreciated. Tom's men will be here tomorrow to help, too."

The crowd continued to ask questions to better understand what would happen, but it was obvious to Hank that they were excited. For all of them, it was the first time they had begun to have hope.

The next day, Hank and George began cutting trees. It was demanding work, but Hank knew he couldn't expect the others to work if he wasn't willing to. When they had cut three large oak trees, George began cutting off the limbs while Hank cut the trunks to be used for a rustic cabin he and his brother would live in that winter. When spring came, they would take their cabin apart and have the logs cut into boards. Hank wanted to stay at the property in case there was any trouble from the mining operators. Offering housing to black miners could create a problem for them.

Back in Clayton, Tom had arranged for a construction crew to begin building houses on the property Samuel and Finn had prepared. Since Fred was interested in becoming a carpenter, he joined the crew to learn as much as he could firsthand. Archie hired Clyde to help at the mill. Clyde had never worked at a sawmill but was a hard worker who caught on quickly.

The construction crew stayed in a large tent on the land but often came to the restaurant for dinner. They were a good group of men who were very talented at their craft. Fred was happy to be learning more about carpentry.

One afternoon, Widow Henry, Nancy, and Sarah loaded Tom's wagon with food they had prepared and rode to the job site around lunchtime. "Gentlemen, could you put some tables together so we can unload your lunches?" asked Widow Henry.

Surprised, the men scrambled to get things arranged for the ladies. Widow Henry spoke when the food was placed on the makeshift tables," Men, while you are in Clayton working, we wanted each of you to know how much you are appreciated. We hope you will consider Clayton your home away from home for the next few months. So, as new neighbors, we wanted to bring you this food as a welcoming present. Before you eat, let's thank God for his abundance."

Most of the men removed their hats while Widow Henry prayed a blessing over the meal and the workers, asking God to protect every one of them. When the prayer was completed, the men dug in. As each filled their plates with food, Nancy and Sarah poured iced water for them to drink. The job foreman spoke for the men and thanked the ladies for welcoming them to Clayton and for the delicious food.

"In all my years working construction, I have never been treated this nice. Thank you, ladies, it really does mean a lot."

After eating, the women cleared the table and put the dishes on the wagon. The men quickly jumped up to help, thanking them over and over. Widow Henry stopped the horse when they were leaving and gently invited them to worship on Sunday. As the women rode away, the men shook their heads. Some were walking back to work, saying, "Boy, that was something."

While Clyde was working at the sawmill, Meg went to see Carol to continue learning to read. Over the summer, the two of them became friends. Meg realized what Carol and Seamus were doing to help backwoods folks and how she loved teaching. Carol learned that Meg had never traveled far from where she was raised.

"I've always stayed around these parts. I didn't need to go anywhere else if I was happy where I was."

Carol could tell Meg was having trouble reading, but it took her a while to determine what was causing the difficulty. One day, a quail and her little chicks walked across the garden near the shelter at the edge of the woods. Carol saw them and turned to Meg, putting her finger over her lips, and motioned for her to be quiet. Carol turned to look at the little ones, and when she looked to see if Meg was enjoying seeing them, she saw her squinting.

"Meg, are you having trouble seeing?" asked Carol.

"I've always had a little trouble seeing things clearly, but it's not a real problem; I've gotten used to it."

On Friday, Carol asked Meg if she would like to visit Clayton with her. "I've got something I want to show you, plus I need to check on something at our house."

Meg agreed, so the two women and little Nancy began their walk into Clayton. When they arrived, Carol said, "Why don't we stop by the restaurant to get something cool to drink and then go to the general store?"

After enjoying a cool iced tea, the three went to the general store across the street.

"Hi, Nancy," said Meg as they entered the store.

Quickly, Nancy rushed over to see her favorite little girl.

"Nancy, could you hold Nancy for a minute?" asked Carol.

"That sounds funny," said Nancy.

After handing the little one to Nancy, Carol took Meg to the reading glass display.

"Meg, why don't you try these on and see if they help?" requested Carol.

After trying several pairs, Meg found a pair of glasses that brought everything into perfect sharpness. Meg began to cry. "I've never been able to see this clearly. It's wonderful!"

Nancy asked her how they felt on her face and made a few minor adjustments so that they would set straight and not slip down her nose.

"How much are they?" asked Meg.

When Nancy told her, Meg slowly took them off her face and began to put them back on the shelf when Nancy stopped her. "Meg, you need those glasses, don't put them away. You can have Clyde give me a dollar a week until they are paid for."

"Are you sure?" asked Meg.

"Of course, Meg, now go to the sawmill and show Clyde your new glasses."

Clyde was thrilled that Meg could see better. He knew it had been a problem for her, but he didn't know how to help her without a job.

"Don't you look fancy?" quipped Clyde.

Meg excitedly explained how well she could see with the glasses.

"Why don't you wait until I'm finished with work and ride back on the horse with me?" said Clyde, smiling.

Being able to help his wife with some of the money he was now making made Clyde proud, but it also made him sad that he hadn't done something earlier. Sensing what was going through his mind, Archie put his hand on Clyde's back and said, "I know how you're feeling, my friend; I've been there. Widow Henry once told me not to look back at what might have been but to look forward with hope, trusting God with everything. You're a good man, Clyde, and an even better husband."

CHAPTER 46

SAMUEL AND FINN loaded the wagon from Widow Henry's Charleston sawmill and headed for the settlement Tom had taken Samuel to earlier. Traveling east on the Kanawha Turnpike toward Cabin Creek, Samuel noticed all the train cars full of coal and the coal piles reaching as high as forty feet. The coal stacks were used to fill train cars, and barges headed down the Kanawha River to New Orleans. The entire eastern part of Kanawha County was consumed by one industry or another.

When they arrived at the site, Samuel found Hank and George cutting down a large maple tree. After greeting one another, the men moved the fallen trees to the sawmill wagon to be taken to Charleston. When the wagon was filled, Hank and George took it to the lumber yard in Charleston while Samuel and Finn began clearing the land. They started pulling tree trunks using their equipment and the two additional horses they brought.

On his way home from the coal mine, Jonna noticed two men on the property Hank had told everyone about. Curious, he slowly walked over to see what was going on. "Hey, what are you doin'?" yelled Jonna.

Hank had warned Samuel that the locals weren't comfortable with strangers, so he stopped what he was doing and slowly began walking toward Jonna.

"Hi, my name's Samuel, and that fellow up there is Finn; we work for Widow Henry. We're starting to clear the land so the sawmill can be built," Samuel said confidently.

"Where's Hank?" asked Jonna.

"He went to Charleston to take the first load of trees to be cut into lumber," replied Samuel.

"When's he coming back?" asked Jonna.

"Well, he left around noon, so I expect he'll be back by sunset," replied Samuel.

When Jonna turned to head back down the hill to his shack, he mumbled, "Good meetin' ya."

When it was almost dark, Finn heard a wagon coming up the little road. Hank and George were back and, to their delight, had brought food they had purchased at the farmers market, along with a ham.

As the men sat around the campfire Samuel and Finn had started earlier, Hank told them about their visit to Charleston.

"Boy, that place sure has changed since I was last there. The sky is full of soot from all the smokestacks, and I've never seen a place so crowded."

"How can anybody live there?" said George, not knowing that that was where Samuel lived.

"It does take getting used to," said Samuel, "but you have to go where the jobs are to take care of your family."

"I suppose," said George, "but I sure wouldn't want to live there, job or no job."

The next day, all four men worked together clearing stumps. It was demanding work, but with four horses working at a time, the land began taking shape. All the stumps were pulled to one place to be burned after they had dried so that they could start moving dirt to level off the site.

Friday, after they had worked all week, a couple of the men from the settlement stopped by on their way home from the mines. They were curious to see what had been done. When they saw the amount of work Samuel and his "crew" had accomplished in just five days, they were convinced that what Hank had told them was true. Widow Henry didn't want free labor to clear her land at all; she must be serious about helping them out.

Word got out in the settlement that evening, and eight men showed up to work on Saturday morning. Samuel and Finn divided them into two teams. George and Hank worked with separate teams, so everyone felt equal. Finn's team moved logs to the wagon while Samuel's team cut more trees. The tree branches were then cut into smaller pieces to use as firewood once dried. By the end of the day, five more trees were down, stripped of branches, and readied for shipping to Charleston.

They also removed two stumps, leaving only three more for Monday. Hank couldn't have been happier. He never expected this many men to help on the first weekend, but that evening, as he lay in his sleeping bag, he had another take on it. All these men coming to help showed him how desperately they hoped for change. The severity of their plight and subsequent trust in him weighed heavily on his heart. "Thank you, Father, for bringing me to this place."

The following week, the men continued to work as hard as the week before, and on Saturday, even more men from the settlement came to help so that by the end of the day, enough land had been cleared to build the sawmill and several houses. As the men were leaving that Saturday, Hank thanked each of them individually and told them that he and George would use his wagon to bring the branches all of them had cut to their cabins to be used as firewood later that winter.

The process continued for the remainder of the summer until there was enough cleared land for the settlement to relocate entirely. The sawmill foundation had been set, and the stakes had been measured and placed for the schoolhouse and church. The folks from the settlement wanted to do something to thank Samuel and Finn for all the work they had done, so even though they didn't have much, they decided to have their first community picnic and share their food with the men.

Samuel had been going home on Saturday nights to be with his family on Sundays, but Finn had stayed since he didn't have anyone he wanted to see; besides, being around Hank and his brother was always a good time.

On this Sunday, however, Samuel brought Ruth and the children to the picnic to meet the people he had gotten to know over the summer. Ruth and Liz hit it off right away and spent most of the afternoon talking about how wonderful it would be to have a real community. Hank's heart was filled with joy as everyone laughed and told stories. These people were beginning to understand real freedom.

Samuel and his family rode back to Charleston, and as they were riding along, Samuel couldn't help noticing a change in Ruth. She seemed much happier, and the children were more playful than usual. That evening, after the children had gone to bed, Ruth explained what she had started in their community. "After spending time in Clayton, I learned that people want and need friendships. Widow Henry opened my eyes to what it means to give yourself to others. She cared for me and the children and Samuel; it felt good, really good. After coming back here, I realized that I needed to do the same thing, or else I would go back to living in the little protective shell I had been used to.

"I decided to visit our neighbors to get to know them better and see if they needed anything. Samuel, it was amazing; you could almost see a veil being lifted. Before I knew it, we all started going to one another's homes and visiting, sharing receipts, and telling stories about where we came from, but what I didn't want to happen did, so I stopped it right away.

"When they started talking about their past, some began saying how white people are evil and such, so I tried to tell them that not everybody is the same. At first, they didn't like what I said, but after I told them about Widow Henry and the people in Clayton, they began to listen. Anyway, now we take walks together and watch the children play. It's been wonderful," said Ruth, full of excitement.

"That's great, Ruth. It reminds me of something Finn said the other night. We were getting ready for bed, and he told me he was frightened the first few days we were working with Hank. He said he knew he was the only white man for miles and asked me if I had felt the same way when I came to Clayton to work. It's a shame how we all have notions about people different than us. This has been a good time in our lives, Ruth; we're starting to see people differently. I guess you would say it took a little elderly white lady to open the eyes of a lot of us," said Samuel, reflecting on his times with Widow Henry.

Doctor Hunter and Sarah continued their courtship, having dinner at the restaurant every evening after all the guests left. It was clear to both of them that their relationship had grown to a point where they knew how they felt but hesitated to say anything to one another for fear that their feelings would not be shared.

One Friday evening, Jim reached across the table to hold Sarah's hand. Looking into his eyes, Sarah knew she had to tell him how she felt because he was still concerned that she wasn't ready to commit to a lifelong relationship.

"Jim, you are a wonderful man, and over these last few months, I have struggled with letting go of my past and allowing myself to feel free to love again. I struggled with guilt at first, but as time passed, I realized that I loved you, and to deny that would be a mistake I would regret for the rest of my life. I love you, Jim." said Sarah as a tear ran down her cheek.

"I love you too, Sarah. I have loved you for a long time," said Jim.

Just as Jim had finished telling Sarah that he loved her, there was a squeal in the restaurant. Lizzy had been listening to their conversation. Unable to control herself any longer, Lizzy ran out to their table into her mother's arms. "I'm glad you two finally told each other how you feel; I've known it for months!" The three of them laughed, hugged, and cried with pure joy.

The next day at work, Mary noticed how radiant Sarah looked. Her smile never left her face.

"Sarah, you have never looked so happy," exclaimed Mary.

"Mary, Jim told me that he loved me," said Sarah as she hugged Mary.

Mary told Sarah how happy she was for her as the two sat down and enjoyed a cool glass of water. "Tell me all about it," said Mary. The two talked about the evening, and everything said for a long time. It was evident to Mary that Sarah had allowed herself to move forward with her life, and she was very happy for her.

For his part, Jim shared the news with his friend David Smith. David congratulated Jim and suggested he take Sarah to Charleston to look for a ring. Overhearing everything, Nurse Wallace was glad for Doctor Hunter and said, "Congratulations" as she continued her work, unable to relate personally with either of the doctors.

Jim and Sarah made plans to go to Charleston the following weekend. Mary agreed to watch Lizzy while the two of them had time alone. It was a day that Sarah never thought she would experience in her lifetime.

That Saturday, when the couple was away, Nurse Wallace was having breakfast at the restaurant. When Mary served her usual food, Peggy asked if she would like to join her. Shocked, Mary said, "Of course, I'll be back just as soon as I take care of the other guests."

After a few minutes, Mary sat down with Peggy, bringing a cup of coffee. Mary couldn't imagine what Peggy wanted, and after exchanging pleasantries, Peggy asked Mary what it was like for her when she moved to Clayton.

"I understand that you used to live in the backcountry, so I would imagine that it was a difficult adjustment."

It was evident to Mary that there was more to her question than it first appeared, but she replied. "Yes, it was tough at first. I was ashamed of who I was, but I was at a point where I didn't have enough energy to fight anymore."

The answer surprised Peggy. She had expected Mary would have said something about being hungry or something along those lines, but instead, Mary had utterly opened up about the severity of her emotional state.

"What do you mean, if you don't mind me asking?" asked Peggy.

"Nurse Wallace," using Peggy's formal name to make a point, "you have been going into the backcountry with Doctor Smith for some time now. What do you think about the people you meet? Do you think they are lazy, uneducated, dirty people? They are anything but lazy. Uneducated, yes; dirty, only because it's hard to find a creek large enough to wash off in; but lazy, no! Every day is a fight to survive, every day! When I lived in my little shack in the woods, all I could think about was having enough food for me and Rusty. I needed to make sure I had enough firewood to keep us warm in the winter. To have good drinking water, I had to walk over a hundred yards to a spring, regardless of the weather. So yes, I was exhausted, afraid, and embarrassed when Carol and Seamus rescued me.

"The way they cared for me and Rusty didn't save our lives but our very souls. So, I beg you, when you see these people, please try to understand that they are all afraid. They all need someone to come alongside them and ... care."

When Mary finished talking, her lip was quivering, and tears filled her eyes.

"Mary, I didn't mean to offend you, but I am having trouble understanding why people would choose to live like they do. Why don't they get jobs and send their children to school? I was brought up by parents who insisted that I do nothing but my very best in school so that I could take care of myself if I had to. Still, these people seem to be happy doing nothing about their position in life," said Peggy, opening herself up more than she intended to.

"Ma'am, your world was completely different than theirs has been. You were raised in the city by wealthy parents who could afford whatever they wanted. Their insistence on getting an education was very forward-thinking since most women never got an education beyond high school. These folks came to this country because they were hungry and poor, but when they arrived, no one would give them work, so they moved west. Most of them had been farmers in Europe, so when they settled down where they felt safe, they farmed.

" People in the cities frightened them because of how they had been treated in the East, so it was more comfortable for them to stay to themselves and care for their families the best they could. Wildlife has migrated with more and more people moving west after the war to work in the factories and mines, so hunting is more difficult than in the earlier days. Peggy, they're not lazy, but they are exhausted," replied Mary.

Peggy began to see that her perception of these poor people was from the perspective of her background and not theirs. She realized that they didn't know how to get out of the backwoods and survive; they didn't have the skills and, most definitely, the education.

"Mary, you know Earl and his wife are about to have another baby. I've been going to their place to check on them daily and even brought them a pie I had made with Widow Henry. I need to go out later today to see how she's doing. Would you come with me? I've felt sorry for them and tried to help, but maybe I should treat them respectfully and like Carol cared for you. Until just now, I had never thought about my attitude toward them. To care for somebody, I need to take the time to get to know them. Their needs are more than food and medical help; they must find a way out. Will you help me, Mary?"

"I'm sorry, Mary, for the attitude I have had toward them, and for that matter, you. I guess I have always looked down on people less educated than me, or maybe people with less money, I don't know, but what you said has opened my eyes more than you can imagine.

"When I came to Clayton, I didn't think I could stay. Going out with Doctor Smith wasn't something I liked, and at one point, I had written my letter of resignation.

" Some people in town must have been able to tell I wasn't happy and have come alongside to see if they could help. Nancy invited me over to meet people a few times, but Widow Henry saw the depth of my lonesomeness and invited me to her house to bake. At first, I thought it didn't make any sense, baking? What she taught me was to take time to do things just for the enjoyment of it. That's why I now take cookies with me when I go with Doctor Smith to the backwoods. She has helped me learn to relax and have a little fun. Mary, you have shown me how to care and not judge people. Thank you."

That afternoon, Mary, Rusty, Lizzy, and Peggy Wallace visited Earl and his pregnant wife. Rusty and Lizzy played while Peggy and Mary sat and talked with Earl's wife, Kathy. She had been having labor pains, but she knew it was too early for her to give birth. Peggy told her that it was normal for some women to have these pains, but she did warn that since this was going to be her second child, she probably wouldn't go full term.

After discussing her medical condition, Peggy asked where she and Earl had come from. It was easy to see how much Kathy missed her homeland of Scotland.

"We settled here because it reminds us of Scotland, but we didn't have enough money to buy cattle or sheep like we raised back home," replied Kathy. "We do our best, growing vegetables and hunting, but without livestock, it's hard. Sometimes, I'm afraid that Earl is going to give up. He works so hard every day. See him out in the field? He's been out there since sunrise. It's like that every day."

Peggy saw her patients differently than before and realized she could help them with more than their medical needs.

On their way back to town, Peggy considered how she could help Earl and his family.

CHAPTER 47

DURING THE SUMMER, after Samuel and Finn had completed their development work and the construction crew had begun building homes at the Campbell's development, Tom had been very busy finding a teacher for the school. The county seemed to be dragging its heels in finding a replacement, so Tom had gone to a little teacher's college in eastern Ohio and found a wonderful young lady looking for an opportunity to work in a small town.

Lauren McFarland was a spunky young lady in her early twenties looking for an adventure and teaching in a small town in West Virginia seemed to fit the bill. Once she had completed all the required certificates for the School Board, she packed her bags and came to Clayton. When she arrived in Charleston, Tom met her at the train station and escorted her back to Clayton.

After Lauren had settled at the boardinghouse, she came down to the restaurant to have dinner, but to her surprise, most of the people from Clayton were there to greet her.

"Everyone, I am very pleased to introduce Lauren McFarland, our new schoolteacher," said Tom, smiling.

Seeing that she was a little taken aback, Nancy approached her and softly said," Miss McFarland, everyone wants you to feel welcome, and the only way we could show you was to have a welcoming party." The crowd parted to display the desserts and drinks on two of Sarah's tables.

Lauren was speechless; these people are so lovely! "Thank you very much. Mr. Campbell told me how wonderful the people of Clayton were, but I never expected anything like this. I was a little nervous going so far from home to a place where I didn't know anyone, but you have taken all that fear away. Thank you."

"Carol and Maggie have agreed to work with the younger children so that Miss McFarland can best serve the older students," said Tom.

Maggie had told Tom that even though Alma Gay was only nine months old, she felt she would be helpful to Carol. Tom had agreed but had another idea that he kept to himself.

Later that evening, Tom and Nancy sat on their front porch having iced tea. "Nancy, what do you think about opening a kindergarten for the children too young to begin school? I think it would be helpful to get them prepared for grade school, plus we may be able to get more of the children from the country to attend."

"Tom, that's a wonderful idea, but where can we have it, and who will work there?" asked Nancy.

"I think Maggie can do it. It's a lot to expect her to help Carol and care for Alma Gay, but if her students are also young, Alma Gay will be less of a problem. She'll need help eventually, but I think it will be perfect for her and the young ones. I'm going to ask Seamus if we could use the church," said Tom enthusiastically.

That year, seven new students attended school solely because of Carol's work helping the folks in the backwoods that summer. It had been arranged for the children to meet at Archie and Maggie's home to be taken into town on their wagon. Archie had built benches along the side of the backboards so that there would be seating for all of them. Later, Tom purchased a cover for the wagon so the children would be protected from the weather on their journey to town.

Mary was working all day at the boardinghouse and restaurant, helping more than ever before, while Sarah began slowly to back away from doing everything. Her extreme exhaustion had opened her eyes to the importance of maintaining her health to be there for Lizzy and Jim.

Doctor Jim Hunter alternated visiting people with Doctor Smith so that everyone who needed healthcare could easily get it. The annual exams Doctor Smith had done with folks helped six people discover some health issues they were now treating. Clearly, the community, including the people from the backwoods, needed two doctors. On more than one occasion, there were two emergencies requiring all three medical personnel to attend.

Although Jim enjoyed living at the boardinghouse, he knew it wasn't a place for his soon-to-be family. Sarah needed to get away from the continual interruptions from guests to maintain her health, so on Thursday, after the clinic closed, he headed over to the general store to see Tom.

"Hi, Doctor Hunter. " Nancy said as Jim entered the store, "What can I do for you today?"

"Hi, Nancy, I would like to talk with Tom about the houses you two are building," said Jim with an excited tone to his otherwise calm nature.

"I'll get him for you. I think he's in the back sorting inventory," said Nancy.

In a few minutes, Tom made his way to the front of the store, where he greeted Jim, "Nancy tells me you're interested in looking at the houses."

"Yes, sir, I would like to see them, "said Jim.

As the two men walked down the street toward the new houses, Jim explained that he wanted a home where he and Sarah could raise Lizzy, away from her work.

"I know exactly what you mean," said Tom. "Before we built our house, we lived in the back part of the store, where I keep inventory now. Something was always needed in the store, making it almost impossible to relax after a long day's work."

Walking up to the first house, Tom told Jim it was a one-bedroom home and that Peggy Wallace would purchase it in the next few days. The next house was a two-bedroom house that Jim said he wanted to look at but was also interested in a three-bedroom model.

"You never know if our family will be expanding," laughed Jim as they walked up the front walk of the two-bedroom home. Jim looked all through the house and appreciated the quality workmanship and attention to detail that was very evident.

After looking at the smaller house, Jim asked to see the larger three-bedroom house. "We can go through it, but I must tell you, it won't be finished for another month. The men have been working hard to finish it but still have some interior work that needs to be completed."

Walking through the house, Jim knew that this would be perfect for them. "I can't wait to show Sarah," said Jim as the two returned to the general store. After discussing the price, Jim felt he could put a substantial deposit down with the money he had saved while working in Charleston. "I'll just have to meet with the bank in Charleston to get a mortgage for the remainder," said Jim as he was about to leave.

"You know, Jim, if you want, I can finance the rest for you, and you can avoid all of the bank fees associated with getting a mortgage," said Tom.

"Thanks, that would be great, Tom, thank you," exclaimed Jim.

That evening at dinner, Jim told Sarah about his house-hunting adventure. "Saturday, when we're both not working, Tom said we could look at it together. I think you're going to love it, Sarah."

Jim was excited, as was Sarah, but the thought of leaving the boardinghouse and moving away seemed oddly difficult for her. She and Charles had built the business from nothing. Every month, in the early years, it was a struggle to make ends meet. With his handyman income and the few guests they would have, they were able to slowly pay off their mortgage and keep the business going. It seemed odd not to be there, yet she knew it was the right decision.

When Saturday came, the whole soon-to-be family walked down Henry Way to the southern end of town to see the new house. When they walked through the front door, Sarah couldn't believe how beautiful the house was. Walking through each room, she visualized living there.

"Lizzy, I want to show you something," said Jim excitedly. Walking down the hall to the last door on the right, Lizzy walked into the room, and before Jim could say a word, she screamed, "Is this my room, my very own room?"

Lizzy rushed into the room and looked at everything. She would have her own closet, two windows, and plenty of space for her dolls to play.

"Sarah, if this is what you want, we can get it or wait until next year. Tom said he could adjust the next house to make any changes we would wish to."

"No, Jim, this is perfect," said Sarah as she hugged Jim tightly, tears running freely down her face.

On their way back to the boardinghouse, they stopped by the general store to tell Tom their decision.

"Just as soon as it's ready, I'll let you know, Jim. In the meantime, if you want, you can pick out the paint you would like, and the men will paint the inside and out for you."

"Oh, that would be great," exclaimed Sarah. Lizzy jumped up and down excitedly, saying she wanted a pink bedroom!

Returning to the boardinghouse, Sarah ran into the kitchen, where Mary gathered food to prepare lunch orders. "Mary, I've got something to tell you, "Sarah said excitedly.

"Jim and I are going to buy a house in a month or so. We visited one of Tom's new houses and found the perfect house for us."

"That's wonderful," exclaimed Mary. "I'm so happy for you!"

"Mary, this means you and Rusty can live in our apartment downstairs. No more sharing a bathroom with guests!" "Are you sure?" was all Mary could say. She had never had a place to live that had a bedroom, living area, and bathroom. "There's a second little bedroom that Rusty can live in, too. It's been Lizzy's room since she was a baby," said Sarah.

"Mary, living downstairs, you must always be available for anything guests might need. Most of the time, it isn't a problem, but occasionally, you will need to bring them something they might want. With that added responsibility, I want to increase your pay. Knowing that you are here and caring for things will mean a lot to me. What do you say?" Sarah asked.

"Thank you, Sarah, thank you. Not only do I get a new apartment but a raise. Thank you," cried Mary.

Jim and Sarah's wedding plans began taking shape. Both wanted a small, quiet ceremony at the church with only a few people from town invited. Lizzy, on the other hand, had her own ideas. Over a period of two weeks, Lizzy managed to tell everyone living in town about the "little" wedding at the end of August.

The annual Fourth of July picnic was the largest ever. People from all around came to enjoy the celebration. Widow Henry, as always, entered an apple pie into the baking contest, and as she stood next to the display of deserts, she noticed all the young families with their babies. It was so good to see how the community was growing with more and more younger people moving to the area.

Sarah brought her pie to the contestant's table, but as she started to walk back to where Jim was standing, several ladies asked her what date she had picked for her wedding.

"We're going to wait until the house is finished and we can get things moved, so not until late August."

"Late August," exclaimed Carol, "there's so much that has to be done!"

"No, no, we're just going to have a small wedding, nothing big," said Sarah, smiling. Everyone laughed as they told her what they would do, some in jest, others not. Widow Henry listened and kept her thoughts to herself.

As everybody was about to watch the pie-baking contest, one more family was riding into town. Samuel and his family had been invited by Widow Henry to the picnic. As soon as the wagon stopped, Liza and her brother, Willie, jumped out and ran over to Lizzy and Rusty. The children had missed their friends. After tying up his horse, Samuel and Ruth walked over to say hello to Widow Henry. All the ladies welcomed them to the picnic and told them how glad they were that they had made the trip from Charleston.

"Well, the last time we were here, Widow Henry told me we needed to come to the picnic and that I should bring a pie for the contest," said Ruth as she pulled a cloth covering off her blackberry pie.

"I'm glad you got here when you did," said Nancy, "we were just about to begin the contest."

Most adults gathered around as Seamus, David, and Sheriff Griffith sat down to begin tasting the pies. The three men had stayed away from the table at the park so they wouldn't know whose pie they were trying. After much discussion, the winner was announced.

"Ladies and gentlemen, all three of us agree that this year's winner is this delicious blackberry pie," said Seamus.

Ruth was overjoyed. Tears streamed down her face as she took the ten-dollar grand prize. After gaining some composure, she thanked everyone for allowing her to participate in the day.

"This is more special to me than just a pie baking contest; it's being included that means the most. Thank you, everyone," said Ruth as she humbly approached where Samuel stood.

As people slowly left that evening, not wanting the day to end, Widow Henry asked Ruth if she and Samuel would like to spend the night and travel back the next day. Looking at her children and how much fun they were still having, playing at the park, Ruth thanked Widow Henry and agreed to stay.

After the children had calmed down for the evening, the three adults relaxed in the parlor. Ruth told Widow Henry how she had started getting her neighbors together occasionally to help build community. "It's taking longer than I thought it would, but people are beginning to join us as we sit outside and visit or take walks to the park. The children are playing more with other children now, too. I only wish it could be as wonderful as this," said Ruth.

Widow Henry told her how glad she was that she was reaching out to her neighbors and encouraged her, saying, "Ruth dear, these things take time. People must learn to let go of their pasts and enjoy what they have now. It took a long time here, too. Remember, almost everybody here came from different places and some from tough pasts. Trust takes time to build, but people slowly discover that they need one another."

Samuel said that during the picnic, Tom mentioned that when the Cabin Creek project was finished, he would like us to prepare another ten acres for his housing development.

"When do you think you will be done?" asked Widow Henry.

"Well, we've cleared enough to build the sawmill and all the houses, but there is still work to be done to build roads. But we'll wait until the houses are finished before doing the rest, so it will probably only be another few weeks."

"So, you're ready to begin the sawmill?" asked Widow Henry.

"Yes, Ma'am, we're just waiting for the lumber to dry," replied Samuel.

"That's much sooner than we expected. I will give you a letter telling my manager to give you the lumber from our inventory, and we can replace it with the new, undried lumber you have brought; that way, they can start building. I'll talk with Tom in the morning and let him know. This is exciting, Samuel; I never thought you would get so much done so quickly," said Widow Henry.

"Well, Ma'am, men kept coming every Saturday, and before long, every able man was helping us. They are the ones that did most of the work. They're so excited. Those folks sure are grateful, too, Ma'am. I heard that they are planning to have a community picnic in a couple of weeks to thank me and Finn for everything we have done," said Samuel.

"Before you leave tomorrow, I have something I want to give you to give to Hank for me. Ruth. I want you to know that when Samuel comes back here to work, you and the children are invited to stay with me; I miss you."

Before going to bed for the evening, Widow Henry got out her Bible and had Samuel and Ruth read scripture to discuss. Their reading was much improved from earlier, but more than their reading ability was their understanding. The scriptures were alive to them now, and Widow Henry could see how hungry they both were to learn more.

Widow Henry thanked the Lord that night for allowing her to share with Samuel's family.

"Tom, I need to talk with you when you have a minute," said Widow Henry, walking into the general store. Samuel and his family had just left, and she couldn't wait to tell him about the sawmill.

"Sure, just give me a minute to put this away," said Tom.

"What is it?"

"Last night, Samuel told me he would be done in two weeks, and they could start building the sawmill. I know you wanted Samuel and Finn to begin working on clearing land, but if they could go there for a month or so and help Hank and his neighbors get started on the sawmill, we might be able to get it finished before winter."

Tom, too, was surprised at how quickly the clearing and landscape work had gotten done and wanted to help as much as possible. "Sure, I can wait to have more land cleared. We won't be able to begin construction until late spring anyway."

On their ride back to Charleston, Samuel and Ruth realized that after all that had happened to them over the last year, something bigger than they could imagine was happening in their lives. Though they talked about it, neither could put it into words.

CHAPTER 48

BY LATE AUGUST, school had begun. Carol moved to the younger children's room, and Lauren took over teaching the older children. After the first week of classes, Lauren asked Carol if they could discuss the children after school on Friday. When school had closed and the children had gone home, Carol went to her old office to meet with Lauren.

"Carol, I know that this must be a little difficult for you, and to be truthful, it is for me as well, but I need to ask you about a couple of the students."

Carol tried to help Lauren understand what she knew about each of them so that she could better help them.

"Thank you, Carol," said Lauren, "that information will help me greatly. My last question has to do with Rusty. He lacks some basics, yet I feel he is very bright. Can you help me understand his situation?"

Carol explained that she, too, felt that Rusty was a very bright young boy, and after telling Lauren that a little over a year ago, he couldn't read or do any arithmetic, she was shocked.

"Lauren, he learned to read and basic mathematics in just a couple of months. I was going to move him to more difficult novels to help him expand his vocabulary and his understanding of science. He has come a long way. I've never had a student work as hard as he does."

"I think giving him more difficult books and advanced subjects during the next year will show me just how advanced he is. If he's as intelligent as I think he might be, I'm thinking of seeing about sending him to a finishing school that I know of in Ohio."

"Lauren, that sounds wonderful, but his mother doesn't have the money for that. She just learned to read and do mathematics this past year, too. She's the lady who helps Sarah run the boarding house. Mary, I'm sure you have met her."

"Yes, I've met her. She's a very nice lady, a little awkward speaking with people she doesn't know, but very nice," said Lauren.

"Lauren, I know you're new here, but you need to understand how far she has come in such a short while. If she had grown up in the city and had been educated, living her life around other people who were also more refined, then I would completely agree with you; however, if you knew her history, you would have a better appreciation for her."

Carol went on to tell Lauren about Mary and how this tough woman had worked to provide for her family. When Carol was finished, Lauren had a completely different opinion about Mary.

"You know, sometimes it's easy for all of us to judge people before we know them, but if we take the time to walk beside them, often our opinion changes. We've all done it; the most important thing is to learn from it," said Carol softly.

"You are young, Lauren, and I admire you for striking out on your own. From what I've seen, you're an excellent teacher, so excuse me if I've offended you; I just wanted to help you."

Lauren shook her head, acknowledging that Carol's advice was right and she wasn't offended. "Thanks, Carol; I can use all of the advice you can give me," said Lauren.

After they finished discussing Rusty and some other students, Carol asked Lauren if she would like to go to the restaurant for a glass of iced tea. When Mary came with their tea, Lauren asked if she would like to join them since no other guests were in the restaurant.

"Sure, just let me put a couple of things away, and I'll be right out," said Mary.

For several minutes, Lauren told Mary how excited she was to have Rusty in her class. "Mary, he's very bright, so I will push him slightly this year. Please let me know if he starts to struggle; I don't want to discourage him. I think he has an excellent future ahead of him if he chooses to focus on his schoolwork."

Mary's reaction was mixed; she was pleased about Lauren's assessment of Rusty, but she was frightened at the thought that she would soon be unable to help Rusty with his schoolwork. After Lauren went to her room, Carol asked Mary how she felt about Lauren's assessment of Rusty. Carol could see the concern in Mary's eyes as Mary tried to respond with gratitude.

Reaching her hand to Mary's forearm, Carol told Mary she had an idea. "Why don't you and I look at Rusty's school assignments before he gets them, and I will help you understand how to help him on Sunday late afternoons when things have settled down here."

Mary looked gratefully into Carol's eyes and, as she shook her head, whispered, "You're always here for me, Carol. Thank you."

That same Friday, Tom was told by the construction manager that they had finished the third house. Tom went with him to inspect it and saw Jim on his way to the boardinghouse. "Hey Jim, want to join us?" yelled Tom across the street.

"Sure, where are you going," replied Jim.

"We're headed to inspect your house, and I thought you might like to come along."

"Of course, I would," said Jim excitedly.

The three men slowly walked through the house, ensuring everything was done according to plan specifications. Both Tom and Jim were pleased with the quality of workmanship and made sure to tell the manager. After completing their inspection, Jim rushed off to tell Sarah while Tom talked with the manager about the sawmill project.

"I want you to take all the time you need to get that sawmill and lumber yard built. From what I hear, you will probably get some help from the local people, plus my friend Hank lives there now and has built a sawmill before. It's very important to me and Widow Henry that this mill and lumber yard gets finished as soon as possible."

The following week, after work, Jim moved what things Sarah wanted to be taken to the new house. On Saturday, he borrowed Tom's wagon and headed for Charleston to get the things he had stored with a friend while Sarah stayed behind to work with Mary at the restaurant.

That evening, before Jim returned, Carol, Mary, and Sarah sat down to plan Sarah's wedding. Carol didn't tell Sarah that Lizzy had invited everyone in town. She remembered how surprised she had been when everyone came to her wedding.

They discussed having the ceremony at the church and a small reception at the park if the weather permitted. Everything seemed manageable and under control until the door to the restaurant swung open, and Jim came staggering in, collapsing on the floor.

On his way back to Clayton, Jim had been robbed and beaten by two men outside Elkview. It had taken him a while to regain consciousness and crawl on the wagon to head home.

Carol ran to the clinic to get Doctor Smith while Mary and Sarah cleaned the head wound with cool clothes. When Doctor Smith arrived, Nurse Wallace was at his side, and together, they examined him to see how badly he was injured.

Thankfully, his head wounds were only superficial, but his arm was broken. Doctor Smith set the arm and made a cast that evening at the clinic. "I'm afraid you will need to keep the cast on for at least six weeks, Jim," said David.

Sherriff Griffith talked with Jim as David made the cast to get a description of the two men. "They've been having more and more trouble in Charleston, and now it appears it's working its way upriver to Elkview," said the Sheriff with a concerned expression.

After everyone left, Jim and Sarah sat in the restaurant and talked. Sarah was upset at what had happened, and though Jim was as well, he tried to direct their conversation to the wedding.

"I don't want this to delay anything, Sarah. I'll strap my suit coat around my chest, and everything will be fine," he said, smiling.

They talked until late that evening, but by midnight, both were tired and ready for bed. Sarah attempted to help Jim up the stairs to his room, but Jim resisted. "I'm fine, Sarah; get a good night's sleep, and I'll see you in the morning."

After worship, Sheriff Griffith saddled up his horse to go to Elkview and visit his friend, Matt Lincoln, but before he left, Fred asked if he could go with him. "I used to know many of the hoodlums in Charleston; maybe I can help."

"This is official business, Fred; I don't want you to get involved; I'll take care of it," said the sheriff.

"Sir, I may know who it is. I used to be in a gang in Charleston, and maybe I can talk with a couple of guys I know and help you out. I won't be in the way, I promise," said Fred, wanting to help repay the kindness he had received since moving to Clayton.

"You have to follow my orders, "said Sherriff Griffith firmly with a stern look.

When Sheriff Griffith and Fred arrived in Elkview, they immediately went to see Matt Lincoln, Elkview's sheriff. After telling him what had happened to Doctor Hunter on his way back from Charleston, the sheriff shook his head.

"Yeah, we've been seeing more and more trouble around here lately. The police in Charleston have been going after the gangs, and it looks like they're moving in this direction.

"Doctor Hunter said one of the two men had a large scar on his left cheek and was missing one of his front teeth."

"Did he say anything else?" asked Fred.

"Only that the other guy was short and looked like he had a limp," replied Sheriff Lincoln.

Fred paced around the office floor, knowing his life would be in danger if he told them who it was.

"Look, I remember those two from a couple of years ago. I want to help, but you have to understand that if they find out I had anything to do with this, their entire gang will be out to kill me," said Fred, frightened.

"No one will ever know we even talked to you, Fred, I promise," said Matt.

"Those two used to hang out on the west side of town. My guys and I used to get into fights with them all the time over territory and stuff. My guess is they have come out this way because of what you said the police were doing. Also, I understand that Shorty used to have connections with somebody in the river precinct. They go by Shorty and Kirk. These guys are bad news, sheriff, really bad. Remember, you didn't hear anything from me, OK?"

After talking for another half hour, Fred and Sheriff Griffith left for Clayton. As they headed out the door, Matt thanked them for the information and said he would get on it first thing in the morning. When Fred was mounting his horse, the sheriff's deputy walked by and went into the office; turning back to look at Fred as the door closed,

Riding back to Clayton, Fred seemed nervous to Sheriff Griffith. "Are you alright, Fred?" asked the sheriff.

"Those guys are bad; if they find out it was me, I'm dead," said Fred nervously.

When they returned to Clayton, both men went about their day as if nothing had happened.

Jim rested while he recovered from the shock and trauma of the robbery. Doctor Smith kept checking on him to be sure he wasn't concussed. By Tuesday of the following week, Jim was back practicing medicine at the clinic, and Sarah was busy at the boardinghouse.

Jim insisted that the wedding be on Saturday, as originally planned. He felt fine but found his left hand clumsy, which made everything he did take longer, including getting dressed for the wedding.

Sarah and Mary were in the back of the church putting the finishing touches on her dress and veil, while Jim was at Seamus and Carol's, attempting to get dressed.

Doctor Smith was going to be his best man, but he had been delayed at the clinic.

Mary went to Carol's to see what was wrong, since it was already ten minutes after the wedding was supposed to begin. When she saw the problem, she quickly tied Jim's shoes and tie and put his coat on him. Jim rushed out of the house and through the side door of the church, and as he made his way to the front of the church, he was shocked by all the people in the sanctuary.

Meanwhile, Sarah left the back room and walked around the front of the church. She, too, couldn't believe how many people were standing in the church's front yard that couldn't get inside. As she slowly made her way up the four stairs to the door, she thanked everyone for coming.

Finally, as Sarah stood in the back of the church and the music began to play, everyone stood as she went down the aisle to start her life with Doctor Jim Hunter.

The ceremony was simple yet moving. Reverend McConnell shared how God had moved in their lives to bring them together: "God moves in all of our lives, sometimes in obvious ways and other times in very subtle but still important ways that sometimes you have to look back to see."

After exchanging vows, the couple turned to walk down the aisle, followed by Lizzy carrying a Bible. In typical Lizzy fashion, she waved to everyone as she slowly walked to the back of the church, smiling.

Since it was a beautiful day, the reception was at the park in one of the shelters. An old friend entered the line while the newlyweds greeted all their guests. Doctor Smith slowly pushed a wheelchair carrying Doctor James Stephenson. Doctor Smith had corresponded with Doctor Stephenson over the last few months to let him know how Jim was doing. Doctor Stephenson had written David, letting him know what a wonderful young man he thought Jim was, so it only seemed natural for David to let him know that Jim was going to get married.

Doing his best to greet everyone, Jim hadn't noticed the wheelchair to his left. Turning to greet his next guest, Jim saw James and bent down to hug his old friend and professor. Jim couldn't have been more surprised. The two talked for as long as it felt they could, given the circumstances.

"I'll see you in a few minutes,' said Jim as David wheeled the doctor to one of the picnic tables.

Lizzy stood between Sarah and Jim during the reception, happily greeting everyone and thanking them for coming. When all the guests had blessed the couple, Sarah looked for Mary to especially thank her for all she had done, only to find her serving cake to the guests while Rusty poured punch. She was a dear friend that Sarah cared for more every day. After everyone was served, Rusty walked over to Lizzy and gave her a glass of punch, causing her to blush a little.

Jim went to see his old friend and introduced Sarah while pointing out her daughter, Lizzy.

"Oh, I've met Lizzy!" exclaimed James. She brought me cake and punch and told me how glad she was that I had come to your wedding. She's something!"

"She sure is," said Jim, smiling. The two friends talked for about a half hour before David took him to his place for the evening. During their conversation, Jim learned that Doctor Stephenson had developed a weakness in his leg that kept him from walking very far. If he wasn't in the wheelchair, you wouldn't have been able to tell anything was wrong.

"He's always had such an incredible attitude," said Jim as they walked to their new house for the first time. Lizzy stayed in her room one last time so Mommy and Daddy Jim could be alone.

Again, the community had come together to be there for one of their own. It was clear how much they all cared for Sarah and Jim. When they opened the front door to their new house, a new Bible was set in the parlor on top of a table between two chairs. The furniture and Bible were gifts from Tom and Nancy, who wanted to give the new couple something they hoped they would use every evening for the rest of their lives, just like they did.

CHAPTER 49

In the fall of 1894, the community gathered at the community garden to harvest the vegetables they had grown and to have a picnic under the shelter. This was the first time some of the backwoods folks had met people from town.

At first, everyone seemed a little awkward until Carol introduced some of them to one another. Soon, they began talking about what they had done in the garden. They started sharing ideas about next year's crops; some mentioned planting winter crops. After about an hour, the food was served, and everyone spread out blankets and had a picnic.

For most, it was the first time they had shared food, and as they continued talking, it was obvious that they were beginning to bond. After eating, some men who had brought plows began turning the soil to prepare it for winter, while others started planting winter crops.

Archie, Tom, and Fred had filled their wagons with the vegetables to deliver to the backwoods. Each made several trips until they were sure everyone had all the food they needed. Tom purchased squash and pumpkins for the store, Sarah bought vegetables for her restaurant, and another load was taken to the church's cellar to distribute to the poor. Archie and Tom took the remaining vegetables and filled their wagons for their trip to Charleston the following day.

The farmer's market was bustling with people, but to Tom's surprise, Howard and Vivian came looking for food to supply their church's food pantry. Seeing Tom, Howard, and Vivian ran over to see what he was doing, and once they saw all the food they had, they bought every squash and pumpkin along with the other vegetables.

"Why don't you two come to our place before heading back to Clayton," said Vivian.

"That would be wonderful," said Tom.

Archie hadn't spent much time in Charleston, so following the McDougals to their home took him through parts of the city he had never seen. Vivian served an excellent meal as usual, but what was even better for Tom was enjoying seeing his friends so happy. They had always been good people, but this last year, they had discovered what filled their hearts with real joy.

On his way out the door, Tom thanked Howard for all his help doing the drawings for the settlement in Cabin Creek.

"You know Howard, they are building the sawmill and lumber yard now so that next spring they can start on the houses."

"That's exciting, Tom. Please let me know when they begin; I want to be there to help. I've had a few ideas I want to use to improve it," said Howard excitedly.

"Maybe I can get some people from our church to come with me to help build the houses. I'll see."

On their ride back to Clayton, Archie kept thinking about how much Tom and Nancy had been doing for people behind the scenes. He always knew they had money and were helpful in Clayton, but he never knew until then how far their influence went and how God was using them to mend bridges between different groups of people.

With Clayton in sight, Archie once again thanked God for the people He had brought into his life who had helped change him forever.

The next day, after school had been dismissed, Tom met with Seamus and Carol to ask them if they could help him divide the money.

"Can you give me an idea how much time different people worked in the garden? I know you were there until school began, Carol, so you probably have a pretty good idea," asked Tom.

"Tom, many of the people came from the backcountry and did what needed to be done, but usually, there wasn't more than an hour or two's work that was needed. One day, I got up extra early to watch the sunrise and read my Bible, and I saw Archie working. I went out to say hello, but he seemed surprised and disappointed that I saw him. It took a while, but he finally admitted that he had been coming to the garden four or five times a week to take care of it before work, and when I asked him why, all he could say was that it was the only way he knew to help. He asked me not to tell anyone. He said that he was following what Christ had said to do in the Bible, to care for the poor."

They continued to talk about the work people had done in the garden until Tom had a clever idea of how to divide the money. Leaving, he stopped by the sawmill and asked Archie if he could speak with him before he headed home.

"Sure, Tom," said Archie, "what can I do for you?"

"I was talking with Carol about how to divide the money between the people who worked in the garden, and I thought maybe you would like to go with me Saturday morning."

"Sure, I'd be glad to go if you want," said Archie.

Archie and Tom headed out the following Saturday to see the folks who had worked throughout the growing season to ensure the garden was maintained. Their first stop was Karl's place, and as usual, his dogs kept them at bay until he recognized Archie and called them off.

"What can I do for you, fellers?" asked Karl.

"Karl, I understand that you worked at the garden this season, and I wanted to give you your share of the money we got from selling the crops," said Tom as he handed Karl his share.

"Why thank you, but I never had to do much, but if this is what you think I should get for what I did, I appreciate it."

The look on Karl's face was priceless. He had never had that much money. He kept looking at it and thanking them for stopping by. When Archie and Tom were leaving, Karl walked into his cabin, looking at the money as if it were treasure. As they continued making their rounds, the reactions were all the same. People were rewarded for their work, but more importantly, they realized that Seamus had told them the truth.

Heading back to town, Archie told Tom how good it made him feel, seeing how much the money meant to everyone, but then he stopped his horse and, looking Tom in the eyes, said, "I know exactly how they feel, Tom, it's the way I felt when you and Widow Henry helped me. All of them know they're loved by the people living in the area. Sometimes, that's all that people need.

I can't wait to see what happens next!"

Author Notes

MANY, IF NOT most of you who have taken the time to read this book don't believe this type of real community can exist. I would agree with you if we continue living at the fast pace we currently do. Every person I have met responds to someone taking time to care for them. It's our time that means so much to the frightened single mother who wants someone not to judge her but to listen, the schoolchild who doesn't have the clothes others do or finds himself struggling with schoolwork who needs someone he can trust. It's nice to give money to a charity that helps the poor, but your one-on-one time with someone will be the most crucial gift you could ever give them.

I have tried to discuss how a loving community can affect people. The single mother who struggles to feed her family and who herself is so terribly lonely. I've attempted to discuss racial issues from both a black perspective and a white point of view. Prejudice is learned and often fueled by the lack of genuine love. Poverty is the worst enemy in our society. The poor lose self-respect and dignity. Many give up hope and settle for things as they are. Still, if only someone would come alongside them, get to know them, and care for them as the Good Samaritan did in Christ's parable, much like Carol did with Mary or Widow Henry with Archie, their lives would dramatically change. Allow yourself to imagine this kind of world.

We have, instead, delegated whatever can be done to the government, and while the government can spend money trying to change things, it is not possible for the government to love people; only we can do that. If these issues, and I am aware they are multilayered and complex, could be broken down into small communities, we will begin seeing change, one community after another.

I don't want to belittle any of the efforts made by large corporations, non-profits, wealthy people, and the church over the years. Each has done many wonderful things to help people, but it will fail without each of us taking the time to help our neighbors.

In the book, the wealthier people, like Widow Henry and Tom and Nancy Campbell, took time to get to know folks. They invested time, not just money. They provided people with opportunities, not handouts, and just as important, they continually encouraged their new friends. Nonetheless, those with less money also got to know people and spent whatever time was necessary to help them. I don't believe this was just a late nineteenth-century model so much as it reflects how a real community can work. People caring for their neighbors never becomes obsolete. We have time to stare at a television or a smart device for hours a day, so why not use our time more wisely? It will take courage at first. People will think you're weird, but if you are patient, God will allow you to see how people will begin to change.

Not everyone in the story is a believer. Some came to faith, and others still struggled to believe; however, everyone was affected by the loving kindness shared without judgment. Loving others like Christ is what all true believers are called to do, yet it is often very difficult.

We are all different, having our likes and dislikes. The way some people act or dress, perhaps it's their political stance or worldview that grates against everything you stand for, yet, once again, we must follow Christ's example. He did not condemn or condone prostitutes; instead, he forgave them, telling them to "go and sin no more." While dying on the cross, barely able to breathe, he begged God to forgive the people who had done this to him. It's hard to separate the person from the actions they may be part of, but we are called to love them because they, like us, are all made in the image of God.

Imagine what the world would be like if we took our faith seriously and loved one another as Christ first loved us.

In the part of West Virginia where this story is based, in 1905, the Horton mine caught fire, suffocating five miners. In 1912, the Mine Wars broke out, where miners and hired "enforcers" engaged in war, and men were killed because they simply wanted to be treated fairly. U S Marshals were called in to end the conflict, yet the miners struggled years later. Despite the dangerous working conditions, this part of West Virginia grew from 93,000 in 1880 to 446,000 by 1920, largely due to the coal industry.

Worldwide, the twentieth century saw more people killed than at any other time in the history of the world. There has never been a time of peace, and there never will be. There will always be a struggle for power and control by nations and people groups. The internet and the news media expound on our differences, driving us further and further apart. The radicals from both sides seem to have overtaken the internet with their hate, forcing people to choose one side or the other. Yet, if there were a truthful representation of our population, most would be somewhere in the middle.

The only solution is to love each other with a sincere brotherly love that seeks the betterment of one another. God has made us different yet the same. We are all made in God's image, and we need to look for ways to understand one another better so that living in harmony can be possible.

Although this story is entirely fictional, some characters are real. Archie and Maggie were my great-grandparents, and though there wasn't much information to go on, I knew that they lived in Clay County and that Archie farmed. Alma Gay was their firstborn who tragically died when she was sixteen. Archie and Maggie's eldest son was my grandfather, who worked in the oil fields of Cabin Creek where, sensing there was about to be serious problems, sent his pregnant wife to live in Dunbar, where my father was born. As I mentioned, there was little information to go on, but if Archie was anything like his grandson, my father, I think I have represented him well in this story.

I beg you to please take time away from your everyday routine and spend it with people who need a loving, caring hand to help them. To those who know Christ on a personal level, pray; it's the only way real, loving change will happen to people's hearts. Search your soul for the peace that only comes from knowing Christ Jesus.

Milton Keynes UK
Ingram Content Group UK Ltd.
UKHW011123050624
443649UK00006B/505